PRAUSPRESS

The
Seventh
Trumpet

JOSEPH DEHNER

FIRST EDITION

Published by Praus Press

FOR NOËL

ACKNOWLEDGEMENTS

Life is relationship, past and present. We create from what comes before us. We polish with the help of the living.

A gauntlet of readers suffered through early drafts, offering much more kindly worded suggestions than the drafts deserved. A Writers Circle from The Literary Club (America's oldest continuously operating organization of its kind, located in Cincinnati) offered important comments at various stages. A roundtable of Writers in Paradise, a remarkable annual conference held at Eckerd College, critiqued initial chapters, and forced craft and other changes. Fred McGavran, Prof. William Pratt, and Prof. Sam Greengus receive special Circle recognition. George L.M. Bustin, James Buchanan and others provided editorial encouragement.

Background reading is abundant on apocalyptic religious texts and the forces at work in what Americans call the "Middle East." Much is either/or — religious or political. My friend, the late Dusty Anderson, author of *Biblical Interpretation and Middle East Policy* (2005), convincingly linked the two in non-fiction. How freer it is to write fiction!

Gatekeeper Press provided a professional copy edit that influenced the final form of this work. My publisher, Richard Hunt, merits great thanks. No better coach could one find to get to publication's finish line.

There is one person who should be listed as co-author, though that might blame her for faults the reader may ascribe to this work. She labored for years at my side, providing piercing criticism when warranted, offering stylistic and substantive suggestions, going immeasurably beyond what editors do. She is my muse, inspiration, and love — the Rev. Noël Julnes-Dehner.

This work is fiction. While I worked on it, at least two tragic events occurred that I had written. The time came to surrender the draft before it became a further prophecy. That is not its intention. My hope is that you enjoy it, dear reader, and perhaps take from it ideas and actions that will advance our common hopes as People of the Book.

– *Joseph Julnes Dehner, December 2020*

1

VATICAN CITY
Saturday, April 15

DIO SANTO!

Father Alessio Brondini fumbled for his gym shorts after an abrupt awakening. *Discipline*, he scolded himself.

The dream had returned. A blonde woman in a translucent nightgown approaching his bed with an index finger placed vertically across her lips.

Frantically, he launched into his routine from soldier days. One hundred crunches and fifty one-hand push-ups on each side, counting on sweat to flush temptation. Finishing his workout, he mumbled the Holy Rosary of the Virgin Mary and reaffirmed his vow of chastity as a priest of the Holy Catholic Church.

After a shower purposely bordering on cold, he threw on his cassock and fastened around his neck the chain with a gold cross presented to him when the Holy Father asked him to serve as the pontiff's personal aide. The job was a perfect match for his skills, a fitting blend of his service in the Italian Army and the priesthood. There was an established hierarchy anchored in unchanging faith, a commanding officer, and eternal reward for loyalty and service.

Though this morning, Alessio worried about his commander. The night before the Pope assured him that a headache was nothing aspirin couldn't fix, but the pain radiating from the tired eyes of the 82-year-old pontiff was unlike anything Alessio had sensed before. Age charges increasing dues to popes, shepherds of a multitude in this life and into the next. Alessio had prayed sleep would heal.

As he does every morning since ordination two decades ago, he crossed himself before the black iron crucifix hanging above his bed and uttered the Jesus prayer — *Lord Jesus Christ, Son of God, have mercy on me, a sinner.*

He glanced at the only other adornment on the room's white walls — a photo of the Holy Father in radiant all-white regalia, arms stretched out, embracing the crowd at St. Peter's Square. It was taken the day of his election ten years earlier, vital, smiling, eyes aglow. Finally ready for another day of service, Alessio walked the brief distance to rouse the Pope and prepare him for the day's hectic schedule. There might need to be changes.

Before even reaching the Pope's quarters, he sensed something was wrong. He turned the bronze doorknob, and instead of the usual snore, there was the silence of a tomb. Drawing close to the bed, he saw the Holy Father's head rigid on the pillow, eyes open, staring up as though watching his soul fly home to heaven. Departed was this Vicar of Christ, spiritual leader of over a billion Roman Catholics worldwide. Gone was the man he loved and served.

May Christ who called you take you to himself, he prayed.

Always a soldier at heart, he pushed aside tears and grief to fulfill his duties. The Swiss guard stationed down the hall must be notified. But before leaving the room, he spotted something on the nightstand. A blue note stuck atop an inlaid box. **Fatima 3 > 1 7 !** was scrawled in the late Pope's handwriting.

He had been unusually reticent this week, shuffling files out of sight when Alessio entered the room. Obeying the pontiff's strict instructions about guarding anything to do with Fatima, Alessio pocketed the note.

A final message ... for me?

2

NEW YORK CITY, USA
Friday, April 14

THE REV. DR. RUTH WALLER found it hard to believe she was in the chief guest's chair at a glamorous Rockefeller Center studio in midtown Manhattan. She was there for the Harry Black Show.

Cameras were poised to catch every angle, while production assistants scurried to do the will of the infamous host. A gregarious middle-aged man, he was famous for arguments on controversial topics that often ended with shouting, shoving or worse. Against her better judgment, Ruth had succumbed to her publicist's request.

"A television appearance on cable's most popular show is the perfect cap to the book tour," she'd cajoled. "We'll sell more from this than all your events combined."

Black's antics were not what Ruth had in mind when writing her surprise best-seller.

"I'm an academic and don't care that much about the royalties," Ruth hedged, looking for a way out.

"But your publisher does," the publicist countered. "And besides, you're off to Rome tonight. We need this TV appearance to keep sales going."

Ruth marveled how her effort to write for serious theological readers had climbed to third on the New York Times' nonfiction list. *Visions of the Apocalypse* attracted a mass readership eager to know how prophets of the three great religions descended from Abraham foretold the End Time.

Was it from a search for ultimate answers in a time of fear and spiraling violence? A yearning beyond global breakdown, clashes of faiths and civilizations? Or, pray not, of an acceptance that the end truly was drawing near?

On her book tour, believers thanked her for bringing alive their prophetic heroes. Ruth's book confirmed their convictions about an imminent supernatural intervention. Many were certain that God was about to put things right one final time.

As a priest in the Episcopal Church, Ruth did not embrace a literal interpretation of the Bible. Understanding sacred scriptures involved knowledge of historical setting, ancient poetry, Hebrew and Greek. Dismayed at mainstream ignorance of the Bible's context, it was her mission to explain that sacred stories began as oral traditions full of symbol and metaphor, and when first transcribed, were written in Hebrew, Greek and Arabic. Not English, which didn't begin to emerge until 500 years after Jesus walked the earth. She delighted in pointing out nuances in the original languages that English did not express.

Harry Black was neither a linguist nor a scholar. She wondered what circus he had planned.

Too late to back out now.

The camera lights blinked red. The packed audience hooted and clapped on cue. Harry Black waved Ruth's best-seller while grinning.

"Terrorists kill thousands. The Middle East explodes. Is the Apocalypse near? Here with us is Dr. Ruth Waller, Episcopal priest and author of *Visions of Apocalypse*. Help us sort it out, Professor. How's the world gonna end?"

She began to contrast literalism with the use of poetic language in biblical prophecy when Black cut her off.

"What's God telling you? Will it be a ball of fire?" Ever the showman, Black mimicked an explosion. Black laughed, and his audience responded in kind.

Resolving never to be on television ever again but determined to redirect the conversation, Ruth continued.

"For people of faith, what's important to remember in these troubled times is that visions from Jewish, Christian, and Islamic traditions all offer hope."

"Hope, you say." The concept held no interest for Harry the ringmaster. "Let's welcome a rabbi, a pastor, and an imam to explore which vision is right."

Black greeted his other guests, each in traditional garb, as they settled into armchairs. "Let's start with Islam. Imam Sahib, you head a mosque in Dearborn, Michigan. How's the world gonna end?"

The Shiite cleric turned to the audience.

"Dr. Waller put it perfectly in Chapter 4. In a final battle, the Mahdi will emerge to lead victory over the ignorant forces of darkness. Then the Book of Judgment will be read out by Isa, the English name is Jesus, and the righteous will have their eternal reward. For nonbelievers — eternal torment."

"Hope for some but the rest of us roast," said Black in mock horror. He turned to the Christian minister, whose title flashed on the screen as leader of a 10,000-member fundamentalist congregation in Oklahoma. "Pastor Stone, does the imam have it right?"

"You know, Harry," said the pastor, "only through *Jesus* can you be saved. At the Rapture, the chaff will be incinerated with a great *conflagration*, and the elect will be lifted into the heavens to be with our Lord and Savior. *That's* how it'll end — in *glory*!"

"Lifted clothes and all?" prodded Black, with a barely suppressed smirk.

"Why yes," nodded Pastor Stone. "Without doubt."

"Hope for the elect it is. Check if I'm on the list," Black chuckled, wide-eyed. "Rabbi Bernstein, thanks for joining us. So what's the Jewish time's-up story?"

"At the end, there will be a cosmic battle against the great dragon, a final struggle of good and evil. All the nations will be judged. The Mashiach will appear as a Third Temple is built in Jerusalem. The Torah will rule over the Land of Israel where all will worship the one true God."

Ruth wondered where Black had found Rabbi Bernstein, a proponent of messianic Judaism, so different from the broad-minded spirit of reform Judaism and an outlier in the diversity of Jewish thought.

Black challenged. "The one true God? Which one is that?"

"HaShem," glowed the rabbi.

"The Messiah is Jesus Christ," blurted Pastor Stone. "Turn to *Him* to be *saved*!"

"Israel's the one to be judged!" the imam shouted. "It strangles Palestinians with the help of our own President. That must end!"

Black grinned at the brewing rancor. The imam, rabbi and pastor proclaimed that whoever did not accept their doctrine faced eternal damnation, each raising his voice to drown out the others.

"All three can't be right," Black provoked, leaning forward in his chair.

Pastor Stone pulled a pocketbook from his trousers and held it aloft. "This **Qur'an** is the problem. Look at the terrorism it spreads."

"Islam is a faith of peace. Its enemies are the evildoers," countered the imam.

"Muslims aim to wipe Israel from the map," the rabbi snapped, "and **you** claim to be a peacemaker!"

The three jabbed fingers at one another. Black leaned back to relish the spectacle. The audience erupted as though picking sides in a pro wrestling match.

Ruth was appalled, but she had experienced this more quietly, personally, at book signings. Some were enraptured by visions of ancient prophets of their selection and ignored what others had to say. Worried her book could be associated with this disastrous bickering, Ruth loudly interrupted.

"Stop! Jews, Christians and Muslims all believe in one compassionate and merciful God."

"Perhaps Professor, but that's not what we're hearing today," said Black, waving for the others to cut their banter. "For a guide to different paths to the coming Apocalypse, give this a read," he said, holding up *Visions of Apocalypse*. Ruth's publicist nodded approvingly off stage.

The director gave the ten-second hand signal.

"Thanks to our guests. Monday, we'll dive into human trafficking. Social injustice or job creation?"

Ruth did not disguise the horror on her face that this was a question.

The camera lights turned dark as applause faded. Ruth quickly unhooked the microphone from her clergy blouse. Her job in Rome would be to represent the Anglican Communion, the worldwide denomination that included America's Episcopal Church, and to seek common ground with the Roman Catholic Church.

Although the two had been antagonists for almost 500 years when the Church fractured into Roman Catholic and Protestant, her new role would be a thousand times less stressful than the Harry Black Show.

3

VATICAN CITY
Saturday, April 15

THE VATICAN PHYSICIAN, Secretary of State, and two other cardinals somberly gathered in the papal bedroom. They closed the door, leaving Alessio to return to his room.

He knelt to pray a litany of mourning. He had not known his biological father, and now grief for the only father he had ever known left him unable to speak.

A kaleidoscope of images came to mind, starting with his mother combing his hair at age five, before she left their Sicilian apartment early one morning. A victim of omicidio, said the policeman. Alessio was shuttled to an orphanage run by nuns whose creed was iron discipline.

Escape at 12. Life on the streets, meals from back alleys.

At 13, a hired man, moving crates on the docks.

His first time with a woman at 15, with a tavern owner's wife two decades his senior who called him "my charming boy."

Enlistment in the Italian Army at 16 with a fabricated birth certificate that said he was 18.

At 19, duty with a UN peacekeeping mission in a Lebanese city. The brotherhood of soldiers, late night carousing, gambling, midnight outings to relish life's sensual offerings.

His chest began to tighten as a memory slithered around him like a boa constrictor on the hunt. The night that changed him.

Get away from me, Satan, he commanded, as the Holy Father had taught him. *I have confessed and been forgiven.*

It was that confession that led him to the Vatican. After ordination, Alessio was posted to a dwindling Tuscan hill town, an anemic remnant of its Renaissance incarnation, its population averaging age 60. The ghosts followed him there, and the sleepiness of the parish did nothing to distract him.

One day when he could take no more of the waking nightmare, he drove to Orvieto's

Cathedral, where no one knew him. The confessor hidden behind the curtain that day was a cardinal who traveled incognito to parishes to keep a finger on the Church's pulse. A cardinal who would become pope. Through the bond forged that day Alessio found his place in life, to serve the Holy Father to the end. And now, the end has come.

A sharp rap on the door shattered the reverie. It was the Camerlengo, a cardinal who'd been a fierce conservative opponent of the late Holy Father. He now served as the temporary executive director of Vatican operations pending election of a new pontiff. He entered before Alessio could open the door.

"A terrible loss," he said.

Alessio made the sign of the cross.

"You were with him last night. Anything out of the ordinary?"

"He was preoccupied with some sort of research." Deciding to play it safe he added, "But he did not confide in me his interest."

The Holy Father had warned him about the intrigues of the Vatican inner circle that was determined to resist change that threatened their fiefdoms or their version of doctrine.

"We appreciate your service to the Holy Father. That has ended," said the Cardinal. "We will let you know your next assignment. And remember, whatever he told you as his assistant, you are forever sworn to silence."

Alessio agreed, hoping he looked compliant.

What was the message of the Miracle of Fatima?

4

NEW YORK CITY, USA
Friday, April 14

RUTH CHANGED in the station's dressing room for the overnight flight to Rome. Black jeans, white blouse, black sweater and black flats, the practical traveler's uniform. She polished her tortoise-shell glasses, pulled her light brown hair into a ponytail, and exited the studio.

Waiting in the lobby was Cindy Wallace, one of Ruth's closest childhood friends from

Zoar Village, Ohio, the historic small town they both escaped at age 18.

Ruth opened her arms. "Thank you so much for coming to cheer me on."

"I had to see the famous writer. Congratulations." They hugged. "You look wonderful." Cindy tugged her sweater over tight-fitting slacks.

"You need glasses if you think that," Ruth countered, reminding herself she needed to find a gym in Rome. She would be forty soon and didn't have childbirth as an excuse for needing to squeeze into her jeans.

It had been years since they'd seen each other at Tim's memorial service, when Cindy flew to Virginia to comfort Ruth on the loss of her fiancé, an Army chaplain in Iraq. A passage from John 15 was inscribed on his gravestone, "Greater love has no man than this, that a man lay down his life for his friends."

"Now you're off to Rome for pasta, gelato and Italian men."

"Yes to the first two. As for men, I'll be dealing with Roman Catholic priests."

"No romance there," Cindy agreed. "First trip to Europe?"

"I was in Portugal last year to give a talk at a conference about Our Lady of Fatima." Seeing Cindy's puzzled look, she explained. "A hundred years ago three Portuguese children saw Jesus' mother Mary and reported that she told them secrets. They were locked in a Vatican vault and published over time. Some believe there are prophecies not yet revealed."

"Well, I'm sure you were a hit," Cindy replied. Forestalling any further theological discussion, she pulled out her smartphone. "These are my girls, Rebecca and Esther," she said, pointing at each.

Cindy flicked through photos of her twins and husband in front of their sprawling home on Long Island. While delighted for her friend, Ruth wondered, not for the first time, what might have been if Tim had not been killed, if they'd married. Sometimes she dreamed Tim was about to come home to her, their infants squealing with delight. But in daylight, the door never opened and children never arrived.

A studio assistant interrupted to say the taxi was here. He handed Ruth the leash restraining a dog that looked to be a poodle and basset hound mix.

"Cindy, meet Gabriel, the only guy who could put up with me. I'm so sorry we don't have more time. Come visit us in Rome."

"Just might surprise you one day, Ruthie. Tomorrow I head to Ohio for our high school reunion. Zoar High — Rah! Rah! Sorry you can't make it."

Though she'd been anxious to leave the confines of her small town, Ruth had looked forward to seeing old friends.

"Give everybody a big hug for me. Here's my new email address." She handed Cindy a card embossed with a gold Anglican Centre crest.

"Fancy," Cindy admired the card. "Any message for Noah?"

Ruth thought of her nerdy high school boyfriend. She read he'd become a tech mogul. "Live long and prosper," she chose, remembering his passion for Star Trek.

Ruth and Cindy embraced as the assistant hefted Ruth's suitcases, led her to the yellow cab and stuffed the luggage in the trunk. Ruth coaxed Gabriel into the airline carrier with a treat, then placed him beside her in the back seat where she could reassure him. The Manhattan traffic unsettled Gabriel.

A professor at Virginia Theological Seminary, Ruth had enjoyed its tree-lined suburban campus in Alexandria, Virginia. It was an oasis of order in contrast to her scholarship that focused on the Middle East's cauldron of religious and tribal warfare. Spinning its web of violence globally while spawning terrorist cells, the conflict scattered refugees by the millions to overwhelmed, anxious hosts and stoked fires of populist backlash. In 2001, terrorists crashed an airplane into the Pentagon only a few miles from Ruth's home. And closer to her heart, the violence swallowed her fiancé.

One morning, she was reading the Washington Post in her breakfast nook when a UK phone number flashed on her cell phone.

"The Archbishop of Canterbury is calling for the Reverend Ruth Waller," said a British accented voice.

"What?" she sputtered, thinking it was a prank call. "This is she."

"I'll put him through now," said the caller.

And indeed it was — Archbishop Okello. He said he'd consulted with the Presiding Bishop of the Episcopal Church. They agreed she would be an excellent choice to become Director of the Anglican Centre in Rome.

She was aware of this outpost of Anglican churches to pursue dialogue with the Vatican. She was ready to leave associations with the Middle East behind. But she hesitated. The Roman Catholic Church did not ordain women, and she had no desire to be a second-class citizen in a city dominated by men.

The Archbishop cajoled. "A strong woman in Rome would prove the priesthood is not reserved for men."

She knew Tim would have given the same advice. What could she say but yes?

Looking out the cab's window she saw blockades around the United Nations snarling the chosen route to JFK. The driver quietly cursed himself in Arabic for heading to FDR Drive instead of turning due north.

"Palestinian?" Ruth guessed from the name on the medallion. She saw his surprise in the rear-view mirror when she reassured him in conversational Arabic, *"It's okay."*

Switching to English, she said, "My flight's delayed an hour."

The driver nodded. "I hope you not go to Israel," he said. "Dangerous."

"No, Rome," Ruth replied while watching street demonstrations for and against Israel's expansion of West Bank settlements that prompted bitter UN wrangling.

The prior Democratic Administration had abstained on a vote that resulted in passage of a UN resolution which condemned Israel for declaring its annexation of large swaths of the West Bank. Ike Palmer, who moved from Vice President to the Oval Office upon the sudden death of his victorious Republican running mate, vowed to veto any measure Israel did not support.

"What brought you to America?" Ruth continued in English.

"Our children. We lived in Gaza. Because of Israelis it is jail." The driver edged skillfully between competing vehicles, like a jockey on a champion racehorse heading to the finish line. The driver looked at her in the rear-view mirror. "I was surgeon there. Now I drive."

Ruth glanced and then immediately looked away from the report streaming across the small TV in the back of the car — bomb blasts at a Sunni mosque in Iraq, dead children and body parts strewn about the foreground, rescue workers poking with sticks to find survivors.

How ironic that the painful battles among and within Judaism, Christianity, and Islam would boost her book. A book that tried to show their common source of Abraham as a bridge across their differences. She'd become a sought-out source when a reporter wanted religious commentary to explain who was killing whom and why.

In Rome, religion would be less perilous. Theology would be served as the main course at polite dinners. She would carry her team's banner in difficult dialogues ranging from the role of women to joint worship to same-sex marriage. She would navigate the currents of division between Rome and the Anglican Communion that included her own branch, The Episcopal Church. It would be challenging to collaborate with a Vatican wedded to an all-male hierarchy and orthodoxy on many social issues, but as a woman, perhaps she could make a difference. And Rome might open a path she'd missed for years — a quest for life beyond words, beyond lectures and writing of the ambiguities of faith. She'd have time to find herself.

As the car exited for the airport, Ruth leaned back in the seat and pictured herself drinking espresso in a café near the Coliseum. *Roma*.

5

ROME
Saturday, April 15

The early morning taxi from the Rome airport swerved through traffic like a wild bumper car at Coney Island, with lanes mere suggestions and horns surrogates for brakes. Prayers for survival answered, Ruth was delivered to the smog-stained marble mini-palazzo where she and Gabriel would be third-floor tenants.

As she unloaded her suitcase, she received a text message from DHL. Her books and furnishings would arrive Monday. Time to take Gabriel for a brief walk. Then back to the apartment to feed him Italian dog food.

For her first day, she decided not to wear the traditional black clergy shirt that the Italian priests would be wearing. Instead, she pulled out a light blue cotton clergy shirt and a clerical collar to go with black slacks and grey blazer. She was excited to see the Centre, which was only a short walk from her apartment. Jet lag could wait.

Holding a guidebook map while tracing the path, she passed the Pantheon and read that it was commissioned by Marcus Agrippa and rebuilt around one hundred years later by Emperor Hadrian in 126. Topped by the world's largest unreinforced concrete dome, it took its name from the Greek for "to every god." Romans must have been startled when Emperor Constantine converted the Empire in the fourth century, transforming the pantheistic temple into a Christian church without altering its pagan personality.

A cordial three-person staff greeted her at the Centre — an Amazon-height woman who presented herself as Secretary Lucrezia Ponelli, a diminutive assistant with shocking pink fingernail polish named Maria, and an elderly man with deep forehead creases, white shirt and thin black necktie introduced as Antonio.

Lucrezia Ponelli, the Centre's Secretary in her early 60's, leather-bound pad in hand, ushered Ruth into the Director's high-ceilinged office. It was fit for a magistrate or business chieftain, with an oversized carved solid alder desk, sofa and sitting area and a cleaned-out humidor on a Corinthian plant stand. A faint cigar odor lingered.

"We are so happy you arrived, Mother Ruth. I hope your trip was pleasant."

"A little bumpy but right on time," said Ruth.

Ah, the problem of titles. Not only had Jesus said in the Gospel of Matthew "Call no one your father on earth," but also using parental titles made everyone else a child. Then again, a situation in which all the men had ecclesiastical honorifics and she used the academic 'Doctor' would be awkward.

Sensing that Lucrezia was a woman of formality and Rome a haven of hierarchy, she accepted the ecclesiastical address and replied.

"It is an honor to follow Father David. He spoke very highly of you."

"Shall we review the schedule for tomorrow's service here and the week ahead?" asked Lucrezia. The matronly Secretary poured tea and offered Ruth a tray of exquisite pink and yellow Ladurée macaroons, sent the day before as a welcome gift by the Dean of the American Cathedral of Paris.

Maria swung open the door, mouth agape, and while Secretary Ponelli glared over the interruption's impropriety, Ruth heard her whisper to Lucrezia, "... Papa e morto."

Switching to her rusty Italian, Ruth moved toward Maria to give comfort. "Your father died? I am ..."

"No," Secretary Ponelli gasped. "*Il Papa.* The Pope died."

"*Sì. E 'vero,*" Maria confirmed, crestfallen, tears seeping down her cheeks.

The three women held hands as Ruth recited the Episcopal prayer said at the moment of death.

"May his soul and the souls of all the departed, through the mercy of God, rest in peace. Amen."

Signora Ponelli patted her eyes with a handkerchief.

"The Pope was a wonderful man. Father David knew him well. And the day you arrive, Mother Ruth!" She breathed deeply and swung into action.

"I will clear the schedule. I have been through the deaths of three popes and the resignation of Benedict," she said briskly. "The Archbishop and a few other Anglicans will be invited to attend the funeral. I suggest you contact Father Alessio Brondini, personal assistant to the late Holy Father. He is our official liaison at the Vatican."

Ruth was reassured that like her, the Secretary was married to her job. Things would get done.

"Had he been ill?" Ruth asked.

Secretary Ponelli deliberated. "His age was showing. There were rumors he planned an encyclical about a major change to Vatican doctrine and was pouring his energy into it. But there was no thought of death."

The Secretary glanced out the window, then shifted her gaze back to Ruth. "The cardinals are bitterly divided over change. They will not easily agree on who comes next."

"Is there an obvious candidate?" asked Ruth, having expected the late Pope to out-last her time in Rome.

"He will be conservative, in things that matter to most cardinals. I don't...."

The desk phone jangled with a ring familiar to the land-line generation. Father David had advised Ruth to answer the Director's phone herself. It was a private number known only to a few persons who needed to know. After a nod from Lucrezia, Ruth picked up the receiver and said, "Buongiorno, Anglican Centre."

"*Ciao*, hello, *scusami*," intoned the male voice in Italian-British-accented English. "Father Alessio Brondini from the Vatican. Who is speaking?"

"Good afternoon, Monsignor. Director Ruth Waller here."

"Ah, the new director. Welcome to Rome."

"I am sorry for your loss, Monsignor."

"Grazie, Mother Waller."

Ruth replied, "Our prayers are with you. How can we help?"

"Father David, he was a close friend. I have an urgent request. Could we meet — tonight?"

In light of the circumstances a meeting seemed sudden, and she was starting to feel the heaviness of jet lag. Still, she was intrigued.

"I apologize for the short notice. I will explain at dinner. The restaurant Tamerici. Secretary Ponelli knows it. 19:00. Incognito. No collars, please. Until then."

The line disconnected.

Ruth turned to Signora Ponelli. "Father Alessio Brondini."

Secretary Ponelli paused. Putting her right forefinger to her right ear and thumb to cheek, as she often did when perplexed, she said, "To call you now, it is not about Anglican invitations. You see, Father Brondini's role with our Centre is only one of his tasks. He is --was-- the Pope's right-hand assistant, like a son, someone on whom the pontiff relies — relied — for anything any time."

It seemed to Ruth that Secretary Ponelli looked at her with new respect, that she rated an urgent call from someone that close to the late pope on this day. *But what could be so urgent?*

6

KIRYAT ARBA
Saturday, April 15

THE ROMAN POPE'S DEATH meant nothing to Haim Etzion, founder of a clandestine group named 4K. Stroking his gray flecked beard, Etzion sat alone on a stone bench in Kahane Park in the West Bank settlement of Kiryat Arba, waiting for a 4K lieutenant who was two minutes overdue.

A meticulous man, he pulled a file along his fingernails to remove any trace of grit, then flicked lint from sharply creased slacks. In the blazing sun of mid-April, he prided himself on not sweating despite his traditional dress. He wore a spotless starched buttoned-up white shirt and black suit of Haredi Orthodoxy and wool kipa atop a head of curly black hair. Gazing over his community's gleaming white homes with their red-tile slanted roofs, verdant vegetable and flower gardens and orange trees, Etzion envisioned the Jewish enclave spreading outward until it replaced the flat-roofed, crumbling Palestinian hovels and minaret clinging to a nearby hill. The filth of non-Jewish culture would be erased. The Torah would be the center of life. The realm of King David would be restored.

4K was his creation, and he kept its derivation secret from all but a few confidantes. The K's stood for the Hebrew words *kodesh, Kach, Kabbalah* and *Kook. Kodesh* for "holy or set apart." *Kach* for a former Zionist organization that aimed to restore the biblical Land of Israel. *Kabbalah* from a school of Jewish mystical thought. Last, Kook for the late Rabbi Zvi Yehuda Kook, leader of a yeshiva that inspired the Israeli settlement movement into Palestinian territory after the 1967 War.

From the moment Etzion envisioned it, the organization's central mission was to restore the Land of Israel to its ancient boundaries under King David by wresting land from Syria, Lebanon, Jordan, and the Palestinians. With the Land of Israel purged of unbelievers and a great Temple rebuilt in Jerusalem, 4K would herald the Mashiach to reign over an eternal Torah-based kingdom. Etzion briefly fretted that the papal funeral, with its speeches about charity, peace and good will, might delay Project Redemption. Fortunately, the world would quickly revert to its natural state of combat among tribes.

The perfect timing for 4K's strike.

Etzion flinched when the tardy lieutenant tapped him on the back.

"You're late," Etzion scolded, silently chiding himself for not sensing the approach, a mistake that could be fatal in other circumstances.

"At your command," saluted the lieutenant, also in a Haredi black suit and white shirt but with an unbuttoned collar.

Israeli flags proudly unfurled over what had been Palestinian land for centuries. Kiryat Arba was Etzion's choice of home, which was also known as "The Town of Four" because of its proximity to the Cave of the Patriarchs. Some believed Adam and Eve, Abraham and Sarah, Isaac and Rebecca, Jacob and Leah were all buried there.

Etzion pointed toward the cave. "Our politicians let Arabs patrol the most holy tombs of our faith." *Disgusting!* They scowled and shook their heads.

"Picture this Land restored," said Etzion, sweeping his right hand toward the Arab community that should be bulldozed, its tenants evicted and banished to other lands. "Kodesh," he exclaimed. "And once they are gone, when we rebuild the Temple, Israel's destiny will be achieved."

"You will succeed where your father stumbled," said the lieutenant.

Etzion nodded.

When he was a boy, his father Yehuda and an underground group plotted to demolish the Dome of the Rock. This gold-domed Jerusalem landmark was their target as a Muslim shrine built above two sites sacred to Judaism — the stone where Abraham offered Isaac in obedience to God and the home of the Holy of Holies, where the Ark of the Covenant rested in ancient times. But their plans were uncovered and thwarted. 4K would atone for the botched attempt to excise this Islamic wart from the face of the holy city and cleanse the Temple Mount.

"Chief, why not broadcast 4K's meaning to the world? It would rally others to our cause."

"Soon," replied Etzion. "The world will sing our name. *Selah.*" He instructed the lieutenant to summon the Inner Circle. The lieutenant saluted and left.

Etzion neatly folded the newspaper headlining the death of a popular pope. Within days heads of state and religion would gather in Rome. The late pope's efforts to build bridges with the Muslim world meant that Sunni and Shiite leaders would attend in a spirit of reconciliation. This heightened the risk that the two warring branches of Islam might unite against Israel. Etzion marched to his two-room brick apartment to place a call on a secure device that skirted Interpol, Mossad, Shin Bet and other surveillance, used for communications not shared with anyone else, not even 4K's Inner Circle.

"Ibn, I have a job for you," he said as the call connected and before the recipient answered. "The Imam of the Umayyad Mosque. Damascus. ... Right, the one bending over to the Sunnis. Fifty thousand for his termination. Half now. Half when the task is complete. ... And it must be blamed on Iran. ... You can arrange? ... How soon?"

7

ZOAR, OHIO
Saturday, April 15

CINDY WALLACE delivered bad news to Noah as they entered the Tuscarawas County American Legion Hall for their 20th Zoar High School reunion: Ruth could not attend because of her appointment as Anglican ambassador to the Vatican.

"She asked me to give you a message — 'Live long and prosper'."

Noah laughed, masking his disappointment. A wealthy tech entrepreneur, he was used to success as a matter of will. This was his first time back in 21 years, having left after junior year when his mother moved to Southern California to escape the winters of Northern Ohio. He'd planned to reconnect with Ruth.

"A signed copy of her book." Cindy handed *Visions of Apocalypse to Noah*, who read the inscription, *For your spiritual journey, Ruth*. "Here's her address in Rome." Cindy handed him the Anglican Centre card.

School had been a struggle for Noah, the teachers mistaking his dyslexia for a low IQ. He transcended his limitations and what he considered the intellectual wasteland of small-town Ohio through a computer's portal. He mastered software languages, including seminal but extinct COBOL by age thirteen. Obsession with digital code and cross-country running earned him a nerd reputation. Now portraits of Leonardo da Vinci, Alexander Graham Bell and Dilbert creator Scott Adams graced his Mountain View home office, all dyslexics who turned innate genius to brilliant success.

The hall hosted a cocktail reception festooned with floating balloons and blown-up black-and-white yearbook photos. Beer-drinking cross-country teammate Hank Slimmer regaled Noah with tales of running a tattoo parlor in Youngstown.

"A Hell's Angels gang used a Groupon for my Heaven's Gate special. Kept me busy for a weekend!" He guffawed. "How 'bout you, man? Heard you made it big."

Should he try to explain that he devised a software language linked to the open-source movement of the late 1990's and turned that into a tech business sold for ten figures? His classmates seemed so proud of accomplishing so little. He'd overheard Jack Schmidt bragging about how big his used car business had grown to be in Wooster. Big deal.

"I've done okay, Hank. Sold the business a couple years ago. Gives me time to find the next thing."

"Kids? Divorced?"

"Nope. Too busy."

"California didn't turn you gay, did it?"

He repeated what he told others who asked. "I'm still looking for the one. She's out there, somewhere."

"Sorry Ruth's not here," said Hank. "You two were close."

Noah smiled. "Those were the days." Wasted days, he did not say.

Dating was an area where his willpower did not achieve the target. His most recent website match could talk about artificial intelligence and big data applications, but she looked at her watch repeatedly during church services. Women outside the IT field always wanted to talk about their feelings and eventually would let him know that he lived in the digital world so long that his brain became detached from his body. He denied it at the time, but the more he spent weekends alone, the more he realized something was missing.

Now at age 38, he would launch a quest for love. He would pursue it with the same zeal as a new tech product. He'd create Noah version 5.0. On the trip to Zoar he planned to reconnect with Ruth, to see if he could reboot with her.

But she was in Rome. Noah knew little of the Episcopal Church, but from what he read about it on Wikipedia, it straddled Catholics and Protestants. Ruth was the only woman Noah could think of to talk deeply about what replaced business as his ultimate obsession born of a faith journey begun four years earlier after two decades of worship at the altar of software. In light of her absence, he resigned himself to 36 hours of backslaps, cold cuts and potato salad.

All was not wasted. After the Reunion he would host in Zoar a gathering of the New Jerusalem Alliance, the NJA.

Noah's turn to religion began when he was 34 and accepted his Chief Innovation Officer's invitation to attend an evangelical mega-church outside Mountain View. Perhaps it was the congregation's fervor, vaguely reminiscent of the early days of his company when caffeine substituted for cash. Attendance became a Sunday habit, and within two years he was anointed Captain of Christ in an immersion pool. This led to membership in CEO's for Jesus, entrepreneurs whom God had blessed with financial success. This group incubated the elite New Jerusalem Alliance. An invitation-only corps of businessmen and women who sold their companies' shares for a minimum of eight figures and were ready to lavish some of their wealth on a heavenly purpose.

NJA members needed no robes or hymnals full of songs a hundred years out of date. They spoke directly to Jesus, and Jesus came to dwell directly within them. They accepted Holy Scripture as written. Like every great work, the Holy Bible saved its best book for last — the Revelation of John, the NJA's guidebook to the second coming.

The Zoar meeting would convene Sunday evening. Noah was preparing to host the other 23 Elders when he heard on i-Radio the Pope died. That would not change the Elders' plans. The NJA's agenda was as fixed as the North Star. Only tactics needed consensus after prayer.

Noah's mind remained fixed on the NJA gathering as a way to endure the reunion dinner of fried Amish chicken, mashed potatoes laced with butter, lima beans, and the obligatory lime Jell-O with mandarin oranges, reflecting the green and orange of Zoar athletics. Trapped at a table between a life insurance salesman who couldn't help but look at Noah as his biggest potential sale in years and a former football star who wanted to talk Cleveland Browns trivia, Noah excused himself with a headache as the pretense. He departed before the video of the glorious victory twenty years earlier of the Zoar Separatists over the Massillon Tigers, one of the greatest upsets in Ohio football history.

Noah walked through the village toward the Zoar Hotel. A 3-story 1833 wooden structure looking as though it belonged in Nantucket's whaling days, white walls, lime-green and red painted door, gray slanted roofs, crowned with an observatory and widow's walk. Here the Elders would convene amidst other 19th century wooden buildings preserved by the Ohio Historical Connection to evoke the era of communal, separatist societies that helped settle the Northwest Territory.

As he passed the greenhouse where early Zoarites grew the Midwest's first grapefruit two centuries earlier, Noah began humming a Byrds hit of the 1960's. "To every season, turn, turn, turn … a time for war, a time for peace…." As lyrics and melody occupied half his brain, a quiet voice filled the rest — "It is time, it is time, it is time." He held tune and voice in unison and then halted in front of the concrete steps leading to the Hotel's registration desk. Through the song Jesus revealed to him that this is the final season. All was instantly clear, certain, urgent.

Time for the NJA to hasten the Second Coming.

8

LE TAMERICI, GAMBERO ROSSO, ROME
Saturday, April 15

RUTH TOOK A TAXI to the restaurant Alessio selected for their meeting. It weaved through traffic along a streetscape of blended centuries. Rome was a flirt, full of sound, light, fountains, fashion, a beckoning earthly garden of delights except for the honking and fumes. So far from Virginia Theological Seminary, so far from Zoar.

She dressed business casual — black skirt with a tailored white blouse, accented by a thin white gold necklace with no pendant and as requested, no clerical collar. Ruth wondered if this Vatican priest would be able to see her as a clergy colleague.

The taxi slowed as the Trevi Fountain came into view. "*Three Coins in a Fountain*," Ruth quietly hummed the theme to the 1954 movie starring Clifton Webb and Dorothy McGuire. She fell in love with Rome's fountains when the film played at a Zoar film series, "Romance in Europe." And now she sat before it, the most stunning water sculpture in the world. "Le Tamerici," said the driver, pointing to a sign across from the fountain. At the restaurant's entrance stood a man of her generation in a navy pullover, gray slacks and highly polished black wingtips.

As she drew near, he said "Good evening, Mother Ruth. I am Father Alessio Brondini."

Even priests here look like GQ models. His ramrod posture suggested a military upbringing. Why the priesthood?

He was about six feet tall, not including the thick wavy black hair, and appeared to be anything but a man who wanted to spend all his time with other Roman Catholic priests. *Unless he's gay.* She'd been hazy about official Vatican rules since a Roman Catholic clergy academic told her that as long as he wasn't having sex with women, other encounters didn't matter.

"It's a pleasure to meet you, Father Alessio."

He presented his card with an embossed coat of arms of two crossed keys and a papal tiara. She fumbled in her purse for hers. "I left mine at the Centre."

"Thank you for seeing me," said Father Alessio. He was stiff, hesitant. "Father David and I sometimes met here when we needed private time. I avoid the media, especially now."

Alessio opened the door for Ruth to enter the dimly lit room punctuated by candles on each table.

"I am pleased to be of assistance," she replied. *Friendly and collegial,* she congratulated herself on her first greeting to the Roman patriarchy, though she wondered how she could possibly help anyone after being in Rome less than a day.

The maitre d' nodded. "Buona sera, Padre Brondini," he whispered. He smiled in Ruth's direction, said "Benvenuti nel Tamerici," and seated them in a quiet corner, a single candle within an orange translucent vase illuminating the table.

This was a place where people could talk quietly, without the din of a gastropub or sports bar, acoustical touches muffling the voices of others. Lace tablecloths and a formally attired wait staff forecast a four-star meal.

After review of the menu, agreement that the wine would be red and consensus on the meal, Alessio leaned back, visibly uneasy. He put his hands palm down on the table and leaned forward.

In almost a whisper he said, "May I start by asking confidentiality? Father David and I kept our talks between us. That helped in our roles for Rome and Canterbury."

"Agreed," she replied. "Unless you and I say otherwise, our conversations will be in confidence. As we say in America, 'What happens in Vegas stays in Vegas,'" Ruth replied with a smile she quickly erased. *Too flippant.*

Alessio smiled weakly and leaned further forward. "Okay, as you Americans say."

He asked about her flight, where she had settled. She expressed sympathy for his loss. They discussed immediate details to be addressed, how funeral arrangements would unfold.

As the second course was served, Alessio looked right and left, seeming to be certain no one else was listening.

"You must wonder why it was urgent that we meet on this terrible day. Before he left, Father David told me about your background — and he mentioned your work on the Miracle of Fatima."

Ruth was startled by the reference to her research from five years ago, when she was writing about twentieth century Christians' ecstatic experiences of the divine.

"Tonight I ask to draw upon your work, not as Anglican Ambassador but as a scholar ... to solve a mystery."

"Go on," she encouraged, curious that he wasn't discussing this with colleagues at the Vatican, where the documents pertaining to Fatima were archived.

After a slight hesitation Alessio proceeded. "I was the one who found the Holy Father this morning. On his bed stand he left a note, a very strange note, and I am trying to know its meaning." He unfolded the blue note from his pocket and handed it to Ruth.

She studied the scrawl of ink — **Fatima 3 > 1 7!**

"Can you help me understand Fatima?"

"Very well," said Ruth. This was within her comfort zone, like a seminarian asking about the interpretation of a biblical passage. "The Miracle of Fatima. It arose during World War I, in the days of the First Portuguese Republic, when the government repressed religion, especially the Roman Catholic Church. Three shepherd children said that a heavenly Lady dressed in white and shining brighter than the sun visited them in the hills, directed them to pray the rosary, and promised to return every month for six months. Officials claimed they were possessed by demons and arrested them for fear they would stir up religious fervor."

Alessio listened intently, taking notes in a booklet that appeared to be a journal.

"October 13, 1917, the last of the visions. 70,000 people gathered with the children in a field. Clouds parted, and the crowd watched the Sun dance and spin with color, though historical accounts differ. The girls said the Lady was Mary and they saw the Holy Family blessing the people."

"Mary gave prophecies to the children."

"So they said. At least three. They said that Mary shared them three months earlier. They were published much later after Lucia, the one who became a nun, wrote her memoir."

"That could refer to 3 in the note," Alessio theorized. "Three prophecies. Maybe 17 is the year it occurred, 1917. But how can 3 be greater than 17? And what would it mean?"

"That's the challenge, isn't it? To interpret the meaning of an extraordinary vision."

"What if there is a prophecy not yet revealed?"

"A secret?" Ruth put down her fork as the waiter cleared the table and prepared it for the third course by combing the tablecloth of crumbs.

Alessio exhaled deeply. It seemed he was about to leap from a cliff. He lowered his voice to a whisper.

"There exists a secret page. The Holy Father confided this to me. I may be the only living person who knows this. And now you."

9

DAMASCUS, SYRIA
Saturday/Sunday, April 15-16

WHILE RUTH AND ALESSIO DINED in Rome, Vali Qalil arrived in Damascus near midnight after a harrowing journey that began in the folds of Iran's Zagros Mountains, where Qalil lived as a recluse. He'd acquired a white Kia Bongo truck with an Arabic decal of a sewer supply company on each side to avoid suspicion as he and his driver traveled through Iraq and Syria. Qalil had summoned the Officer Corps of the Army of the Mahdi to assemble in Damascus to witness first-hand Syria's destruction.

The journey featured rubble of ancient ruins, wrecked hulls of mosques, markets and dwellings, cities now stalked by ghosts of the protracted Syrian civil war and the Islamic State's suicidal marauding. Assad's Army, Russia and a disjointed combination of Kurdish, Iraqi, Iranian and American forces had cleared vast areas of Syria and northern Iraq of ISIS fighters, scattering millions of residents. The remaining inhabitants cowered behind shuttered windows, terrorized by roaming bands of scavengers and warlord gangs, sucking remaining life from Syria following President Bashar al-Assad's assassination by his own guardsmen.

The hadith, sayings, and stories of the Prophet 1,400 years ago, foretold this moment. Muhammad called Syria "Allah's favored land" and described how a Grand Battle would be fought near Damascus as the End Time approached, when the Mahdi would reveal himself to lead the forces of the light to victory. The Officer Corps of the Army of the Mahdi, AM for short, would see for themselves that Syria's destruction was complete, a final signal that the Mahdi would emerge for the final struggle.

Qalil was in his 60s, gray haired, thin but not scraggly, as though his form was chiseled by a tragedy that squeezed any softness from the body. It was his eyes that impressed, black pupils against pure white, that sharply focused vision like that of a desert falcon searching constantly for prey.

Early the next morning, Qalil's driver delivered him to the Great Mosque of Damascus, the Umayyad Mosque. An armed sentry met Qalil at the southern gate that dated to the Temple of Jupiter during the time of the Roman Empire. He was led to a second-story office. Wearing a long black robe and white knitted *kufi* atop a thinning head of gray hair, the Mosque's imam motioned for Qalil to join him at a mosaic table where tea steamed.

"*As salaam alaikum,*" Qalil greeted the imam humbly with the traditional salutation of peace.

"*Wa alaikum salaam,*" the imam replied perfunctorily. "You may sit."

"I bring warm greetings from your colleague in Isfahan." Qalil probed for a connection, uncertain whether the Syrian imam would be open to help AM. Syria enjoyed a convergence of interests with Iran, but the imam was known to aim above politics or the Shi'a-Sunni divide.

"Thank you. He said you would come."

"We know your troubles and come to help." Qalil decided a straightforward approach was best. "We aim to summon the Twelfth Imam from occultation and restore the true caliphate."

The imam's face brightened. This signaled agreement that Islam's rightful leadership was from the Prophet's bloodline. It confirmed Qalil's bet that the imam believed as he did that the last of the twelve infallible imams who had gone into hiding in the ninth century would return as a savior warrior to lead the righteous to final victory.

Qalil continued, "As you know, the terrible devastation of Syria is the final sign of the approach of *Al-sa'ah,*" The Hour. "We gather the Army of the Mahdi for the struggle. I am its Emir."

"Why have I not heard this?" The imam's skepticism surfaced as he stared at the unprepossessing man in front of him who claimed to know something an imam didn't know.

Qalil's stare locked on its target.

"The truth is before us. The people no longer offer prayers. Dishonesty replaces virtue. Worldly gain rather than faith commands the people's attention, and corrupt imbeciles rule. So frequently has the blood of innocents been spilled that streams flow red in the streets. Pride is celebrated through torture and physical oppression. Titled scholars are hypocrites, adultery rampant, famine widespread. There is no shame or respect for the elderly."

The words mirrored the imam's beliefs. He appeared ready to listen.

Qalil continued, "All is planned. A great march will come to you."

The imam placed his gold-rimmed alabaster cup on its saucer. Nearby gunfire rattled the windows.

"What bullets do not kill, disease and famine take. Our people brave snipers to buy a loaf of bread. Wild dogs feed better than our children. Only on Fridays is it safe to walk the streets. Allah grants us this."

Both men had watched the Arab Spring melt into a scorching summer of inciner-ated hope. It seemed demonic spirits arose from their corner of hell to haunt Lebanon, then Iraq, then Egypt and the rest of the Middle East, then exploded their fury on Syria. The country had become a card table for outside powers and warlords to play deadly games. Students marched to demand a new order, though their hopes were a mirage. All the divided United Nations could muster was humanitarian support for refugee camps, but without a functioning Syrian government, aid money was funneled to Swiss accounts of predators who escaped to luxurious exile.

"Alawites must join in a great arc of Islam from Iran to the Sea, with its capital one day here in Damascus," Qalil pressed.

"A noble vision, but Sunnis will never allow it. I preach unity but evil blocks their ears," said the imam with a mix of anger and sadness.

"We have found the way to unity."

"How is that possible?" Suspicion clouded the imam's face.

"You are a great man," Qalil flattered and leaned forward. "When you receive the signal, you will know what I say is true." Qalil stood.

The imam remained seated. "May it not be too late — if what you say is true."

Qalil departed to a sullen city. He was driven in the Kia to the Talisman Hotel in the old town, near souks and street markets that escaped the devastation of the business center. He sat for coffee in the courtyard, gazing at the pool and palm trees that evoked the splendor of Islam's golden age.

Soon the officers of AM, the Army of the Mahdi, would meet in Damascus. They would see beyond question that Allah's final sign had flashed — Syria was destroyed. Once this was affirmed, they would activate the plan.

AM operated as a tight cabal with a sparse website calling for Islamic unity to restore the vision Allah revealed to Muhammad in the 600's C.E. The vision to live by divine law, to strive for the exemplary life that Muhammad's was to all Muslims. After the Prophet's death, his grandson Hussein was assassinated, leading to the great split of Islam into Sunni and Shi'a ever-after at war with each other. Shiites claimed that a descendent of Muham-mad should rule, while Sunnis believed the Muslim community should choose the caliph. Aiming above the fray, AM would call on Muslims to put these differences to rest.

Qalil conceived AM's plan for transcending the Shi'a/Sunni divide, based on the power of women. All twelve original imams in Islam were infallible, as had been Mu-hammad's daughter Fatima, but because she was a woman, she could not be seen as an imam in that age or even now.

But times were changing. AM interpreted Fatima's infallibility to mean in the current age there should be no distinction between the sexes, except for references in the Qur'an about family law. Had not Allah spoken through the Prophet, may Allah's peace and blessings be his, "Women shall with justice have rights similar to those exercised against them"? So long marginalized by men, women were hidden in plain sight. They would initiate the final battle.

The veil of time would vanish. Vali Qalil would reveal himself as the Mahdi. He would extend Islam's righteous rule throughout the world, bringing justice and peace for the End Time. But before that timeless eternity loomed the battle against the greatest enemy, the Dajjal, leader of the forces of darkness.

He had revealed himself — Israeli Prime Minister Aaron Feldman. AM would prevail. *Al-sa'ah* drew near.

10

LE TAMERICI, ROME
Saturday, April 15

"THIS UNPUBLISHED PAGE from Sister Lucia's account — have you seen it?" Ruth asked Alessio after Le Tamerici's waiter served a lamb dish.

"No. All I know is what's been published."

"Well, let's consider what's been released, what Sister Lucia transcribed as the prophecies of Mary."

Alessio nodded.

"The first was about the coming of a terrible war. Some say that was the Great War then afflicting Europe. But most interpret it as a vision of what was to come in 1939 when Hitler invaded Czechoslovakia and the Second World War began."

"The prophecy became a revelation," said Alessio.

"The second was published in Sister Lucia's memoirs. It was about the return of Russia to Christ. Communism fell, and the Russian Patriarch now heads a large flock. That fit the prediction that Russia would be consecrated to the Immaculate Heart."

"Though Russian Orthodox is not what God had in mind," frowned Alessio.

The waiter gently interrupted about dessert. After ordering cassata Siciliana for them both with Ruth's consent, Alessio whispered, "The first two were prophecies that came true."

"Not so accurate if you remember Mary told the children the way to prevent war was to pray for Russia's conversion," Ruth countered. "World War II had nothing to do with that. Let's go on to part three."

"John Paul II released it in 2000," said Alessio. "It spoke of a bishop in white who would be killed. He believed it referred to the assassination attempt, and he credited Our Lady of Fatima for saving his life. Again, an accurate forecast."

"Not so. Sister Lucia wrote of a bishop being killed by bullets and arrows, along with priests, men and women in religious orders, and lay people. None of that happened." Ruth paused. She was being too harsh. As Director of the Anglican Centre she must be open. She shifted to a conciliatory tone.

"As you said, the third piece does describe a bishop in white. He ascends a mountain with a cross on top, and when he reaches the foot of the Cross, the Bishop is attacked by soldiers. But its wording is so different from the others that some believe Lucia could not have written it."

Alessio nodded. "I have heard this."

"People like Father Kramer, who wrote *The Devil's Final Battle*. And *The Secret Still Hidden* by Christopher Ferrara."

Sicilian cassata arrived.

"The secret page," said Ruth. "What do you know about it?"

"Only that it exists. It must relate to the final note." Alessio looked down at his plate, seeming to withdraw.

Ruth wondered if he feared it was wrong to enlist her help. She was not of his Church. She sensed he had no alternative. She was not subject to the intrigues of the Vatican, where knowledge was power subject to manipulation and misuse. She'd heard stories of how cardinals spent more time on politics than in prayer. Alessio must have gambled that Ruth would not betray his trust. She would not.

"Espresso?" asked the waiter.

"No grazie," said Ruth.

"Sì, espresso," said Alessio.

"Well, if you will, I will."

Alessio leaned forward. "One more thing I can share. The Holy Father had me swear that after his death I must deliver it to his successor and no one else." His expression changed to acceptance of her as worthy of his trust. "But the note — what does it ask of me?"

"If we can read the page together, I might be able to help you interpret the note's meaning." Ruth shifted the blue paper sideways. "And look here, maybe it's not about how 3 can become greater than 17. It could mean 3 will become 1, with an emphatic 7 after that. Three into one — perhaps meaning Father, Son and Holy Spirit. Seven is a fabled number. Seven days of creation, seven battles of the War Scroll, seven trumpets of Revelation. Seven expresses a climax, an ending. Some who saw the dancing sun in Portugal interpreted it as Mary sending a sign that God would return to Earth as Christ to reign over a New Jerusalem."

Alessio's eyes widened. "The end time?"

"The Bible ends with the Apocalypse of John. It's possible the unpublished page is an Apocalypse."

"A prediction of the world's end!"

"The word means revelation, not that life on earth ends. We need to study the secret page to understand what the late pontiff was trying to tell you here," Ruth said as she handed back the note.

Alessio took a deep breath. "I must retrieve the file. I will pray we can read it before the next Holy Father is chosen, whoever he may be."

"Perhaps one day it will be a she," said Ruth, smiling.

Alessio smiled too. "Ruth the First, sì?"

11

ZOAR VILLAGE, OHIO
Sunday, April 16

THE SUNDAY MORNING after his reunion dinner, Noah Stoll used www.finda-church.com to locate an evangelical church only 15 minutes from Zoar Village. Another example of technology serving God. Noah approved.

Driving along a two-lane road in his Tesla rental, Noah reflected on classmates whose lives followed paths so different from his. How could they be content with minor promotions and leased SUVs when there was the Kingdom of God to expedite? The reunion was like being frozen in high school, classmates stuck in a world of football Fridays, Walmart bargain days, and 19th century hymns sung on Sundays. He had explored frontiers, mastered digital code, turned a start-up into a global giant, and gained the ear of politicians. Not stopping there, he was on a final quest beyond worldly pursuits, a mission beyond all he had accomplished in his life until now.

Our Church of the Seeker featured a rock band and colored streamers dangling from the rafters of a former Home Depot. The denim-clad pastor preached that the worst sin was sloth.

"Success," he thumped on the lectern Bible. "Focus on what will make you the most you can be — like our Savior! Remember the parable of the talents. They must not lay fallow. You must multiply them. There is no shame in plenitude, for when you have much, you can give back to God a greater measure of what He has given you."

Amen. Noah affirmed. Done that.

When he pulled out of the Church's driveway, Noah noticed a familiar fellow with a thumb out at the side of the road. He pulled up and opened the window.

"Sam, it's me."

A fabled American means of mobility, hitchhiking had virtually disappeared since the 1960's. Perhaps because of its rarity and the willingness of strangers to give a neatly dressed 30-year-old a lift, Sam Turrain, youngest of the NJA Elders, made it to Ohio in 26 hours from Boise, Idaho.

"Noah, my man, the Good Lord provides," said Sam.

They caught up on how their former businesses were doing. Sam created and sold for a fortune rights to technology that collected and mined data of in-store purchases. Customer loyalty to stores using Sam's technology skyrocketed, and he cashed out at age 29 for more than a billion dollars. Hitchhiking was a spiritual discipline in learning to trust the Lord.

As they neared Zoar, Noah began to describe the 19th century Society of Separatists of Zoar that emigrated from southwest Germany.

"It survived as a commune until 1898, based on rigid standards set by the leader. The modern age made it a dinosaur," Noah explained.

After parking the car, Noah led Sam around the village. Left behind were sturdy buildings organized around a central garden and a community legacy of equality and sharing with an eye on salvation. Zoar Village was now an offbeat tourist destination for the AAA and AARP crowd in search of lost America.

"When I lived here, I didn't know anything about the group. Now I admire their belief that each person must have a direct relationship with God without a lot of ceremony."

"Unchanging belief can be its own demise," Sam commented, surrounded by artifacts of a creed that had not survived its rigid Germanic separatist life, a victim of urbanization, industrialization and the call to break free and grow rich.

"Let's have lunch at the Hotel," said Noah, happy he could justify skipping the brunch that remained as the final offering of the Zoar High School Reunion. God comes first.

Over sauerbraten and scalloped potatoes, Sam asked Noah for a preview of the night's agenda.

"It'll be a turning point," said Noah. "Don't want to give away too much. Tell me, Sam. Do you think it's Time with a capital T?"

"Affirmative. Facts, friend. The Middle East in flames. Nature in a death spiral. Unmistakable, as Revelation predicts. If only others could see it as we do."

"And they will," Noah affirmed.

"Once we offer what they're looking for, Noah, they'll buy. People know this world's not gonna last forever. They're just waiting for the signs."

Later that afternoon Noah welcomed the other NJA Elders as they arrived at the historic Zoar Hotel. They were assigned drafty rooms with hexagonal quilt designs on bedspreads and rag rugs scattered over gnarled floorboards.

The Elders were the uber-rich of America. One was a Hollywood star who fled Scientology when it demanded she give it her millions. God led her to an Evangelical pastor who taught that financial success was a blessing showered by heaven. Another was a retired Navy Seal, who corralled his colleagues into a private security firm guarding US assets in combat zones. Yet another developed a business that packaged romance devices and sold them through house parties. The Elders were eighteen men and six women.

After dinner culminating in a hefty slice of the hotel's legendary sugar pie, Noah convened the Session of the NJA Elders in the Bümiller conference room, named for Zoar's founder.

"Destiny draws us," Noah began. "We have witnessed the portents. Volcanoes erupting in Washington and Iceland. Another nuclear meltdown in what's left of Ukraine. Terror throughout the Middle East, massacres in Nigeria, genocide in Burma." He paused as the Elders reflected on recent fire, smoke, darkness, slaughter, violence, and strife plaguing humankind. "The epidemic of rabbit flu, the resurgence of AIDS — all signs the hour nears."

The Elders leaned forward, attentive, when the plank floorboards began to wobble, as though a supernatural force was shaking the flooring to smooth it out. The tremor lasted about ten seconds. Other than a Rookwood vase sliding off a bookcase and shattering to bits, there was no harm to person or property, and the rumble ceased abruptly.

While Elders glanced about, some fidgeting and the Navy Seal alumni chief stoically indifferent, Noah said another sign had flashed. Since fracking hit northern Ohio, quakes had increased dramatically. God using technology to warn the Kingdom.

"All things are gathered together in the final days as the divine purpose is revealed," said Sam Turrain reverently.

Noah continued, "Last night Jesus came to me. He spoke as clearly to me as I speak now to you." Noah shared Jesus' instructions on how the NJA would hasten His Second Coming. "As our Lord said, 'I came to bring fire to the earth, and how I wish it were already kindled.'"

"Luke, Chapter 12," Sam Turrain exclaimed.

In a break from unwritten tradition that Elders speak in seniority sequence, Sam pronounced a loud Amen. There was a collective nodding of heads and a decision that followed the leader's question, "What say you — Yes or No." For no, one simply had to remain seated. All stood. Operation Apocalypse would begin.

12

VATICAN CITY
Sunday, April 16

ALESSIO SHOOK OFF the returning dream of the temptress, this time with raven hair, and slipped on his exercise shorts before dawn. There was no need to rouse a pope or confront tasks a personal assistant performs for a great person, but his inner alarm clock was set.

The end of one papacy and the start of another comes less frequently than in earlier centuries, when some popes were consecrated and died within weeks, often under suspicious circumstances. The modern routine of burial and renewal has a script downloaded from a digital folder. While invitees confirm flight plans and the Vatican prepares to host them, only details need tweaks. The Vatican bureaucracy rolls along, each cog functioning smoothly.

But for Alessio, the Pope's death was a dead end. As the Pope's private aide, he was there to support the pontiff without questioning. Duty encrusted any personal feelings.

They were dulled to the needs of the Holy Father, who had meant as much to him as any earthly father could. Now what?

Doing an extra twenty minutes of reverse crunches, butterfly kicks and bicep, tricep and lat exercises with dumbbells from his weight bench, Alessio allowed himself to replay the Lebanese tragedy.

After returning to barracks around 3 a.m. from a night of carousing, his convoy moved out four hours later to patrol a dense urban cluster contested by warring factions. Without the benefit of a telescopic lens, he spotted a rooftop sniper ready to fire at the platoon's vehicles flying the blue-and-white UN flag. Alessio scored a bull's eye with a single shot. The terrorist plummeted to the street six floors below. Alessio bounded from the convoy to identify his kill. Turning over the body, he saw with horror a child's face, a red splotch over the boy's heart where the bullet claimed instant death. The child's right hand clutched a TV antenna, not a rifle.

An accidental casualty of undeclared war. His sin, his alone.

Waves of guilt threw him to his knees, and he threw up. He could barely make it through the following weeks and avoided other soldiers.

Once after guard duty, he headed toward the barracks. It was a clear night. Stars blazed in the black sky, as though beaming upon him like searchlights. Maybe the Wise Men had followed one to Bethlehem to see Jesus newly born. He collapsed against a wall, rifle falling to the ground. He had killed a child, one born precious like Christ.

"I'm sorry," he cried, "so sorry," until he could no longer speak. He remembered that the baby Jesus had grown to be an innocent man crucified dead before his time. He called out from the cross, "Father, forgive them for they do not know what they do."

At that moment he heard Christ say, "You are forgiven, for you knew not what you did." Very gently a sense of peace relaxed his breathing and filled him with acceptance.

His new life in Christ led to seminary. Ordained a priest, he was sent to serve as pastor in a forgotten Umbrian hill town. He could not have predicted what happened a year after arrival at his assigned outpost while visiting Orvieto. The confessor that day was a visiting cardinal. Without knowing the confessor's august identity, Alessio spoke openly about his sin in shooting the Lebanese boy, grieving he could never make amends.

Deeply moved, the confessor was a man used to taking charge. "My son, you were a soldier in man's army. Now you serve a higher commander."

Thus began his relationship with the cardinal, his father in God who would become Pope and summon Alessio to serve as his personal assistant, a soldier for Christ.

He placed the 15 kg weights back into position on the rack, knowing he wasn't the only soul disquieted by the Pope's death. Outside the Vatican, the Roman Catholic Church was in turmoil. The gap between Vatican doctrine and public practice widened daily. Basilicas were museums, with boxes "for repair of Cathedral" more prominent than alms for the poor collectors consigned to side altars.

Parishioner unease, or worse — apathy, reflected a growing, unspoken self-doubt about how the Church could be relevant in a world increasingly secular, diverse in its flock and split on issues ranging from contraception to poverty to climate change. Without his commander Alessio felt neither anchor nor direction.

Showering, cool water rinsing sweat away, he wondered if the pharaohs had it right — bury your attendants with you. After a breakfast of oatmeal, strawberries, and yogurt, Alessio resolved to secure the file marked "Fatima/1917/AFR," the suffix shorthand for "Access Fully Restricted." It was the Holy Father's one remaining command. Perhaps with Mother Ruth's help, he could unlock the final note's meaning.

Since 1957, the post of Vatican Archivist was combined with the office of Librarian of the Vatican Library. Giani Mercati would be a challenge. His insistence on precise protocol in who could access archival material was legendary. To Alessio's annoyance, the Librarian was not in his office when Alessio arrived at the Leone XIII Index Room so that he could consult the digital device that replaced 20th century card catalogs.

But the Admission Secretariat Chief was present.

"Buongiorno, Father," he greeted Alessio and walked through a doorway to embrace him. "A sad day. Do they know more?"

"Nothing I can say," equivocated Alessio, projecting insider status to make information more available to him. "I have a mission to complete, one from the Holy Father himself before he died." He shut the door quietly.

"This is for your ears only," he flattered the assistant. "I was instructed to retrieve a file marked 'Fatima/1917/AFR.' The Holy Father sent me here with a brief note written two days ago." Alessio handed the Secretary the creased blue note taken from the late Pope's bed stand.

The Secretary inspected the note carefully, nodding affirmation of the handwriting but finding no mention of the file.

"This would be irregular. No file number."

"It is a matter of grave import," coaxed Alessio. "The file relates to the circumstances of the Holy Father's death. My access was ordered by him. I will wait in the Meridian Hall," the loggia of the Tower of the Winds as the meeting point for the file's hand-off.

Strumming four fingers of his left hand on a binder, the Chief of the Admission Secretariat vacillated under Alessio's unwavering gaze before seeming to yield.

"I will call you. No need to wait in the Hall," he said, lips drawn taut as a private ordered to privy duty.

13

VATICAN CITY
Sunday, April 17

Alessio returned to his spartan room to await the call from the archives. He would have gone to his office, but he had none. None was required for the priest whose job had been to be at the Pope's side at all times.

A rap on the door. Alessio opened it.

Staring at him was the Camerlengo, a cardinal who served as acting Vatican head of state during a papal interregnum but with no authority to make changes in doctrine or staffing. It was he who had confirmed the Pope's death, removed the Ring of the Fisherman from a lifeless finger, and began the process of calling the conclave to choose a successor. Alessio tensed under a stare like that of a prosecutor at a murder trial.

"Your computer," demanded the Cardinal.

"Yes?" replied Alessio, unsure of the request's intention.

"We require it."

Shocked at the intrusion, Alessio unplugged his laptop and presented it for inspection.

"We will return it tomorrow," said the Cardinal.

"Is there a problem, your Eminence?" Alessio shifted to diplomacy. "How may I help?"

"By your silence." The Camerlengo's face softened. "We are grateful for your service to the Holy Father. You will have two seats in the Square for the mass. Choose another priest to be with you."

"Thank you, your Eminence," Alessio replied formally.

"And your cell phone."

Alessio fingered it, knowing the call would come to it about the Fatima file.

"I am expecting a call from the sisters about eucharist today," he said, using his one remaining assigned duty as an excuse to keep the phone.

"Then deliver it to me by noon," said the Camerlengo.

"Is there a problem, your Eminence?"

"Routine. We must document all aspects of the Holy Father's last days," said the Camerlengo.

"Of course."

Alessio knew the Cardinal's priorities lay with Vatican forces that had resisted the late pontiff's reform efforts. He regretted mentioning to his interrogator research the Pope had been doing.

"One last matter," said the Cardinal. "We found in the bed stand drawer funeral instructions in the Holy Father's hand. Did he give you a copy?"

"No, your Eminence," said Alessio.

"We will respect his wishes about the rites," said the Cardinal. "Did he ask you to communicate with others about his instructions?"

"That was not my role, your Eminence."

The Cardinal narrowed his eyelids to a suspicious squint, then appeared satisfied. "And that is not your role now." The Cardinal moved to leave, then turned. "We will find a place for you."

Alessio shuddered as the door closed. The late Holy Father had offered hope to reformers and been an inspiration to the poor. His writings proclaimed that materialism was a false idol, that service to God was all that mattered. In contrast, the Vatican's vast conservative bureaucracy continued to punish critics of orthodoxy, especially those urging women in the priesthood and nuns who strayed from the settled path. The Pope had opened the door of change, but only a crack.

Am I being investigated? Left with no one in the Vatican he could trust, Alessio sent a text message to Ruth, inviting her to sit with him at Friday's mass. *The Camerlengo did say to invite a priest.* She texted acceptance minutes later.

As noon approached, having not received a call, Alessio phoned the Admission Secretariat's Chief but got a voicemail message he would be away several days. A call to Archivist Mercati got a similar response. The assistant had obviously talked with the boss. He was being stonewalled.

Before presenting his phone for inspection, Alessio deleted calls and texts since Saturday morning despite worry that an empty record would be suspicious.

His mind turned to the blue note. **Fatima 3 > 1 7!**

What does it mean? Is Mother Ruth right? Conversion of 3 into 1, and then 7 follows? But what three into what one? And what seven comes next?

He pulled the New Testament from his bookcase and began to read Chapter 1 of its final Book, one not studied before.

"Blessed is he that readeth, and they that hear the words of this prophecy, and keep those things which are written therein: for the time is at hand."

14

JERUSALEM
Monday, April 17

4K'S INNER CIRCLE gathered in a private room at Moshiko, a kosher restaurant on Ben Yehuda Street in the City Center of Jerusalem. In the heart of a tourist area, the location was typical of 4K's mode of operation. It was behind closed doors in a public place, where the authorities would never suspect subversive plots being hatched.

Serious discussion began after lunch of lamb shoulder, Israeli couscous and *labne*. Plates cleared, waiters dismissed, room swept for surveillance, a sentry guarding the door, Haim Etzion opened the meeting with assurance of success.

"The people rally to our cause."

The proof, Etzion reminded 4K's lieutenants, began with a 2010 Channel 99 poll finding 50% of Israelis favoring construction of a Third Temple on *Har haBáyith*, the Temple Mount. Each year support edged upward. Despite this, every government since the Israeli takeover of 1967 allowed an Islamic group called the Waqf to control the Mount. Such an affront to the most holy part of the Old City, where lay the Foundation Stone, the Rock where Abraham was prepared to sacrifice Isaac upon God's command and then was spared by divine grace. The site for centuries was defiled by the oldest Muslim structure in the world, the Dome of the Rock. Har haBáyith, or Haram al Sharif as Muslims called the Mount, was Islam's third most holy site, where Muslims believe the Prophet climbed a ladder to heaven with the Angel Gabriel.

"Many rabbis embrace that the Third Temple's time is now. Our Prime Minister will act if we strengthen his resolve to do what his heart knows is right," said Etzion. "We are the instruments of destiny."

The Inner Circle murmured encouragement, a team revving up for battle.

Each member of the Inner Circle recited his assigned role and confirmed readiness to carry out each scrupulously designed step. Tunnels were cleared for entry. An engineer graphed the placement of detonation devices to be wired under the base of each pillar. An architect meticulously charted stress levels required from each ignition to cause the Dome's collapse.

Satisfied that years of planning had prepared well, Etzion closed the meeting.

"The guard of our nation will be down while the Prime Minister is in Rome for the funeral. The eyes of the world will be distracted while we demolish the Dome. Then the path will be clear to build the Third Temple. May God protect us in our mission."

After benediction, the Inner Circle dispersed into the humid air of the Holy City. As they scattered for separate lodging, not to be together again until their day of triumph, each gazed upward at the illuminated *Har haBáyith*.

Etzion paid the guard and dismissed him, locking the door behind. Using his secure device Etzion phoned a private number in Damascus. After a single ring, Etzion asked in Arabic, "Ready?"

Assured that his conversant was set to execute his instruction, Etzion spoke.

"First payment tomorrow morning. The other half on success. 10% bonus if you leave clues that blame Iran for the hit. Agreed?" Etzion grinned when the bonus offer received enthusiastic acceptance. "Wait for my signal."

Etzion congratulated himself. Lacking the bold instinct that a leader needs, the 4K lieutenants would have disapproved of killing a religious leader to advance 4K's aims. This would be a personal gift, not the last, to maintain incessant fighting between Shiites and Sunnis, a schism vital to Israel's survival. Civil war within Islam kept Muslims from forming a united front to prevent restoring the Land of Israel as it was under King David. Divide and conquer, then erase from the Land of Israel any memory that Islam had ever polluted it.

15

DAMASCUS, SYRIA
Wednesday, April 19

VALI QALIL, Emir of the Army of the Mahdi, greeted its Officer Corps in an abandoned factory on the outskirts of Damascus. A grant from the European Bank for Reconstruction and Development had converted the former Syrian Army compound into a space where 500 destitute Syrians were supposed to make chicken processing equipment. Instead, funds were siphoned off to enrich the rich, padding officials' Swiss bank accounts. The site was a cavernous concrete shell, a temple of corruption, a perfect gathering place for AM's Officer Corps.

Qalil opened the meeting with *salah*, the physical and spiritual exercise of Islamic prayer. An imam from Qom gave a blessing.

"We recognize Feldman as the Dajjal from the signs foretold in our *hadith*. An eye patch covers his right eye, and he has the blood of the Tribe of Khuzaa, though he denies it. He expels us from our land and builds walls around territory he usurps for Jews. I call you, Officers of the Army of the Mahdi, to jihad! Under the leadership of Vali Qalil you must hasten *Yawm ad-Din*, when the Judgment Book will be read, the righteous will be exalted, and the unrighteous will be sent to roast in an eternity of flame."

"In the Name of Allah, the Compassionate, the Merciful," the Officer Corps resoundingly chanted.

Qalil raised himself from his prayer rug. His taut physique and piercing black eyes demanded submission.

"We are Shi'a, but we are not the enemy of our Sunni brothers and sisters or any righteous person. We are soldiers of Allah. Our foe is the Jewish Dajjal and his legions of evil."

"In the Name of Allah, the Compassionate, the Merciful." The Officer Corps repeated.

Qalil's face reddened. "We have seen for ourselves Syria's destruction. The spirit of the people is torn apart. From the weak ranks of the Saudis arose Osama bin Laden, who captured the attention of the West but painted our Shi'a faith as vile." Qalil's diction accelerated as his pitch rose. "We shall succeed where others failed. We prepare for victory in the final battle."

"In the Name of Allah, the Compassionate, the Merciful!"

Qalil's neck muscles throbbed. "You ask me — correctly — why have the masses not rushed to our side? As our *hadith* instructs, the Mahdi will appear after Syria is destroyed. On Friday at the Great Mosque, when it is revealed to the faithful that the Mahdi will return, supporters will beg to follow us."

"In the Name of Allah, the Compassionate, the Merciful!"

"Our holy magnet will be A'ishah, my blessed daughter. She will lead a great March of the Innocents. This will be our message that Islam is on the move." Qalil bowed in the direction of a young woman who appeared as if from nowhere in dazzling white muslin from head to covered toe, chestnut brown eyes aglow, like a dervish ready to whirl in ecstasy. "The March will unify Islam as we gather the forces of righteousness. The battle plan is written. We have only to obey the Mahdi."

"In the Name of Allah, the Compassionate, the Merciful," the officers cheered.

"And the wrath of Allah will be upon those who shirk the true commands, those who are doomed at *Yawm ad-Din*. A fiery death will be theirs. Eternal bliss will ours and for all the righteous."

"In the Name of Allah, the Compassionate, the Merciful," the officers exulted as one.

16

VATICAN CITY
Friday, April 21

AS FRIDAY DAWNED in Rome, the papal funeral was set to broadcast throughout the world. Pope John Paul II's 2005 funeral held the record, viewed by about two billion people. Attending his mass were the Archbishop of Canterbury and the Ecumenical Patriarch for the Orthodox Eastern Church. It was the first time the heads of these churches traveled to Rome for a pope's funeral.

This mass would be far more inclusive, a celebration of all faiths, intended as a call for humanity to embrace its full self. Following the late pope's directions, the Vatican erected enormous screens in front of St. Peter's Basilica, city squares and other places where people gather for such passages. Invitations went to every head of state, including Cuba, the Democratic People's Republic of Korea, and East Timor. Invited faith leaders included television evangelists, Sufis, Tibetan and Thai Buddhists and a Zoroastrian priest.

An overnight drizzle ended before dawn, *heaven remembering to dry its tears*, thought Ruth, admiring the teal blue canopy above the city. Shops and offices emptied as people filled the streets to enjoy April warmth and watch an historic ritual.

Sitting next to Alessio on a wooden folding chair in St. Peter's Square, Ruth commiserated with the police. With unprecedented attendance of heads of state, including the recently sworn-in U.S. President Ike Palmer, European Union President Angela Schmidt, and presidents or prime ministers of over 80 countries in Rome, security forces faced a daunting challenge to prevent a terrorist or crackpot from wreaking havoc. She gazed at metal detectors stationed around St. Peter's. She'd read that the Italian Army deployed anti-aircraft missiles to protect Vatican City. The Tiber River was reserved for gunboats poorly camouflaged as fishing vessels, the muscular sailors looking as though they'd never fished and didn't expect to catch anything in the murky fluids.

The Dean of the College of Cardinals began the Mass of Repose and Rite of Visitation inside the Basilica precisely at 10:00. Ruth and Alessio watched as large screens broadcast the face of the late pontiff being covered by a white silk veil. The body was lowered into a cypress coffin into which were placed a Latin scroll detailing his works and 85 euros in coins, the formal compensation earned as Pope, payable on death.

Commentators highlighted the presence of the Supreme Leader of Iran, Ayatollah Mahdavi Mousavi, the third Grand Ayatollah since the 1979 Iranian Revolution. Alessio had told her that only after fierce debate within the Invitation Committee had the Camerlengo decided that the Ayatollah should be included in the private initial rites, as the late Pope's plan had specified. Alessio explained the placement of the Ayatollah between the Archbishop of Canterbury and the Ashkenazi Chief Rabbi of Israel, a symbol of how the Vatican could bring together faiths as no other earthly power could.

Alessio whispered that having the ecumenical visitors inside before the Mass of Requiem began outside was a major break with history. Only the College of Cardinals and patriarchs and presiding metropolitans of Eastern Catholic Churches in union with Rome were previously permitted for this intimate time before the casket passed through massive doors to the world beyond. This was the direction of the late Holy Father — to gather the world's spiritual leaders for all aspects of his earthly farewell.

Continuing to whisper, Alessio leaned closer. "When he was a cardinal, he visited Qom, where he secretly met Ayatollah Mousavi before he became Supreme Leader."

"I had no idea. Did he tell you what they talked about?"

"Wish I knew. Recently, he planned to invite the Ayatollah to Rome."

A brass orchestra signaled mass would begin. Large screens projected the casket lifted for its final journey to the public.

Ruth leaned toward Alessio and asked softly, "Did you get the Fatima file?"

"*Mi dispiace!*" Alessio said in a louder tone than intended, then reverted to a whisper. "I forgot to tell you. I checked the records. The Holy Father returned it to the Secret Archives with instructions that only a pope can have access."

The Papal Gentlemen as pallbearers walked through the Basilica's huge doors.

"You must get it," Ruth urged. "Fatima was Muhammad's favorite daughter. Given the pope's ecumenical spirit, could she have something to do with the blue note?"

The procession entered the blazing light of a cloudless day. The moment commanded silence, prayer, and contemplation.

"Requiem Aeternam" sang the men and boys choir, captivating an estimated 2 1/2 billion television audience. Readings from Acts of the Apostles and Psalm 22 followed, then a second reading in English from a Letter of Saint Paul to the Philippians.

"Verbum Domini," concluded the reader.

Congregants sang in reply, "Deo gratias." Ruth sang instead in English "Thanks be to God," dutifully playing her role as the Ambassador from the Anglican Communion rather than doing in Rome precisely as do the Romans.

As she witnessed the tears of many gathered on Vatican Square, she was taken by the radiance on their faces. Alessio sat transfixed, enveloped in the majesty and order of the Roman Catholic Church. Certainty, unchanging principle, glorious ritual. Ruth banked the moment as evidence of the power of fixed faith. And then she felt envy. She wondered how faith without doubt would feel.

17

ROME, TEL AVIV, ATHENS & PARIS
Friday, April 21

IN THE PREDAWN DARKNESS before the papal funeral, scrolls bound by golden cord arrived at the city halls of seven great cities. Each bore a cryptic message printed on vellum, with an urgent cover note that it be read immediately.

Mayor Jeffrey Chomsky of Tel Aviv, a secular business city, was the first to read his scroll. Thinking it was a wedding or bar mitzvah invitation from a wealthy constituent, he carefully untied the gold cord and smoothed the vellum, on which was written something shockingly different. In florid two-columned Hebrew/Greek script, the scroll read:

Those who say they are Jews and are not, they are but the synagogue of Satan. Do not fear the things you will suffer. You will have tribulation for ten days. Be faithful unto death, and I will give you a crown of life, and you will not be hurt of the second death.

Mayor Chomsky immediately called Security and demanded to know who delivered the bizarre message. The head guard rushed in.

"I am sorry, Mr. Mayor, but our video system malfunctioned. The guard recalled that the delivery boy was a teenager wearing a yarmulke who came and left on a bicycle."

"Security malfunctioned?" shouted the Mayor.

"It must have been a hack. The camera's working now," said the guard.

Mayor Chomsky phoned on the dedicated line supplied by Shin Bet, Israel's intelligence service. Connected with the Deputy Director, he demanded, "Look at this — now!" He snapped an image with his iPhone and sent it to the secure address used only twice before, once when a bomb ripped apart a dozen people in a shopping mall, the other when explosives were found in the basement of the Tel Aviv International Synagogue.

"Keep this between us," instructed the Deputy Director.

The first mayor to report a gold-bound parchment to the media was Yannis Kyriakopoulos of Athens, Greece. His scroll read in 2-columned ancient and modern Greek:

Your two-edged sword is sharp but unused. You allow apostates to flourish and to fornicate. You tolerate those who teach falsehood. Repent. If you do not repent, I will come and defeat the apostates with the sword of my mouth. I will award a white stone to the one who conquers.

The Mayor guessed it must have come from the youthful band of Greek students who picketed London's British Museum outside of class hours, demanding the return of the Parthenon Sculptures to their rightful home in Athens. What other explanation could there be for the "white stone"?

The only media mention of a scroll before the papal funeral began was during a BBC slot reserved for humor, which followed news highlights at the top of the hour.

"Mayor Pierre-Emmanuel Chantal of Paris criticized his opponent for the French presidency of stooping to a new low by delivering a mysterious scroll accusing Chantal of jilting his second wife for money. Mayor Chantal declared that he married only for love, not for the assets of his third wife, the perfume heiress. His rival denied having any part in the caper, claiming, '*Amor* is above politics.'" The scroll read:

You, who are rich beyond measure, abandoned your first love. Remember from what you have fallen. Repent and do the work you did at first. If not, I will come and remove your lampstand.

The mayors of four other global centers received similar gifts with varying messages about sin and consequences. In Los Angeles, the Mayor assumed a Hollywood activist wrote the odd message about "walking through the city as a thief in white garments." He assumed it was a protest of the city's ordinance banning discrimination against transgender workers.

The Mayor of Canterbury, England took his scroll to mean that a political rival was upset over his pragmatic politics. The words accused him of being lukewarm, "neither cold nor hot," called him rich, and urged that he zealously repent. The Mayor perceived no advantage in sharing this with the press. Not recognizing a biblical connection, he did not alert the Archbishop of Canterbury.

Oslo's Mayor was offended by the words citing Jezebel and said the writer would "kill her children with death" and would "give him the morning star." He fretted it was a warning from a copycat follower of the 2011 assassin who attacked the youth camp of Norway's progressive party. He handed it to the security chief for analysis.

Unfamiliar with Christian texts, Istanbul's secular Islamic Mayor had no idea what the scroll meant. It spoke of open doors that could not be shut. It denounced hypocrites who formed a synagogue of Satan and called for a New Jerusalem to be written "on the one who holds fast." The police chief could not make sense of it either, so they deposited the parchment in a box full of oddball missives.

The New Jerusalem Alliance had launched Operation Apocalypse. The seven scrolls echoed the early pages of Revelation, John's letters to Christendom's early churches of the Near East. The NJA did not identify itself from a hope that the content of the scrolls would be the news rather than the group that delivered them. The NJA Elders would that afternoon exchange encrypted texts of disappointment that the mayors and the media did not grasp the scrolls' meaning. The time to repent as the end of the world approached. The mayors should warn humanity that time was short. Didn't anyone read the Bible anymore?

As he monitored the papal funeral from a Rome hotel room, Noah Stoll received a secure call from NJA Elder Sam Turrain. Sam reported he personally handed the scroll before dawn to a shocked Mayor of Paris as he arrived at the Hotel de Ville before dawn. Sam described the Mayor as rumpled and red-eyed, as if he'd been out all night before returning to his official residence.

"He must have thought I was serving him with divorce papers," Sam laughed. "But I think he found the scroll more shocking. Are you all set there?"

"Affirmative," said Noah. "The world will know this morning."

18

VATICAN CITY
Friday, April 21

THE DEAN of the College of Cardinals extolled a magnificent papacy.

"Humble, yet strong. Valuing tradition handed down from the Apostles. Decisive. A rock in uncertain times."

Ruth listened as the Dean, a candidate for next Vicar of Christ, ignored the late pope's ecumenism. Orthodoxy and obedience would be the Dean's election slogans.

The choir sang Psalm 129 as the huge crowd before the Basilica and those standing throughout Vatican City and Rome received consecrated bread from cardinals and priests of the Roman Catholic Church. *Of course, no women distributing bread.*

The Requiem's finale was the Commendation, beseeching that the late pope enter heaven. The choir sang the Litany of the Saints. To Ruth's surprise, ecumenism reappeared in an historic edit of an ancient script that limited participation to cardinals and the patriarchs, archbishops, and metropolitans of the Eastern Catholic Churches. Rows of other religious leaders, including Iran's Grand Ayatollah, were invited to approach the coffin and express farewells according to their traditions. Incense wafted through the air.

Silence descended as cameras zoomed in on the Papal Gentlemen, who gently lifted the coffin where it would begin its journey back into the Basilica. From there, it would be interred beneath the altar near John Paul II.

This gave the television commentators an opportunity to talk about likely successors, including the Dean. Speculation centered on two rivals, both Italian, both conservative. One focused on writing about compassion for the poor. The other podcasted daily about the never-changing Gospel. A Daily Digital Rosary was offered by the latter, while the former's recent campaign was to raise funds for African pandemic orphans.

As the casket moved slowly onward, the enormous screens shifted from the Papal Gentlemen to a lone musician projecting his trumpet from the north central point of Bernini's Tuscan colonnades. Dressed in black, he pierced the air with a triumphal cadence that sounded more like the start of an Olympic flame lighting ceremony than a mournful brass Amen.

On the screens and television stations of the world, images began to flow as the trumpeter blared his call: hail and flame, forest fires, African grasslands burning. Interspersed with natural catastrophe were black and white newsreels of World War II bombers dropping cylinders of death and Dresden aflame. Then appeared color napalm explosions from Vietnam in 1969, followed by Baghdad buildings burning at night under bombardment during the 2003 American invasion.

Ruth stared with wonder. *A modern capstone to a traditional mass? Audiovisuals during services were the province of start-up megachurches, not the Vatican.*

The crowds watching from beyond St. Peter's Square began to clap, certain this must be a message from the late pontiff that war was immoral and Mother Earth must be saved. This Pope had preached against all wars, including against the planet.

Ruth looked towards the top of the southern colonnades where a second trumpeter began without a pause. This solo was higher pitched, allegro rather than the prior andante. Projected images responded in kind: rapid flashes featuring gushing waters that extinguished flames. An enormous rock cliff rimmed with burning trees crashed into a sea. Waters churned and changed from aquamarine to blood red. Ocean vessels sank as rogue waves covered them, and close-up snapshots along beaches revealed dying and dead sea creatures. The Hiroshima mushroom cloud and a tsunami crashing into a Japanese nuclear plant flashed across the screens. The onslaught of catastrophe unnerved the crowd out of its bereaved silence. Amid the rustling some stood while others gawked motionless at the spectacle.

A third player took the lead on the northwestern point of the colonnades' tile roof. He started with a staccato riff at the highest pitch imaginable, then tone by tone descended the scale. Images appeared of shooting stars falling towards earth in clear winter skies with iridescent green Northern Lights undulating in the background.

Before the fourth musician appeared and blew the lowest tones a trumpeter can summon, images of the 1986 nuclear meltdown at a Soviet power plant appeared, captioned "Chernobyl" and "Wormwood" in ten languages. A star streaked downward with two names emblazoned on a Bible. Script explained that Wormwood or Chernobyl was the star that fell to Earth in the biblical Revelation to John. It poisoned rivers and springs, and many thousands died from the bitterness it spread.

The fourth virtuoso slowed to largo in a low-pitched dirge accompanied by scenes of dense smoke billowing outward toward the crowd. It dissipated to reveal the collapse of the World Trade Center's Twin Towers, followed by the massive darkening of noonday skies when Saddam Hussein lit the oilfields of southern Iraq.

A fifth trumpeter beckoned from the northeastern corner of the roof and blurted the equivalent of a bumblebee's buzz. Film clips streamed of gigantic helicopters spitting fire into jungle huts, with close-up flashes of fierce pilot faces intermingled with bombs being dropped onto protesters in the streets of Libya, Egypt, and Syria in 2011 and 2012.

The screens shifted to a Google map depiction of a desert from a decreasing distance, as though a camera were hurtling from space towards Earth at warp speed. As the image neared ground level clarity, a river formation appeared. Instead of a ribbon of green along each bank, the waterway was virtually dry.

"Euphrates" flashed across the bottom of photos depicting people walking across what had been the longest river of Western Asia. The sixth trumpeter bellowed a military march while intermixed images of ancient, medieval and modern battles accompanied the majestic music as visual rap.

When the first and second trumpet solos sounded, the Papal Gentlemen dutifully paused in their recessional cadence. By the third, they noticed Swiss Guards in traditional ribboned pantaloons conversing with men in black suits wearing earpieces. Before the fourth trumpeter emerged, a Swiss Guard whispered to the lead pallbearer, who began a race to the bronze doors of St. Peter's. By the time the sixth trumpet sounded, the coffin, cardinals and other religious dignitaries were inside the Basilica, doors slammed shut when much of the world witnessed the desiccation of the Euphrates River.

Media commentators were baffled. There was no advance script for this. Some glibly informed viewers that Hollywood had come to Rome. The Church must be trying to connect to the youth through an ending meant as a summons to return to it. Others guessed the images portrayed the awful power of death and speculated there would soon be a sequel, once a new pope was consecrated, showing the path to faith and an afterlife that conquers death. Some babbled about celebrities in the crowd.

Ruth sat transfixed throughout the spectacle, keeping track of how the trumpets and images embodied Revelation's Chapters 8 and 9.

When the brass was silent and the screens black, Alessio turned to her.

"What in the world?" he asked.

"Definitely not of this world. We've been visited by angels of the Apocalypse."

"Why six trumpets?" Alessio wondered.

"It means something dramatic is about to happen. In one part of Revelation, what occurs between the sixth and seventh trumpets is called the third woe. Some say this will be worse than the first two of demonic locusts and angels, while others interpret the 'loud voices in heaven' in Chapter 11 as something more positive — Christ's reign. The chapter ends with, 'And the destroyers of the earth will be destroyed before God's temple in heaven is opened.'"

Alessio was grim. "We need the Fatima file fast, before someone brings on the third woe."

19

DAMASCUS, SYRIA

Friday, April 21

RUTH HAD AN HOUR between the bizarre end to the funeral and the 1 p.m. luncheon for Anglican delegates the Centre arranged at a hotel near the Vatican. She scanned news reports and was shocked by what appeared first on the Al Jazeera channel and immediately spread to other media. Recaps of the funeral and the trumpets and horrific images on Vatican screens shifted to reports from Syria.

"We interrupt our Rome coverage for a special report from Damascus," CNN's Breaking News flashed. Its senior Middle East correspondent solemnly reported, "A nuclear device was found around noon Syria time in the Umayyad Mosque. Authoritative sources describe it as a detonation receptacle for a nuclear bomb. Retired Air Force General Robert Slevin joins us."

The general explained, "The casement would hold sufficient material — if loaded and we understand it was not — to vaporize the City of Damascus."

The reporter continued, "Security forces at the Mosque are withholding comment. Speculation centers on Israel. A paper left at the scene declares that Israel will not tolerate a nuclear Iran. The Imam of the Umayyad Mosque announced an investigation and called on Sunnis and Shiites to pray together for peace and unity."

Fast News Network posted six commentators on its screen, each interrupting the other before any had a chance to finish a complete thought, one claiming this was the fault of the prior weak-kneed U.S. Administration that failed to occupy Syria when it had the chance, another arguing that this was obviously Iran staking its claim on eastern Syria and signaling that it already had a nuclear weapon. The third and fourth commentators debated whether to blame a Shiite or Sunni group.

The BBC took a different approach, offering a professor from the American University of Lebanon to discuss the significance of the Umayyad Mosque.

"Syria's Great Mosque," explained the Professor, "the fourth most holy place in Islam, the first mosque visited by a Pope. It ...."

"If it wasn't the Israeli Government, who else would have placed a nuclear device there?" The BBC interviewer interjected.

With a scholarly curl of lip the Professor responded.

"It would be a sacrilege for a Muslim to defile this site. But it could be a warning to Israel and the western world that Islam has a right to nuclear weapons. Or a final Israeli signal to Iran to stop its nuclear program. Then there are Christian sects who deplore the persecution of Syria's Christian minority, about 10% of the population. They're under attack, and it may explain why the casement was planted at the shrine of John the Baptist inside the Mosque."

"You're saying it could be anyone seeking to stir up trouble. But why at the Great Mosque?"

"This Mosque is important. It's where Muslims believe Jesus will return at the End of Days to read the Book of Judgment. According to Christian and Islamic scripture, the world must go through hell before it arrives at the final millennium."

Ruth glanced at the Vatican site before rushing to the luncheon. The Press Office posted a release that the screen shots after the Requiem Mass were not part of the service and an inquiry had begun to find who was to blame.

A morning full of signs of a coming Apocalypse. In Jewish, Christian and Muslim terms. But what did it mean, and what forces were behind this?

20

EAST JERUSALEM
Friday, April 21

HAIM ETZION WAS FURIOUS.

4K's mission failed because of one misstep — a message not delivered. Addressed to the Waqf chief who controlled access to the Temple Mount, it instructed him to close and clear it of visitors overnight and the next day. Because the message did not get to the chief, guards remained on the site and the Mount opened to visitors as usual the morning of the papal funeral.

Proceeding with the plan would have placed tourists at risk, and the site of the Holy of Holies would have been desecrated. The rabbi who blessed the plan was emphatic that his blessing depended on no blood spilled. So the Dome of the Rock remained standing Friday, its gold dome glistening in a heat wave of late April.

As he walked to the café to meet Adlay Epstein and Daniel Alion of 4K's Inner Circle, Etzion recited from memory a verse from Chapter 9 of the Book of Daniel.

"May the right hour and destiny merge in our effort, as you have willed. We ask protection as we try once more to bring forth your Word into the wholeness of time."

Careful not to stumble over the paving stones and cracks of the Old City, Etzion scrolled for news on his smartphone. He paused before skirting the Shuk, an ancient shopping mall where at the entrance, kids kicking around a soccer ball dodged vendors shouting out prices to passersby.

He read with astonishment about the nuclear device discovered at the Umayyad Mosque and was startled to see a Jerusalem Post report that an unnamed Jewish group was suspected, based on a scroll found at the Shrine of John the Baptist. Not our doing! Reading further, Etzion saw the call of the Umayyad Mosque's Imam for Muslims to unite.

He could wait no longer. His private contractor in Damascus must proceed with the hit. He texted the assassin and scurried to the Quarter Café within the Jewish Quarter. The owner nodded, a silent recognition, and led Etzion up the stairs to a table in the upstairs room. It looked across the Kidron Valley to the Jewish Cemetery of the Mount of Olives, where over 100,000 mauve stone tombs filled the hillside, dating from the time of the First Temple three millennia ago.

Epstein and Alion were waiting. Etzion asked if they'd heard about the nuclear device. They agreed it must have been placed there by Iranian agents as a message to Israel that Iran already had the bomb — a warning to back off, and a call to all Muslims to unite in defense of Islam. They shook their heads at the botch of their plan, agreeing that the lieutenant responsible for delivering the message should be removed from the Inner Circle.

Epstein pledged to see to it personally that the next time instructions to the Temple Mount chief would be not only delivered, but obeyed, so there would be no human beings on the Mount on the rescheduled date for 4K's operation. Elected to the Knesset from a minority party pledged to protect the right of orthodox schools to be exempt from state requirements, Epstein was a reliable blood brother.

"Our best opportunity will be in about three weeks when a new pope's installed," said Etzion, as he drummed his left-hand fingers on the gnarled wooden table with onyx inlaid geometric symbols. "It will again draw attention away from Jerusalem, and we can make our move."

"Agreed," said Alion without his typical "but what if" retort that could make meetings last hours instead of minutes. "The red heifer's doing well," he said, referring to a young cow of perfect red color. The Book of Numbers specified that a rabbi should sacrifice it to ensure success. "It's eating like a bull."

"No need to meet this week," declared Etzion. "Activate the chain. Once a pope is elected, Rome will announce the date of the consecration. That will fix our timing."

Etzion turned to Epstein, who was munching his second poppy seed bagel. "Did you know you can fail a drug test from eating those?"

"I've heard that — opium comes from poppies. But you won't find me running an Olympic race," Epstein guffawed and took a large bite.

Alion eyed Epstein's ample girth.

"We're counting on you to move quickly, Adlay. We can't afford another failure. Are you certain you can do it?"

"I won't be running around the Mount, but I have just the right person to clear it. Does it matter if a Muslim guard is there when the explosion happens?"

"I don't care," Etzion responded, "but the rabbi who blesses our mission insists that no human blood be spilled. Muslim blood is blood to him."

"So it will be," said Epstein.

They finished their lukewarm coffee dregs and left a hefty tip for the waitress, though her dress was much too short for their standards of feminine modesty.

21

ROME
Friday, April 21

RUTH RETURNED to her third-floor walk-up around 5 p.m., or as Alessio would say in military time, 17 hundred. She was exhausted from fulfilling the Archbishop's requests, attending to Anglican bishops and scrambling to post an Anglican Centre message of prayer for the departed pope.

When she stepped onto the red tiled apartment entrance, Gabriel jumped up and down in an ecstatic greeting with tail wagging. Ruth noticed an envelope nibbled by Gabriel at one corner, Crane stationery, an American brand, sealed with red wax bearing the Christian fish symbol. It must have fallen from the pile of documents she was carrying yesterday.

It was not an invitation to a post-funeral function as she expected but a letter from Noah Stoll — the first communication between them since his move to the West Coast after Zoar High School junior year other than a flurry of letters that dwindled and ended by graduation. It ended with, "Join me for a drink this evening at 6 — St. Regis Grand Rome. Yours, Noah."

Cindy Wallace had alerted her that Noah might resurface after asking about her at the reunion. Cindy provided details about how Noah had achieved enormous financial success through a tech company called Butterfly.

"He looked great — finally un-hunched his shoulders." The awkward teenager Cindy remembered had matured into a man in charge of himself.

Cindy's message took Ruth to her teenage days in Zoar, when the future beckoned, everything was possible. Nothing held you back — except for small-town thoughts that could imprison those seeking global adventures.

As she hustled Gabriel on a brisk walk around the block, she remembered Noah's self-doubt, loneliness, and fear of rejection. He asked Ruth whether he was a freak or whether it was Zoar Village that was strange. "Look beyond Zoar," Ruth assured him, assuring herself at the same time that Zoar was a beginning and not the end.

He named his tech company Butterfly. *Did he remember my secret?*

When she was ten, she took her father's butterfly collection from a closet. It was a black-lacquered box containing Tiger and Zebra Swallowtails, a Monarch and a Luna Moth, each specimen neatly pinned against deep purple velvet. She imagined them prisoners and carried them into the maple and oak woods along Stanberry Creek, where she gently placed each atop ostrich ferns, dreaming they would flutter away to butterfly heaven like Jesus. Her first attempt at eternal life?

Noah was the only person she told.

In the apartment with Gabriel, Ruth dashed off a postcard with a photo of the St. Peter's Basilica and stamped it for delivery to her parents, recently retired to Florida. She scrapped meditation time, took a brief shower, accepted Noah's invitation and texted Alessio about their dinner location.

One quick look in the mirror before leaving to meet Noah. She detected a worry line forming as a crease above her nose, faint but apparent in the magnifying mirror. Wrinkles would spread and one day crowd her face. She pictured herself in a retirement home. *What will I accomplish by then? Will I be an old maid?*

22

VATICAN CITY
Friday, April 21

LIKE THE ORPHANAGE. As he lay on his bed Alessio recalled nights alone in the small room he shared with a succession of other boys. After the bizarre tumult of the trumpet extravaganza, the massive hallways encased an eerie silence. Gone was the usual bustle of personnel with papers, huddled conversations and the rhythm of a bureaucracy that had both temporal and spiritual work to perform. In the celibate all-male environment of the Vatican's inner sanctum, calm ruled through bureaucratic discipline.

He would be assigned a new post after a new pope was consecrated, his service no longer required within Vatican walls.

Siena? Venice? Milan? A small town again, the only priest? Will I remember what to do?

The Fatima mystery demanded action. Unlocking the black 15th century Florentine cabinet by his bed stand and opening the leather-bound Volume XXI of a journal he would bequeath to the Vatican archives, he thumbed through pages to find notes about a conversation with the Holy Father seven months before.

He found the entry for the eve of Advent. The pontiff was exhausted from a schedule that took them to a monastery for an ordination, lunch with members of the Italian Parliament, a diplomatic reception for the first Ambassador of China to the Holy See, a blessing for 25 American Knights of Columbus, two hours of correspondence, and finally vespers. The Pope relaxed with a crystal glass of his favorite Argentinian dessert wine. This was when the Pope could reflect freely, with Alessio serving as a trusted sounding board, there to help the Pope clarify his thoughts without argument or challenge.

His notes recorded that the pontiff walked to the Secret Archives that morning before mass and brought back the Fatima file. From several feet away, Alessio could see the formatted sheets that every file contained to mark its contents, its date of deposit and other critical archival data. The folder held several sheets of 100-year-old faded handwriting.

The Pope held them reverently. He spoke gently of how he discussed Fatima with John Paul II shortly after that sainted pontiff visited Portugal and published "the Third Secret," in hopes of ending speculation about it.

Ridiculous rumors ensued about how the Third Secret called for the priesthood of women, or the end of the Vatican's leadership of the Church, or the rise of Islam, or other baseless speculation of uninformed fanatics. The Pope held a single sheet apart from the others and declared that it must be left to his successor.

"We cannot release this!" he instructed sternly. Alessio pledged at the Pope's insistence that after the pontiff's death, he would inform the successor immediately about the unpublished page. Nothing more was said except for the Pope's comment that burned in his memory even now — "This holds the final revelation. Show it to no one except the one who follows me."

Alessio returned his journal to the cabinet and locked it. He hurried to the Vatican Archives hoping to find Archivist Mercati, though he knew that on this day no one would probably be on duty. The Archives were deserted and the library dim as dusk. With late afternoon sunlight filtering through glass designed to preserve ancient texts, Alessio located the search function on the archive's central computer. Using the late pontiff's private key, he gained full access. Scrolling to the Fatima listing, he found recent entries. The Pope's withdrawal of the file appeared seven months earlier, matching the date in his journal. On the next day, a final entry showed the return of the file to its "*Solo PM*" status, meaning it could be retrieved only by *Pontifex Maximus*, the pope.

His cell phone buzzed with a text from Ruth asking which restaurant tonight. He replied with the name of a taverna near the Coliseum.

Alessio paused, thinking there was one other place to check — a cross-file that recorded each deposit and withdrawal of any item within the restricted access category. Inserting the code number of the Fatima file, he found the chronological listing of every time anyone removed or returned the file.

Final listings were the day before the Pope's death. The Holy Father personally withdrew the volume early that morning and returned it late that afternoon. The last entry showed a withdrawal. The person marked as removing it was Archivist Mercati.

23

ZAGROS MOUNTAINS, IRAN
Friday, April 21

VALI QALIL scanned media reports of the discovered nuclear device, starting with the outraged comments of Fariborz al-Hasani, Imam of the Umayyad Mosque.

"Sacrilege! An affront to Islam," he thundered. An immediate investigation would be launched to find who was responsible for planting the device at the shrine of John the Baptist. "Islam is a religion of peace. No weapon belongs within a mosque," he fumed.

Imam al-Hasani was a beacon of Islamic unity. Throughout the troubles that put Syria on the endangered countries list, he regularly hosted dinners that brought together bitter enemies, following the Qur'an's injunction that evil should be met with reconciliation. The nuclear device planted by AM would stir hope for unity.

Qalil was thrilled to see widespread blame directed at Israel, given a document found at the scene with a blue and white Star of David on otherwise blank stationery. He read that the weak Syrian Government took possession of the device and refused to let anyone else inspect it. Offers of help from the United States and European Union were quickly rebuffed. A call offering forensic assistance from Russian President Mikhail Mikhailovich Goudonov, an ally, received no immediate acceptance. It was obvious that a viewing of the casement was worth something substantial in return. Qalil envisioned high-ranking Syrian officials vying privately to trade information for euros, dollars, yen, Swiss francs, gold, or cryptocurrency. Israel announced that it had nothing to do with the incident.

As the AM Officer Corps gathered again in its sanctuary within Iran's Zagros Mountains, Qalil watched the day's developments on an Iranian channel.

"Tension rises like desert heat on a cloudless day," he said to himself. All Muslim countries denounced the incident as an Israeli provocation. AM had avoided the media's list of suspects charged with placing the nuclear casement at the Umayyad Mosque. The bogus document AM planted falsely implicated Israel, with the aim of rallying Sunnis and Shiites in support of AM's plan once announced.

Once the AM officers arrived, Qalil brought the group to order with prayer and a recitation from the Qur'an. Then he stated triumphantly, "In the name of Allah, the

Compassionate, the Merciful. We witnessed first-hand Syria's destruction, as foretold in the Qur'an, the final sign for us to act. Peace is a mirage. The forces of the Dajjal strengthen."

A colonel spoke. "Syria is not yet destroyed. Should we not wait for its total collapse before we launch the March?"

Debate erupted. Since the suicidal struggle of the Assads to hold power by blasting whole cities to bits, it was plain to the AM officers that Syria was not a functional country, but the timing of next steps was not obvious.

Qalil settled the argument. "Syria is in its death rattle. Mustafa, is the call ready?"

"Yes, my Emir."

"Then the call goes out tomorrow immediately after *Fajr*," the dawn prayer, first of the five daily prayers.

The webmaster assured the officers he had tested the site with a far-flung network of Islamic internet specialists. He projected the test-site announcing the Innocents project on the conference room's wall. As the webmaster reviewed icons on the home page, an officer on the technology team whispered into his ear, and the webmaster switched to an Al Jazeera news stream. "Imam of Umayyad Mosque assassinated by suicide bomber" was the report.

The room erupted, "Death to Israel!"

"We must act now," said Qalil. Jerusalem would be retaken, starting with the March of the Innocents as the key to unite Islam, following in the footsteps of *Salah-al-Din Yusuf ibn Ayyub*, Saladin to the western world. That great Kurdish warrior united Egypt and Syria and took back the holy lands from the Crusaders. Now AM must lead.

After AM's Officers departed, Qalil sat alone at his command desk. He unsheathed his dagger and, picturing his enemies, began to stab the desk which was already pockmarked with cuts of prior ruminations. He would unite Islam against the forces of evil. The venom of revenge coursed through him as he recalled a U.S. drone strike ten years earlier that destroyed a Syrian school for girls he had founded. He sliced into the wood. All but one student were killed. The survivor was remarkably unscarred. Another jab. He adopted the girl, a child whose parents were killed in the Syrian civil war. A'ishah — she would lead the March of the Innocents.

He thrust the blade into the center of the desk, then twisted the dagger into a widening hole. The world would soon discover that he was the heroic Mahdi of the End Time.

24

ROME
Friday, April 21

CENTERED BETWEEN the Moses and Najada Fountains, the five-star St. Regis Rome looked more palatial residence than hotel. A bellman in a blue double-breasted uniform with silver buttons stood between white pillars. He opened the heavy middle doors for Ruth to reveal a dazzling white and gold interior.

She recognized Noah, who was checking his smartphone in the middle of the lobby. No longer a gangly adolescent with tousled hair, Noah wore a tailored grey suit, with a starched white shirt and pink silk tie. He stood at broad-shouldered attention, thick brown hair waved to the right. She marveled at the crystal chandelier, the Roman busts, gold timepieces and artfully spaced sitting areas.

Noah looked up as she entered and strode towards her with a broad smile. She extended her hand, which he confidently turned into a hearty hug.

"Ruth, you haven't changed a bit. It's so good to see you."

"Your eyes are kind," she laughed, marveling at his self-assurance.

"Let's have a drink," he said, maneuvering her gently toward the library bar off the lobby. "When I last saw you, you were headed to college in Ohio. And here you are in Rome. You're a minister."

"We say priest in the Episcopal Church," Ruth corrected. "You know me, always wondering why we're here on the planet."

"Thoughts I've been having," said Noah. "How did you end up ordained?"

"A long story to be told another time. How about you, video gamer to titan of industry. How did you manage that?"

"Luck and persistence," he said. "Riding the digital wave. Five years earlier or later and it wouldn't have happened. I patented software that ended up worth a fortune. We sold the business for a price I couldn't refuse."

"I always knew you had it in you," she said. "And what do you do now in California — surf?"

"Surf the web," he laughed. "I'm into running. My car has a 26.2 plate, for my first marathon."

"I like to run — but 26 miles! I'm in awe. What was your time?"

The years melted away. A red-vested waiter brought to their table Campari and sodas Noah pre-ordered.

"Give it a try, small-town girl."

"Campari? Now I know I'm in Italy."

She reached eagerly for the dark red cocktail that worldly characters drank in novels. It took supreme effort to endure the shockingly bitter taste. *So much for attempting Roman sophistication, she thought as she looked around unsuccessfully for a place to spit it out.*

"Can't take the Zoar out of us," he laughed, putting down his glass. "I had the same reaction on the first sip." He signaled to the waiter and ordered two glasses of Brunello. "So how'd you end up in Rome?"

"The Archbishop of Canterbury decided it's time for the Church of Rome to enter the 21st century and interact with a female priest. I'm a professor with a specialty in visions from different faiths. He asked me to be the emissary from Anglican churches here."

"Do you have spies?"

Ruth tossed her hair, narrowed her eyelids and leaned forward. "I'd have to shoot you if I shared the details." Remembering the centuries of church versus heretic, she added, "or put you on the rack." Noah pretended to grimace in fear. Relaxing in the presence of her old friend, she leaned back onto the soft cushions. "So, how's retirement?"

"I wouldn't call it that. After selling the company, I felt like Midas counting his gold, but for what? I started attending a church in Palo Alto, and that led me to the quest I'm on now. I'm part of a group that takes the Bible as a call to advance the Kingdom."

Ruth was intrigued by this religious side of Noah that she did not expect. But advancing the Kingdom had evangelical overtones. He might believe that God dictated the Bible, or that people had to have a specific born-again experience. She didn't, so she would tread lightly.

"I'd love to hear more about your faith journey," she encouraged, certain this was a safe approach.

"Cindy gave me your book. Brilliant. You brought the prophets to life."

Ruth was surprised to feel herself blush. "It's great material," she said.

Noah nodded. "The Christian group I belong to reveres the Bible's last book. You summed it up so well in your final chapter."

"Poetry really." Thinking how Revelation underlay the theatrics and trumpets at the end of the Vatican ceremony, Ruth asked, "That reminds me, were you at the funeral?"

"Nearby," Noah answered vaguely.

"What happened at the end — the Vatican seemed stunned."

The bartender whisked away the Campari and showed the bottle of Brunello to Noah, who nodded approval.

Noah offered her the glass to taste.

She approved.

He asked, "What did you make of the trumpets?"

"There's no mistaking the biblical roots. Revelation."

"There were only six trumpets," Noah probed cautiously.

"A man of the Bible," she said, impressed.

How refreshing, an engaging entrepreneur who knows the Bible. Her academic colleagues were mostly men who sat at desks or stood in front of students, and the men friends introduced showed no interest in theology.

"Ruth, can I share in confidence?" He leaned forward and hushed his voice.

"Like old times." Ruth leaned in.

"At my church I'm a member of the '9'ers.' Membership's restricted to those who amass at least a hundred million before age 45."

Noah recounted how at a 9'ers retreat in the Russian River area of California the group had an intense discussion about how to do good in the world, and the conversation revolved around the Bible's final Book.

"The New Jerusalem Alliance, have you heard of it? Or maybe by its initials — the NJA?"

Ruth scanned her memory of evangelical movements in social media and came up blank. "Sorry, no."

"You will once we go public. The NJA's goal is simple — to hasten the coming of the New Jerusalem as described in Revelation. If we do it properly and if the time is right, the final stage that God intends will arrive." He paused. His right eye twitched slightly, a sign Ruth recalled from Zoar days when Noah was nervous about something.

Ruth decided to draw him out. "What would it mean to hasten the coming of a New Jerusalem?"

"The trumpets and screen shots this morning — we orchestrated that to show the world that most disasters that precede the End Time have happened, that we're at the dawn of the End Time. Unfortunately, the media were distracted by the nuclear device in Damascus and portrayed the trumpets like a Dixieland send-off. They missed the point." He shook his head.

Ruth reacted. "You desecrated the Pope's funeral? What were you thinking?"

Noah replied defensively. "We want the world to recognize the chaos that's already been unleashed, and to prepare."

"Prepare for what?"

"Why, for the coming of New Jerusalem," he replied. "Its time is near."

Ruth frowned. "It's one thing to read John's ancient dream. Quite another to think you should bring on the apocalypse."

"Ephesians 6:12," Noah argued, "'For our struggle is not against flesh and blood, but against the rulers, against the authorities, against the powers of this dark world and against the forces of evil in the heavenly realms.'"

Ruth was silent as he finished the verse. "Spiritual principalities and powers — there's more to life than what we can see, and more God wants us to do than sit in church."

"My specialty is religious visions," Ruth replied cautiously. "I do believe there's more than meets the everyday eye. But we mortals can't take charge of God's calendar."

"I can explain more if you're free for dinner," he suggested hopefully.

"Love to, but I have an appointment." She must be misunderstanding him. Noah didn't seem like a crackpot. Perhaps she wasn't up to date on how technology is used to communicate faith.

"I'm flying out tomorrow morning, but let's stay in touch." He held her hands. "Please," he added.

"I'd like that," she said.

"Time is short."

She nodded.

Noah walked Ruth to the front. The bellman opened the heavy bronze door to the dusk of early evening. Noah accompanied her to the sidewalk and said softly as she escaped hearing range, "Enjoy the fireworks tonight."

Noah watched her depart along the Via Vittorio Emanuele Orlando. He gazed at the Fountain of Moses, looking for each feature the hotel's guidebook described. Built in the 1500's by Sixtus V as the terminus of an aqueduct, the Fountain's centerpiece was a colossal statue of robed Moses striking a Wilderness rock to bring forth water. In the background lions watched Pope Sixtus V's mounts carry a large iron cross. On one side a triumphal sculpture of Aaron led the Israelites to water, shielded by tabernacles and trees of life. On the other, the warrior-prophet Gideon adorned in Roman gear led his people across the Jordan River. Noah felt inspired by the marble of ancient Rome with the majesty of Moses, his spiritual ancestor who led his people to the Promised Land.

"Yes, the signs are everywhere," Noah spoke silently to the ancient prophet. "And more to come, even tonight." He suddenly wondered if Moses ever married. He could not recall. But Moses had his mission. And that was everything.

Almost everything.

25

ROME-LA TAVERNA DEI QUARANTA
Friday, April 21

RUTH UNFOLDED her pocket map of Rome's impossibly zig-zag streets. The taverna Alessio selected for dinner was within walking distance of the St. Regis, which gave her time to absorb her reunion with Noah. He'd grown up to be a successful businessman and a spiritual pilgrim, but she was uneasy about his talk of the Book of Revelation.

Why was he saying time was short? A strange comment if he meant to rekindle a relationship.

She passed the neoclassical monument to Victor Emmanuel II, an enormous white marble edifice built in honor of Italian unification and its first king. She chuckled at the guidebook's note that some Italians called it *la torta nuziale* (the wedding cake) or *la dentiera* (the dentures).

Ruth wondered if Noah suffered from grandiose delusions. Nearby Forum columns that once supported temples to long-forgotten gods and goddesses stood as reminders that religions too can crumble. Faded election posters competed with advertisements for baroque music concerts pasted on walls along store fronts. A couple slowly pushed a twin baby stroller. A black Mercedes angrily flashed headlights at a Fiat straddling two lanes.

Searching the map for the twisting, ever-changing names of streets, she scanned for Via Claudia, named for Rome's Emperor in the time of Jesus of Nazareth, where the appointed restaurant was at number 24. The Coliseum glowed as dusk met night.

When she arrived at La Taverna dei Quaranta minutes before the agreed time, she mentioned the name Father Alessio Brondini, prompting an insider nod from the host, who led her to an outside table. Gazing at the colossal ruin where gladiators entertained the elite two millennia ago, Ruth worried about the NJA and what it meant about Noah.

Alessio arrived looking unlike the stereotypical priest in his open collared navy polo shirt over black jeans. Ruth noticed the fit of his clothes and wondered if he ever had trouble with the vow of celibacy or if the nuns for whom he celebrated mass struggled in his presence.

"A place my superiors never come," he explained. "Father David and I always dressed off-duty to avoid being recognized." The menus arrived in Italian only. He pointed on the page listing house specialties. "The cod is what to order if you like fish."

He told her about Italian culture, why pasta is not an entrée in Italy, the ingredients of a good fish rub, and why Romans honk their horns incessantly. Ruth felt Italian ordering the house Insalata Caprese. At home it would bear the less charming title of "tomatoes and cheese."

The restaurant dimmed as twilight darkened to reveal faint stars and a brilliant full moon hovering on the horizon. Alessio turned to the subject of the evening.

"The Archivist took the Fatima file. He doesn't trust me now that my role at the Vatican is ended."

"What does the Vatican say about the trumpets?" Ruth asked.

"Security is on a hunt to know how the trumpeters got access to the colonnade and who hacked into the transmission lines. They suspect atheists ... or Protestants."

Ruth winced. Roman Catholics and Protestants had been adversaries for five hundred years since the Great Schism. Images flashed through her brain of the medieval Inquisition and instruments of torture that the Roman Church used to suppress heresy.

Unaware of Ruth's reaction Alessio continued.

"It was the Holy Father's wish that his funeral might bring together people of faith. To have his friend, now Iran's Supreme Leader, present for his parting — that was a tribute to his quest for a universal faith community. But the finale?"

"I heard a rumor that the people who did this were acting out the Book of Revelation." She felt that much was safe to say.

"Revelation?" Alessio questioned as salad was served. "That book does not receive much attention from the Church. Ever since Protestants and emperors began interpreting the Beast or the AntiChrist as the pope, we keep it on the shelf."

"Interpretation swings both ways," Ruth explained. "Beginning in the 1500's several popes claimed Martin Luther was the AntiChrist. But back to Revelation, where the six trumpets calling forth demonic events match the images flashed on the screens. The message is that the horrors on the screens have scourged the earth, and six trumpets have already sounded."

"And then the third woe. You mentioned that — and what a seventh trumpet means."

"Most scholars say it would herald the return of Christ to earth."

"The kingdom of our Lord and of his Christ. And he shall reign for ever and ever," Alessio sang softly to the strains of Handel's Hallelujah Chorus.

"That's the optimistic view. 'The mystery of God will be accomplished, just as he announced to his servants the prophets.' Revelation, 10: 7," recited Ruth. "But there's a dark side to this interpretation."

"Something terrible?"

"Revelation says that only when one City's citizens 'were terrified and gave glory to the God of heaven' would the seventh trumpeter call forth the kingdom of the world as having become the kingdom of our Lord and of his Christ."

"Which city is targeted for this terrible fate?"

"Early Christians thought it was Sodom or Egypt's capital."

"Could it be Damascus today? Maybe that's the link to the device found at the Umayyad Mosque."

"Who knows? The City of the final revelation is Jerusalem. That much is clear."

"A new Jerusalem. If the reign of Christ is near, I hope the seventh trumpet sounds soon," said Alessio, as entrées were served, lightly fried codfish, specialty of the Taverna.

"I'm not so sure you'll like it. After that glorious day in Chapter 11, Chapter 12 opens with a woman clothed with the sun and the moon under her feet. Your Church interprets her to be Mary, while others see the woman as the universal church, persecuted and hunted by the Beast, and she's forced to hide in the wilderness for 1260 days. Then red dragons and other creatures do battle, toward the ultimate end of God's final triumph, and Satan is banished forever. Picture Jesus holding his threshing fork, separating the elect from the chaff. And you know where the chaff goes."

"Into the fires of hell. What about the beast numbered 666?"

"The Dead Sea Scrolls and other texts say the number's either 666 or 616, through the Greek practice of assigning numbers to letters and adding them up."

"Gematria," Alessio named it.

Ruth nodded.

"Bingo. Most likely the author of Revelation was referring to Emperor Nero, whose letters in Greek add numerically either to 666 or to 616, depending which variation of his name and title is used. Every generation identifies someone new. Today you can find a Gematria 666 calculator in multiple languages on Google."

They talked about the conclave to elect the next pope, points of dialogue between the Anglican Centre and the Vatican before Ruth's arrival, the warmer than usual weather of Rome. Torta della Nonna arrived, along with strong Italian coffee in demitasse cups. Ruth took a sip.

A brilliant dark red burst over the Coliseum flashed and exploded in sound. This was followed by spectacular sparks high in the air with multiple repeating flowerhead figures, arcing streams that shot off comet-like spirals, smaller bouquets with more gentle ruby spurts. The magnificent display continued for fifteen minutes, one crimson burst after another without a pause, no interruption for ground displays, as far as they could tell from their seats. Finally, a rat-a-tat round of twenty giant zinnia-like images seared the skies, with ruby sparkling trails falling from the sky and fading to dark before touching ground. The firework filter turned it blood red.

"'The full moon became like blood' in Revelation 6: 12, after the sixth seal was opened, with the stars of the sky falling to earth. 'Fall on us and hide us from the face of him who is seated on the throne, and from the wrath of the Lamb, for the great day of their wrath has come, and who can stand before it',"" she quoted, wondering if this was Noah's work.

"You read too much into a colorful display." Alessio shook his head. "Tell me about your Archbishop."

Ruth explained how the Most Reverend Crispus Okello, first African-born leader of the Anglican Communion, became a priest in a country of unspeakable genocide. When the tribal and religious violence spiraled into a terrible vortex of Islamic-Christian hatreds, Archbishop Okello led a march of Hutu and Tutsi priests down a highway, claiming peace in the name of God. The violence subsided.

His charismatic leadership attracted worldwide attention, and he was soon called to England, where he became a confidante of Archbishops Rowan Williams and Justin Welby. Canon Okello helped each navigate the course between conservative African Anglican churches and liberal North America, with disputes over homosexuality, the role of women and other issues threatening to fracture the Anglican Communion that began 500 years ago under Henry VIII, when the Church of England split from Rome.

"Who do you think will be the next Holy Father?" Ruth turned the discussion.

"Many say it will be one of two Italian cardinals. I'm not so certain. The Church today primarily belongs to believers in Latin America, Africa, Asia. A second pope from outside Europe could emerge."

"Whoever it is, I look forward to working with you, Alessio. Please call me Ruth. I don't use Mother."

"Agreed. But Ruth, I no longer have a post. I reported only to the late Holy Father. I continue in my role with the Anglican Centre only until a successor is named."

Ruth sighed. Alessio's replacement would be an older conservative priest who looked askance at ordained women. She finished the final drops of Grappa. At least she had enjoyed the Fatima adventure with Alessio for a brief time.

Very early Saturday morning, Ruth took Gabriel for a walk and purchased *la Repubblica* at the corner coffee shop that never seemed to close. The paper had a beautiful spread of fireworks reflected in the Tiber River, blood red in tone. On page one a column reported that the Vatican denied the fireworks were an official postlude, saying they must have been an anonymous tribute from the faithful.

The spirit of the Apocalypse is in our midst. Signs all about. Noah's words.

In the local section, there was a column about overnight pranksters who put dark red gelatinous ingredients into seven basin fountains of Rome — the Trevi, the Four Rivers, the Neptune, the Egyptian Lion, the Fountain of the Moor, the Palazzo Venezia and the fountain at St. Peter's Square. No lasting damage was reported, but thick liquid jammed the pumps to move the fluid like a pulse, as though the fountains came to life.

Noah's attempt at the fulfillment of Revelation's description of what would happen to rivers of the world before the seventh trumpet sounds?

Later that day, not reported by *la Repubblica* but picked up by Islamic media and spread virally by social networks and bloggers, including one Ruth checked after feeding Gabriel, was another Damascus incident. On the day after the nuclear device was discovered, black smoke billowed through the City of Damascus from twelve directions, covering the sky around the Mosque and its environs, blotting out the sun. In a city used to bombings, snipers and shelling, the fire department did not respond with trucks and brigades but sent a captain to investigate. He reported no fire where there had been a dark cloud, and the fumes did not seem harmful. The impact was more like that of a gigantic smoke bomb.

Noah again?

Ruth's Muslim media feed cited a Shiite leader invited to participate in an Islamic unity service at the Great Mosque, who gave a stirring summons to the greater jihad. He was quoted, "Although only Allah knows when the Day of Resurrection shall be, we would be fools to ignore the signs foretold in the Qur'an and the hadith. When Syria is destroyed and ashes cover its skies, Isa will return, and the Mahdi will appear. *Inshallah.*"

Were Christians and Muslims being called to accelerate the end of the world? How far were Noah and his group prepared to go? And who or what was playing a similar role for Islam?

26

ROME, WASHINGTON
MOSCOW & JERUSALEM
Sunday, April 23

ALESSIO FELT LIKE AN INTRUDER at early morning mass in the Vatican chapel, a private service for those not experiencing the splendor of Basilica worship. He had not been there on Sunday for years, given his duty always to be with the pontiff, whose calling was to be the central figure at public worship somewhere in the world. The homily was titled "Search and thou shall find," referring to the Holy Spirit at work in the Sistine Chapel where the cardinals were in conclave. For Alessio it inspired an online quest.

Returning to his room, he booted his pc and searched the web for Revelation and Apocalypse. Up popped a dizzying array of sites predicting the end of the world drawing near. As he scrolled through the list, he added "Islam" to the search and found a striking video of explosion after explosion in the Middle East, followed by a woman who emerged from a cloud dressed in pure white robes and repeated two phrases in Farsi over a world-fusion Arabic chant. "It is time, it is time, it is time," read English subtitles. Its final scene zoomed to the Umayyad Mosque of Damascus, first bathed in sunlight and then shrouded in smoke as the image faded to black with the phrase in Arabic and Farsi — "Islam Unite!" and in crimson letters — "AM."

Alessio searched "AM." Wikipedia offered an array of meanings including a calendar era based on the biblical creation of the world, a method of numbering years in the Coptic calendar, a climate classification code, the Aston Martin luxury car, and a fictional supercomputer in the short story titled "I have no mouth, and I must scream." A biblical scholar pointed out that "AM" if written as "Am'" meant in ancient Hebrew the nation or tribe of Israel, but if used as "Am ha-aretz" it meant the common people, pagans in ancient times.

Alessio browsed to the highest trending YouTube video, a collage of six trumpeters and scenes of destruction broadcast at the end of the Vatican rites, capped with booming blood-red fireworks over Rome to strains of the Hallelujah Chorus. The visuals paralleled visions from Revelation.

Skimming blogs, he was unsettled to find Doomsday predictions receiving mainstream attention. Never had these topics come up in the Vatican. *The world is more on edge than I realized.* Groups like the Kingdom Warriors, Atlanta Zombie and skeptoid. com posted timelines of an impending cataclysm.

What if the time for the Seventh Trumpet really is near?

USA President Ike Palmer's daily intelligence briefing was a blur of the political tinged with the religious. A pope buried amidst Revelation scenes projected by unknown hackers. The nuclear device planted in Damascus. Assassination of Imam al-Hasani of Damascus' Great Mosque. Threats by Arab leaders against Israel. Elevated to President a month earlier after a heart attack took his predecessor, Palmer made an impromptu visit to the press room to stake out his position. Calling for "irreversible actions" to prevent Iran from getting a nuclear weapon, he declared all options ready for use.

"Sanctions are for the sandbox. We're serious now," he said.

After this public statement, Palmer met with National Security Advisor Arnoldo Coulter and Director of National Intelligence Maureen Sullivan. Each was newly installed after Palmer shocked the establishment by choosing an entirely new foreign policy and defense team within a week of becoming President.

"A nuclear device takes us by surprise in a Damascus Mosque, and the Pope's funeral is penetrated by crackpot trumpeters and hackers. What do you know?" he demanded.

Security Advisor Coulter reassured him, "The device was from Iran. It was the regime's way of bluffing that they have the bomb or are so far along that there's no time left to stop them."

DNI Sullivan was not so sure.

"The stunt was too ambiguous to be Iranian. There's an upsurge in web traffic among Muslim extremist groups. Al Qaeda, ISIS and their clones were not involved, that much seems clear. Hamas and Hezbollah aren't operative in Damascus."

Palmer drummed his fingers on the Lincoln Desk. "I didn't hire you two for printouts of the New York Times. Figure it out. Israel's worried. Mossad confirms Iranian labs are working overtime."

DNI Sullivan chimed in, "The Fordow plant near Qom is where enrichment is handled. Shall we destabilize the centrifuges, same as in 2011?"

Palmer quickly rejected that idea. "They strengthened their tech defenses. They're too smart to be burned a second time."

"We cannot know that doing nothing for another month will not expand our options," Coulter cautioned.

"You know I hate double negatives, Arnoldo. That was a triple. Say what you mean."

Knowing the President's close affinity with the Prime Minister of Israel, Coulter stated, "It's time to strike Iran, sir."

Part of Palmer's appeal to conservative and Jewish voters as a vice-presidential candidate was his close personal connection to Israeli Prime Minister Aaron Feldman. They became friends while spending a post-graduate year together at Oxford.

During Palmer's first press conference after assuming the presidency, he spoke of the "inseparable" bond of the U.S. and Israel and of Jerusalem as "the City of God." He used the phrase "Land of Israel." Those with linguistic nuance noticed "Land" capitalized in Palmer's public releases, indicating alignment with Feldman's position of Israel's right to expand to King David's boundaries, which already claimed huge expanses long occupied by Palestinians before the 1967 war.

The election had been razor close. Like his running mate, Palmer railed against Muslim terrorists and runaway liberal justices. Catholic, Evangelical and Jewish voters put the Republicans over the top.

"We'll meet at 7 p.m. Tuesday. Tell me then who masterminded Rome and Damascus, and give me a plan to stop Iran once and for all."

Determined to rebuild Russia into a world power, President Mikhail Mikhailovich Goudonov was ready to take far bolder steps than his predecessor, who seized Crimea but grew distracted by pursuit of popularity and fortune rather than restoring the Russian empire. No bare-chested photo ops or flights with migrating cranes for Goudonov. He would reverse the disastrous breakup of the Soviet Union. A grand alliance with Islamic countries would lure Central Asian republics back into the Kremlin's grip. Ukraine would follow, then the Baltics.

On the same evening the Americans held a state dinner for Israeli Prime Minister Feldman, Goudonov hosted a lavish Kremlin dinner for Iran's President Al-Rabani. Non-alcoholic juice toasts proclaimed Russia's eternal alliance with the people of Islam and a pact to counteract the U.S./European alliance with Israel. Silk banners festooned with standards of ancient Persian kings Cyrus the Great and Darius I intermingled with Shiite and imperial Russian imagery.

In a show of solidarity, President Goudonov announced Iran had the protection of Russia's nuclear arsenal if any nation dared attack it. The Iranian President looked startled by this news but smiled broadly and raised his white grape juice glass to toast his country's new ultimate guardian.

Upon return from Rome, the Israeli Prime Minister gave a 5-minute report to the Knesset. Aaron Feldman used a teleprompter, as the camera angle when he read from notes focused attention on his eye-patch and bald spot. Feldman spoke more like an impassioned rabbi than former Army commander that earned him hero status.

"My friends, we built walls for peace. We offered painful concessions to those of Palestinian heritage. The time for compromise is past. The Book of Daniel of our *Ketuvim* guides us. We will not allow a new Persian empire to inflict unholy disaster upon our people. We will act."

At first the chamber was silent. Seconds later, thunderous applause erupted. Defense and restraint had only led to suicide bombers in market stalls and rockets dropping on schools. There would be no more of that.

27

LEBANON, SYRIA, JORDAN, SAUDI ARABIA, & EGYPT
Week of April 24

WHEN THE NJA'S SAM TURRAIN VISITED the isolated Lebanese village of Sir ad Dinniyah, the local chief was baffled as to why anyone would want to construct a massive arch. But jobs were scarce, money was offered, and the design was impressive. Drawings showed an enormous marble gate, an architectural echo of an ancient civilization's projection of immortality. Thinking it could become a tourist magnet for the shriveling village, the chief approved it after extracting baksheesh and jobs for relatives.

The first public mention of a white marble arch surfaced in an April Israeli newspaper that a massive gate was being built in the Sinai near Elat at the southern tip of Israel, just outside the Egyptian town of Taba. The mayor refused to reveal details but proclaimed it would project the glory of Egyptian civilization.

 of the NJA orchestrated the creation of nearly identical monuments. Connecting the dots between them would plot a line that started just outside Bur Sa'id, the northernmost seaside terminus of the Suez Canal, headed straight south to near Fanara and continued in a straight line south to Bir Nakhail, Egypt, just west of the Gulf of Suez, then taking a 90-degree turn due east to Taba, Egypt, traversed east to Al'Aqabah, Jordan, continued all the way to Al Mughayra, Saudi Arabia, then veered due north to Qa al Wisad in Jordan, to an area southwest of Bi'r Irziq, Syria, then pointed straight west in northern Lebanon to the Sir ad Dinniyah site.

Drawing lines between these points on a map revealed a two-dimensional diagram of about 70% of a square's perimeter. Each side stretched about 333 miles in length, so that the square, if completed into the eastern Mediterranean Sea, would measure about 1,363 miles all the way around. Directly in the center was Jerusalem.

Construction proceeded at breakneck speed at each site with hundreds of craftsmen and officials well paid to get the work done on time. There was no trace of the source of the crisp 100 Euro notes and US $100 bills used for payment.

28

WASHINGTON, D.C.
Monday, April 24

SAM TURRAIN MET NOAH STOLL in a Georgetown coffeehouse after returning from his tour of the arch sites.

"They're on schedule," he reported.

"Great. You didn't hitchhike over there, did you?" asked Noah.

"Only once, but I was with my driver. Flat tire."

They discussed the media's failure to understand the warnings the NJA issued during the papal funeral or to grasp the significance of the seven scrolls delivered to astonished mayors.

"We have to go public," said Noah.

"Why haven't we before now?" asked Sam.

"We wanted the world to recognize the signs as coming from God. Now we'll have to reveal the NJA as the intermediary."

"Roger. It's like the passage from Hebrews you texted me," said Sam. "We owe it to humanity — give everybody the chance to believe and repent before the Time arrives."

"For Christ will come a second time, not to deal with sin, but to save those who are eagerly waiting for him," Noah quoted from Hebrews' Chapter 29.

Drawing on the considerable resources and talents of the Elders, Noah and Sam had worked for months to prepare an internet campaign through www.nja.org, drafted as a dazzling site that gave browsers a 3-D guided tour of a New Jerusalem as described in Revelation. Noah gave Sam a pre-launch tour of the site.

"A glorious city on a hill, with the river of life flowing through it, lighted not by moon or sun but from a holy figure sitting next to a brilliant white lamb," read the banner.

It was never dark in the New Jerusalem. The Garden of Eden was reinvented with a global citizenry and no fruit forbidden. Amiable residents chatted under banners of the Almighty and Christ the King. Simply worded text asked readers to imagine a world at peace, full acceptance of everyone, no illness, no sin and no need for it, harmony, abundance. And after imagining, the reader was asked — *What will you do today to bring about the New Jerusalem?* An invitation to join a network committed to the mission beckoned, with an unexpected bold notice — "Financial contributions not accepted."

"What d'ya think, Sam?" asked Noah.

"Wow."

"Then it's a go."

Noah clicked a button and launched the site. Within hours interest percolated. The pace quickened when the NJA offered a prize of $250,000 for the best proposal for how a New Jerusalem could be expedited — with instruction that this be stated in no more than 500 words and submitted within ten days. Preachers used the prompt in their Sunday sermons to urge congregants to enter the contest. In two days, the site achieved 3,467,532 hits, and by the sixth day about 10 million visits.

Submissions poured in from around the world. On deadline day, a clock ticked away the seconds, and a counter blurred past the 55 million hit mark with more than a million submissions. www.nja.org promised to crown the victor within a month.

29

ROME
Wednesday, April 26

AFTER THE ANGLICAN DELEGATES to the papal funeral left Rome, Ruth took Gabriel on long walks through Rome's Non-Catholic Cemetery. It was a peaceful respite from the turmoil of the City, the resting place of poets Shelley and Keats and of many other Protestants. She worked with Secretary Ponelli to adjust the Anglican Centre to her style, the cigar humidor the first item sent to storage.

She spent hours researching details of the Miracle of Fatima and scanning news reports from Syria, Israel and Iran, all projecting a rising level of tension. One find seized her attention — a YouTube video by AM. From the mists of a whirling cloud a woman in white named A'ishah emerged and stood next to Navid Kosari.

Ruth searched Kosari's background to find he was the mega-star of Iranian film, Islam's heartthrob, with bulging biceps, jet black hair and cropped beard. His square-jawed face and deep-throated voice projected sincerity. His stature in Iran grew from refusing to leave the country's modest film sector despite offers from Hollywood and Bollywood. The Wikipedia profile reported that he scrupulously obeyed Iranian censors, obsessed about any showing of excessive female skin that might let a camel's nose poke too provocatively into the tent of Revolutionary Iran.

Within days of its launch AM's post garnered a top viewed rating, the first time any segment from Iran rose to such heights. Rhythmic background music by a noted Iranian composer who catered to the young without offending the Revolutionary Guard drew viewers in, as scenes of ancient Persia dissolved into a stunning picture of the Qaaba, the black cube-like building that is Islam's holiest place, considered the House of God to which able Muslims journey on the Haj.

Ruth was captivated as Kosari praised male pilgrims circling the Qaaba. Then the screen focused on Kosari, who looked directly into the eyes of viewers. Each sentence was accompanied by a closer image until at the end only his dark eyes appeared while his voice intoned, "It is time for the Innocents to lead in the teachings of the Prophet, peace be upon him and his family. We will follow in Fatima's footsteps." Ruth knowing this referred to the Prophet Muhammad's daughter.

"Women of Islam — you are the Innocents who must lead. You hold the mightiest weapon of all — righteousness. Together we will summon the 12th imam to come forth as the Mahdi. He will call Isa to return and fight with us against the Dajjal. Women of Islam — join the great pilgrimage — the March of the Innocents."

The screen dissolved to an azure sky. Music faded to silence as a gold script emerged in two lines in Arabic and Farsi — "To join click here."

On Wednesday Ruth was astonished to read that thousands of Islamic women had signed up, pledged to join AM's March with no declared destination.

30

EAST JERUSALEM
Thursday, April 27

PESTILENCE!

4K Chief Haim Etzion sprayed insect repellant along the floorboards of the Jerusalem apartment lent by an ultra-orthodox Russian turned Israeli, who amassed a fortune by supplying Siberian oil oligarchs with Chinese-made pressure valves. No matter where he was, Etzion was vigilant in defense against contamination. The thought of cockroaches ready to crawl out from the floorboards made him shudder.

He put away the disinfectant and congratulated himself on the Damascus imam's assassination. Thanks to documents planted by the assassin, blame for the murder fell on the Sunnis. A reciprocal cycle of Shiite attacks on Sunni mosques followed. A bloody struggle between the two major branches of Islam guaranteed that Muslims would never unite against Israel, which would be free to extend its borders to King David's Land.

He needed to impress his vision upon Prime Minister Feldman, who was more sympathetic to 4K's cause than any leader in Israel's history but hesitated to attack Iran's nuclear bakery and had not yet called for building a Third Temple.

And there was still danger that Sunnis and Shiites would not remain divided. Etzion was troubled by YouTube videos of Navid Kosari and his call for Muslim unity. A

March of the Innocents could bring Muslims closer. He would learn about this group, maybe infiltrate. Israel's restoration depended on him.

Later that day Etzion met with the 4K leadership inside an Orthodox synagogue. Specifics of the operation were checked off like a shopping list:

- Blessing by Rabbi Epstein on the condition no human blood be spilled on the holy site;
- Plans for the red heifer's sacrifice to ensure success this time;
- Double-checks of measures to clear the Temple Mount of people;
- Precise placements of explosives below each pillar of the Dome of the Rock;
- Reconfirmation of all actions to climax on the day the next pope is installed.

Etzion appointed a team to work with him on a 4K marketing effort. He then led a reading of Psalm 137, which fit the event for which they were preparing.

Remember, O Lord, what the Edomites did on the day Jerusalem fell. 'Tear it down,' they cried, 'tear it down to its foundations!'
O Daughter of Babylon, doomed to destruction, happy is he who repays you for what you have done to us — he who seizes your infants and dashes them against the rocks.

After the meeting, Etzion returned to the disinfected luxury apartment. Sipping kosher grape juice from a glass Etzion fastidiously wiped clean, he pondered 4K's three-fold PR plan: avoid blame for destroying the Dome of the Rock/promote building the Third Temple/secure donations. The Army of the Mahdi had its movie star. What dramatic step could 4K take to accomplish its aims once the Temple Mount was cleared of infidel debris?

His cell phone vibrated. Pulling it from the left pocket of his traditional black pants, he answered, "Etzion talking."

The Damascus assassin confirmed receipt of the second payment for the hit on the imam of the Umayyad Mosque.

"Well done," said Etzion. To the question of whether there was more to be done, Etzion did not hesitate. "Soon."

31

ROME
Sunday, April 30 - Friday, May 5

ALESSIO KNEW IT WAS POINTLESS to follow gossip about the next pope. The Holy Spirit didn't give interviews. The Roman Catholic Church locks its eligible cardinals in the Sistine Chapel to find a new leader of Christendom's largest denomination, an elite electorate that communicates to the outside world through puffs of dark smoke to indicate "not yet" until white smoke curls out of the special chimney created for observers.

For days since the conclave began, he was amused by how the internet had turned the Vatican's search for a new leader into a casino. An offshore website — www.bet-on-the-pope.com — took gambler's stakes on the next pontiff. On www.olbg.com/next-pope.htm, real-time odds favored two Italian cardinals, alongside other contests such as who would win the next Eurovision competition.

Gambler support spiked and crashed for a Jesuit who headed the Indonesian bishops' conference, a Franciscan bishop from Brazil who daringly suggested in 2000 that condoms might be acceptable to fight AIDS, and a Ukrainian with a U.S. passport who led six million Ukrainian Greek Catholics. The Ukrainian's support skyrocketed when a blogger reported that John Paul II left a secret message that he would one day be pope and collapsed after a Vatican denial.

Senior media commentators assured listeners that after popes from Poland, Germany, and Argentina, it was time for the safety of an Italian. One cardinal described as "roly poly," whose noted quotation was that "a single African child sick with AIDS counts more than the entire universe," led the betting. A Venetian patriarch was called "unyielding but no fanatic," leaving listeners to wonder what that meant. A columnist described him as a strong curial enforcer, having demanded disciplinary action against an Italian priest who participated in a pro-gay-rights rally.

On the conclave's third afternoon, black smoke rose twice from the chimney and on the fourth three times. This must mean that minor candidates were being eliminated, leaving the favored Italians battling for two-thirds support.

Alessio clicked on a news report about a 2012 book, *Petrus Romanus* subtitled "The

Final Pope is Here," with sales spiraling upward. It was wrong about the prior papal election, but the re-issue caused conspiracists to wonder whether the St. Malachy "Prophecy of the Popes" might finally be realized. These writings from 1595 held that "Peter the Roman" would be the last pontiff, ushering in the "great apostasy" followed by "great tribulation" including the rise of a false prophet who would merge church and state and set in motion events to destroy Rome itself.

Alessio laughed at the twisted speculation. Revelation was the only apocalypse in the Bible. The Holy Catholic Church was eternal, the Bible unchanging. The Church only needed her new leader.

On the fifth day again, dark smoke belched forth. A reporter quipped, "The cardinals must be electioneering more than praying for the Holy Spirit to choose." The reporter mentioned a TV series that depicted Rodrigo Borgia bribing fellow cardinals and later as Alexander VI being hailed as the most effective diplomat pontiff in history.

Alessio clicked to the daily Vatican news release and read:

After full investigation, it was decided that the trumpeters who disrupted the end of the papal funeral will not be prosecuted. Through their music they meant to pay homage to the late Holy Father.

From discussions with Ruth, Alessio doubted this. But this is what happens when a bureaucracy operates without a commander. A new pope will set things straight.

Ruth closely followed media reports about the conclave. When the announcement about the trumpeters appeared, knowing what Noah told her in confidence, she marveled at how the Vatican converted an embarrassing security lapse into a tribute to the departed pope.

Ruth wondered what Noah would make of the Vatican release. The NJA had not succeeded in getting the world to grasp that tribulations that precede the New Jerusalem had already occurred. This might compel the New Jerusalem Alliance to take more drastic steps to broadcast its message. As she browsed the internet, Gabriel jumped onto her lap, alert to a noise outside, growling a warning for her protection.

"It's okay, sweetie," Ruth comforted. She cradled Gabriel on his back and tickled his chest, his hind legs twitching as if running in air. "I'll take care of you, baby dog."

32

IRAN, IRAQ & SYRIA
Late April/Early May

AM'S CALL FOR WOMEN to join its March roared across Islam. From Iranian villages to Iraqi cities, from Isfahan to Basra to the Kurdish part of northern Syria, Shiite and Sunni women were captivated by Navid Kosari's invitation to join an unprecedented pilgrimage. It began in late April from Kosari's summer home in northwestern Iran near Tabriz, an ancient Persian capital, location of the Garden of Eden some claimed. By May 1st, the March of the Innocents passed around Lake Urmia and entered Iraq at its eastern border.

Kosari appeared on AM's web channels in Arabic and Farsi, each interrupted only during *salah* in Arabic, *namaz* in Farsi, the five daily Muslim prayer sessions. Dressed in a pure white muslin shirt with a widely open collar, Iran's film star began with a short quotation from the Qur'an, then delivered his message.

"*Allahu Akbar*. Women of Islam, you suffer from violence, injustice, and war. Our mothers, our grandmothers, our sisters, and our daughters, for centuries you have endured the tyranny of men who seek their own glory and not the people's welfare.

"Now is your time, the time of the Innocents. You must lead where many men have failed, those who spoke boastfully but acted in petulance and cowardice. The time for unholy aggression is past and for godly action is now.

"Join the March of the Innocents. We go to Damascus on our *darb al-hajj*, our pilgrimage of peace.

"You may hesitate, fearing your husbands will curse you or interpret our journey as an abandonment of duty. This is not so, any more than the *Hijra* of the Prophet, peace be upon him, abandoned Mecca. His journey was and ours will be the righteous response to the evils of our time.

"The path will be challenging. The journey will be long. But is it worse than what we suffer now? Attacks in the night, bombs in our marketplaces, our children taken by famine and bullets, no reward for the faithful, riches for the undeserving. We raise no flag of nation or tribe. We join instead in what the Prophet recited, calling forth an age of peace and justice for our children and generations to come.

"Wear white — the color of purity. I will be your companion and the Army of the Mahdi is our guard.

"Onward to Damascus, *Inshallah. Assalamu alaikum wa rahmatullah.*"

With that, the hypnotic image of Navid Kosari faded to gilt-etched instructions over a jet-black background, evoking the Qaaba. The site gave details, online registration, articles to pack, routes to take by car, bicycle, camel, horse, and foot. AM expanded its server capacity to meet the registration demand and enriched its site with images of smiling Muslim women in all phases of life. From holding their infants, to leading a business session in a Qatari office tower, to praying in mosques, to walking arm in arm in parks, and then to feeding the hungry. Sunni and Shiite images mingled to project indivisible Islam.

By the third day after Kosari's startling appeal, AM's leader Qalil received a count of a hundred thousand signed on to march.

Women will restore Islam to what we embraced 1300 years ago, when the Word first spread like fire through the world, burning away impurities and preparing for Judgment Day.

33

EAST JERUSALEM
Saturday, May 6

4K'S TASK FORCE CHAIRMAN Jeffrey Magnitsky entered the lobby of the midrise apartment building Haim Etzion used in East Jerusalem. The building's plain exterior hid any suggestion that occupants were plotting an attack. The doorman pointed the visitor to the bird-cage elevator that marked the opulence of French Second Empire in multi-story luxury dwellings of the late 19th century.

"*Shalom,*" Etzion greeted Magnitsky and offered tea.

"The Task Force report." Magnitsky opened his laptop, ignoring the offer of a drink. He ran through the test site, marketing plans and details of a campaign that could start instantly. "A contest for the best design of the Third Temple. With a 2-week deadline and a viral campaign, we'll seize center stage. In no time 4K will be known throughout the Land of Israel."

Etzion sat silent, not moving. It took restraint for Magnitsky not to shake him. But he'd seen Etzion before in this trance and knew that all one could do was wait.

Etzion's eyes opened.

"Great idea, but we can't tip off anyone about the start of Project Redemption. You need to put the Dome of the Rock back in the sketch. Show space for the Temple between it and the Mosque. And you misspelled two words here."

Etzion scowled and pointed to offending letters.

"All must be perfect."

"Got it. Good news about the prize money. Abraham Rosenthal pledged 4 million. Funds are in our account."

"Four million shekels?" Etzion asked, raising his eyebrows.

"Every shekel," Magnitsky confirmed.

"Make it one million euros. The public will think it's from a wealthy European."

"Excellent," beamed Magnitsky. "We'll make the changes and be set to launch tomorrow, if the leadership approves."

"I have the votes. And run it by Leibowitz one last time. He knows web media better than anyone. You can trust him. With his okay, launch."

After Magnitsky departed, Etzion looked out the window, over the marble balcony that faced the Temple Mount, to where the Third Temple would rise. *Yes, we will restore your home, Holy of Holies.*

He scanned news reports he followed daily. Grim reports from the Muslim world, mosque bombings, street fighting, demonstrations, retaliation and suppression by regimes and rogue groups. Civil war, said commentators.

All good news. Lebanon was disintegrating further. Beirut's Green Line, the tree-filled boulevard separating Muslim from Christian sectors of the capital, was once more turning red with blood, buildings, and plantings victims to the fighting. Syria was anarchy. Iraq's Chamber of Deputies featured more fistfights than debate. Retaliatory bombings of Shi'a and Sunni mosques made for spectacular news coverage, gold domes collapsing and minarets falling — played over and over to burnish images into the followers of the two warring branches of Islam, each wishing for the other to be excised from Muhammad's tree.

What remained of organized Palestinian leadership was impotent. Palestinian Authority President Arafat, a distant relative of the original PLO leader, struggled to be taken seriously. Palestinians were the lepers of the Middle East, degraded by their neighbors. Unemployment among Palestinian men hovered at 80%. Israeli blockades ensured shortages of everything, exemplified by a Save the Children shipment of vitamin supplements sunk in a harbor, something the Israeli Government described as regrettable but prudent.

"Terrorists were hiding with the vitamins," said the Israeli spokeswoman.

If Hell could come to the people of Islam, this was its dress rehearsal. The time was right. Etzion would lead the triumph of the Jewish people.

34

ROME
Monday, May 8

STANDING AT THE KITCHEN SINK, Ruth reflected on surprise. She'd anticipated a comfortable post, a break from the fervent response to *Visions of Apocalypse*. She had planned to research female mystics who centuries ago envisioned a faith world free of patriarchy. They understood God not to be male or female but an encompassing wholeness. And she'd envisioned a fresh start, time to pursue life beyond academics, dinners with new friends, perhaps romance.

Instead, within days of arriving in Rome, she'd become reacquainted with her childhood friend turned tech mogul and hopefully not Revelation zealot. She was brought into the confidence of an enigmatic Vatican priest. Rather than quiet nights she expected, six rogue trumpets sounded at the papal funeral and blood red fireworks burst over the Coliseum while fountains gurgled red gelatinous ooze. To top it off, she was consulting about the Miracle of Fatima while papal mystery swirled. Seminary did not prepare her for this.

As she scrubbed canned food remains from Gabriel's bowl, Alessio phoned with an invitation to a meeting of a book club.

"What sort of books do you read?" she asked, hoping it wasn't an academic group where everyone vied to be resident know-it-all.

"Not what you expect. A cardinal founded it over 200 years ago. He called it 'The Book Club' to avoid suspicion that its membership would invite a charge of heresy. A dozen theologians from other faiths dined with him regularly, with no agenda except to talk about what's going on among those who claim Abraham as their spiritual father — People of the Book."

"Battling Jewish, Christian and Muslim theologians have been getting together over a meal for two centuries?"

"Out of the spotlight," Alessio replied. "There is a fixed membership of 36. Father David belonged," referring to Ruth's predecessor at the Anglican Centre. "As the host I can invite a guest. The scholar I invited broke his arm cycling, and he cannot attend."

After learning another woman was a member, Ruth accepted. While she was determined to succeed in a field dominated by disapproving men, she didn't want to fight the battle every hour.

Uncomfortable jogging the smoggy, traffic-choked streets of Rome, so different from bucolic Virginia, she was disappointed not to have found a nearby park with a running path.

She pulled out her mat and began a yoga routine. Gabriel wagged his tail, begging her to play the game of throwing a squirrel toy and watching him shake and return it. As she moved into the Downward Dog position, she felt a pain in her lower back.

Age? Stress? She tried to stretch further, winced, and resolved to do yoga more regularly. Gabriel emitted a sound like "Whrrrrr." Ruth stroked his back. "It's been a whirlwind all right."

She spent the day at the Centre planning what the tasks would be once a pope was elected and she would manage the Anglican presence at his installation. Secretary Ponelli offered detailed summaries of the prior three ceremonies but warned, "This one could be most challenging. Everyone wants a trip to Rome in May. It's our best season."

"Will we get a crush of requests from bishops wanting to be here?" asked Ruth.

"The Archbishop will inform inquirers; it is invitation only. Our role is to communicate with the Archbishop's choices and arrange good seating and lodging."

"*Grazie.* I appreciate your help with this, Lucrezia."

"*Prego*," the Secretary replied with a grateful smile.

Ruth had an hour before the Book Club after returning to her apartment. Recognizing her approaching steps, Gabriel uttered his distinctive call that was between a bark and a screech. After a hurried walk, Ruth gave Gabriel his favorite scratch near his tail, then turned to read *la Repubblica*'s page 3 summary of Middle Eastern events headlined "Arab world aflame."

Assuming that clergy wore clerical garb for most occasions, she decided she would too, adding a soft blue sweater over black clergy shirt. She debated between the pearl earrings her grandmother bequeathed or the filigree drop set that was a gift from the Altar Guild of the only congregation she served before accepting a seminary professorship. She chose the more adventurous filigree.

Arriving at the Vatican guard post on time, Ruth was escorted to a room where she found about twenty men and one woman holding wine or water glasses with colored glass markers clinking as they chatted. As the Swiss guardsman in bright striped pantaloons and black armband bowed and departed, Ruth was virtually tackled near the door by the only other woman.

"Thanks be to God," her new friend exclaimed. "I'm Eugenia Portman, professor of Church History at the American University of Rome. And you must be Ruth Waller. Father Alessio speaks highly of you."

Ruth suppressed a blush. "I'm honored to meet you, Eugenia. Your works on female prophets are on my bookshelf. You were an inspiration when I was in seminary and deciding on doctoral studies." She hoped she hadn't made Eugenia sound ancient.

Eugenia smiled graciously. "I just know we're going to be great friends," she said, easing Ruth into the group. "I'm the Club's original female member, the first of what must become a wave." She leaned toward Ruth and whispered, "Men can learn. They need us."

Alessio made his way over, bowed to Eugenia, and began introducing Ruth to others one by one. When he came to Steven Friedman, Ruth preempted the introduction.

"You're from Cincinnati, Rabbi Friedman. I attended your lecture on Revelation last year." Ruth knew Rabbi Friedman as the Herbert Thompson Jr. Professor of New Testament studies at Hebrew Union College, the first Reform Jewish seminary in the United States.

After a three-course dinner of vegetable soup, chicken Milano and non-lactose sorbet prepared to satisfy kosher requirements, Alessio clinked his crystal glass with a dessert spoon and called the session to order with the invocation written by the founding cardinal.

"We gather as People of the Book. Lord of all, bless and unify your people." He conveyed regrets of eleven absent members. "As you know, Cardinal Fleitas is at the conclave."

"Probably trying to talk the other cardinals into backing his candidate," Rabbi Friedman called out. The Club laughed in acknowledgment of Fleitas' relentless power of persuasion.

"Here is tonight's subject — what is the faith significance of recent events, including what happened at the funeral and in the Middle East?"

Views crackled like sparks from a bonfire. Saudi Grand Mufti Feisal Al-Sheikh, on an extended sabbatical to Rome, spoke with fixed conviction: "Israel is about to attack Iran. That will unite Islam. The Qur'an does not approve wars of aggression. But defensive war is Iran's sacred obligation. We are headed for trouble, serious trouble."

Rabbi Ehhud Krusch of the Great Synagogue of Rome spoke next. "The Imam of the Umayyad Mosque is killed for preaching Islamic unity. This AM group hires a movie star for a Muslim women's march to Damascus. A contest by a Jewish group is launched to design a new temple for Jerusalem. Chaos I see."

"The trumpets and screens at the funeral," said Patrick Mason, a Salt Lake City Bishop on extended assignment to open the first Mormon Temple in Rome. "Right out of Revelation."

Eager to welcome Ruth to the discussion, Alessio announced, "Our guest tonight is a scholar of apocalyptic visions. The Rev. Dr. Ruth Waller has a recent book on the subject and an article published in *The Anglican Journal*. Dr. Waller, do recent signs align with ancient texts about the end of the world?"

Nervous about her debut, Ruth entered the dialogue, mindful of the presence of three faiths.

"There were many other apocalypses written 2,000 years ago, but only John of Patmos' version became part of the Christian Bible. It's obvious that those who staged recent Vatican events followed the Revelation of John as though bringing it to life. The trumpets and screen footage at the funeral come directly from Chapters 8 and 9.

"Other events — the device planted in Damascus, Syria's collapse, the murder of the imam of the Umayyad Mosque, the way the March of the Innocents was announced — all derive from Shiite beliefs about *Al-sa'ah*, The Hour." Ruth nodded in the direction of the Grand Mufti.

A Sunni imam, the Grand Mufti nodded and expanded on Ruth's remarks. "These events form a pattern familiar not to Sunnis but to the dominant thinking among Iranian Shiites known as Twelver theology. Twelvers believe the great Book of Judgment will be read at the Umayyad Mosque in Damascus, where the March is headed, the same destination where the Prophet's daughter Fatima sought haven after the Prophet's grandson was killed at Karbala. The call for the Mahdi to emerge and for Isa to return means to Shiites that the world nears its end."

A Shiite scholar on the faculty of Rome's Sapienza University agreed. "These are signs that *Yawm al-Qiyamah* is drawing near — the Day of Resurrection that precedes *Yawm ad-Din*, the Day of Judgment."

"There's a recent push within Israel to build a Third Temple on Mount Moriah. What do you make of that?" Ruth turned to Rabbi Krusch.

He frowned. "Most Jews do not dwell on the End Time. But there's a group that recently emerged, 4K, that declares the way must be prepared now for the Mashiach, the Jewish Messiah, to come and be enthroned in the final Temple."

"So, one can trace recent signs to similar beliefs about the Last Days in our three faiths," Ruth summarized, satisfied she had not embarrassed herself and involved others in conversation. As a professor it was so tempting to pontificate.

The Shiite scholar asked, "But help us understand, Dr. Waller. What did it mean that six trumpets sounded at the pope's funeral? I thought your Bible spoke of seven."

"It does. There are many ways to interpret Christian scripture," she replied. "In John's Revelation the seventh trumpet could mean an end to one cycle of violence and the start of another. Or it could be reserved for just before Judgment Day, when the Temple of God opens in heaven and the ark of his testament is revealed."

Rabbi Friedman shifted the conversation back to the original question. "If you consider John's Revelation literally and if you add what happened at the funeral, we are in the period after the Sixth Trumpet. In the text, this is a time when four angels are let loose near the Euphrates, armies of 200,000 do battle, a third of humankind perishes in fire, and other disasters afflict the earth. Isn't that the warning from the funeral?"

Ruth shifted in her chair, unwilling to disclose what Noah had told her was the NJA's intent. "For those who take a literalist approach perhaps, but I am not among them."

"I wonder what you make of this," the Grand Mufti interjected. "Our sources report enormous marble arches being constructed in desert towns of Lebanon, Egypt, Iraq and Saudi Arabia. Each has a name emblazoned in Hebrew and Greek."

"What names?" asked Rabbi Friedman.

"I hear that each bears the name of an ancient tribe of Israel," replied the Grand Mufti.

Ruth and Rabbi Friedman spoke simultaneously, "The twelve tribes of Israel?"

Rabbi Friedman asked, "Are twelve arches being built?"

No one knew.

Ruth, Rabbi Friedman and Alessio looked at one another. Revelation described twelve gateways to greet the elect as they enter the New Jerusalem.

Noah was not the only one pushing an apocalypse, Ruth thought. *And how far were they willing to go?*

35

VATICAN CITY
Tuesday, May 9

EARLY TUESDAY MORNING Alessio arrived at the Vatican archivist's desk. This time a light was on, and Alessandro Mercati was there.

Alessio began casually, "Alessandro, good morning. Any prediction about the next Holy Father?"

"I am a librarian, Father," was the Archivist of the Vatican's stern response. "But it could be between Milan and Naples. Both represent stability."

"Not the Archbishop of Venice? He offers continuity with the benefit of youth."

Sensing that Alessio might favor reforms promoted by the deceased pontiff, Mercati shifted in his chair and changed the subject.

"How may I help you, Father?"

"Oh, I need to retrieve transcripts about the Holy Father's foreign travels. To assist the press office. I can search myself, so I won't trouble you." Feigning an after-thought he added, "By the way, did you locate the Fatima file?"

"It is secure. Until there is a new pontiff, I cannot grant access, not even for you."

Alessio bristled but maintained a stoic visage as he coaxed. "As there is nothing secret there, you won't mind if we look at the pages together."

Mercati drew in his sizeable paunch and puffed out his chest, then exhaled in a gust. "I am sorry, but that requires papal approval."

"Yet you have the file and did not yourself have papal approval to take and keep it."

Mercati scowled and snapped, "I am charged to protect the Vatican's greatest treasures — not the buildings and the art but texts of the ages. The Holy Father ordered me to keep the Fatima file secure. I withdrew it to protect it beyond what even our security system can ensure. It is safe and will remain so until a successor is on the throne of St. Peter."

"Have you read the unpublished page?" probed Alessio, hoping to catch him off guard.

Mercati blinked twice. "It must remain in the control of the next pope. I trust you will not tell anyone about the page."

"Agreed that neither of us will reveal to anyone that we discussed this matter," said

Alessio, extending his hand to seal the pledge.

Mercati exhaled and completed the handshake. "Pledged on my sacred honor."

Alessio tried one more time. "I too received instructions about the Fatima file.'

"Yes, I know, you are the one to deliver it when the time comes."

Alessio nodded. "For the protection of us both, tell me where the file is, in case you are not available."

Mercati paused. "Here." He pointed to a dark wood file cabinet next to his desk — "Middle drawer. The label is 'Trumpet 7,' a code the Holy Father gave it the day before he died."

Alessio stifled a gasp. 7 — like the note.

"*Mille grazie*," he said calmly and departed the Archives, forgetting the pretense of collecting files about the late pope's trips.

36

JERUSALEM
Tuesday, May 9

NOAH STOLL AND FOUR OTHER ELDERS of the New Jerusalem Alliance gathered in the King David Hotel, the legendary five-star lodging opened in 1931 by a wealthy Egyptian Jew for travelers to Jerusalem. Overlooking the Old City, it hosted notable celebrities from Margaret Thatcher to Madonna. It suffered spectacular bombings, the first in 1946 by Irgun, a militant Zionist group in an attack against British rule. When independence came in 1948, the imposing hotel was on the Israeli edge of the no-man's-land armistice line that split the City between Israeli and Jordanian control. The 1967 Six-Day War reunified the King David and the rest of Jerusalem through Israel's victory. Five NJA Elders gathered in a lavish suite on the top floor, where Mount Moriah beckoned in the distance.

"Who's the winner?" Noah asked the Prize Committee Chair Fred Scribner, heir to the fabled publisher before it faded and was acquired. Fred invested in a company that migrated public domain books to the internet and sold it to Google in its quest to digitize the world's knowledge.

"We'll announce that in two days. The response was beyond belief. Most submissions were, let's say, not ready for prime time, but thousands were publisher quality."

"So what's the media plan?" asked Bip Schroth IV, a 40-year old wizard of global sourcing. His qualification for membership came from a decision twenty years ago. Instead of finishing Yale like his three namesakes, he dropped out and developed an enterprise that sourced industrial products at Chinese prices.

Noah reported for the public relations expert of the Elders, who was recovering from shoulder surgery on Orcas Island, Washington. He communicated by encrypted video with Noah, but not for this meeting — too much cybersecurity risk for that.

"The plan is to fly the winner here and present the prize near the Western Wall. We'll issue a tease the day before."

"Are we set on phase two, building the Third Temple?" asked Schroth.

"We're trying to determine where it can be built," said Archibald Kinney, whose architectural firm had 37 global offices. "A Muslim group called the Waqf controls the Temple Mount, and it would never approve a Temple there. We've found five places off the Mount where it could be built."

"We can't rewrite Revelation," Noah explained patiently. "The Third Temple must arise on the foundation of the others."

"Then we'd better get the world's best zoning attorney," said Kinney.

Scribner raised a new subject.

"Did you all see what this group 4K is doing? A contest to design a Third Temple. Anyone know them?"

Social media expert Celia Gamble reported. "My team's trying to figure out what the acronym means. Looks like an extreme Jewish group pushing the Government to expand Jewish settlements. Their 'Design a Temple' contest calls for restoring the Kingdom of David, which would mean the Temple has to be built on the Mount."

Noah nodded. "So 4K wants to build the Third Temple. Did I get this right? God must want these two pieces of the New Jerusalem puzzle to come together. Send me their contact info."

As yellow lights of the Old City gradually replaced the orange of sunset, the Elders turned to a reading of Chapters 21 and 22 of Revelation. While hearing "and I saw no temple in the city, for the temple is the Lord God the Almighty and the Lamb," Noah's mind strayed, troubled that building a Third Temple seemed to conflict with verse 22's "no temple in the city."

How to square a plan to construct a physical Third Temple with Revelation's description of a heavenly temple that has no earthly substance but only the Light of the Holy One?

The answer must be that laying the cornerstone of the Third Temple would serve as a beacon gathering the faithful to Jerusalem. As the Bible says, only then can the Last Day occur.

Praising God for solving that puzzle, Noah bowed his head as Scribner read.

"Blessed is he who keeps the words of the prophecy of this book."

Blessed are they who hasten the prophecy's fulfillment.

37

QOM, IRAN
Tuesday, May 9

VALI QALIL ARRIVED an hour early to meet with Iranian President Al-Rabani on the sixth floor of Qom's Mar'ashi Najafi Grand Library, home to over a half million texts sacred to Islam. Ensconced in a small reading room used by scholars to inspect delicate scrolls, he was entranced by a 9th century tract about The Hour, reveling in its vivid prophecy of how the Mahdi would vanquish the armies of darkness.

Not even Al-Rabani's or Qalil's closest aides knew of their personal relationship. Years ago, they had studied the Qur'an together at a Tehran madrassa led by a devoted follower of Ayatollah Khomenei. For the past year they maintained private collaboration by unmonitored cell phones. The President never placed his rare in-person meetings with Qalil on his official schedule and used the pretext of an hour of hadith study to conceal his meeting with the Emir of the Army of the Mahdi.

Upon arrival through a service elevator to avoid public notice, President Al-Rabani withdrew a 10th century tract. He carried the parchment scroll to the reading room where Qalil waited. Once the Library Director supervised the delivery of tea, deviating from his iron rule of no food or beverage in the reading rooms, the Director withdrew, and Al-Rabani made certain the door was securely closed.

Embracing Qalil, Al-Rabani was congratulatory. "Vali, your March attracts Sunni and Shiite women, as you said it would."

They sat across from each other sipping their favorite rose petal chai from an alabaster gold-handled cup the Director provided for presidential meetings.

"Innocence is a powerful weapon," Qalil grandly affirmed.

"And well done at the Umayyad Mosque — a double masterstroke," Al-Rabani nodded, referring to both the planting of the unarmed nuclear casement at the Shrine of John the Baptist and the assassination of the Mosque's peace-oriented imam.

Out of respect for listening devices that could be present anywhere, installed by any number of powers internal or external to Iran, Qalil was careful not to acknowledge the praise.

Puzzled by credit for the assassination he replied, "You must have information we do not have."

Mistaking lack of knowledge for discretion, Al-Rabani, shrugged. "He was not one of us."

Qalil changed the subject. "How is our Supreme Leader's health?"

"He is not well. He could use some 'assistance'."

Qalil nodded. "I can help."

Al-Rabani walked to the window, where beige minarets and gold-leafed domes of Qom spread before him like geometric patterns in a Paul Klee painting. He remembered the midwinter night when he dreamed Allah sent the angel Gabriel to visit him as a youth. Touching him with a golden staff, the divine being recited. "You are chosen — to lead the righteous to *Yawm ad-Din*."

The Iranian President turned to face Qalil. "In Damascus the March will announce its final destination — Jerusalem."

"The holy place where the Prophet, peace and blessings be upon him, ascended a ladder to heaven," said Qalil. "There will we restore the reign of the righteous after the defeat of the Dajjal." He lowered his voice. "Others in AM do not know the sacrifice that is planned."

President Al-Rabani nodded, picturing the Islamic world uniting before him. *Soon all Muslims will see that I am the Mahdi, returning from a thousand years of sleep to lead our final triumph.* Unaware that his colleague had a similar plan, for himself.

38

EAST JERUSALEM
Tuesday, May 9

HAIM ETZION SAT at the claw-foot antique table in the East Jerusalem apartment's dining room with three members of the 4K Inner Circle — Jeffrey Magnitsky, Mort Leibowitz and Eytan Osnat. Leibowitz reported on media preparations for what would follow destruction of the Dome of the Rock.

Osnat addressed the message to be delivered to the Waqf commander to clear the Mount this time. Now a Knesset member, Osnat had a trusting relationship with the Islamic guardians of *Har haBáyith*. When Israelis protested Muslim excavations of "dirt" as an effort to eradicate archeological proof of the existence of Solomon's Temple at the site, Osnat calmed both sides, leaving Jewish archeologists free to sift the rubble dumped off-site, which revealed thousands of coins from the time of Herod and Jesus. Osnat negotiated a secret protocol between the Waqf and Israel that any further excavations would be strictly by agreement. The Waqf commander called Osnat "My brother, a Jew we can trust."

Etzion started the review. "As you know, Eytan, the Rabbi blesses our plan on the conditions that there be no bloodshed and that this time we sacrifice the red heifer." Though no guarantees about the bloodshed.

Taking the paternal tone of a grandfather congratulating his grandson, the college graduate, Eytan reassured Haim.

"All is arranged. Do not worry."

Mort Leibowitz, the journalism executive, had not been privy to the latest plans. "What exactly are we asking the Waqf chief to do?"

Etzion nodded.

Osnat explained, "I will deliver to the Waqf commander a secure message stating there is a rupture in water pipes beneath the Mount, making it essential to close it to everyone, guards included. Because of bacteria spreading in the system, a rupture in the pipes could contaminate the holy sites. He'll smile when he reads I convinced the City to pay for it. He'll clear the Mount for an entire night and day. Trust me."

39

VATICAN CITY
Tuesday, May 9

THE MORNING AFTER the Book Club meeting, Ruth, Alessio and Rabbi Friedman were to meet for coffee at 10:30 at a café along Borgo Santo Spirito near the Piazza San Pietro. A narrow, gray cobblestone connector between the Tiber and St. Peter's Basilica, the street was lined with four-story unmarked apartments, boutique hotels, the Santo Spirito Church and the headquarters of the Society of Jesus. From the café one could almost see the chimney where black smoke had disappointed crowds hoping this would be the day that rewarded their vigil.

Having spent until 2 a.m. browsing for information about the mysterious marble arches discussed the night before, Ruth was bleary eyed. What little sleep she got was interrupted by a recurring nightmare of treading water alone in a choppy ocean far from shore, gasping she would sink into oblivion, until Gabriel barked and daylight pierced the shutter slats she had neglected to close.

Ruth arrived fifteen minutes early to skim the morning's *la Repubblica*. A reporter speculated that the two leading Italian candidates for pope were deadlocked, and with a supermajority required, spiritual arm-wrestling was in its final stage — who would yield?

Alessio and Rabbi Friedman arrived at the same moment. Ruth rose to greet them and before one could ask what she'd learned, she begged for the results of their research.

"Ladies first," said Alessio as he sat down.

"The Lady asked first for your reports."

As the waiter delivered cappuccinos and biscotti, Rabbi Friedman and Alessio spread downloaded papers on the red-checkered tablecloth, using the sugar bowl and silverware as paperweights to keep notes from scattering in a light wind on a very hot May morning.

Friedman broke the deadlock. "I found references to seven arches. The descriptions were remarkably the same except for the name over the top of the arch. Each was one of the twelve tribes of Israel."

"Not to boast but I found eight," said Alessio. They shared notes. Together they had references to nine monuments. Ruth was relieved that was the number she'd found.

Combining research, they found mention of ten arches. Plotting locations on a map Alessio brought, they drew lines forming a square with Jerusalem at its center. Someone was building gateways to a New Jerusalem as described in the second to last chapter of the Revelation to John, at distances specified in that Apocalypse.

"Seconds anyone?" asked Rabbi Friedman. "My treat. I found the fewest."

Ruth took his absence as an opportunity to thank Alessio for the invitation to the Book Club. "How did you become a member?"

Alessio laughed. "Not because of my scholarship, that's for sure. I joined as a spy. The late Holy Father felt he could not continue as a member when he was elected pope, or the Club would be exposed to publicity. So he proposed me in his place, and I took notes for him. As you know, he hoped to be a force for unity among faiths. He would remind me that his honorary title Pontifex Maximus means greatest bridge builder."

"The Club sees you as a full member. I could tell."

Friedman returned, and a few minutes later the waiter delivered steaming second cups. As they discussed the import of arches being built to Revelation specifications, a mass murmur arose from the direction of Piazza San Pietro, then a burst of shouting and clapping.

They dashed to the Square. Bystanders excitedly explained that a cloud of white smoke had drifted into the heavens from the most watched chimney in the world. A new Vicar of Christ would soon reveal himself.

As they stood among thousands, Alessio described Vatican preparation for this moment. Papal cassocks and white skull caps awaited in every size, vertical and horizontal, delivered weeks before by the Gammarelli tailor shop that for centuries supplied papal garments. The moment of election is followed by the embrace of cardinals, some crestfallen but outwardly cordial. While press announcements are rushed for release, the cardinals pledge loyalty to the new pontiff, a tailor makes a quick fitting, and a stunned cardinal transforms into pope.

Alessio, Ruth, and Friedman sweltered in the blazing sun, looking upward towards the portico where a man would emerge soon to bless the crowd. It might take minutes or hours, but no one there would relinquish a glimpse of history.

Just before noon there was movement at the portico. The sound system came alive with baroque orchestral music. The Vatican coat of arms glowed on erected LED screens. Shutters opened, then doors. A short man emerged in a blazing white cassock and skull cap. The crowd squinted, not immediately recognizing the figure.

Ruth overheard an elderly woman standing next to her gasp and say with disappointment, "He's not Italian."

Her husband asked, "How do you know?"

"Too thin," she chided.

The diminutive, dark-skinned man began blessing the crowd with the sign of the cross and upward and downward movements of his hands, turning his head left and right, with an exuberant smile that filled screens so the crowd and hundreds of millions of television and web viewers could see his face.

Alessio turned to Ruth, voice choked with excitement. "It's Cardinal Francisco Fleitas."

The announcer said, "Pope Sixtus the Sixth." And then the new pope did what none had done in recorded history. He prostrated himself on the balcony's red rug, dipping three times in different directions, each time touching head to floor. He arose, taller than before, and blessed the crowd, the sheep of his flock.

Ruth grasped Alessio's arm. "From the Book Club?"

40

THE WHITE HOUSE, WASHINGTON, D.C.

Tuesday, May 9

PRESIDENT PALMER sent a congratulatory note to Pope Sixtus VI. An Evangelical who might have viewed any pope as the AntiChrist had he lived 300 years earlier, Palmer embraced conservative Vatican views against abortion. During the campaign as a Vice Presidential candidate, he proclaimed to thunderous applause that any justice his ticket would appoint to the Supreme Court must be committed to overturn Roe v. Wade. "Roe must go!" was the punch line.

Palmer gathered in the Oval Office with his IQ, shorthand for "Intelligence Quintet." The IQ met every Tuesday evening for dinner from the time Palmer was sworn in as President. MBA educated, Palmer started each meeting with a short briefing by Director of National Intelligence Maureen Sullivan, a tough-as-nails veteran of the Rand Corporation. Other IQ members were Secretary of State Wym Shulman, Secretary of Defense Studs Bancroft and National Security Advisor Arnoldo Coulter.

No matter where the five were on any Tuesday evening at 7:00 p.m. Washington time, they met over a single question — "How do we protect the American people?"

DNI Sullivan took three minutes to review North Korea, the China Straits and Venezuela, each with a "no change" marker.

She turned to the Middle East.

"We've seen major escalation this week both in Syria and throughout the region. Iran moves from orange to red by mobilizing ground troops along its western borders. After we dumped the farce of easing sanctions for peace, our hackers hit their centrifuges, but they were back up and spinning in no time. CIA says the regime is within a month of having its bomb. Israel's ready to strike."

"I asked Aaron to give me until Sunday, and he agreed." Palmer and the Israeli Prime Minister had spoken the day before.

Coulter reiterated his blunt conclusion. "It's time. The margin of error's slim as it is."

Defense Secretary Bancroft took his turn.

"Operation Meteor, the mini-drone strike aimed at Iran's nuclear brain trust, is ready. We reviewed it with our Israeli counterparts last week and calculated 90% chance for success. With luck we'll be incognito. That should delay Iran's getting a bomb by at least six months. A last chance for Iran to yield before a strike on the factory."

Given the loss of American lives in Iraq and Afghanistan, Bancroft advocated selective killings as unquestionably superior to sending American personnel to another Muslim country. He hated meeting the caskets, a ritual he faithfully practiced as Defense Secretary.

Secretary of State Shulman in his usual matter-of-fact style reported, "Our Ambassadors in the region are briefed."

Palmer combed through his salt-gray hair with his right hand three swipes at a time, a clue he was having trouble making a decision. The IQ members privately joked that hair stroking was Palmer's way of summoning wisdom to penetrate a thick layer of political calculation that shielded his brain. But this time politics had little to do with presidential pondering.

"You know, when I was in eighth grade, my pastor gave our teen group the single best sermon I ever heard," he said, surprising the team with theology rather than the expected order of military action. "There we were, with soft drinks, eating popcorn, flirting with the girls. What stuck with me was the message — that God's kingdom is ours to create. He won't do it for us. Now, here we sit, with more power at our fingertips than all the emperors of history. And what does the Lord want us to do with it? Drop the ball? Kick it out of bounds for someone else to score a goal some other day? No, I'm here for a reason."

Palmer looked out the window towards his constant inspiration, the Washington Monument, with scaffolding around it to repair recent damage from earth tremors. He turned back to his IQ.

"I'll be in Rome for the installation of the new pope — from Paraguay, who would guess. What do we know about this Sixtus the Sixth?"

The IQ members shuffled papers without a formal briefing about this extraneous subject. DNI Sullivan came to the rescue.

"Francisco Fleitas came to fame by bucking convention in Paraguay. Dictator Stroessner tried to control the ordination of priests because he believed the Vatican was anointing troublemaking Liberation Theology types who thought God was on the side of the poor. Fleitas applied for seminary but wasn't on Stroessner's approved list, so he cobbled together airfare to Rome. In a twist of what the Vatican calls 'divine fate,' Pope Paul VI overheard a hallway conversation about a visitor from Paraguay. After a two-hour conversation, ranging from the need for interfaith dialogue to the primacy of the Church, he placed Fleitas in an expedited ordination process.

"When Fleitas commits to something, he's all-in. After returning to Asuncion, Father Francisco went to the chapel where he was assigned and scheduled his first mass. Stroessner ran Paraguay like a mob boss, and when he heard Fleitas was back, he sent armed men to silence him. Peasants in the pews stopped them at the door. They say the crowd literally shamed the soldiers into leaving their weapons outside the church, and so the thugs waited unarmed in the rear of the nave. When the mass was about to end, Father Francisco called them to come forward. He embraced each, pronounced collective absolution, and gave them communion. At first the astonished crowd wondered whose side Francisco was on. But when the chastened thugs bowed to the young priest, they applauded. The chastened men became regular parishioners. After that no one dared interfere with him. Francisco began a climb to the top, not one we hear that he sought."

"Nice story, Maureen. But a pope from Paraguay?"

"He was probably a harmless choice of cardinals tired of being deadlocked between two Italians, and so they picked someone in his 70's to hold things together for a while, without any risk he'll disrupt the status quo," Sullivan responded, visibly discomforted to speak in maybes. "I've read he's an arch-conservative about Catholic doctrine, which probably endears him to conservatives who thought his predecessor was far too liberal."

"Back to the Middle East," said Palmer. "We're not sending troops. Send the mini-drones with the foreign name."

"Abaddons, Greek for 'Destroyers'," said the Defense Secretary. "About the size of a softball, but with the wallop of an artillery shell and the precision of an Olympic archer."

"Deliver them tomorrow," Palmer commanded. "Coordinate on the blue line," referring to the direct phone connection with Feldman and his Defense Minister. "You decide when they're unleashed. Clear?"

"Yes sir," was the crisp response.

"One last thing, my friends," said Palmer. "What do you know about a web contest to design a Third Temple in Jerusalem?"

"There's a lot of crackpot millennial thinking that the End Days are near," Sullivan smirked.

Palmer looked uncomfortable but said nothing.

41

DAMASCUS
Wednesday, May 10

NAVID KOSARI, Iran's most famous actor, set out cheerfully on the March of the Innocents atop a white mare. He underestimated what happens to a body when it rides a horse for days in dry heat. But he bore the saddle sores as a great actor can, rewarded by pain relief cream, an astonishing multitude of women and a flood of media attention.

AM Emir Vali Qalil had phoned Kosari a fortnight earlier as Kosari was about to leave his Tabriz compound.

"Ready for a crowd?" asked Qalil. "I expect you'll attract at least 50,000 female fans by the time you get to Damascus."

"I'm flattered," Kosari replied, adding modesty to his voice. "We only had 25,000 extras in the arena for the finale of Darius the Great," a popular film that recast the iconic Persian king as a wise monarch practicing Islamic-like rituals, despite the historical fact that the Prophet Muhammad was born centuries later.

"Keep the spotlight on A'ishah. You're the man, but she's the star. Understood?" Qalil sternly demanded.

"If only I could control my fans." This time he chose a wistful tone.

"It's an essential part of the plan," Qalil reminded Kosari. "A'ishah the beautiful, swaying groups of devout women. It will be a glimpse of heaven."

"Of course the lovely A'ishah will ride beside me." *Though perhaps a bit behind.* Kosari would not waste an opportunity for a profile shot.

As they pierced the Syrian border and headed toward Damascus, Kosari and A'ishah rode side by side. Kosari was amazed to be surrounded by more than a hundred thousand women and children and constantly being interviewed by reporters from around the world.

"Who is the sponsor, this AM?" a television reporter asked in English.

"AM is a noble group dedicated to righteousness," Kosari dramatically proclaimed.

"What does AM stand for?"

"The Army of the Mahdi," replied Kosari, holding reins in his right hand and turning his profile to the ideal camera angle. "A force of good in this troubled world. It calls on the 12th imam to return from centuries of deep sleep and lead us to victory over ignorance."

Gazing at the women in white following him and the mysterious A'ishah, he wondered what he had taken on. Actors rely on scripts. The March was improvisation.

"On to Damascus," he called out, confident this was how the scene should play out.

From the first announcement of the March, AM's website was overwhelmed with enlistees. Women bade farewell to angry and confused husbands. An interview with a 26-year-old mother of two taking her children along with her mother, ensconced in the family Land Rover, explained:

"We are tired of the corruption, the fighting, the hopelessness, the nonsense of leaders who lost their way. We want peace, a future for our children. The men had their chance. It's our turn."

"And what do you hope to accomplish?" asked the male reporter for Al Jazeera's English language site.

"Everything," she replied earnestly. Off went the Land Rover toward the Iraqi border, as the ranks of pilgrims swelled by the hour.

Press reports covered the phalanx of women and young children trailing A'ishah and Kosari. Television coverage featured women from Saudi Arabia, Iraq, Syria, a few from Pakistan, several from Indonesia. An elderly grandmother from Tehran was interviewed, standing alongside her daughter and a grandchild.

"We walk the path set for us by the Prophet, blessings be upon him and his family. There will be no more babies until the world is safe for them." Her message morphed into a headline in London's *The Sun* tabloid: "No more sex 'til violence stops — Granny to men." "Sexual jihad" screamed a headline in *The Star*. A revolution was under way with no precedent from the history books.

42

VATICAN CITY
Wednesday, May 10

SIXTUS MOVED to the papal bedchamber the night of his election. After his spectacular elevation, donning white vestments, blessing throngs of adoring followers, receiving pledges of obedience from those who were once fellow cardinals and now were his College, he finally was alone. Profound silence in the vast room led him to his knees. Unprepared for this new role, he must find a vision for his papacy at once.

A voice whispered, "You made it. To you are the power and the glory."

The same temptations Satan dangled before Jesus in the wilderness. As he prayed for power to resist, an image of Jerusalem as a gleaming white city on a hill floated to mind. Shafts of sunlight pierced clouds above Mt. Moriah. Mist shrouded its architecture. But unmistakable, anointed by beams of light, was a starkly white cross rising from a silver orb atop the same lantern, cupola and drum that crowned St. Peter's.

A Catholic Cathedral for a new Jerusalem.

Energized, the Pope emerged from prayer and walked down the hallway to Alessio's room. He softly rapped on the wooden door. Alessio opened it, startled to see the new Holy Father standing before him.

"May I come in, Father," said the Pope.

"Of course, Holy Father." Alessio bowed.

"You look surprised, Father Alessio. Well, so am I," said Sixtus. "I witnessed your loyalty, your discipline, your ... discretion. I ask that you continue your service. Nothing will change except for the person you serve."

"Your Holiness, I am honored," Alessio said quietly, shocked. He assumed the Pope would install his own men. Now he would become Sixtus' man.

"Thank you. As for the Book Club," the Pope added, "I must resign. You must continue."

"I will at your command, your Holiness," replied Alessio. He knelt and kissed the papal ring.

As the Pope turned to depart and prepare for meetings with Vatican officials and press planners, Alessio stopped him with the message he'd been waiting to give.

"Holy Father, I am sworn to deliver to you a file for your eyes only. It concerns the Miracle of Fatima held in the Secret Archives." Alessio explained the late pope's interest and the mysterious blue note.

Sixtus clasped Alessio's shoulder. "Bring me the file tonight."

43

JERUSALEM
Wednesday, May 10

THE MOOD in the Israeli Prime Minister's conference room was electric as Aaron Feldman met with the Cabinet members who mattered to him, those involved with defense and security. Feldman's goal was to preserve his people from mortal danger and advance Israel's territorial destiny. The greatest threat was Iran, whose President called for wiping Israel from the map. Intelligence reports were conclusive. Iran was within days of having a nuclear weapon.

On his recent visit to Washington, Feldman finalized a plan with Palmer to eliminate the brain trust of the Iranian nuclear program and then destroy the facility where the bomb was being hatched. The fractious election that put him in power created ideal conditions to eliminate the Iranian threat and advance his relentless push to expand Jewish settlements into areas King David had ruled. Only that would protect the Jewish people, drawing exiles back to Israel, making way for the Mashiach to appear and lead the final struggle to restore the Land of Israel as it was promised.

The far-right parties in coalition were sure to support his plan, including the unspoken subtext that over time non-Jews would be evicted from Israel, moved to areas where they and their offspring would be more comfortable. Israel would not be accused of a reverse Babylonian captivity, referring to what the ancient Jews experienced in the 500's BCE when conquered by King Nebuchadnezzar. It would be a voluntary exodus, sure to occur when Arab youth accepted the truth that their opportunities lay outside the Jewish state, not within. There were ways to make that happen.

With his military and security advisors assembled, Feldman drilled each participant like a general preparing for battle.

Satisfied, he announced, "We'll eliminate the nuclear brain trust as soon as the mini-drones arrive."

Key business concluded, Mossad's Director asked what Feldman made of the March.

"It's an Iranian diversion to draw attention to a ridiculous mob of women and a movie star pretending to want peace, and away from its final preparations in the Fordow bunkers where the Iranian bomb is being born."

"Ridiculous as it is, there is a risk," said the Mossad director. "If the Damascus rally ends with people streaming south into Israel, we'll have to stop it."

"There will be no march across our borders." Feldman slammed his fist on the desk. Turning to his Foreign Minister, he barked, "Get me a map showing the defensive buffer we need to the north, east and west beyond which nothing passes — no equipment, no massed groups, no women in white. That's for their protection as well as ours. And find out everything about this AM group, obvious terrorists."

Mossad's Director took notes of his instructions. "Anything more, sir?"

Feldman switched from command to reflection.

"According to Shiites and some Sunnis, this Mahdi figure is supposed to make the world safe for Muslims by getting rid of Jews and other nonbelievers. They say that in the final conflict the Mahdi will battle the Dajjal, a word for the devil incarnate. And who's the Dajjal? They say he will have only one working eye. Because of my eye patch, they see me as a perfect symbol of the Dajjal. I'm a target."

"Absurd," the group murmured, deriding such primitive superstition.

"The Lord our God gave us this Land. We will possess it, all of it."

44

JERUSALEM
Thursday, May 11

NOAH HURRIED from his room at Jerusalem's American Colony Hotel to join his fellow NJA members. Today would be a breakthrough for Operation Apocalypse.

Adrenalin flowed as in the early days of his company Butterfly, when sleep was but a brief respite from the brain's compulsion to create. Now body and spirit were fused to force the world that God ordained into bloom. *Hallelujah!*

Obviously, most of the world had ignored the crowning book of the New Testament. Only a few grasped signs the New Jerusalem Alliance flashed. Seven scrolls to global mayors weren't recognized as echoing the epistles to seven ancient churches of Anatolia. No mainstream story reported the magnificent twelve gateway arches built along the precise perimeter laid out in Revelation, beckoning Jews to come to Jerusalem for conversion now. Though the trumpets and screen images at the Pope's funeral were witnessed by billions, most missed the point — that the time for the Seventh Trumpet is near. Red fireworks over Rome and blood-like fluids in its fountains, orchestrated by the NJA, were misunderstood as a post-funeral salute rather than a signal that the Last Day is nigh.

Noah had hope for the temporary alliance he forged with the leader of 4K. When they met, Etzion explained they were a Jewish group whose goal was to build a Third Temple. Another sign that God was bringing all things in creation to fulfillment. Once the Temple's cornerstone was laid, the NJA could part ways with 4K — Jews would know the light of Christ and join the elect for the Second Coming. According to Revelation it would take only 144,000 Jewish conversions to herald the return of Jesus.

Public recognition of Operation Apocalypse would expand exponentially with the announcement of the NJA's essay contest winner. In addition to architects and city planners who wrote how to refashion Jerusalem's urban fabric, many entrants understood that the end time approached.

The winner was a 26-year-old contributor to a web-based magazine called "Onward Movement," an offshoot of the Southern Baptists dedicated to practical application of the Bible's literal text. Her essay declared that the New Jerusalem was emerging but invisible to people hypnotized by material wealth and military power, false idols worshipped like a golden calf. She called for a Third Temple that would awaken spirits.

At breakfast in the King David Hotel, Noah reviewed progress with fellow Elders. "All 12 gateways are complete?"

"The last will be finished in time for our press conference," said Sam Turrain.

"The prize winner cleared Israeli immigration yesterday," said Fred Scribner, head of the Prize Committee. "Text, music and graphics are set. It'll spread like spiritual wildfire."

Celia Gamble reported. "Noah contacted the leader of the group called 4K. Its activities are aligned with ours, for now. They seek a design for the Third Temple and pledge to build it. They're open to our help. The devil's in the details, or should I say the details provide the pleasure of negotiation?" The small group chuckled.

With the desperate civil war in Syria, rumors of a strike on Iran and other omens, prophetic signs were flashing like lightning. NJA reminders would force even the most oblivious to pay attention.

"Are we ready for Rome?" asked Bip Schroth IV.

"Roger," said Noah. "This time the media can't mistake what will accompany the Pope's installation."

"Why the Pope's tongue twister name?" puzzled Fred Scribner.

"Sixteenth century Sixtus V may be the answer," said Noah. "He was one of the most energetic popes of all time. He completed the dome of St. Peter's, took the Vatican from bankruptcy to a hefty bank account and led the Counter-Reformation. On the other hand, he issued a bull declaring that contraception was a mortal sin and was about to destroy the Jesuits when he died. He called for annihilation of the Turks and the conquest of Egypt, and he wanted to move the Holy Sepulchre from Jerusalem to Italy."

"And that's a reason for the new pope to use the name?" asked an incredulous Fred Scribner, thinking about the marketing challenge of banking on a predecessor's nefarious past.

"Atonement? Who knows what goes on in the papal mind," said Noah.

45

NEAR QOM, IRAN
Thursday, May 11

THE CERULEAN SKY over the holy City of Qom was so uniform a blue that a painter would have needed a single tube of acrylic to capture it on canvas. At the nearby Fordow underground facility, where international inspectors had not been allowed since President Palmer's predecessor reimposed crippling sanctions on Iran, security was on highest alert. Iran's senior scientific team was ensconced in Qom, working on "Firebird," a program to electrify the country, said the regime. Foreign intelligence officials scoffed at that, certain Iran was preparing to test a bomb.

A day earlier, Israeli and U.S. intelligence teams conversed in a secure Vienna safe room. They agreed there were at most weeks before it would be too late to stop a test that must be in its final planning stage. Once it occurred, the genie would be out of the Persian lamp. Iran would be a nuclear power, and the security of the Middle East would be irreparably unsettled.

Recommendations to the Israeli and U.S. governments were agreed. First, eliminate the scientists. Then, if Iran did not immediately stop its program and give international inspectors free run of the country, destroy the oven. The two-step method would give Iran one final opportunity to see the madness of its obsession to join the nuclear club. Phase one was set. Phase two would be as simple as pulling a trigger.

As the Iranian scientists gathered for breakfast at their Qom hotel, they enjoyed a view through the enormous plate glass window that drew the eye to the Fatima al-Masumeh Shrine, with its multiple minarets and gleaming golden dome. Qom was a city of pilgrimage and scholarship, where ayatollahs, imams, other clerics, and students gathered for meditation, study, and inspiration. The Fordow uranium enrichment plant was built deep into a mountain about twenty miles to the northeast.

As traditional cheese, jam and lavash bread were served, a buzzing sound like a swarm of hornets began a crescendo. Before the scientists could look outside, a barrage of iron-like globes with slits for wings and scorpion tails shattered the glass and blazed into the dining room. The lead mini-drone struck a dumbfounded waiter and exploded, shattering his head, the rest of his body dropping to the floor in a heap spurting blood from the severed neck stem.

Before anyone could kick back a chair to escape, the flying devices found every human target in the room, shattering each at head point. Walls and tablecloth were splattered with blood, bone, and brain. The carpet puddled from an incessant flow from decapitated bodies crumpled on the floor like headless rag dolls.

The mini-drones missed one target. The leader of the physicists, a 62-year-old with benign prostatic hyperplasia, unable to get a supply of medication because of sanctions. He had excused himself to the restroom after orange juice and was about to re-enter the dining room when the first mini-drone shattered the window.

"*Saved by my enlarged prostate! May Allah be praised,*" he thought. His mind immediately turned to prayers for the departed and then to jihad, not the greater jihad of personal struggle and submission to Allah the Qur'an demanded of all Muslims, but the lesser jihad fueled by anger and revenge.

Within an hour the Iranian regime was on the web, television, and radio, denouncing the unprovoked murder of innocent civilians, accusing the great Satans, Israel and the United States, of using a demonic new weapon. The spokesman reiterated the belief of most Iranians that this was the work of the Dajjal, who had begun his attack in the great battle.

The righteous must unite to defeat him and his allies.

The spokesman declared, "The Dajjal is one-eyed, but we are not. We see perfectly. We will prevail. *Allahu Akbar! La illaha illa allah.* There is no God but God."

46

ROME
Friday, May 12

NO ONE WILL AGAIN BE SAFE, anywhere, any time.

Ruth stood motionless as she held a coffee cup and watched Gabriel lick his dog bowl. The television screen broadcast grainy bystander footage of the Qom attack — blurry images of wasp-like drones crashing through a hotel window. English captions told how Iran's top nuclear experts, a Revolutionary Guardsman and a waiter had been blown apart, that neither the United States nor Israel claimed credit, leaving commentators to speculate which of the two it was or whether a rogue group had created and deployed this new robotic assassin.

Ruth booted her computer. A *Le Monde* editorial expressed outrage that the flying head-bombs unleashed a new epoch in human violence. Russia's *Commersant* offered an admiring analysis of their per unit cost, estimating they were cheaper by a factor of thousands than human armies. If the technology became generally available and affordable, The *International New York Times* warned, mobsters, drug lords and solo actors could eliminate a target at will, with defenses difficult and detection of the drone operator virtually impossible.

As she browsed further, Ruth got a message that an emergency meeting of the Book Club was called for 9:30 and she was invited.

How will members react?

She googled "Third Temple" and clicked on the 4K site, which had moved beyond seeking designs of a Third Temple to a call for funds to build one. She checked her archived folder of references to marble arches and discovered a mainstream story about mysterious arches said to be the work of an unnamed apocalyptic Christian group. *The Economist*'s daily post featured a scowling Russian President Goudonov facing off against a stern U.S. President Palmer, each threatening the other with missiles held in cartoon hands. She closed her computer and flagged a taxi to the Book Club.

Alessio met Ruth at the door of the Great Synagogue of Rome on Lungotevere Cenci and joined twenty other members at a long table. After a blessing Chief Rabbi Ehhud Krusch began, "The dogs of war howl after yesterday's killings in Qom. How does faith respond?"

"The Crusades return — with a twist," said Grand Mufti Feisal Al-Sheikh. "12th century Christians slaughtered Jews and Muslims alike. Now Judaism and Christianity unite against Islam."

Alessio was quick to the defense. "My Church admitted the excesses of the Crusades. The late Holy Father worked to build bridges between Islam and Christianity."

80-year-old Rabbi Abraham Wiesel, an Israeli war veteran turned pacifist rabbi, did not often speak. When he did, the combination of turtle-paced diction and a deep pitch caused everyone to lean forward.

"My friends," he began, as a member silenced a cell phone, "Israel's leaders have one sacred mission — to preserve the Jewish people. We cannot have neighbors with nuclear weapons. But tell me, my friend from Iran, what do Shiites say?"

Imam Barzani, the sole Iranian member, appeared startled by the question. Anger melted from his face as he explained.

"Shiites believe that the great prophet Isa will return at the End Time to join forces with the Mahdi. Together they will slay the great deceiver, the Dajjal. Isa will kill all swine and wars will end. Perhaps that time draws close, for the Qom attack unmasks Prime Minister Friedman as the Dajjal."

Before the rabbis could take offense, Alessio quickly directed the group to a rising flow of social media material focused on the Last Day.

"Take a look at the website of the New Jerusalem Alliance, an American evangelical group. They read the Second Letter of Peter in the Bible to mean that Christians have a duty to hasten the Second Coming of Christ. And marble arches built in the Middle East are patterned after what the Book of Revelation describes as gates to the new Jerusalem."

Ruth flinched at mention of the NJA. She couldn't bring herself to add that the drones used in the attack looked like creatures with scorpion tails described in the Book of Revelation. She was unwilling to fuel a rising and irrational apocalyptic fever. Now even members of the Book Club were projecting fiction as though it were prediction.

Rabbi Wiesel resumed to make his point. "In our faith the Mashiach will appear and unite the People of the Book in the final days — final because God will finally have had enough of mankind's transgressions."

The Chief Rabbi stroked his beard. "Does death haunt us all, eager for a final harvest? Can our faiths bring peace or salvation?"

Mormon Bishop Patrick Mason offered no comfort. "New Testament passages foretell that a new Jerusalem will be born of an all-consuming fire."

The Book Club disbursed with grim and worried faces, not the camaraderie of scholars. Ruth's mind spun.

Is religion the cause or the hope? Is there a way out of this apocalyptic spiral?

47

DAMASCUS, SYRIA
Saturday, May 13

EYES FIXED FORWARD, indifferent to the movie idol at her side, A'ishah led a river of white into Damascus. Ethereal, a wisp of a young woman, she wore a dazzling white hijab and a kaftan rippling in a light breeze. Militias paid homage by suspending their bloodletting as the March of the Innocents entered the city — women and daughters smiling, crying, greeting their Syrian sisters, arriving from all points on the compass for the destination of this historic female pilgrimage, projecting throughout the Muslim world the power of female witness and sacrifice. A'ishah and Kosari steered the throng toward the gleaming Great Mosque of Damascus.

Kosari recalled a movie he made here. In the 2008 Iranian classic, *The Mahdi*, he played Isa. From the film he learned the history of Damascus, claimed by some as the world's oldest continuously inhabited city. Approaching the Mosque, he recalled the final scene — standing erect atop the Minaret of Isa with the Book of Judgment in one hand, separating the righteous elect from those he banished with a stern forefinger to eternal flame.

As Kosari neared the wooden stage erected for a ceremonial benediction for the March of the Innocents, he marveled that the March had achieved spectacular coverage, elevating his persona to global heights. His agent begged him to return to Tehran for a starring role in a new film — *Saladin*, about the 12th century Muslim leader who vanquished the Crusaders and restored Jerusalem to a city that welcomed all People of the Book. The agent had succeeded in doubling Kosari's price, crediting his bargaining skills rather than the March.

A huge photo of the assassinated Imam of the Umayyad Mosque gazed over the crowd from stage left. The interim imam and three other clerics greeted A'ishah and Kosari as they dismounted from their horses and ascended the steps. Through loudspeakers installed in minarets, the entire city listened as shops closed, men emerged from coffee houses onto the streets, and women stood on balconies.

The imam began by reciting the Qur'an's teachings on the equality of souls. Women are not property of men. Marriage is a matter of agreement.

"Just as Fatima, the Prophet's daughter, came to the Umayyad Mosque, so you have come here today," he welcomed the pilgrims. "Allah, the compassionate, the merciful, led you to this place where your burning devotion will scorch the face of evil that afflicts us beyond the limit of our despair." He called to the podium a woman barely five feet in height with vibrant green eyes and a voice as full-throated as a mezzo-soprano diva.

A'ishah had emerged from obscurity. Reportedly an orphan adopted by what she would only name as "the teacher," she would not speak of the past. Her beauty, diminutive stature and poetic statements in the style of Rumi vaulted her to fame as the March progressed.

She stood before the vast crowd and gently waved a hand to conjure silence. "The time of violence is past. We reject it.

"The time of corruption has expired. We will not stand for it."

With each couplet, high decibel shouting and clapping roared through the crowd.

"The time for deceit is banished. We are not fooled.

"The time for ignorance is over. We are informed.

"The specter of anger tempts us. We respond with unbounded love.

"Our weapons are words — swords of truth and justice.

"The time for hiding is no more. We are in the streets ...

"Until Allah's will be done."

A verbal staccato of 1-2 punches, words crescendoed. The pitch rose with the crowd's excitement. All Damascus swayed to a common rhythm.

An unexpected conclusion followed. "Last night Fatima, beloved daughter of the Prophet, may blessings and peace be upon her and him, visited." A hush swept the crowd.

"Fatima instructed that we must march on to Jerusalem, blessed city of all People of the Book."

Marchers jostled to hear her startling call. "For our children's sake we will create a New Jerusalem, free from occupation. Allah commands. We submit."

A'ishah paused, head bowed, exhausted as an oracle spent. There began a murmur that swelled to a cadence, "Jerusalem! Jerusalem! Jerusalem!" Navid Kosari bowed to A'ishah, projecting a gleaming white smile. Fatigue was cast aside. Many mapped routes to Jerusalem, with no thought of a visa or what would happen when they approached the walls and electrified fencing of the Jewish State.

48

ROME
Saturday, May 13

ON A BRISK DAWN WALK with Gabriel, who busily sniffed the intoxicating scents of Roman sidewalks, Ruth stopped at a panetteria near the Pantheon. While Gabriel gnawed a biscotti offering from the proprietor, she watched a couple with their adorable little girl in a white frilly dress arise from a nearby table. The toddler outstretched her arms as her father helped her take wobbly steps in white booties.

Ruth glanced through the International New York Times and la Repubblica. The Times offered a quick summary of what was important to the western world, and la Repubblica kept her current on Vatican developments while aiding her quest to be reader-fluent in Italian. Front page stories raised the fear that time itself might soon end, so dire were the portents of war. la Repubblica balanced grim stories of suicide bombings and attacks on synagogues, mosques, and churches with speculation about the "Paraguayan crusader turned Pope."

Would he continue as a doctrinal dogmatic or embrace reform? Would he change the Vatican's stance on Liberation Theology? What were his views of women and their role in the Church? What of his bout with cardiac arrhythmia? Was he a caretaker? In his mid-70's, Sixtus VI would have little time to accomplish anything.

As she walked Gabriel back to the apartment, a text message from Noah signaled from a harp glissando. Even his cellphone was programmed for heaven.

"In Rome Tues. Let's meet. U pick time/place — before install. Txt me N."

A reply could wait until after her meeting with Alessio.

Arriving at the café early, she ordered her new favorite, a vanilla no-fat cappuccino, and chose a table for two. Rabbi Steven Friedman waved from the counter.

"I'll be with you in two minutes — caffeine calls!" Before an awkward explanation that she was expecting someone else, Alessio entered, pulled up an extra chair and apologized for failing to mention Rabbi Friedman would join them.

Laden with coffee and biscotti the two men joined her. Alessio said, "Last night Steven and I proposed you as a new member of the Book Club. You are unanimously invited to join."

"And what would I bring to this gathering of men plus one token woman?" she asked bluntly.

"Are you like Groucho Marx, who said he wouldn't join a club that would have him as a member?" Steven teased.

"Eugenia is no token!" Alessio added.

Regretting her earlier lack of grace, she accepted. Alessio was her first friend in Rome. It would be good to stay in touch, especially as they wouldn't be working together once the new pope chose a Vatican liaison for the Anglican Centre. She meant to ask him what his new assignment would be.

After they clinked cups, Alessio asked for their take on the March.

Rabbi Friedman shook his head and described how the apparent turn of the March from Damascus south to Jerusalem invited collective suicide.

"Israel won't let a million Muslims cross its borders. No visas, only a vague cause to promote, one not friendly to Israel. A united Islam is Israel's worst nightmare."

"Could Israel attack a March led by an unarmed woman? Is the Iranian regime provoking Israel into doing the unthinkable?" Alessio wondered.

"Perhaps the women of Islam are creating an entirely new way of thinking, not only within Islam but for how we in the west understand the region," Ruth suggested hopefully.

"Iran is not known for gender equality," said Steven.

"Whatever the reason for the March, you can build a dam to hold back water, but there's no stopping a million committed women." On that Ruth held firm.

Without waiting for a response from Steven, Alessio turned to a new subject.

"I arranged for the Book Club to have seats in the Piazza for the installation of our former member."

Ruth and Steven marveled at the good fortune that brought seats better than some ambassadors were able to wrangle.

"How did you manage that?" asked Steven.

"I have news," Alessio turned to Ruth with a broad smile. "The Holy Father asked me to continue in my post."

"That's wonderful, Alessio," said Ruth.

"Do you expect trouble this time?" asked Steven.

"The Swiss Guard will prevent a repeat of trumpets from the colonnades," said Alessio.

Ruth averted her gaze downward, wondering what Noah and the NJA were planning. Her phone rang with organ music fit for a British cathedral, signaling it was the Archbishop.

"Ruth, how is your morning? Raining here, but that's jolly England." Despite living in England for years, the Archbishop had not warmed to its dreary drizzle.

"We're preparing, your Grace. What can I do for you?"

"Get out your map of the Holy Land. Have you been there before?"

"Only once. With a seminary group."

"This won't be a tourist jaunt. Something's afoot. Pope Sixtus is planning a meeting in Jerusalem. He wasn't clear about why or what. But he asked me to meet him there soon. I'll need you to observe the conditions and give me a report. I'll send you questions. Let's leave it at that for now. Can you depart the evening of the installation?"

"I'll prepare," Ruth replied, puzzled why she was being asked for such an enigmatic mission, given Anglican clergy present throughout the lands of the Bible.

Ruth apologized as she rejoined Steven and Alessio.

Alessio nodded understanding that the two of them each had one caller who could never be ignored. "Anything exciting?"

"Preparations," Ruth said, but her face messaged there was more to it than getting ready for a papal installation.

49

JERUSALEM, WASHINGTON D.C., MOSCOW & TEHRAN
Sunday, May 14

BLOGS, TWEETS, TELEVISION and newspapers speculated that the March was a cover for Iran's final preparation to test a nuclear weapon — or a sincere call to rid the world of male tyrants — or a protest against Zionist expansion — or ....

Prime Minister Feldman was in a foul mood but steeled as always to achieve his ends, most well-known to the public, others hiding in the secret chambers of his mind. While Israel was in the final phase of destroying Iran's ambition to join the nuclear club, this rogue band of women in white, accompanied by a two-shekel movie star, threatened to divert his country's security forces. They were needed at the border to defend against Muslim troops poised to invade, the major risk if Feldman ordered the destruction of the underground bomb factory near Qom.

But the wave of white undoubtedly hid suicide sisters. He could not let killers into the country. Perhaps he could appeal to the Palestinian leadership, invoking the ancient truth that the enemy of my enemy can temporarily be my friend. Palestinians were Sunnis who viewed Shiites as traitors to Islam and received no help from Iran. If Palestinians rebuffed the March, it would never get near Jerusalem. Perhaps he could invite to the capital the movie star and this new female celebrity and give them a photographed welcome on the Temple Mount, then fly them home with their horses while the women in white tired of waiting and dispersed.

President Ike Palmer fumed daily that the media's coverage of events in the Middle East dominated the news instead of focusing on him. His staff assuaged him that photo ops at the installation of him with the new pope would solidify the Catholic vote.

He scanned the daily security briefing but read every word about how the March was anything but innocent. Intercepted messages confirmed its orchestration from Tehran. CIA analysts linked the March and the nuclear device at the Umayyad Mosque to the Tehran regime's imminent test of a nuclear weapon.

Palmer paused on page 3. Russia was increasing arms shipments to Iran, including long-range missile launchers and air-to-air missiles. By supplying these Russia was upping the stakes beyond its declaration of alliance. Palmer sent a demand for details to Director of National Intelligence Sullivan.

Noah couldn't believe it. Reports of the Temple design contest of 4K and the NJA essay contest appeared on newspaper back pages, if at all. A few architectural critics debated the aesthetics of 4K's winning Third Temple design. The NJA's chosen essay about how to create a New Jerusalem received over a million hits but generated no mainstream coverage. Psalm 78 came to mind. "A stubborn and rebellious generation, whose hearts were not loyal to God, whose spirits were not faithful to him."

What will it take for the signs to be understood?

Russian President Goudonov talked with the Syrian Ambassador about the March. They concurred it was a cultural blip with no real significance. The Ambassador predicted a resumption of civil war as soon as the women left the Syrian capital. There was an immediate need for more Russian military aid.

Goudonov looked at him through impenetrable grey eyes. "Yes, it always seems so, Mr. Ambassador. What are allies for? How much?"

Iranian President Al-Rabani told a television interviewer that the March was a grapevine rooted in rich soil displaying the strength of Iran's women. As usual Al-Rabani boasted that the Great Satans would be crushed if they attacked Iran.

"We moved forces to the west," he said, not needing to remind viewers that this meant closer to Israel.

The Supreme Leader was on retreat at Qom, silent, unaware that President Al-Rabani had tested a handful of Revolutionary Guards to see whether Al-Rabani could count on them if the Supreme Leader confirmed his inability to preserve the dignity of Iran.

50

THE VATICAN
Monday, May 15

THREE SHARP RAPS on the door awakened Alessio Monday morning at 4:45. Wrapping a robe about him, he opened the door, shocked to see Pope Sixtus standing before him in papal pajamas, white cotton with gold Vatican seals.

"Join me for breakfast," commanded the Pope.

Fifteen minutes later a showered and fully dressed Alessio joined his new boss in his private chamber. The Swiss Guard standing watch stiffened to attention as Alessio entered. Sixtus wore a simple white ankle-length cassock and a mozzetta, a short cape as a symbol of his papal authority, as his predecessor preferred. A painting of Paraguay's patron Saint Blas, a silver-encased icon of Our Lady of Guadalupe and a large portrait of a dour looking Saint Ignatius Loyola rested on the red tiled floor ready to be hung. Rows of santos, Paraguayan wooden religious sculptures painted bright colors, claimed the bookcase where the prior pope had stocked writings of Augustine of Hippo and other Doctors of the Church.

"Mate cocido and chipa," the pontiff offered. "See what you think of Paraguayan cuisine." His eyes sparkled as he offered Alessio a plate and encouraged him to help himself to a cheese-flavored roll and sweet yerba mate tea.

"Thank you for agreeing to stay in your post. Heaven knows I need your help."

Alessio bit into the chipa. "This is better than Italian bread. Corn?"

"No, cassava, the sweet kind — Guarani style — with cheese." Picking up the Fatima folder Alessio delivered from the Archives, the Pope switched to business. "There was a note from my predecessor that you are the only man he could trust in the Vatican."

Alessio had always been proud of his service. "It was an honor to serve him."

The Pope nodded and sipped mate cocido. "Did you read the extra page?" asked Sixtus.

"No, Holy Father. I was not asked to read it, only to deliver it, for your eyes only."

"Please read it." The Pope handed Alessio the file.

Surprised, Alessio looked at the page on top, written by Sister Lucia, the last survivor of the Miracle at Fatima. Unable to read Portuguese, Alessio carefully turned the sheet to find an Italian translation created when typewriters had a black ribbon punched by individual keys that hammered ink onto paper. A minute to read but a lifetime to absorb, he thought.

"Father, we must keep this between us. My predecessors kept this secret, and I understand why. But, frankly, I don't know what to make of it."

"Excuse me for a moment."

Alessio hurried to his room and took the late pope's blue note from the locked cabinet. Presenting it to Sixtus, he said, "This was left on the bed stand over there. I think he meant it for me."

Sixtus stared at the note with its **3 > 1** scrawl. "And also for me. What do we know about the Fatima Miracle?"

"I have been studying it," said Alessio, thinking of his collaboration with Ruth. "Sister Lucia warned us to repent, to pledge Russia to Mary, to turn away from communism, or disaster would befall."

"Tell me more," urged the Pope. Alessio summarized the Book Club's intense discussion of recent events, of Jewish, Islamic and Christian concepts of Apocalypse, of how signs were flashing a coming cataclysm. "We discussed groups who believe the End Time approaches and are acting to bring it on."

"What do you make of this note?" asked the Pope.

Alessio explained how it might be read to mean three must join as one before a final ending, like the seven in the last day of creation week, or the seventh trumpet sounding at the end of time.

"Just a thought," he added. It was unthinkable that he would tell the Pope what or how to think.

"Three into one?" Sixtus scratched his head. And suddenly his puzzlement vanished with an emphatic extension of his hands, palms up. "I see. We must unite Christianity — in Jerusalem. There's little time left."

They sat in silence while Sixtus closed his eyes in prayer. Opening them he took a sheet of papal stationery, wrote two lists of names and handed the paper to Alessio.

"I will invite these leaders to meet with me Friday."

Alessio was startled to see Jewish, Christian and Muslim religious leaders on the first and an odd grouping of presidents and prime ministers on the second.

"What will you ask them?"

"To gather in the Holy City."

"They will be here, in Rome."

"Not Rome. Jerusalem, where our Lord and Savior was crucified, was buried, and rose from the dead. Where he will soon come again. We must gather our flock under one roof." The Pope seemed to look through Alessio to a distant place. "What you discussed at the Book Club — prepare a presentation of signs that time is short. I need it for Friday."

Alessio nodded, suppressing astonishment at the Pope's sudden certainty of what the Fatima page and the blue note meant.

"And pack your bags. You leave for Jerusalem Sunday," commanded the Pope.

51

TEHRAN, IRAN
Monday, May 15

IRANIAN PRESIDENT AL-RABANI felt he was skidding on thin ice, an odd image in the unusually hot late spring of Tehran. The surge of youth and pent-up frustration of an increasingly impoverished middle class in the capital fomented daily demonstrations that required insistent suppression. American sanctions resulted in frozen bank accounts, shortages, and economic suffering. The culture police detained individuals for an ever-widening variety of offenses, even an errantly erotic glance through a veil. The scope of arrestable sacrilege expanded to western lettering on a T-shirt or a designer label on a polo shirt — anything the culture police found suspect, given President Al-Rabani's order to trample any sprout of rebellion.

Complicating politics were the super-zealots, complaining that the Government's steps to boost employment were apostasies. One man's corruption was another's elbow grease. Worst of all, Al-Rabani was stymied by the indecision of the third Grand Ayatollah, who held supreme power but sat on his hands in Qom, lacking the fire of the first Supreme Leader or the rigor of the more taciturn second.

How could a president exercise his powers when the Supreme Leader dawdled and equivocated?

Infuriating to Al-Rabani, was the skyrocketing popularity of Navid Kosari. Commentaries circulating on the Iranian internet featured a photo of Kosari's handsome profile with A'ishah to his right. Why was an imposter getting such coverage when it was he, Al-Rabani, who would soon emerge as the Mahdi to lead the people of Islam to glory?

The Iranian President's most immediate worry — that the spineless Supreme Leader might halt his drive to give Iran a nuclear weapon. Iran claimed its nuclear program was to bring electricity to the poor. But to the west and Iran's elite, this was a tale told to a third-grade teacher by a boy holding one hand behind his back with fingers crossed. The end game was obvious. Only when Shi'a Islam had the bomb would Iran and its Revolution be safe from the Great Satans of the West and from Saudi Arabia and its Sunni allies.

Iran was enraged by the massacre of the scientists at Qom. A strengthened hand encouraged Al-Rabani to take his case to the Grand Ayatollah. Let us do only a test, he would argue, so Iran would have leverage to bargain from strength with Israel, America, and Europe.

He wouldn't stop there. Unleashing those mini-drones against Iran, those lethal bats from the depths of hell, ratcheted up the stakes. Al-Rabani would call on all Muslims of the region, who outnumbered Israelis overwhelmingly. Zionism would be crushed by Islamic unity.

The President ordered 80% of Iran's military to positions along its western border, reassuring the leaders of Iraq, Jordan, Syria, Lebanon, Egypt, and Saudi Arabia that the build-up was not unfriendly to them. He urged them to post troops along their borders with Israel. Thus began a mobilization of tanks, artillery, men, camels, ammunition, tents, portable kitchens, mobile toilets, and the other entourage of war targeting Israel. This time no Muslim leader would call the Israeli Prime Minister to claim peaceful intent.

52

BETWEEN DAMASCUS AND ISRAEL
Monday, May 15

VALI QALIL and two Army of the Mahdi officers pored over maps and reconnaissance, strategizing how the March of the Innocents could best approach Jerusalem. Qalil ordered the marchers to remain in Damascus an extra day before embarking toward its newly proclaimed destination. Kosari and A'ishah led the women in prayer, visits to shrines around the Umayyad Mosque and an ongoing peace fest that kept local gunfire at bay.

AM's leadership plotted a path due south toward the eastern bank of the Jordan River, which by May was more dry bed than watercourse. There the March would pause for photographers to capture the massed white assemblage gazing longingly into the West Bank, conquered by Israel during the 1967 War and now under a checkerboard mix of Palestinian and Israeli control that disadvantaged Muslims.

The March would enter the West Bank near Jericho across the King Hussein Bridge, force its way into lightly guarded agricultural land where date palms and bananas grow, then hurry westward into an area under Palestinian control, and from there turn north. Here boundaries were marked not by concrete walls but by electrified fencing that separated Palestinian controlled land from what Israel considered reserved for Jewish settlers. The women would move along this perimeter to a point most amenable to crossing into what world maps considered Israel proper. If it penetrated the pre-1967 borders of Israel, the March could trek peacefully through Israeli territory to complete its pilgrimage to the city visited by the Prophet on his Night Journey.

The March of the Innocents left Damascus at 9:00 as the temperature hit 80 degrees Fahrenheit. A cavalcade of press vehicles preceded Kosari on his white mare and A'ishah on her pale beige mare as they led the spirited crowd of a half million out of the Syrian capital south toward Jordan. Damascus residents waved flags and held Qur'ans aloft. They projected relief that life could soon return to normal, despair that life would return to normal, fear that bloodlust would resume as the March departed.

Well-wishers greeted the multitude in Jordan, offering tents, opening homes, serving meals, and greeting the marchers like relatives visiting for a wedding. That evening gilt-edged envelopes were hand delivered to A'ishah and Kosari. Inside were identical invitations on the stationery of the Prime Minister of Israel.

They silently read the words, provided in double-columned Hebrew and Farsi. The letters began with a personal message congratulating them on efforts to bring peace and to elevate the status of women, including a quotation from the Book of Isaiah about arms beaten into ploughshares. After this flattering start, the page got to its point.

"You understand it is not possible to permit a March to enter Israel. To our knowledge no participant holds a visa. In this time of extreme tension, we must keep order and avoid tragedy.

In the spirit of reconciliation, I invite you both to be my personal guests two weeks from today in Jerusalem. We can discuss all matters. May our common God guide us to understanding in this way.

Faithfully yours, Aaron Feldman, Prime Minister of Israel"

A'ishah finished reading and sat quietly while Kosari scoured the lines twice to comprehend each nuance. He turned to her with the penetrating gaze so powerful in films and asked what she made of it.

A'ishah answered dutifully, "We must refuse."

Kosari hesitated, considering the risk of perishing in the desert. But his fans would be outraged by a photo of him with Feldman.

Choosing his most heroic voice, he declared, "Yes."

Together they asked the AM communications officer to send a short reply declining the invitation, thanking Feldman for the sentiments, and requesting a blanket visa for the March to enter Jerusalem. It ended, "We come to Jerusalem in peace as People of the Book." Nothing was released to the media about this exchange.

When Vali Qalil took a call from A'ishah about the declined invitation, he was alone in a safe room in Jordan lent by the patron of an underground group dedicated to overthrowing the country's Hashemite monarch. The owner's family traced direct descent from Muhammad's daughter Fatimah and viewed the King as a puppet of Britain, which created Transjordan in 1921 and installed the dynasty from afar. Qalil confirmed she acted righteously by declining Feldman's invitation.

"Lead on," he told her.

Qalil's plan was unfolding as designed. *The sacrifice will be soon.* Qalil recited Qur'anic verses about Abraham's submission to Allah's command that he slay his son Ishmael, an order reversed by Allah's mercy.

"Peace be on Abraham," he prayed.

He had cared for A'ishah since she survived the orphanage bombing of a girls school. She would soon fulfill her destiny. He felt a moment of sadness but only a moment.

Yes, the sacrifice of innocent A'ishah will be my bitter submission, and peace will be unto all our people.

After prayer Qalil phoned a Palestinian confidante. Assured the guards were within reach of the March, Qalil inquired if the instruments were in place. "Remember, Kosari first, then A'ishah."

53

WASHINGTON, D.C.
Tuesday, May 16

PRESIDENT IKE PALMER had unsalted mixed nuts, kale chips and a mango smoothie for Tuesday night's dinner with the IQ, his four senior security and defense advisors. The aides struggled with unwieldy chicken caesar wraps that threatened to squirt white dressing onto the navy-blue Oval Office carpet as they gathered for their weekly discussion of how to protect the American people.

"I always gain weight on these trips. Can't insult the hosts about toasts and dessert, you know," said the President. The group was used to his sporadic dieting to fit the lean, tough conservative image he aimed to project.

Providing the weekly summary, Director of National Intelligence Sullivan dispensed with second-tier foreign concerns. The President dubbed Russia during the election campaign "America's chief threat." Palmer had demanded a report about Russian arms supplies to Iran.

"Russia's supplies to Iran are confirmed." She handed a page to Palmer. "This was clearly a move to stop Israel from daring to strike Iran's nuclear facility. The first phase of Operation Meteor was a success eliminating the Iranian brain trust, but it prompted this reaction. Iran moved Army units to its western border, a second warning to Israel."

"Feldman won't flinch," said the President, referring to Operation Meteor's second punch to bomb the Qom nuclear bakery.

National Security Advisor Coulter added, "This March is an Iranian trick to divert attention from its nuclear program. Pathetic — to slog these women and children through the dust. The barrier around the West Bank will turn that group into a pinball searching for an opening at the bottom of a case with no holes."

Palmer moved to the next topic.

"I'll be in Rome in a few days. Anything from the new Pope we should request?" he asked, tossing the plastic cup into a dark, intricately carved wooden waste basket. It was a gift from the Emperor of Japan to Franklin Roosevelt in 1938. Palmer would have preferred a Republican waste bin, but even minor changes in the White House seemed to upset one or another voting bloc prone to hysteria over such trivia.

With shrugs from the IQ about spiritual matters, Palmer dismissed the group. He stood at the window and watched a full moon begin its rise across the skies toward the lighted obelisk of the Washington Monument. He picked up his private line to one of the 25 people on speed dial. Each of these elite had encryption on their phones that made calls untraceable.

"Noah, good evening. You're in the States? ... Right. ... Listen, I have a mission for you."

54

ROME
Tuesday, May 16

ON THE TUESDAY BEFORE Pope Sixtus' installation, Alessio and Ruth met for breakfast at the Albergo Del Senato opposite the Pantheon on the Piazza Della Rotonda, where Alessio's cousin was the manager. A quiet meeting place where hotel guests shared a buffet, it was a world apart from the Vatican, an oasis from frantic preparations for the papal installation.

The day before, a Rome paper ran a photo of Alessio with the headline "Papal Continuity," reporting he would continue in his unique role for the new pope. To avoid recognition, Alessio decided he and Ruth should pretend to be tourists staying at the hotel.

Ruth needed to be at the Centre by 9:30 to prepare for the arrival of Anglican delegates flying to Rome for the first Paraguayan and by some historians' assertions the first person of "indigenous blood" to be seated on the throne of St. Peter. Alessio intrigued her by the urgency of his breakfast invitation with a vague request to work together on a presentation.

Alessio was in the breakfast room when she arrived. Ruth slipped in, hesitated before putting her hands on Alessio's left shoulder, then cheerfully greeted him, like a tourist wife joining her husband.

He sprang to his feet and pulled back a chair for her. "Ready to see the sites?"

After selecting English muffins, strawberry preserves, and soupy mixed fruit from the buffet, they settled into business, careful not to be overheard.

"Sorry for the disguise — but you probably saw the news story yesterday with my photo." Ruth lifted her coffee cup as if making a toast.

Alessio glanced around. An elderly English couple was scouring an English language guidebook of Rome, and a family of five was dealing with squealed complaints from the youngest child that sugared corn flakes were not available. No reason to think a journalist or interloper was listening.

"I've seen the missing Fatima page, Ruth. The Holy Father had me read it."

Ruth stopped spreading strawberry preserves onto her muffin.

"Did you bring a copy?"

"I could not. The Holy Father wants to keep it secret."

"Then I'm sorry I can't help — you or Pope Sixtus." Ruth put down her knife.

Alessio nodded with a troubled expression. He looked up at Ruth and grinned. "Let us try it this way. Let us assume I heard a story."

"Hypothetical only," Ruth returned a mischievous smile.

"Let us pretend the story is about a father who gathers his three before the throne in the Holy City."

"And just pretending, is the number seven in the story?"

"Not directly. But assume it ends by saying that the faithful will gather under one roof before the Final Day." Alessio took a sip of coffee.

"Seven days of creation. Seven days in a week. Anything else in this hypothetical tale?"

"Let us say there is a warning against following the false manual and a call for twelve dozen centuries to change, and a reference to the second from the south. And the skies of Babylon turn black for the sheep and goats to gather, and a great blaze lights the path."

Ruth took careful mental notes. "False manual. 144 centuries. Sheep and goats. A great blaze. The Final Day. Did Pope Sixtus conclude anything from this — hypothetically?"

Alessio looked about to ensure no one was listening and leaned forward to whisper. "He is fixed on one thing — to unite Christianity on the Temple Mount. To him the Holy City is Jerusalem, and he must gather leaders there. He sends me to Jerusalem Sunday."

"Well, hypothetically, there will be a meeting in Jerusalem, and he needs you to take a look and report back. What does he plan to do in Jerusalem?"

Alessio held the cup suspended in his hand. "A meeting first, the faithful gathered under one roof. He wants to unite Protestants and the Orthodox with Rome."

"One meeting won't do that."

"He will propose building a Vatican Cathedral on the Mount."

"Build a Roman Catholic Church on the Temple Mount?" Ruth asked, visibly astonished.

"Yes."

Ruth was stunned. She whispered, "Have you been there?"

"Never."

"There's no room for a Cathedral to be built there."

Alessio appeared perplexed by this. "He will invite your Archbishop, and a group of Jewish and Muslim leaders also."

Ruth paused. An attendant cleared plates and refilled their cups with steaming coffee.

Quietly Ruth said, "Confidentially, he already invited the Archbishop. Jerusalem's a bomb ready to explode, with the women's March heading there, the killing of the scientists and everything else. And Sixtus wants to build a Vatican church on the Temple Mount? Does he have any idea how incendiary that would be?"

She folded her hands on the table and was silent for a minute, thinking. "Jerusalem's sacred to Christianity, Judaism and Islam. Why invite all three to this meeting?"

"He needs their support to build a church there?" Alessio shrugged his shoulders. "Maybe he sees the people of all three as the faithful? It fits who is invited. A rabbi from Israel, and you must hold this between us, the Grand Ayatollah of Iran, your President, other heads of state. Your Archbishop is the invited Protestant, and the Russian Patriarch for the Orthodox. The Holy Father is driven to reunite Christians into one church and maybe he sees it as a way to offer Jews and Muslims a path to heaven."

"Anglicans split from Rome but never left *the true Church*," Ruth corrected. "And there are more than three Christian groups." Ruth added cream to her coffee and took a sip to compose herself, thinking how Three into One on the blue note related to the Fatima page, at least parts of it Alessio shared hypothetically, and how preposterous it was if the Pope thought he could convert Jews and Muslims to Roman Catholicism.

"I need time to think about this."

In hushed tones Alessio said, "God chose the Holy Father to fulfill the Fatima prophecy and unite Christianity while there is still time."

Ruth leaned forward. "So what does he intend to accomplish at this meeting in Jerusalem beyond getting everyone to agree on a cathedral there? He'll probably fail at that."

"He prays about it. He believes the End Time draws near. He needs to show the leaders the recent signs and get them to take urgent action."

"Religious leaders may understand signs of the Apocalypse, but heads of state? And you know that other faiths have their own stories about the End Time."

"That's where I need your help. He asked me to create a video for Friday's dinner to convince the leaders to come to Jerusalem." Alessio seemed to hesitate. Perhaps he had said too much, but Ruth was the expert. "The Miracle of Fatima and apocalyptic traditions are your specialty. Will you help me?"

"Of course I will. But what will this presentation show?" asked Ruth.

"Everything you have helped me to understand."

55

ROME
Tuesday, May 16

RUTH SPENT TUESDAY MORNING confirming arrangements for Anglican bishops flying to Rome so she could prepare a presentation with Alessio that afternoon. The Archbishop phoned to say he'd been invited to an early Friday Vatican dinner and would join the Pope in Jerusalem two weeks from now.

"He called it the summit on the Mount," the Archbishop responded. "He will ask the government and other religious leaders to attend. I said I would."

"Did he tell you who's invited?" she asked, aiming not to breach her promise to keep some of what Alessio said confidential.

"He didn't provide a list, but he said leaders of Judaism and Islam will be included."

"Agenda?" asked Ruth.

"That's where it gets strange. He seemed driven, but asked me to trust him, said it was essential to get the right people there. And when I pressed him about the agenda, he talked about unity, the need for the faithful to gather under one roof before time disappears."

"I'll see what I can find out," said Ruth, feeling conflicted about certain details Alessio privately shared. "I've learned that the Pope is sending a scout to Jerusalem on Sunday."

"Then you need to go as well, Ruth. We can talk more when I see you in Rome."

Before she could work on the video production, she had a lunch date with Noah. But her mind spun pieces of Alessio's story. *A great blaze, sheep and goats, gathering the faithful under one roof before the end — who are the "faithful?" Christians? All those who claim to be? All People of the Book?*

Running late, she caught a taxi to meet Noah for lunch at his hotel. As before, he stood in the palatial lobby's center, and when she arrived, he walked briskly to her. Kissing her on the left and right cheeks, he explained playfully, "Italian style. No more small-town boy."

Effecting a glamorous toss of her hair, Ruth smiled. "Delighted to see you, Signore."

In the hotel restaurant over Greek salads heavy on minced olives, Noah asked if he could share information confidentially. It wasn't a confessional setting where that was sacrosanct, Ruth reminded him, but she promised to be discreet.

Noah's smile halted. "Secrecy's essential."

"Since we were kids, has it ever been otherwise?"

Noah recounted the brilliance of the NJA's essay contest and its disappointing lack of media attention.

Ruth sympathized. "Hard to compete with bombings, famine, a woman's march, mini-drones."

Noah took a deep breath.

"So now we're going to help the winner of another group's contest. An Israeli group called 4K wants to rebuild the Temple in Jerusalem on the site where the first two were destroyed. We'll help fund its construction."

Ruth's eyes widened. "Building a Jewish Temple on the third holiest site in Islam? Have you lost your mind?" *So competing forces aim to cram a Jewish temple and a Vatican cathedral between the Dome of the Rock and the Al Aqsa Mosque!*

"I explained to you that God called the NJA to bring about the New Jerusalem."

"With all the craziness going on, my book club is afraid we're headed for worldwide disaster, not God's shining city on the hill."

"I didn't know you were the book club type."

"It's interfaith, Christians, Muslims and Jews."

"Could I be a guest?"

"Not if you're bringing on the End Time. There may not be time for another meeting from what you're saying. And thinking of doing."

Noah didn't flinch. "Revelation unfolds and the NJA aims to help it along. Our signs aim to help people prepare." Noah looked down at his salad and poked at an olive.

"What do you want from me?" Ruth asked reluctantly, feeling that Noah was courting her brain rather than her.

"Talk with the Archbishop about endorsing a Third Temple."

"I didn't know you were the Israeli ambassador."

"I have nothing to do with politics," Noah replied evenly. "But we're close to the moment when Jews will convert, so Jesus can return to Jerusalem. A Third Temple is a prelude to the Second Coming."

OMG, Ruth mentally texted herself.

"You think if a Temple is rebuilt, Jews will decide overnight to accept Jesus as their savior and that signals it's time for the final millennium and then Jesus appears? Ta-da? What about Muslims enraged that their holy site has been defiled?"

"I want to see the world God planned for us in our lifetimes," Noah replied avidly.

"Let me ask a question about how you read Revelation," Ruth redirected the conversation. "A great blaze — what does that mean to you?"

"The end will come with fire, that's clear. I haven't heard the phrase 'a great blaze,' but it fits. And think what follows. Don't you long for what Revelation 21 describes? 'Death will be no more, crying and pain will be no more for the first things have passed away.'"

"I'm not heartless. But if you're so eager to interpret the Bible literally, there's nothing in it that mentions Noah and the NJA bringing about this brand-new world or incinerating us all in a great blaze."

Noah stared at a half-finished salad. He looked up and into her eyes. "Ruth, I achieved great wealth, but I paid a price. And now I seek what's really important, the glory of God."

Ruth relented. "I understand. You're a new Christian and you're excited about applying Scripture to life." Ready to leave delusional topics behind and without promising to talk to the Archbishop, she teased, "Who would think that one day two people from Zoar Village would be having lunch in Rome's finest hotel talking about the Apocalypse?"

They caught up on their families. Noah's mother had died, and he'd had little contact with his father for decades. Ruth's parents lived in an RV community on US 41 in Estero, Florida. Never married, Noah had no pets because he traveled so much. Ruth revealed the loss of her fiancé without getting into details. She talked about the antics of her dog Gabriel.

Ruth glanced at her watch. She'd delegated to Secretary Ponelli remaining tasks to welcome Anglican delegates. She was due to meet with Alessio at her apartment to work on the video presentation. Before departing she mentioned she would be visiting Jerusalem and asked if Noah could arrange a meeting with the 4K group while she was there.

"I'm researching what drives Jewish fundamentalist thinking."

"I'll try," he said. "They prefer to stay under cover."

56

ROME, JERUSALEM &
WASHINGTON, D.C.
Wednesday, May 17

BACK IN HIS ST. REGIS SUITE after lunch with Ruth, Noah called 4K Leader Haim Etzion on a secure channel arranged by the technicians of 4K and the NJA. Triple encryption devised by an NJA member limited the risk of intercepted communications.

Etzion flattered, "Your essay contest — brilliant. It shines a spotlight on Jerusalem."

"We hoped for wider publicity," Noah admitted. "But we had a great response."

"Thanks to your support the Third Temple will be built."

"Can you get permits?" asked Noah.

"It's under control."

"Can we help?"

"It's handled. When will you visit Jerusalem?"

"I just returned from there, but I'll be back soon. Can you meet someone who'll be there next week?"

"Send me details," said Etzion.

Within an hour, the CIA Director blanched at a top-secret report from the Israeli desk. He immediately reported to DNI Sullivan: "Collusion between NJA and 4K. Noah Stoll ID'd as NJA chief. Plans to rebuild Temple on Mount. Recommend 4K and NJA adds to Red List / tails on leaders."

Sullivan deleted the message. She knew Noah Stoll was a Palmer "Harvester," a secret small group of individuals pledged to gather more than $10 million for Palmer's campaign. Palmer probably had him exploring back channels. She upped surveillance on 4K and instructed the CIA Director to share the message with no one.

The President was on his way to Rome.

57

HAIFA, ISRAEL
Thursday, May 18

THE FIRST FLARE OF REVENGE for the Qom killings of Iranian scientists ignited Haifa. Previously, this northernmost major city of Israel had escaped high-profile suicide attacks of young people promised an express elevator to Paradise by extremist leaders who would not make their own self-sacrifice.

This time it was 14-year-old twins, brother and sister who snuffed themselves and 17 civilians in a shopping mall and wounded 37 others. A second incident followed hours later, when a rusty Fiat driven by a 19-year-old costumed in a vintage Israeli military coat crashed through a barrier at a northern Israeli Army post, killing the driver and a guard. A photo of the guard, arms aflame, took top media billing.

En route to Rome, Prime Minister Feldman detoured briefly to Haifa and expressed outrage at the airport. "We will resist," he defiantly declared. His resolve to strike Fordow was now unalterable. Iran would pay.

Three 4K leaders from Haifa were there during the attacks. They scattered leaflets throughout the city emblazoned with the design of the Third Temple. Calling for war against "those who would destroy us" and urging expansion of Jewish settlements into southern Lebanon and Syria, the leaflets touted a website where Israelis could donate funds or volunteer to be settlers.

Within a day, a thousand Jews declared they were ready to move north into Arab territory to reclaim what had once been part of the Land of Israel under King David, and 1,427,532 shekels were collected to rebuild the Temple on *Har haBáyith*.

58

LEBANON
Thursday, May 18

THE DAY OF THE HAIFA ATTACKS, the remaining 27 Jews living in Lebanon left for Israel, abandoning hope that Jews could have a future there. They were the final remnant of a Jewish community that in biblical times were the tribes of Asher and Naphtali, living as far north as Sidon.

At the start of the 20th century, when Beirut flourished as the Paris of the Middle East, the Jewish community grew to more than 15,000 members worshipping in sixteen synagogues. After the 1975 civil war and Israel's 1982 invasion of Lebanon, Lebanese Jews became an accelerating diaspora. Now the survivors were fleeing.

"Our families come first," said the patriarch, grieving there was no rabbi to pronounce a benediction as they assembled a caravan to head south. "We asked our neighbors to entrust our homes to those who need them. No one would buy them."

Asked what would happen to the Maghen Abraham Synagogue, lovingly restored in 2009-10, with donations primarily from the Lebanese Government and Muslims, including support even from the head of Hezbollah, the leader sadly shook his head.

By the next morning Lebanon lacked a single resident claiming to be a Jew. The same exodus occurred years earlier from Syria with a push by then President Assad, who told Syrian Jews to leave as long as they did not immigrate directly to Israel, so strident was Syrian insistence that Israel's right to exist not be recognized in any manner whatsoever. The countries to the north of Israel were emptied of Jews. Ghost synagogues haunted the streetscapes as reminders of a time People of the Book lived together, synagogues, mosques and minarets, temple spires and church domes creating a mosaic of great and ancient cities. Now the synagogues stood as tombstones of an extinct population.

59

JERUSALEM
Friday, May 19

THE JERUSALEM POST reported on the front page that Prime Minister Feldman would leave Friday to attend the papal installation, amidst stories of the Haifa attacks and a graph showing Islamic forces surrounding Israel.

That same day a 4K technician shut off the water flow underneath the Temple Mount. By 5 p.m. no water reached the Dome of the Rock or the Al Aqsa Mosque. Eytan Osnat had informed the Waqf chief that emergency repairs were needed. The chief ordered signs posted — "Closed — Reopen 14:00 Sunday." Israeli officials blocked the walkway along the Western Wall that controlled public access to the Mount after receiving similar instructions from the Mayor.

With this accomplished, 4K's leadership met one final time before the culmination of years of planning. Etzion confirmed the rabbi's blessing along with the injunction that no human blood be spilled.

The group gathered in the undercroft of the rabbi's synagogue, built in the Old City a thousand years ago. Etzion signaled with a wave of his right hand, and a young man led into the room a red heifer. In accordance with the Book of Numbers 19: 1-22 and Mishnah Tractate Parah, the sacrifice of the calf would sanctify their efforts. Every hair on the creature's body was red. A young cow, it had never been yoked and had no blemish. Color photographs documented the animal's perfect nature. A veterinarian certified the heifer's redness, with hair samples affixed to the certificate. The cow's doleful eyes seemed to project understanding of its fate.

Death came quickly with a sudden slit near the throat. Rituals followed to prepare for the burning that would take place atop the Mount of Olives after darkness descended. The small band that carried the carcass there and prepared the pyre, combining crimson dyed wool, hyssop and cedar wood, sprinkled the heifer's blood seven times in the direction of where the First and Second Temples had stood in the space occupied for centuries thereafter by the Islam's Dome of the Rock. Fuel was added for quick immolation, for fear the East Jerusalem fire brigade might extinguish the blaze before the sacrifice was complete.

Etzion ended the meeting with solemn affirmation. "Jerusalem will again be a glorious city on a hill. We shall build the Third Temple. Then the Mashiach will come to us. May HaShem bless our sacred mission."

60

ROME & VATICAN CITY
Friday, May 19

AN UNPRECEDENTED GATHERING converged on Rome for Pope Sixtus VI's installation. President Goudonov was rumored to be meeting with Palestinian, Iranian, and Syrian officials. President Palmer's press secretary uncharacteristically would not release his schedule. The British Prime Minister was spotted having lunch with the German Chancellor, French President and European Union President, where it was thought they were discussing linking the euro and the pound sterling in a basket to moderate wild currency swings.

Alessio and Sixtus met in the early afternoon to prepare for the evening and review news clippings from the Vatican press office. A tabloid featured color photos of Pope Sixtus as a longhaired rakish teenager joking with Paraguayan schoolmates. An inside spread chronicled his Rome ordination as a young man, celebrating mass in Asuncion's cathedral shortly before he traveled to Rome for the conclave that elected him, and donning white vestments just before emerging publicly as pontiff.

One commentator declared that his theology was rigidly conservative, foreshadowing no shift in doctrine. Another told the noble and tragic story of the Jesuits in Paraguay, who tried centuries earlier to create God's kingdom in its jungles and deserts, teaching Guarani children to sing Latin chants and live in harmonious communes until the pope ordered settlements destroyed. The Jesuits disbanded, under pressure from European landowners who preferred natives as slave labor over their talents as choristers or as equal children of God.

This embedded memory would make the rights of indigenous people the center of Sixtus' papacy, predicted the reporter. There was no mention of the Pope's membership in the Book Club, which remained a secret, no suggestion that the new Vicar of Christ had interests beyond conservative doctrine and Paraguay.

The Pope laughed outright at the newspaper's summaries of his life.

"Did they get it wrong, Holy Father?" asked Alessio.

"No, they spared me. They missed the wild years." Alessio thought he looked pained at the memory. In a flash Sixtus' earnest smile resumed. "Father, this evening we begin our mission to Jerusalem."

Alessio leaned forward.

"The Ayatollah and I meet in a few minutes. If he commits, others should follow."

"They will, your Holiness."

"Is the presentation ready?" asked the Pope.

"I will pick it up in a half hour. I worked with the new Director of the Anglican Centre. She is an expert on the Miracle of Fatima. As you instructed, we used an outside technical consultant sworn to secrecy."

"It was good to keep this between us. No one at the Vatican can know yet."

"She will keep it secret."

"I would like to meet her someday. Amazing what you and she are putting together. I had no idea that the End Time is truly upon us."

"I do not think that is what she believes," said Alessio, but the Pope seemed not to hear. Sixtus glowed with excitement. Rather than feeling inspired, Alessio considered Sixtus' plan to show a video and get agreement for building a second Vatican in Jerusalem to be simplistic. And Ruth's concerns that the Pope was captivated by a hundred-year-old message of a Portuguese nun were beginning to make him think.

Alessio took a taxi to the Anglican Centre to pick up the presentation Ruth had finalized. He entered the Centre, where Secretary Ponelli stood like a waiting sentinel.

"Father Alessio," she bowed and led him to Ruth's office, where a screen and projector awaited. Secretary Ponelli withdrew.

"Let's run through it quickly — and here's a set of notes for the Pope."

They viewed the blend of tragedy and fiction, terrible recent events and signs. Alessio had worked tirelessly since Tuesday with Ruth, fueled by espresso and a deadline. He witnessed the workings of her academic mind. A bond grew beyond anything he'd experienced with another except for his loyalty to the deceased pontiff, an affection utterly different from what he felt with Ruth.

"Until we put this all together," said Ruth, "I wasn't sure how far this had gone. Unless we do something to stop it, the world's in deep trouble."

Alessio was near tears of gratitude.

"Ruth, *grazie mille*," he said. "Thank you. Thank you. It is terrible." His eyebrows rose. "Oh! Not the presentation — it is magnificent. The situation. That is what I mean."

"And now you have a mission as do I. We must find a way out of this."

"I know more about what the Pope intends if the guests agree to meet in Jerusalem in two weeks — that will be his request tonight."

"To meet. And then what?"

"At the summit he will call for a new Jerusalem, with a Cathedral on Mount Moriah."

"One roof, three into one," said Ruth.

Alessio glanced at his watch. "I have to get back."

Ruth gave him notes and two thumb drives. "An extra just in case." She reached for his right arm and squeezed it. "Like all visions, don't take the Fatima page literally. It's like poetry."

Without answering, Alessio thanked her again and rushed back to the Vatican.

The papal installation gave President Palmer and Prime Minister Feldman cover to meet in secret.

"Like the old days at Balliol," Palmer said.

But despite their Oxford camaraderie and nearly identical publicly stated views — Israel and America are inseparable / Palestinian dialogue only if the Palestinians concede in advance that Israel must always be a Jewish State — each had limits to what either would do for the other.

Feldman did not share with Palmer his plan to expand Israel's borders until they reached the full extent under King David. Nor did Feldman want — not yet — to reveal his intention to rebuild a Temple between the Dome of the Rock and the Al Aqsa Mosque.

For his part, Palmer did not declare the limit of support for the contentious expansion of Jewish settlements into lands universally viewed outside of Israel as the domain of Arabs, fearing it could start a war if it went too far too fast. Nor did he expose his deep belief that once the Temple was restored and 144,000 Jews accepted Jesus as the Messiah, then Jesus would return in glory. Palmer kept secret, even from his wife, his fervent hope that he would be present for the Second Coming.

Feldman and Palmer each kept a secret they had in common — each expected to have a private dinner with the new pope that evening.

The President began, "Operation Meteor — the mini-drones — well executed."

"We think that set back the Iranian nuclear program briefly," Feldman replied.

"You were going to hit Fordow on Monday. So you'll hold off for now."

Feldman said nothing.

"Give Iran one last chance to surrender. Do you need anything more from us?" asked the President.

"We have it under control. You'll have deniability," Feldman assured him.

"You sound like an actor from a spy movie," joked Palmer. "What do you make of this March?"

"Shin Bet says it's cover for Iran's final prep for a nuclear test. We won't let this charade of a parade into Israel. Bombs beneath the burqas."

"We do what we must," Palmer nodded.

While Palmer and Feldman met, the Grand Ayatollah of Iran, six years earlier a Book Club guest during a European trip, was with Pope Sixtus. They walked through the Sistine Chapel. The Ayatollah tried to admire its majestic early Renaissance depictions of heaven and last judgment but was dismayed by how Michelangelo painted God as an old man with a beard, personification blasphemous in Islam.

Sixtus asked about the burdens of mixed political and religious leadership.

"My friend, I envy you. Your Vatican predecessors once led armies, raised taxes and at the same time led the Church. Today your charge is simpler. In Islam state and religion are Siamese twins."

The Pope leaned forward. "I am thankful there are no papal armies. But tell me, is there a way to channel the torrents of history down a gentler stream?"

The Ayatollah sat silent before replying. "It will get worse. Our intelligence says Israel is about to strike our Fordow facility. It assassinated our scientists. America's new killing machines take war to an unholy new level."

The Pope ran his fingers over the papal rosary. "For this reason God calls us to a summit. Thank you for your support. We can announce it tomorrow if we get agreement tonight."

The Master Docent of the Vatican art collection gently knocked and entered. He led the Supreme Leader to a waiting black Mercedes limousine, leaving the press to conclude that the Ayatollah had enjoyed an immersion in western art.

As the Ayatollah exited the splendor of the Vatican, he thought about the superiority of the mosque, pure, unadorned by artwork depicting humans as holy. Allah at the center, everything. One God, not the Christian three.

The summit might bring peace. The Iranian people had long suffered. But if the Pope had designs on Jerusalem, there would be a problem.

61

VATICAN CITY
Friday, May 19

THE PATRIARCH of the Russian Orthodox Church, the Ashkenazi Chief Rabbi of Israel, the Imam of the Grand Mosque in Mecca, the Archbishop of Canterbury, the Pope of Alexandria and Patriarch of All Africa on the Holy See of Saint Mark the Apostle, and the Grand Ayatollah of Iran arrived at separate Vatican entrances at the common time inscribed on their personalized invitations to dine at an absurdly early dinner time. The Rabbi's invitation assured the meal would be prepared kosher. The Imam and Ayatollah were informed that halal practices would be followed.

Each was ushered to a dining room where a circular table was set for seven, with an eighth chair by the door. Arriving at the dining room simultaneously, recognizing one another from vestments befitting their stature, they were jolted to see that this would be an unprecedented meeting of leaders of the three great religions stemming from Abraham. As the guests made introductions, hesitant and stiff, an inner door opened and the Pope entered, dressed in a simple white cassock, a diminutive mahogany cross hanging from a fiber necklace, no bejeweled headpiece atop his speckled gray- and black-haired head.

"My brothers, thank you for joining me," he began in Italian, each leader tuning an earpiece for simultaneous translation by Vatican interpreters. The Imam sat next to the Rabbi, who was to the left of the Coptic Pope, to the right of whom sat the Archbishop of Canterbury, who was next to Russia's Patriarch, who pulled back the chair for the Grand Ayatollah, who sat next to Sixtus. "My aide Father Alessio is here." Alessio sat near the door. Sixtus took the hand of Mecca's spiritual leader. "Would you bless our meal?"

The Imam obliged with the traditional Muslim grace. "O Allah, bless the food You have provided us and save us from the punishment of hellfire." To everyone's surprise he added, "Compassionate and Merciful, Adonai, Almighty Lord of us all, we thank you for this gathering. Look with favor on Sixtus as he prepares to serve. Strengthen us to submit to your divine will." Each leader added So be it as pronounced in his faith tradition.

The guests waited for the Pope to pronounce something, but he turned to the Grand Ayatollah and said, "It's been far too long" with a slight wink. A waiter served wine or water according to pre-checked preferences and religious custom, along with appropriate appetizers.

The Pope raised his glass. "The best way to call a meeting, I learned in Paraguay, is to invite friends to a meal. I welcome your prayers, as I will pray for you — and for what I ask tonight." He paused, and except for awkward sounds of root vegetables being chewed, the room was silent. The Alexandrian Pope passed the bread.

"Join me for a summit two weeks from today — in Jerusalem," the Pope said, jolting the group. "The Rabbi is prepared to host. He confirmed arrangements with the Israeli Government. We can meet for prayer and discussion ... and for certain decisions."

Caution swept the room at the word "decisions." Archbishop of Canterbury Okello was the first to reply. "Is there required reading?"

The old joke set off a chorus of muffled sounds among those seated, and a light snort escaped the lips of the Coptic Pope.

The Archbishop continued, "What would be our agenda?"

"My friends, we each lead a branch of faith that stems from a common root, beginning with Abraham, Hagar and Sarah. My hope is that we can occasionally meet to discuss where God, Allah, HaShem calls us. Not to debate creed or ritual, but to find a way forward for our people, People of the Book."

The Grand Ayatollah came in like a viola following a cello. "We would search together for peace and justice."

The Russian Patriarch interposed with a skeptical frown, "Decisions, you said?"

The Pope replied, "I feel the weight of enormous responsibility. Perhaps each of you had similar unease when assuming your position. As I prayed about what I can do with the time I have in this role, the image that came to mind was a New Jerusalem."

"Jerusalem is a nest of conflict," the Imam of the Grand Mosque of Mecca countered, lips drawn tight.

"Our common God does not want our people to continue killing one another," the Pope gently stated more as prayer than plea. The waiter served a pasta course from a flowered Portuguese ceramic bowl.

Sensing a need for the request to simmer, the Pope turned to Archbishop Okello. "Archbishop, tell us what life is like as leader of the Anglican Communion."

Archbishop Okello sipped his wine and looked around the table. "Becoming Archbishop drew me closer to God, but not because I had advanced a rung on some spiritual ladder. The responsibility turns me to God, more so even than as a priest in war-torn Africa."

The Coptic Pope remarked, "The greatest surprise is the bureaucracy, the trivial details! If I had known about that, I would have said no." The entire group laughed knowingly.

Sensing this was the moment to learn more about why they were there, Okello carefully posed his question. "Tell us more about your vision of a New Jerusalem."

"My predecessor preached the necessity of avoiding World War III. He interpreted the world's conflicts as the same 'birth pangs' that Jesus spoke about in the Gospel of Mark," Sixtus began.

"But in the Gospel of Matthew Jesus said, 'No one knows when that day or hour will come,'" Okello reminded.

"My concern is not a date. It's what we do about it."

Alessio noticed Sixtus make no mention of the blue note or Fatima.

The Ayatollah agreed. "I am appalled by blood spilled in the name of Allah, the God we all serve. We must take action."

"Your predecessor opened communication between us. Are you following his path?" the Patriarch asked.

Sixtus nodded. "We are on it together." Sixtus arose and looked around the table. "Will you join me for a summit in Jerusalem? If we attend, government leaders will be led to join." He stretched out his hands.

Archbishop Okello stood. "I will attend."

The Ayatollah rose from his chair, steadying his hands on the table. "My title, Ayatollah, means 'sign of Allah.' I will come as a sign to believers."

Rising, the Ashkenazi Chief Rabbi of Israel explained that Sixtus had asked in advance whether he would be a willing host. "We will receive you all warmly."

"At worst we try and fail. Talking is better than not," said Okello.

One by one the faith leaders stood and concurred, none wanting to remain seated once it was clear that Islam, Judaism and Christianity would be present.

As guests were escorted to separate exits, Alessio wondered what the prelates were thinking — what a summit would mean, whether it was a great mistake, and how they could explain this back home.

62

VATICAN CITY
Friday, May 19

SIXTUS CHANGED into more elaborate vestments for his meeting with government leaders. "Father, half the job is done. Now the difficult part — the politicians."

"You will succeed, Holy Father," Alessio assured him reflexively, though Alessio wondered why the faith leaders had agreed to a gathering that lacked a clear agenda. The heads of state would be more demanding.

They reviewed the presentation he developed with Ruth, a sequence of multiple recent apocalyptic signs and violent events entitled "Warnings." It seemed to Alessio that it had been an academic exercise for Ruth, as she pulled together descriptions of each faith's eschatology and the symbols from each faith's perspective. Though she approached it skeptically, the more Alessio learned, the more believable it was that the Final Day could be drawing near. The Pope believed so. Why shouldn't he. His role was not to doubt, and yet....

"These omens prove what I must do. I must unite the flock before the End Time, as Fatima instructs," said Sixtus. The Pope reached for Alessio's right arm. "Think what we will witness — reuniting the three great branches of Christianity under our roof, making straight the path for the return of our Savior to reign over a New Jerusalem."

The Pope gazed upward to the frescoed ceiling, and Alessio imagined his visualizing the scene that another Michelangelo could paint after this all came to be.

Only weeks before when the prior pontiff was alive, Alessio would have joined in the moment, unquestioning. But now he paused. Granted, Ruth was an outsider and could not be expected to perceive the Roman Catholic Church as the one true Church, but conversations with her caused him to question why the Holy Father was fixated on an improbable vision.

As Alessio tried to gather his thoughts, the Pope glanced at the clock. "Time for round 2. Pray God's will be done." The Pope strode confidently toward his second dinner of the night.

Alessio prayed that God's will be done. He added that only God's will be done.

63

VATICAN CITY
Friday, May 19

ARMORED LIMOUSINES CARRYING HEADS OF STATE pulled up to designated Vatican gates at 7:45. This would be dinner with the Pope without the advance benefit of agenda, attendee list or seating chart, acceptance of a papal invitation unseemly to negotiate.

President Goudonov arrived first and was escorted through the private visitors' gallery where Etruscan, Roman and Greek statuary stood guard over an art collection rivaling any in the world.

Prime Minister Feldman's motorcade arrived at a nearby cul-de-sac and he was ushered through a door for dignitaries wishing to avoid the paparazzi.

The third to arrive was the newly elected head of the Palestinian Authority, the aging and inscrutable Abu Arafat, distant cousin of the late Yasser, who emerged from obscurity when neither Hamas nor Mahmoud Abbas could unify the two split pieces of what one day might become a Palestinian state.

The Egyptian President, who ran as a moderate Islamist in the recent election and once in office proved to be a cautious centrist, arrived at 7:57. At the same time came Angela Schmidt, the first European President elected after the Syrian refugee crisis and a severe recession resulted in an unexpected push towards further European unification, creating the position of an EU President empowered to speak for Europe in foreign affairs.

The last to arrive was President Palmer at the grand public entrance. Understanding the central role of publicity in all he did, Palmer greeted the phalanx of photographers with his patented 2-thumbs-up-and-grin, wearing a bright blue tie that matched his eyes.

"No time for questions. Here for a private audience with His Holiness," he said as two Swiss guards escorted him inside.

The six heads of state were led through hallways laden with priceless artwork to a dining room deep within. Unlike the vast public galleries, the secluded room was spartan, only a single bronze crucifix on the walls. In the center was a plain round table with eight chairs.

The five Presidents and one Prime Minister were rattled to see their dining companions and eight seats, but their puzzlement turned to shock when a door opened and Sixtus strode in with a hearty smile and introduced the others to the Grand Ayatollah, whom none of the guests had met. They settled into seats marked with place cards, each uneasy about the proximity of others, a mix that could not have happened in any other circumstance without excruciating negotiation over preconditions, agenda and protocol.

A waiter brought beverages. The Egyptian President, Palestinian Authority President Arafat and Iranian Supreme Leader received Italy's premier bottled water. President Palmer was served mango juice with a touch of kale. President Schmidt was presented a glass of Alsatian Riesling. President Goudonov received vodka with lime from a frozen tumbler. Prime Minister Feldman got a kosher deep red wine. The Pope's glass held an Orvieto.

"Thank you for joining me. You do me great honor. Tonight is for dinner and conversation. May we keep our discussion strictly among us?"

The guests nodded or uttered monosyllabic assent.

Without asking for more, the Pope continued. "If anyone is uncomfortable, I will arrange for you to have a private tour of the art galleries and a private meal."

He paused five seconds, but none risked a show of weakness.

"I offer a toast to peace and to your good health." The eight raised their glasses. "And *buon pranzo*, enjoy your meal."

As the waiter distributed individually crafted salads and appetizers, Sixtus got straight to his point.

"Our troubles are not anyone's wish," he began, forsaking his salad. "The faiths of our common ancestors have driven us apart. They should bring us together. I believe that if we talk together as People of the Book, we can turn the world from its current path of destruction.

"My request is that you join me in Jerusalem in two weeks for a meeting." That seemed to suspend the group's forks in mid-air. "Joining us will be religious leaders from Russia, Egypt, Saudi Arabia, the United Kingdom, Israel and Iran. Together we can seek peace."

EU President Schmidt broke an extended silence that followed. "This is most unusual, your Holiness. We were not prepared for such a dramatic and may I say bold request. Perhaps by dessert I will digest this first course."

The leaders shifted in their seats, nervously contemplating next moves. President Palmer tugged at his shirt collar. President Goudonov stared at the Pope.

As the next course was served, Alessio entered the room. He hit a button to lower a screen and turned on the computer.

"There are signs," said the Pope. The title slide bore the word **Warnings** in red letters against a black background. "Let us consider recent events."

Scenes flashed of trumpeters sounding the surprise postlude to his predecessor's funeral.

"These are signs that we face great danger," said Sixtus. "In 1973, as you know, the world came close to nuclear war in the Middle East, averted through what some call fortuna. Today our collective ability to destroy the earth is much greater." Scenes of Hiroshima and Dresden in flames flared. Text contrasted the massive impact of current nuclear weapons to the relatively miniscule scale of bombs that ended World War II.

Images switched to the desert. "These are marble gates recently built." Arches erected by the NJA appeared, with up-close shots of the lintel inscriptions. "They are located in precise distances from Jerusalem. If a picture were taken from outer space, you would see this pattern."

A Google photo of the region appeared, zeroing in on each location, then backing out to where each was marked with a Red X.

"If you draw a line, a perfect square appears with Jerusalem at its center. In the final book of the Christian Bible, these gates are the entrance to a New Jerusalem at the end of time."

The leaders stared.

"You see now another apocalyptic sign, this from Shi'a thinking," the Pope continued. "The March of the Innocents began in western Iran and became an enormous pilgrimage of women with Jerusalem its declared destination."

Photos of the March flowed with A'ishah and Iran's leading man at the front and a throng of women and children trailing behind.

"Its sponsor is AM, which stands for Army of the Mahdi. As we know from the Damascus events where the March first traveled, AM argues that the end of this world is near, when an imam will emerge from centuries of sleep to join Isa, Arabic for Jesus, to defeat evil and greet the Day of Judgment." The Grand Ayatollah nodded his head.

As images changed to photographs of the winning design in 4K's contest, Sixtus explained, "This design by a group known as 4K is for a third Jewish Temple on Mount Moriah, *Har haBáyith, Haram Ash-Sharif*," using the English, Hebrew and Arabic names for Jerusalem's holiest center. "You can see that this design cannot fit into open space there." An overlay of the design showed how it encroached upon the Dome of the Rock. The Palestinian and Egyptian leaders shook their heads in anger.

The Pope led the group through other signs, including the return of Jews to Israel, Syria's decimation as an Islamic signal of The Hour approaching, other developments foretelling an approaching End Time in Jewish, Christian and Muslim thought.

"You see here events not well reported the night of my predecessor's burial." Photographs of red ooze circulating within Rome's fountains alternated with blood red fireworks in the Roman sky. "This follows wording from the Book of Revelation."

The screen changed to news reports of golden-bound parchment two mayors received weeks before.

"These are two scrolls delivered to mayors of great cities, using words directly out of the beginning of the Revelation of John, warning that the final revelation is at hand. Is there any question that well-funded Jewish, Christian and Islamic forces are gathering for the end of the world and acting to hasten it?

"And you may be informed that when a nuclear device appeared at the Great Mosque of Damascus, the skies blackened, a final Islamic sign that the End of Time approaches."

President Goudonov scowled and folded his arms on his barrel chest. President Palmer maintained an enigmatic, entranced smile. President Schmidt tilted her head to the left and stared at the Pope as a psychiatrist might when a patient calmly explains that he levitated the Eiffel Tower.

The waiter entered to offer seconds to each guest, but all declined. Sixtus waited until the server departed.

"There is urgent work to be done by us all and little time. I hope this convinces you to accept my request to meet again in two weeks — in Jerusalem."

"You will have my answer tomorrow, your Holiness," stated President Palmer.

"I accept," said President Goudonov defiantly, upstaging Palmer.

The Grand Ayatollah raised his head. "I shall join you."

Prime Minister Feldman, seeing opportunity for political gain, responded warmly. "You are welcome to my capital. I guarantee your security."

"I will attend," said Egypt's President.

EU President Schmidt said, "I will make arrangements. Two weeks from today."

"I will be there," said Palestinian Authority President Arafat.

That left President Palmer to his calculations. Word could spread that the USA was derailing a peace process towards a goal that eluded presidents since Israel's creation. Russia or Europe might upstage the most exceptional country on the planet. And the Pope's apocalyptic theme embodied his own deepest beliefs. Palmer raised his glass, inviting others to do the same.

"Then it's unanimous. I toast the bold vision of Pope Sixtus VI. To Jerusalem."

64

OUTSKIRTS OF ROME
Saturday, May 20

NOAH AND RUTH met for an early breakfast at a café near the eastern corner of St. Peter's Square. For those without privileged access to prime seating, screens and loudspeakers were installed throughout central Rome for multitudes to witness the historic ritual of a pope's installation.

Noah arrived ten minutes early to be certain he would greet her and not the other way around. In high school he was habitually late, and she perfected a scowl for his tardiness that would have vaporized any fly that whizzed by. He rushed to meet her at the door, almost knocking over the table vase with its single salmon rose.

She held out her right hand with a gold-leaf ticket for a seat at the installation. "I was not expecting this," he said.

"Friends in high places," she answered in a mock-dramatic whisper.

They chatted as old friends, as they once had on a Zoar porch swing. They ordered cornettos and coffee. Noah asked, "You probably know more about the New Jerusalem Alliance than anyone outside the leadership. Do you trust what we're doing?"

At the idea of encouraging more NJA action Ruth almost choked on her coffee before deciding on a compliment. "I read the winning essay about a New Jerusalem. Heartfelt."

Noah nodded, holding a smile.

"I don't want to compromise you by getting into too much detail. We'll do what it takes to get people to see what's coming — and to prepare before it's too late."

"No more trumpets! This is a day for celebration. You're not going to muck this up, are you?"

"Our focus isn't Rome," he replied. He looked down at his plate that had a few crumbs left and poked at them with a finger. Looking up at her, he added, "Our sights are on the Holy Land."

"You'll blow into a *shofar* instead of a trumpet?"

"It's no laughing matter. I'm sure you've followed the Temple contest of the group known as 4K. It has aims compatible with ours — restoring Israel and rebuilding the Temple."

"I've been reading about the mysterious 4K. But not even this militant Prime Minister of Israel would dare build a Third Temple. It would be an unthinkable provocation to Muslims."

"Recent polls show a clear majority of Israelis — and this is for the first time ever — support rebuilding a temple. Whether they know it or not, once that project is finished, Jews will convert and then ... the Second Coming...."

Aghast, she interrupted. "We live in this world, not in a biblical fairy tale."

"You're the one not facing reality. Read Letter to the Ephesians, chapter 6, the struggle against powers, principalities, the forces of darkness. Your academic lens is blinding you to what's happening."

Ruth wondered what it would be like to be so convinced of the inerrancy of one's simplistic interpretation of a religious text. *Powers and principalities? Not my area.*

He leaned forward in his chair. The worry line between his eyebrows disappeared. He smiled and gently took her right hand in his, which she quickly withdrew.

"Don't make me sorry I gave you a gold ticket."

Noah paid the tab through the waiter's hand-held credit card device and included an unusually large 10 Euro tip to which the waiter first objected and then said, "Mille grazie."

He pulled out her chair as she stood up and said, "You'll like the horses."

"Horses?" she flinched.

65

VATICAN CITY
Saturday, May 20

THE VATICAN BUREAUCRACY kept installation details a state secret, building anticipation. The ceremony was a coronation until the 20th century, when Paul VI abolished the custom of having a crown placed on his head, dispensing with the image of popes as earthly kings. Since then, a simple pallium is placed on the new pope's shoulders. Paul VI ordered the traditional tiara sold with proceeds given to charity, but it found its way to a shrine in Washington, D.C. as a tourist attraction.

Rumors circulated that a starkly simple mass would be celebrated, with a few details altered to fit the Paraguayan pontiff's folk style. The kneeling of all cardinals to pledge allegiance to the new pope was rumored to resume, though Benedict XVI altered that to twelve clerical and lay leaders kneeling before him as surrogates for the entire Church.

Seated invitees assembled by 8:45, as a prelude of string and pan pipe music wafted a blend that a music critic sneeringly called "New Age plus Baroque — voilà BrokeAge." There was no traditional chanting by young boys, surrogates for eunuchs of ages past, but a mesh of tones that seemed to merge spa music with Bach, with an understated drumbeat at the pace of a human pulse.

"Spach!" the critic jeered. Projected images were close-ups of faces — all kinds of people — smiling, in despair, looking blank, cheering, crying, celebrating — displaying emotions of humankind in its ineffable diversity.

Five minutes before the ceremony was to start, the clop of hooves was heard. Horses appeared at the edges of St. Peter's Square. They were immaculately groomed and moved with precision. Crowds along roadways parted to make way for four identical groups of riders and mounts. They pointed directly towards the Egyptian obelisk brought to Rome by Emperor Caligula in 37 C.E. and moved by Pope Sixtus V in 1586 to the center of the oval that is St. Peter's Square.

Assuming it was part of the script, seated dignitaries craned their necks to enjoy the equestrian display. The first horses to the left were a brilliant white, their riders wearing crowns and holding regal bows, ready to ride into battle as medieval archers to slay a villainous foe. The second set were as red as horses can be, with riders holding large swords in their sheaths. The horses of the third column were stark black, their mounts balancing scales of justice. The horses to the right were deathly pale. Their riders wore beige scarves that masked their faces, each clutching a tall scythe with a blade pointing backwards. All twelve riders sat still as statues.

Bells tolled 9:00. Screens broadcast a group inside the Basilica gathered around the tomb of St. Peter. The camera operator sought the pontiff after scanning red-hatted cardinals dressed in glowing, brocaded vestments. The Pope came into focus. He wore a friar's tunic, as though St. Francis had returned to Rome. The crowd murmured at his plain dress.

After the group inside completed their bows at St. Peter's tomb, the Pope led the group with a shepherd's crook, made of simple wood without jewels or other adornment, down the majestic central aisle of St. Peter's Basilica and out through the enormous front doors. The crowd rose. Cardinals interspersed with clerics from other faith traditions moved into the open air. There were gasps when the large screens posed names and titles of rabbis, the Russian Patriarch, the Archbishop of Canterbury, the Coptic pope, imams, and towards the end of the procession, the Grand Ayatollah of Iran.

The leaders of faith settled behind the Pope facing the crowd. As the liturgy unfolded, a papal ring was presented, with screens showing a silver band on Sixtus' finger. The ceremony's centerpiece was the placement of the cloak-like pallium by a woman who spoke in Guarani, the native tongue of Paraguay. She placed a simple scarf length of lamb's wool on the Pope's shoulders, first kissing and stroking it, saying from a lamb it is given and to the Lamb it will return, symbolizing the pontiff's role as a good shepherd who carries the lost lamb back to the flock. Red crosses sewn into it symbolized bloodstains.

It was expected that the cardinals or a representative group would approach and kneel to the pope. Instead, the pontiff prostrated himself to the crowd. He did this in each direction of east, north, west and south before rising and giving his first homily as Pope.

After prolonged applause he thanked God, asked prayers for the Church, and explained that the silver ring was in homage to the principal source of wealth that South America sent to Europe — silver. Sixtus spoke of the need for the faithful to adhere to what is fixed in rock, a reference that had conservative cardinals nodding their heads. He asked for "the one true church to unite us."

He directly faced the world leaders seated in the front row.

"Today leaders have it in their power to destroy the Earth — just as they have the strength to save it. The signs of our times cannot be mistaken. They are a revelation."

He turned to the prominent leaders of other faiths sitting to his right and left and pointed with outstretched right hand, palm up, to the leaders of Russia, the United States, Europe, Palestine, Israel, Egypt, and Iran.

"Governments and faiths present here will meet in Jerusalem in two weeks. We will discuss how problems that seem insoluble are by God's grace opportunities. For God, Allah, HaShem granted us freedom to make a choice."

This astonishing call became the headlines — announcement of a summit of persons who never before had been willing to meet together, much less agree on the future of the region where Judaism, Christianity and Islam were born. Sixtus ended the service with a simple call for peace and justice, "because without each, there is neither."

The Pope re-entered the Basilica. Special guests were safely escorted into the Vatican. With presidents and prime ministers safely out of public range, the seated crowd was about to be ushered out row by row by Swiss Guards. Suddenly an image of wreckage flashed on the screens seeming to be from a distant place, with a dust cloud obscuring the scene.

The announcer intoned, "Minutes ago, a series of explosions erupted in Jerusalem in the area known as the Temple Mount. The Dome of the Rock was destroyed."

The crowd sat stunned, most collapsing into their chairs rather than exiting. Sitting between the two men, Ruth turned to Noah and demanded if he knew about this. Shaken, he shook his head in denial.

As images from Jerusalem filled the screens, the twelve horses of the Apocalypse and their riders began to move. One row of four headed clockwise from the base of St. Peter's Square to the steps of the Basilica, another counterclockwise, the third in a direct movement towards the obelisk and then around it. In slow precision, riders and horses moved toward the stage. With the news flash, while the crowd continued its dull roar of astonishment, an apocalyptic phalanx halted at the front of the stage. Screen images shifted to them, panning across the group, then shifted back to scenes of destruction in Jerusalem. Swiss guards edged toward the riders and horses without knowing what to do.

Ruth turned to Noah with an icy stare. "I don't like the horses at all."

66

JERUSALEM
Saturday, May 20

"THE DOME IS RUBBLE," Haim Etzion exulted as he opened the meeting of the 4K leadership. "Two minor details. There was a sleeper in the Mosque who might be dead. Stupid. And the Mosque was damaged but not beyond repair."

"Are we cursed if someone was killed?" asked one of the Inner Circle, raising the specter of the rabbi's injunction that no blood contaminate the holy site.

"HaShem demands only our faithful effort. We gave it," Etzion deflected.

"How soon before permits can be filed for the new Temple?" asked Jeffrey Magnitsky, designer of the Third Temple competition.

Knesset member Adlay Epstein fielded that one. "We'll seek a permit without delay. The temptation is to wait for dust to settle. But Torah instructs that we strike when the enemy is in retreat. We act now, before vacillators take control."

"Do you have the votes?" inquired Mort Leibowitz, the journalism executive. His reporter discipline made him the most objective of the 4K leadership.

"There will be no vote," said Etzion, addressing skeptical expressions on faces of the Inner Circle. "Construction approval is granted by the City's Building Department. So long as our plans conform to technical requirements, they can be approved. It would take a Knesset vote to revoke an issued permit, and the Knesset won't stop a new Temple."

"A bureaucrat decides?" asked an incredulous Inner Circle member.

"Yes, and he's our bureaucrat. A classmate of Jeffrey's," said Etzion.

Sitting with the grin of a Cheshire cat, Magnitsky said, "It's been arranged."

With that settled, Etzion announced, "I talked with Noah Stoll, leader of the wealthy American group that sponsored that essay contest about a New Jerusalem. He guaranteed the balance needed to build the Third Temple. In exchange, we agreed to reopen the Gate of Mercy, what Christians call the Golden Gate."

"Why do Christians care about the Golden Gate being opened after Muslims closed it for twelve centuries?" asked a member.

"For Christians this is where Jesus entered on their Palm Sunday. Their Bible says it's where he will return. Such foolishness, thinking a dead man is coming back."

"But Ezekiel 44 tells us the gate must stay closed," said Magnitsky.

Etzion responded, "For us the Gate is where the Shekinah once entered, where the prince alone could eat in the divine presence. We'll close it again when the Temple is built."

Before adjourning, the Inner Circle recited from Pentateuch stories. "To your descendants I give this land, from the river of Egypt to the great river, the river Euphrates," a member read from Genesis.

Etzion reminded them that according to the Book of Daniel the armies of evil would surrender after an epic battle.

"But at that time your people shall be delivered, everyone whose name shall be found written in the book. And many of those who sleep in the dust of the earth shall awake, some to everlasting life, and some to shame and everlasting contempt. And those who are wise shall shine like the brightness of the firmament; and those who turn many to righteousness, like the stars forever and ever."

Zion was on the move.

67

ROME
Saturday-Sunday, May 20-21

RUTH RUSHED to meet the Archbishop of Canterbury at his hotel suite. The shock of the Dome of the Rock's destruction meant the Summit would be delayed and her trip to Jerusalem as well. She was glad. She was an academic, not a special forces soldier. It wasn't raw fear that fed her caution — more the tug of being grounded in familiar territory. Rome had become that.

The Archbishop shattered her assumption after steering her to a quiet alcove off the hotel's lobby.

"Your scouting mission's even more important now," he told her before asking what she would like to drink. "The Summit is on." Minutes later a waiter delivered a skim latte for Ruth and South African rooibos tea for the Archbishop.

They discussed her visit to the Holy Land set for the next day, early morning departure on an El Al flight to Jerusalem. But Secretary Lucrezia Ponelli phoned Ruth from the Anglican Centre to report that commercial flights to Israel were suspended. She was working on an alternative. As if in answer to the Archbishop's prayer, five minutes later Alessio called to offer Ruth a seat on the Vatican's Slipstream jet.

Ruth felt like the time her parents took her to Cedar Point for her tenth birthday, when she thought she'd be thrown into Lake Erie riding the world's first hypercoaster. The Magnum XL-200 that plunged 200 feet at 70 miles an hour left her vowing never to risk death again. Now she neared a turnstile to Jerusalem with no turning back. She pictured being caught in a crossfire of enraged Palestinians and Israeli soldiers.

The Archbishop calmly described how he wanted her to "take the pulse. And find out from your traveling companion what this Pope is up to. There's little transparency from the Vatican." He leaned closer and whispered, "And Ruth, I need your read of recent signs. The Pope gave us a lecture about them at Friday's dinner. It seems certain fanatical groups of Jews, Muslims and Christians are conspiring to bring on the end of the world."

Ruth was silent about what she knew from Alessio and Noah in confidence but led the Archbishop through the efforts of groups from all three faiths that actively believed the End Time approaches and could use their help.

"Some feel the end of the world isn't a bad thing, that it represents a culmination of their faith."

Okello sighed. "Let's hope the government leaders are not among those who feel this way. And Sixtus?"

"I'll see what I can learn."

She returned to her apartment and took Gabriel for a long walk. She gave him an extra treat and began packing lightly for the trip. She put one clerical outfit and summer-weight tourist clothes into her luggage.

The next morning Secretary Ponelli met Ruth at her apartment to take charge of Gabriel. "He will be my companion," the Secretary assured her, leaning over to scratch his ears. "Our office *cucciolo*."

Ruth ruffled Gabriel's back and gave Secretary Ponelli a bag of his favorite food and the squeaky frog toy, the object of his favorite toss and return game.

"I'll be back Thursday night," she assured him, and herself.

Gabriel happily trotted off with Secretary Ponelli, leaving Ruth to complete packing for afternoon pick-up by a Vatican car. She heard a baby's cry from the sidewalk. The image of an hourglass with its sand running out rose to mind. She felt a vibration on her cell phone with a text message from Noah.

"Arranged meet for U w 4K's Etzion. Send me # — he'll call U Mon nt. N"

Ruth emailed Secretary Ponelli for the phone number at St. George's College, where she would stay.

Ruth used the remaining time to browse global news sites that gave her daily exposure to diverse views of what was unfolding. Photos of the Dome of the Rock's smoldering rubble dominated, bumping the Pope's investiture to second placement. Muslim media were in an uproar, reporting furious crowds in East Jerusalem stalking the streets and the heavy presence of machine gun toting security forces forming a cordon around Jerusalem's Old City to prevent a mob from storming the Mount. "Zionist sacrilege" was a Farsi headline of what happened.

Iraqi media made Iranian rage seem tame. The Shi'a-dominated Council of Representatives voted without a single Sunni or Kurdish dissent to condemn the "Zionists' cultural and historic atrocity." It pledged "holy jihad" to defend the place where the Prophet arrived on his Night Journey to converse with Abraham, Jesus and other prophets in heaven. It summoned all Muslims to avenge the destruction of Islam's oldest sacral structure.

Ruth turned to a scan of Evangelical Christian publications. Reminding readers that the Dome of the Rock had stood where the Bible mandates the Temple to be rebuilt, the Bible Institute issued an overnight e-pamphlet proclaiming "The King is Coming," as its best-selling book by Erwin Lutzer promised.

"While regrettable as an historic loss, the destruction of the Dome of the Rock clears the way for a Holy Temple to replace it. Christians rejoice! For it hastens the return of Jesus Christ!" the pamphlet stated, providing the domain name of a website soliciting donations to rebuild the Temple. *Watchtower*, the publication of Jehovah's Witnesses that foretells the world's end, experienced a swell of downloads. "The End Time nears — click here," trumpeted its home page.

The Arab League issued a condemnation drafted by the Hashemite Kingdom of Jordan, which controlled Jerusalem from 1948 until 1967 when Israel captured it in the Six-Day War. During Israeli occupation, King Hussein personally donated $8 million from the sale of one of his London homes to gild the Dome's surface and reinforce it to withstand earthquakes. The release condemned to eternal hell the responsible villains and demanded that Israel pay the full cost of rebuilding it. In obvious reference to the March, the release demanded that all pilgrims be welcomed to Jerusalem unconditionally.

No organization claimed credit. *The Jerusalem Post* printed Prime Minister Feldman's statement, "Israel had no role in this. We have launched an investigation into what occurred, including the likelihood that gas lines ruptured."

Explaining that assigned personnel were absent from the site because of underground work to repair the water system according to an anonymous source, the *Jerusalem Post* reported no casualties. Al Jazeera reported one person taken to a hospital, condition unknown.

The *International New York Times* gave front page coverage to a map of the Middle East. Soldiers were crossing borders to join their Islamic brothers, forming a growing pan-Muslim force of military personnel and equipment along Israel's northern and eastern borders.

She closed her computer and thought about the Fatima page, based on Alessio's filtered hints. *The father — obviously the Pope. With his vision of uniting Christianity, he reads it as gathering Protestants and Orthodox in Jerusalem. Gathering the faithful under one roof. Maybe even Jews and Muslims too. A cathedral on Mount Moriah. That will cause an uproar. Sheep and goats — the chosen and the damned at the last judgment. Like Noah, does Sixtus hope to advance the End Time? False manual — that could be the Qur'an, what else? The Portuguese wording could be critical here. 144 centuries. That's probably a mistake — it must mean 144 thousands — the Portuguese word for thousand is close to that for centuries. Second from the south — an obvious reference to Sixtus, the second pontiff from the southern hemisphere. Skies of Babylon turning black — a reference to the recent smoke over Damascus?*

Ruth closed her suitcase and sat for a moment on her bed, absorbing silence without Gabriel bouncing around. Her mission — to report whether the world was about to end? To help her boss prepare for a Summit called by a Pope inspired by a secret page written a century earlier by a Portuguese peasant girl? Even more bizarre, she would be with a priest from a church that did not ordain women. For a scholar and a female priest, what could be stranger?

68

JERUSALEM & WASHINGTON, D.C.
Sunday, May 21

LEAVING ITALIAN AIRSPACE early Sunday morning, President Palmer phoned Prime Minister Feldman from Air Force One. Using a hyper-secure frequency reserved for Israel, he demanded to know what Israel knew about the Dome's collapse.

Feldman responded wearily. "We have the top intel in the world, but it's like a ghost attacked the Dome."

"What about the group called 4K? A contest it ran?"

"4K's a bunch of harmless zealots. Their web contest had the new Temple squeezed between the Dome and the Mosque."

"You'd better find the culprits soon. Your neighbors are in an uproar, and you're the target now. Tell me — are you planning to rebuild a Temple there?"

"You know that's been a dream of mine," said Feldman. "Building it would be a sign of strength. The Mosque can be repaired to show balance. You're with me on this, right?"

Palmer hesitated, then plunged ahead, "I keep my word, Aaron, but I'm getting calls, worried where this is headed, demanding we not get involved in another foreign disaster."

"Remind them of the Holocaust and how it could happen again. Preach the Bible's vision of Jerusalem with a Temple restored — what they learned in Sunday school. And the old reliable 'We must stand with Israel against terror'."

"Do we postpone the Summit?" Palmer shifted the subject.

"Not my call. Most likely the Pope will go ahead with it. We'll keep you safe."

Palmer emitted a guffaw. "Paraguay. Poorest country in South America. Who would guess a pope would come from that backwater? I'll wager Mossad didn't win the bet on that election."

"We play the cards we're dealt, Ike. We can play the Summit to our advantage. After a photo op, we can restore Israel's rightful borders and achieve real peace for a change."

"Or push everybody over the edge. Why don't you delay the Temple, let it settle down?"

"Ike, if Abraham and Sarah had waited another year, maybe not even God could have given them a son," said Feldman. "I'll see you in Jerusalem a week from Thursday."

69

MOSCOW & TEHRAN
Sunday, May 21

PRESIDENT GOUDONOV RETURNED from Rome to a sweltering Moscow. From his Kremlin window he could see babushkas and old men sunbathing along river embankments in their underwear, driven by a primordial calling to generate Vitamin D after a dreary winter. He turned to face the glum faces of his military staff as they assembled in ribbon and medal laden uniforms. They looked like vodka bingers on a hangover. Knowing they chafed at his spending time with a pope in Jerusalem, Goudonov took charge with an icy stare.

"Our interests lie with our OPEC allies. By going to Jerusalem we honor our commitments and confront the American-EU-Israel axis."

His tone softened. "Maybe Marx was right. Religion is a drug. All this fighting over a strip of dusty land, along with some battling holy texts that claim Jerusalem belongs to one tribe or another — a waste."

A secure-line call came in for Goudonov.

"President Al-Rabani, how nice of you to phone. I was about to call."

The subordinates could not hear the other side of the conversation.

"No agenda, none I have seen."

After a few seconds Goudonov continued, "You know our pledge. If Iran is attacked, that is the same as an attack on Russia herself. Our backing includes everything at our disposal. ... Yes, including our nuclear arsenal. If Israel is so stupid as to bomb Tehran, retaliation would be immediate." He paused. "Measured but devastating."

A long minute on Iranian President al-Rabani's end ensued. The call ended with Goudonov's blanching visibly. Goudonov raised his shoulders, exhaled and said, "My word is Russia's bond."

Goudonov turned to his aides.

"Allies. So like chameleons." He paused and folded his hands. "Reconfigure our nuclear coordinates — code 1989," referring to how targets were programmed in the final days of the Soviet Union. He turned to his press attaché. "Release that for the Americans and Europeans so it can't be traced to us. They'll think the Cold War's back on the stove. Like Cuba missile time. And they'll be right. Russia is back."

70

WEST BANK &
PALESTINIAN TERRITORIES
Sunday, May 21

NAVID KOSARI KNELT in his hot, dusty tent, camped with the March of the Innocents in the center of the West Bank. In an area administered by Jordan until 1967 and after that by a tangled web of control between Israel and the Palestinian National Authority, residents were electrified by the March, dubbed *Tour d'Islam* by the French newspaper Le Monde. Through donations of food, white clothing, water, camels, money and flowers, Palestinians gave the marchers heartfelt support as they trudged northward toward the boundary dividing the West Bank from the rest of Israel. Jewish settlers worried that the fencing and sporadic wall would not deter the marchers and feared that overstretched Israeli forces wouldn't defend them.

On the phone, Kosari's agent fumed that his client was passing up paid opportunities, which meant no commissions.

"What you're doing is not a movie!" The agent fumed.

Kosari quietly thanked him.

"I am sure, my friend, you are only thinking of me. But we are on a divine path. Allah will script the ending. And may I say, I'm getting more coverage now than you were ever able to generate."

Chastened, the agent changed tactics. "Are you really going to Jerusalem? You'll never make it. Seriously, Navid, I worry for you."

"Thank you, my champion," replied Kosari. "Allah will guide us around the barriers, and the Israelis are not crazy to attack us."

Media estimates ranged as high as a half million walking or riding along the Israeli border. An American journalist compared it to Martin Luther King's march on Washington, adding that to match its journey, King would have had to walk from Alabama to Washington.

A'ishah called from behind the carpet that served as entrance to his tent and asked permission to enter.

Kosari pulled back the rug, ushered her inside and offered tea. The attendant rushed to chaperone and brought mint tea in a solar-powered samovar, a gift from a former Mosfilm director who distributed subtitled Iranian productions in southern Russia and central Asia.

"Navid, I wonder if we made a mistake to reject the invitation to Jerusalem. If we make an arc around this barrier, what do we do when we get to the Dead Sea?"

"We can float in saltwater," Kosari joked. "My sister, we did as you instructed."

"Will Israel welcome us with open arms, or just arms?" A'ishah's practical concerns revealed her as less ethereal than the campaign image of a beautiful girl astride a horse.

"They won't shoot us," he declared confidently. "It would be a disaster for Israel — a massacre broadcast live. Unthinkable!"

While A'ishah and Kosari talked, a team arrived unannounced and sought the March captain. They were from Ramallah, they told her, and brought a hundred volunteers experienced in crowd control with local knowledge of the terrain. They would disperse through the March to provide support. Wary at first, uncertain of the group's background, the captain was impressed when presented with a letter of introduction from Vali Qalil. Without further hesitation or inquiry, the captain welcomed them to the pilgrimage.

71

JERUSALEM
Monday, May 22

AFTER A SUNDAY EVENING FLIGHT to Jerusalem on the Vatican jet with Alessio, Ruth was served pomegranate juice, a raisin scone, and coffee with skim milk Monday morning at St. George, the primary Jerusalem presence of the Church of England. Unlike the jolt she'd come to love from Italian espresso, the British teacup offered coffee-laced hot water.

Located a brief stroll from the Ottoman-era wall that encloses the Old City, across the street from the understated and luxurious American Colony Hotel, St. George stamped a distinctly English mark on its neighborhood. Its square dark brown bell tower and Oxford-like walls declared that England is here to stay in the holy city. Ruth felt comfort from its ambience, so similar to the interiors of Anglican churches throughout the world, just as the Book of Common Prayer provides global familiarity for Anglicans.

The receptionist explained the night before that the Dome of the Rock catastrophe caused cancellations, leaving Ruth as the only overnight guest except for a few visiting seminary students and a retired deacon on a month's silent retreat. Ruth was the sole early diner. She gazed across the arched enclosure to a stunning medieval altarpiece of a nativity scene. Mary held a haloed infant, with angels in the foreground. In the background was an older bearded man that must be Joseph.

Ruth pondered what power the Fatima page and blue note held over Sixtus. Her thoughts strayed to what it was like to hold one's own baby, to worship and adore one's own little miracle. After Tim's death, friends encouraged her to date, but no one even remotely possible had come into her life. As years drifted to her late 30's, she contemplated alternatives. The route of a single, pregnant priest through artificial insemination would be difficult in the Church. Adoption did not fulfill her physical longing to bear a child, and to be a single parent was not what Ruth envisioned. There was time for a family, but what were the prospects? Noah, with his Revelation quest? If he was courting her, it didn't feel like it. Alessio — off limits.

The waitress interrupted her reverie to refresh the tepid coffee and asked if she wanted a second scone. Resisting more calories, Ruth checked her phone connection.

Right on time Archbishop of Canterbury Okello called from his office at Lambeth Palace. Even at a distance, the 106th Archbishop of Canterbury had a genial manner like a springtime sun glowing good news. On speakerphone he introduced Ruth to his assistant, The Rev. Canon Willis Dickens, whose reputation was that of a bloodhound on a constant prowl for canonical violations by Church of England clergy.

"Your Grace, Canon Dickens, I've heard so much about you," said Ruth, neglecting to say what she'd heard.

"Ruth, I want you to be with me at the Summit," said the Archbishop. "Your background is perfect for navigating this thicket in which we have become entangled." Ruth imagined Canon Dickens' eyes rolling upward in a sign of how the Archbishop was making a trifecta of errors by involving a junior member of the clergy, an American, and a woman.

"I am honored, your Grace," said Ruth without hesitation. "I'll return to Rome on Thursday if all goes well and give you a full report."

"The Pope's invitation must mean that we Anglicans seem less strange to the Pope than other Protestants."

Canon Dickens interjected piously, "If only the walls between churches would crumble."

"Well said, Willis," the Archbishop commented before steering the conversation back to his point. "Ruth, you're a student of these things. Perhaps Revelation is worth more attention than we Anglicans give it. It seems some groups mean to force it into bloom."

"Which groups do you have in mind, your Grace?" Ruth asked, trying to keep anxiety out of her voice and hoping he wasn't referring to Noah and his New Jerusalem Alliance.

He asked Ruth to pull up on her computer www.rapturepeople.com. Citing First Corinthians 15:51-53, the site proclaimed, "We shall all be changed — in a moment, in the twinkling of an eye, at the last trumpet: for the trumpet shall sound, and the dead shall be raised incorruptible, and we shall be changed. For this corruptible must put on incorruption, and this mortal must put on immortality." The home page blared, "The End Time is here!" urging believers to go to Jerusalem now or prepare to be lifted into the heavens within the next few days from wherever they were as the last trumpet sounds.

Ruth nodded in recognition.

"That group's been increasing its numbers, but it's a minor player. I'll email you a list of other groups I follow. The common thread is a call to be ready, to repent and be worthy of being lifted up to be with Jesus. But this time, well, let's say there's an urgency to it, a stridency I've not seen before. And you should know, this is not confined to Christians."

Canon Dickens retorted, "People who know the end is near are chronically disappointed." Ruth could almost see Canon Dickens' jowls wobbling with sarcastic derision.

"What's new," Ruth replied, "is that some organized groups now believe they are called to hasten the Second Coming, or The Hour for Muslims, or the time for the Mashiach to appear for certain Jewish groups. And they're taking action."

"So it is among the crazies. They won't affect what the Archbishop does in Jerusalem," stated Dickens.

Without addressing the Canon's comments directly, Ruth directed them to the site www.jewstochristians.org. It called for donations to ship Conversion Bibles to Israel.

"144,000 is all we need," the text proclaimed, the number of Jewish conversions that according to Revelation would trigger the Second Coming of Jesus.

"Good Lord," murmured the Archbishop. "What's your tour today?"

"We start with a visit to the Temple Mount. Father Brondini wants to take measurements to prepare for the Summit tent. Then we have a meeting with the leader of a group that plans to rebuild a Jewish Temple on the Mount."

"And enrage every Muslim in the world," said the Archbishop.

Ruth agreed. "And if the Pope wants to build a Roman Basilica there too, it could be quite a jumble."

"What makes you say the Pope has such plans?" asked the apparently startled Dickens.

Thinking she had revealed too much of what Alessio had shared privately, Ruth replied, "Just a thought. He wants to bring Christians together — 'under one roof.' For him this means a cathedral on the Mount."

"A Roman one," said the Archbishop.

72

JERUSALEM
Monday, May 22

4K LEADER ETZION read the headline in the *Jerusalem Post* — "Tourist Invasion!" Two days after the Pope's call for a summit all beds within forty miles of Jerusalem were reserved despite the destruction on the Temple Mount that had mainstream commentators labeling Jerusalem a destination fit only for travelers who craved danger.

Group bookings claimed whole floors and more. One 300-room hotel gave a heavily discounted rate for all its rooms to the Pilgrim Brethren of Minnesota for a 2-week period but was disappointed when they reserved no banquet halls. Instead, the Brethren's agent wanted assurance the roof was available. Bed and breakfasts as far away as Gezer, more than an hour from the Old City, were booked. As word spread of the tourist upswing, entrepreneurial families offered rooms over the internet at prices rivaling 4-star establishments.

Etzion shook his head at Evangelical Christian nonsense about End Time expectation and why foreigners would come just to catch a glimpse of the Pope and other luminaries.

4K's leadership met at Etzion's borrowed apartment to plan the next phase of its campaign to restore the greatness of Israel. After celebrating the prior weekend's success, they reviewed the plan.

"Our friends put this together for us," Etzion announced. At a mouse click a screen descended, and a smiling 20-something couple under the banner "Shalom" began to talk in Hebrew.

"Now is our time. As Torah commands, a Temple will be built on *Har HaBayit*. It will celebrate Israel's spiritual redemption. When the Mashiach comes, it will welcome him as King of all righteous nations."

As the couple narrated, a simulated model of the victorious Temple design was superimposed on a sketch of where the Dome of the Rock stood for twelve centuries over the site of the First and Second Temples.

"You can contribute to this magnificent temple. For every shekel you donate," as an address flashed across the screen, "three times that sum in Euros will be matched by an anonymous donor." The screen projected King David Society and Ark Society giving levels, with a florid deep blue inscription at the bottom: "Build me a Temple and I shall dwell amongst you. Exodus 25:2."

Silence, then rousing acclaim filled the room.

"Wondrous!"

"Hurrah!"

As a journalist Leibowitz exulted, "Almost all Jerusalem will be Jewish. Muslims can have their mosque in the Muslim Quarter. The sixty Jewish families and synagogues there can move. Christians can keep their Quarter. Israel can promise transit for legitimate pilgrims to visit. We need the tourists."

After the group disbursed, Etzion conversed alone with Eytan Osnat, who'd been essential to destroying the Dome of the Rock.

"We'll never get rid of the Muslims," said Osnat, shaking his head, "and if we go after the Christians.... The politics would be impossible."

"It's a process, Eytan. Arabs are leaving now, selling out. Their kids know there's no future for them here. And once our Temple's built, they'll know for sure whose land this is."

"Separation is best for everyone," agreed Osnat.

Etzion changed the subject. "I have a meeting this afternoon with the American who guaranteed funds for Temple construction. He's introducing me to someone who will be at the Pope's summit."

He was tempted to bring Osnat into his confidence about the elimination of the imam of the Damascus Mosque and his other private moves to keep Islamic groups at war with each other. But he resisted the urge.

Did Moses consult with his friends about the Exodus? No, he only described to them the Promised Land, and that was enough.

73

JERUSALEM
Monday, May 22

ALESSIO PULLED the rental Jeep to the curbstone of St. George's College at 8:30. He wolfed down the last of a sesame seed bagel and was finishing off thick black coffee from a Styrofoam cup with the Vatican crest provided by the cook at the Roman Catholic Archbishop's residence where Alessio was a guest. Ruth stood outside the doorway, ready for the first stop on their tour. They were dressed like tourists to avoid recognition.

Because of a security perimeter blocking vehicles near the Western Wall, they parked on the far eastern side beyond the Old City's walls and walked uphill toward the base of the Temple Mount. They were shocked to see a gaping opening through the Golden Gate, which Saladin had sealed with heavy stones after retaking Muslim control of the city from the Crusaders in 1187.

Through this archway, Jesus rode on a donkey on Palm Sunday, and through it he would return one day according to Christian prophecy. Assigned through the auspices of the imam of Mecca's Great Mosque, the Deputy Waqf Commander met them in front of the hastily installed chain-link screen barring entrance through the newly opened double arch. Ruth put on a jacket to cover her bare arms and a head scarf so as not to offend the Muslim officer.

The Deputy Commander compared their faces to photos he held and asked coldly what they wanted to see.

Sensitive to the officer's plight, on whose watch the Dome of the Rock was destroyed, Alessio offered condolences and explained they were scouting for the Summit to start in eleven days. Alessio and Ruth snapped photos of the reopened Golden Gate.

The Deputy Commander silently led them to the traditional staircase to the Mount blocked by heavily armed troops. The Israeli captain glared at them, inspected Ruth's and Alessio's passports and begrudgingly let the trio ascend.

Along the Kotel, the Western Wall, separate areas for men and women were filled with a crush of Jews. Most men were Orthodox, dressed in black and white, some with rounded cloth hats, others rocking their heads up and down in a trance. Green branches protruding from joints in the ancient Wall sprouted pink flowers.

Arriving atop the Mount, Ruth and Alessio gasped at the wreckage from what had been the Dome of the Rock. Gray rock, alabaster, plaster and gold flecks mingled in heaps, strewn about as though Old Testament Goliath had picked up the structure and smashed it to bits. Pillars had fallen outward, leaving the center where the Foundation Stone lay exposed and eerily free of fragments.

The Deputy Commander said nothing but nudged them toward a fence overlooking a depression known as the Well of Souls, an underground cave below the floor where they could easily see the Foundation Stone that had been sheltered for millennia by the First and Second Jewish Temples and then by the Dome of the Rock. Venerated in Judaism, Christianity and Islam by People of the Book as the place where Abraham came to sacrifice his son, the site exuded sacral power.

In the rubble strewn across the Mount's surface was an arch remnant of the Dome with Arabic inscription that expressed the primacy of Islam. Ruth captured cell phone photos of the debris, including a marble fragment warning believers against heresy.

The Deputy Commander explained the plan to clear debris, wash away dust, salvage gold, smooth the surface and erect a large tent for the summit. The officer assured them his forces were working closely with Israeli contractors to prepare for the Thursday after next.

"We can raise a circus tent in one day," he boasted.

Ignoring the implied comparison of a summit to a circus, Alessio began measuring distances. He took notes in a black book with the Vatican seal. When debris posed obstacles to a straight-line measurement, he paced off lengths by meter, a skill learned in the Italian Army.

"What *are* you doing?" asked Ruth when the exercise began to consume far more time than she expected. She was anxious to gather local intelligence about the mood of the population, the religious undercurrents at work in the region, the feel of this troubled place.

"Making sure there will be enough space for the delegates to have separate huddle rooms in addition to the two large meeting spaces."

"Doesn't the Vatican have an internet connection?" Surely the dimensions could be readily determined from published material. Or maybe Alessio was plotting dimensions for a cathedral to be built here. The impulsive Pope must already have a design in mind, one no one will accept.

They spent more than an hour on the Mount, including an inspection of the Al Aqsa Mosque. Damage was extensive but not obviously fatal. Ruth asked the Deputy Commander if, as some press reports speculated, there had been a human victim of Saturday's explosion.

He glared with tautly drawn lips. "There was man in Mosque. Hospital say he may die."

"I'm sorry. I'm glad your men were safe," said Ruth.

Resuming a stance akin to military attention, the Deputy Commander asked if there were anything else.

After thanking the officer, they descended the steps along the Western Wall. Visitors were stuffing small pieces of paper into Wall crevices. Ruth thought how tragic it was that the people of the one God with a common ancestor in Abraham had such certainty about their version of faith that they could treat others as mortal enemies.

"We have a meeting with Haim Etzion in five minutes," Ruth reminded Alessio, hinting that they should they walk faster.

"Onward," Alessio replied as he squinted at a map with Warsaw Café circled in red.

They converged at the entrance at the same moment as a man in a black suit, white shirt and thin black tie. About Ruth's height, the gentleman held open the door and said in English "After you." Ruth and Alessio glanced at the man's black notebook emblazoned with a gold leaf Star of David.

Using the agreed code Alessio asked, "Do you like cream with your coffee?"

Etzion replied, "With two cubes of sugar."

Ruth felt like a spy.

Identities confirmed, the threesome moved to a back table inside the café, a fabled coffee shop run by the third generation of a survivor of the Warsaw Ghetto, who fled to Israel when it was British-controlled Palestine.

Ruth thanked Etzion for meeting and introduced Alessio Brondini as her driver. In his form-fitting olive-green shirt, Ruth thought he looked like a bodyguard. Noah had described Ruth to Etzion as an American minister sympathetic to 4K's cause, who was preparing a report that could lead to financial and other support for building a Third Temple. Ruth thought it best to keep Alessio's identity secret.

"Mr. Stoll's a good friend. What can I do for you, Reverend Waller?" he asked.

"I'm interested to know more about your organization's Third Temple contest."

Etzion appeared to assess what layer of truth to reveal, as though he were a criminal defendant meeting his assigned public defender. Settling on the most cautious course, Etzion smiled.

"I appreciate your interest in our work. Our hope is to restore the legacy of King David." He stopped, waiting to see what Ruth would ask next. As she made notes, he added, "Rebuilding a Temple is a way of doing that."

Ruth asked more about the design and cost, and Etzion more openly described the thinking behind the massive structure of the chosen plan.

"We know more about the Second Temple than the First. Will the Third be a blend?"

"Plans are not final," Etzion offered. "One architect calls it 'Judaic Modern.' Simplicity. Openings for light like the original. Today's construction techniques let us achieve the spirit of an ancient Temple in a modern expression."

"And when can it be built, now that the space is cleared?" probed Ruth.

Etzion was impassive.

"When time is right." He signaled the waiter for round two.

Ruth said, "I understand most of the public favors building a Third Temple."

Etzion seemed startled that a Gentile like Ruth followed polling on this subject. "Yes, but the recent trouble...."

"What have you heard about who was responsible for the Dome's demolition?" Ruth probed gently, bringing the cup to her lips for a sip.

"Who would do such a thing?" Etzion evaded and changed the subject. "What brings you to Jerusalem?"

"I'm writing a piece about the city. I forgot to ask — what does 4K stand for?" Ruth shifted back to interrogation.

"It's just a phrase," deflected Etzion.

"Fortunately, you have 4 K's. 3K in America stands for a terrorist group."

Etzion frowned. "We are familiar with America's racial problem. Our group has a spiritual mission."

Ruth shifted in her seat, finished a note, then decided to provoke a response. "What if Mount Moriah were redesigned to rebuild the Dome of the Rock and add a Temple and a Christian church?"

Etzion's gaze could not hide resentment. "*Har HaBayit* is home to the Holy of Holies. A Christian church there? It would be out of place. Is this what the Pope hopes to accomplish? If so, he is misguided."

Alessio's back straightened. He seemed poised to interject, but Ruth moved her hand to preempt that, glad he could experience this reaction from Etzion.

Ruth asked how Israeli settlers were treated by Palestinians in the West Bank.

Etzion exhaled deeply and shook his head. "In Samaria and Judea?" He refused to acknowledge the words West Bank. "Poorly. Under constant attack by Palestinians. Our settlements cause the desert to bloom. They bring jobs, prosperity in place of poverty, and yet they are treated as the enemy." He returned to being the gracious host and asked about their route.

Ruth showed him her cell phone map through areas to the east and north of Jerusalem, including stops in Jericho and Bethlehem. They planned to meet a leader of the March.

"Will you stay for the Summit?" asked Etzion. "I hope the delegates can absorb the local culture, gain a feel for this place. They should visit local restaurants."

"I understand the delegates will have lunch in local establishments on Saturday."

Etzion walked them out the door before heading back to the recess of the café. Didn't they realize how easy it was to do background checks? Ruth conducted her interview without revealing that she worked for the Archbishop of Canterbury. Ruth and her bodyguard would come to realize the righteousness of the Jewish cause.

Etzion phoned his contractor in Syria.

"Another job. There are a woman and her driver, a green Jeep, license number 55326." A 4K officer had texted Etzion a photo of the Jeep. "Tomorrow morning, they travel east from Qalandia. Intercept them. Tell them to go home. No broken bones. Oh, and send a list of restaurants near the Temple Mount. You have contractors there, right?"

74

WASHINGTON, D.C.
Monday, May 22

AT 85 SIMON MCALLISTER wondered why he'd been summoned to the White House from his summer home in Southwest Harbor, Maine. Decades ago, McAllister was Henry Kissinger's personal aide for Middle Eastern affairs when Kissinger was nursing a heavily drinking President Nixon through his final months in the White House.

Noah Stoll knocked on his door to escort him into an unmarked black SUV. Introducing himself as a private advisor to President Palmer, Noah told him the meeting would be strictly off the record. Palmer wanted details from 1973 when Israeli Prime Minister Golda Meir contemplated a nuclear strike on Syria and Egypt after a surprise attack that began the Yom Kippur War.

On the private plane to D.C., McAllister explained that an invasion would have almost certainly taken Haifa and threatened Israel's very existence. Meir was poised to use Israel's nuclear assets — unless the United States promised a rescue with overwhelming conventional force. Kissinger and Chief of Staff Al Haig fielded her call for help, concerned about Nixon's condition, haunted as he was by Watergate demons. They warned Israel that a nuclear attack would forfeit forever the support of the USA on which Israel relied. American conventional support was pledged, and the Yom Kippur War ended quickly in a stand-off.

Noah asked McAllister what would have happened if Nixon had taken the call. The Rev. Billy Graham was giving pastoral care to the crippled President. Author of *Till Armageddon*, Graham had written that the Rapture was imminent. President Palmer wanted McAllister's recollections of this under-reported history.

President Palmer alone greeted Noah and McAllister in an Executive Office Building underground conference room.

"Thank you for coming, Ambassador. This meeting did not happen," said Palmer.

"Understood." McAllister stiffened. "It's an honor to be here, again."

McAllister detailed the near brush with nuclear war in 1973. McAllister confirmed that his boss had deliberately excluded Nixon from a decision about Israel's use of what it called its Temple Swords.

"We'll never know what Nixon would have done. Billy Graham saw it through a different lens than we did." They discussed current Middle Eastern politics and the religious undercurrents and rip tides in the region.

"In a week," said Palmer, "I'll be in Jerusalem for God knows what the Pope hopes to achieve. We'll have three days to tackle problems that go back millennia. Israel's about to take out Iran's nuclear program, and I support that. Advice?"

McAllister locked eyes on President Palmer.

"If you want to bring on Armageddon, bombing Iran is a first step. If you want to get through the next few weeks without devastation beyond anything the Middle East has ever seen, tell the Israelis to cool it. An attack on Iran could unify most of the Muslim world, except for Saudi Arabia. All the efforts to find a way to peace would go up in fire."

"The survival of Israel's at stake. It can't let Iran get a nuke."

McAllister had maintained a stoic expression but pursed his lips.

"The fact that with our support Israel can beat its neighbors any time and has them outmatched with its nuclear capability, this actually aggravates the situation. Some analysts argue there'd be more stability if Iran tested a bomb. It would be like our Cold War standoff with the Soviet Union. The real mission is to match Iran's self-interest with a path to co-existence. And it's crucial to understand the Shi'a-Sunni divide and the underlying battle lines between the Saudis and the Iranians that keep them from combining against Israel."

Palmer stroked his evening stubble.

"What if you're wrong? We do nothing and then there's a preemptive attack on Israel, with millions killed in a day? Instant holocaust."

"We survived the Cold War. What if Eisenhower had launched a first attack against the Soviets? We may not be here today. Mr. President, may I ask you a question?" McAllister inquired.

"Of course," replied Palmer. His tone indicated he was not used to being asked anything except during annoying skirmishes with the press.

"Sir, you're a devout Christian. I hear rumblings in some quarters about Armageddon. If you could, would you hasten the finale to bring about a New Jerusalem?"

Staring at McAllister as if it were the final question on a big-money quiz show, Palmer answered, "I was elected by God-fearing, Bible-reading Christians who believe as I do that the New Jerusalem will bless the earth one day."

"If the signs were clear, would you welcome nuclear war?" McAllister's voice tightened.

"God's not called me on the white phone from heaven," said Palmer.

"You may need to face the question soon — your faith or the presidency," McAllister warned. "I'm glad we shielded President Nixon from having to choose. God knows what he might have done."

"Noah, share with the Ambassador what we've learned about 4K."

Noah turned to McAllister. "An Israeli group called 4K is ready to build a Third Temple. It could have been responsible for the take-down of the Dome of the Rock."

McAllister asked if they knew what 4K stood for.

They did not.

"I do," he said. "Kodesh, Kach, Kabbalah and Kook."

Noah asked, "How did you...."

"I have my sources," McAllister dodged.

Palmer dipped his head with one eyebrow raised. "That's Greek to me."

McAllister explained, "Hebrew actually. Kodesh means holy or sacred. Kach refers to the ultranationalist party that supports a greater Israel free of Muslims or for that matter Christians or anybody who isn't Jewish inside a purely Jewish State. Kabbalah is a form of Judaic mysticism. But Rabbi Kook is the key. His taught final redemption, which would come only when Israel occupies all the ancient Land of Israel and makes way for the Jewish Messiah."

"So you conclude that 4K was responsible for the Dome's demolition?" asked Noah.

"That's how the hounds are baying."

Palmer switched subjects.

"I assume you've been following this women's march."

McAllister had.

"It's directed from Iran, men using women to advance their agenda. The Israelis view the March as a floating time bomb, ready to explode if it gets near the border."

"That's for sure," said the President.

They discussed intersecting issues of faith and politics, the intertwining of religion and power, uncertainties facing the region and the world.

Palmer looked at his watch.

"Thank you for coming, Ambassador. I'll consider your advice." He clicked a button. A Marine guard entered to escort McAllister to an exit.

"What's your take, Noah?"

"When Abraham took his son up Mount Moriah, he didn't expect the sacrifice to be Isaac. He was rewarded for trusting God. So it is for you."

"You think it's time."

"The signs are clear."

"Thanks for being one of my delegates in Jerusalem," Palmer said and walked through the White House tunnel with Noah, who exited through a basement corridor.

Palmer returned to the Oval Office alone. He gazed out the window to the Washington Monument glowing in the twilight. The President thought of Thomas Jefferson, who once stood in this very spot. It was Jefferson who drew a sketch of the Seal of the United States of America inspired by the Book of Exodus. It pictured the Children of Israel in the wilderness, called by a cloud before them by day and a pillar of fire by night. And Palmer thought of the adopted Seal, with the Eye of Providence at the top of a pyramid. *Yes, America and the Second Coming — nothing inconsistent.*

75

TEHRAN, IRAN
Monday, May 22

GRAND AYATOLLAH Mahdavi Mousavi, Supreme Leader of the Islamic Revolution, donned his black robe and black velvet turban to meet with Iranian President BahrAm Al-Rabani. The greeting was stiff. The Supreme Leader offered a chair across a table where tea was served. The servant departed before a word was said.

Mousavi spoke first. "The Summit is our opportunity to advance Iran's standing in the world. We will do this united."

The President nodded submission to the will of the Guardian of the Revolution. "We are as one," he acknowledged. "I have a suggestion for our third delegate," hoping to preempt the privilege of extending the third invitation, as each delegation was limited to three.

"I invited Navid Kosari," said the Ayatollah.

The President's right eye began to twitch, as it did when he was outmaneuvered in a debate or extremely nervous. "A movie star?"

"I understand your concern, Mr. President," the Supreme Leader placidly stated, as though patting the head of a pupil with words of condescending praise for grasping an easy concept. "It will catch our adversaries off guard. They will know it is not only you and I with whom they contend but an aroused and united Iran."

The President owed his political longevity to the cardinal rule that you fight hard for a minute, and if the opponent doesn't run, you run. The minute was over.

"Did you have the opportunity to review my recommendations for the Summit?" asked the President, yielding to the Supreme Leader's prerogative.

The Supreme Leader listened as Al-Rabani summarized basics — that Iran has no intention to possess a nuclear weapon, that Iran's territory is inviolate, that Israel must cease its suppression of Islam, that Israel should offer Palestinians and all families the right of return to their pre-1948 homes, that Israel should pay to rebuild the Dome of the Rock, that Israel should surrender its nuclear assets, and that if all these points were agreed, then Iran was prepared to consider whether Israel had the right to exist.

The Supreme Leader shocked the Iranian President with his response.

"We Iranians have no quarrel with Judaism. Jews live peacefully here. It was our Cyrus 2500 years ago who ordered rebuilding the Second Temple. We can discuss a Third Temple at the same time the Dome of the Rock is rebuilt. Perhaps a Christian presence also. We will invoke the ancient principle of hospitality, starting with a welcoming place for all People of the Book."

Al-Rabani's right eye began to twitch staccato, this time from a reflexive aversion to any hint of a concession to Zionism.

"That is a religious concern, so you would not expect me to mention this, correct?" begged the President.

"I will handle it," replied the Ayatollah. "I understand that President Goudonov offered to install nuclear missiles near our territory in a defense pact," letting Al-Rabani know that every discussion he had with Goudonov was reported to the Ayatollah. "That eliminates any justification for us to develop nuclear weapons, would you agree? As you know Ayatollah Hismani issued a fatwa that military nuclear devices are contrary to Islam."

"But how can we entrust our security to another country?"

The Supreme Leader did not respond directly. He stood up, signaling the meeting was near its end. He put his right arm on the left shoulder of the President, gazed directly into his eyes and asked, "What do you make of this March, the March of Innocents?"

"It is good to see women marching for Islam," answered Al-Rabani cautiously in an effort to discern the Supreme Leader's position.

The Ayatollah asked, "Are we at the End Time, Mr. President? Is the Mahdi ready to take command for a final battle?"

The President stared, uncharacteristically speechless. A twitch resumed. "I am a mere servant, holding this position by Allah's sufferance. I would say we will know when the Dajjal makes the next move."

"Has the Mahdi returned?" asked the Ayatollah.

"Allah will reveal him in time," replied Al-Rabani.

The Supreme Leader took from this that Al-Rabani envisioned himself as the Mahdi, self-anointed to lead not only Iran but all Islam into cataclysmic combat.

"On to Jerusalem," the Ayatollah concluded, showing the President the door.

76

WEST BANK
Tuesday, May 23

THE DAY AFTER surveying the Old City and meetings with 4K's Haim Etzion and others, Alessio and Ruth sped toward the Qalandia Gate, a major checkpoint built like the guard post of a high security prison. Cars were stopped and occupants questioned one by one as Israeli security forces determined who entered and exited Jerusalem. Alessio and Ruth were set to meet with Navid Kosari as arranged through the Grand Ayatollah at the Pope's request. The Ayatollah phoned Kosari and asked him to leave the March to become a Summit delegate, an invitation Kosari immediately accepted, not sorry to leave the dust and heat behind.

Passing through Jericho, a Palestinian city north of Jerusalem, Alessio eased the Jeep through the holding cell, then sped on, leaving behind the border wall that undulated in the heat as the highway wove through a hilly area mixed with dusty Palestinian villages and gleaming new Israeli settlements with slanted red tile roofs. Women carried water jugs on their heads. Men in native headgear squatted by the roadside, glaring at the Jeep as it failed to stop for trinkets or tea.

"Here we are in the Holy Land, where Jesus walked and called his disciples," Ruth marveled, gazing at a Bedouin herding sheep along a sparsely vegetated hillside as in biblical times. "What led you to become a priest?"

"For me it was a Paul on the road to Damascus moment," said Alessio.

"Sounds dramatic."

"I shot a child." Ruth noticed him swallow hard and his bicep muscles tense. "I was an Italian soldier doing peacekeeping in Lebanon and thought he held a rifle on a roof, but it was a TV antenna." Alessio focused on the road. "As I prayed for forgiveness, a voice called me to become a priest."

Ruth was silent for a time.

"Are you ever lonely?"

"Too busy to be lonely," though that wasn't the whole truth.

"Same here. I have my work, and of course Gabriel."

Alessio leaned back in the driver's seat, his smile melted.

"Tell me about him."

"He's a scruffy little mutt. When I get home, he barks a welcome like I'm the most important person in the world."

"And the one who feeds him." The smile returned.

"I'm more than a meal ticket, you cynic," Ruth laughed. "Gabriel's my little angel. An angel who plays fiercely with a rubber frog."

A roadblock came into view, with men in camouflage clothing and black boots flagging the only vehicle ahead of them in sight and letting it proceed slowly without a full stop. Alessio shifted the Jeep into second gear, slowing down and hoping for similar treatment. Two men held AK-47's pointed at the ground. One signaled with his hands "Halt" and demanded "Passport." Alessio handed over his and Ruth's, one Vatican City, one USA. The lead man inspected them and checked the license plate number against a paper.

Speaking in choppy English, the leader handed the passports back to Alessio, and said, "Car there," pointing to a gravel cut. "You come with us."

Noticing fear creeping across Ruth's face, Alessio assured her this was routine. The men pointed their AK-47's to a cinder-block shack.

The shack was a one-room affair, with a scarred, wobbly wooden table, three battered chairs and a rotary dial telephone on a stand, seemingly a guard post of some sort.

"Dangerous for you here," the leader began. "No place for woman or foreigner."

Alessio responded, "We are tourists."

"You spies."

Ruth shuddered.

Alessio smiled broadly, "We are on a goodwill mission."

"You work for Pope. Pope supports Israel." The leader swung his weapon around and jabbed it into Alessio's stomach.

With a quick prayer to St. Martin, patron saint of soldiers, Alessio grabbed the AK-47 and jerked the man into a chokehold, pressing the weapon against his man's throat until he began to collapse. Hearing the leader's stifled outcry, the other man bolted into the shack with AK-47 pointed directly at Alessio, finger on trigger.

Ruth jumped in front of Alessio. She shouted in Arabic, "Stop! We go to meet Navid Kosari."

Startled at the mention of the film star, the second man kept his finger on the trigger with the rifle pointed at her.

"Release him," demanded the guard.

Ruth glared and said slowly in Arabic, "Put your weapon down now and I'll tell my driver to release your man."

For seconds that seemed like eternity the guard and Ruth froze in their positions, neither blinking. Alessio broke the silence.

"Lower your weapon down and I will do the same."

No reaction. Alessio let go of the leader, who slumped to the floor. Alessio stepped in front of Ruth. He motioned for the gunman to lay down his weapon. Gasping to regain his breath, the leader nodded from the floor, and his companion moved his AK-47 toward the floor as Alessio slowly did the same. Alessio grabbed the second weapon and waved for Ruth to head to the door.

Ruth left the shack first. Alessio backed out clutching both weapons at his side. They ran to the Jeep, Alessio floored the gas pedal, and gravel sprayed the hut. After a mile Alessio pulled to the shoulder, unloaded ammunition from the AK-47's, smashed them on the pavement several times and hurled the firearms into a valley.

"You saved my life," Alessio said as they raced down the highway.

"You saved mine."

"Then we're even. But don't step in front of a loaded weapon again."

"I don't think I was thinking, Alessio." She exhaled deeply.

When he left the Army for the Church, he pledged a life of non-violence, but today protecting Ruth by any means came first.

Was it wrong to make that choice again?

The two men remained in the shack. The lead man called Haim Etzion on his cell phone. "You will not see them again," he lied. Etzion promised payment and disconnected.

77

ZOARA
Tuesday, May 23

PALESTINIAN NATIONAL AUTHORITY PRESIDENT Abu Arafat invited Iran, Iraq, Syria, and Egypt to a secret meeting in Zoara. The ancient site was not on modern maps but had a fabled history. It was once a flourishing oasis town. According to Genesis, God spared it while destroying Sodom and Gomorrah. Here Lot and his daughters took refuge while Sodom burned. Meaning "small" or "insignificant" in Hebrew, Zoara was a perfect place to meet clandestinely, remote from Israeli surveillance.

"Will we stand together in Jerusalem?" asked Arafat. He probed the eyes of the delegates, testing whether the divisions among Muslims would be set aside, at least temporarily.

The Iraqi representative, a Shiite, declared, "If we don't this time, we are damned."

The Iranian deputy of President Al-Rabani agreed. "Defensive jihad is a sacred obligation among brothers. If war it will be, we are with you."

"Our forces mass along our southern border with Israel," said the Syrian general, the only career military man in the group.

"The March," Arafat inquired. "Can it get across the border, even to Jerusalem?"

The Syrian general replied, "Our scouts confirm gaps in the north. When we move our troops, we can divert Israeli forces away from those spots."

The Egyptian deputy was silent throughout a lengthy discussion of how the collective might of the Islamic world along Israel's perimeter could influence the summit's outcome. Asked whether Egypt would unify its forces in a grand Muslim coalition against Israel, he replied flatly that he would seek instructions but said with determination, "There is one Islam."

Arafat invoked history. "Islam once unified these lands. We gave freedoms to Jews and Christians they denied to us. We opened our arms as People of the Book and our adversaries did not. Enough!"

The Iranian diplomat nodded. "If Muslims had lived righteously, the flag of the true caliph would fly over all the world. The banners of Islam must rise above all others everywhere in this holy land. This is our vow."

78

JERUSALEM
Tuesday, May 23

AS THE SUMMIT DREW NEAR, Prime Minister Feldman became unusually agitated. Thoughts burst like fireworks, one explosion after another in an array of colors, clusters, and shapes. He blamed the third cup of Ethiopian espresso.

He tried the meditation technique his cardiologist insisted he learn — let thoughts float away like clouds. Don't fight them. Let them come and go, and the sky would soon be clear blue and he would be ready for the day's focus.

But the imagined clouds that gathered kept turning into epic thunderheads — Muslim March of a million women and a movie star — mini-drones exploding the heads of scientists — nuclear missiles poised to launch at his command — suicide bombers — nightmarish images streamed without ceasing.

He shook his head like a swimmer getting out of a pool. Clarity. He would persevere in evicting Palestinians from lands that belong to Israel, a solemn quest that brought immense pleasure from seeing Zion's enemies brought low and his role in Jewish history enshrined.

When Mossad Director Yehud Siegel arrived, Feldman got straight to business. "Operation David — any rough spots?"

"The destruction of the nuclear oven is ready," replied Siegel.

The Defense Minister enthusiastically agreed. "Not even a haboob could stop it," using the Arabic word for a virulent dust storm that can wreck a village.

"With the enemy massed along our borders, I want all defenses on high alert," Feldman instructed. "24-hour duty for everyone a week from Friday."

"During the summit?" asked Director Siegel, his poker face masking concern that the Prime Minister would attack while delegates were in Jerusalem.

Feldman confirmed.

"I need the Temple Swords ready to launch, coordinates trained on Tehran and Damascus. We must prepare for anything. Our troops must be set to move with lightning speed along the borders."

The Defense Minister affirmed all was ready. His watch would not be a repeat of 1973, when a surprise Arab attack decimated Israeli air bases.

"One more thing. That March of the Fanatics is not setting one hoof or foot in Israel. Do whatever it takes."

"I have your full authority, Prime Minister?" the Defense Minister asked.

"Yes. Blessings on your mission."

"Our mission, Prime Minister, the mission of Zion."

79

JERICHO
Tuesday, May 23

NAVID KOSARI WONDERED if he had the right time or location when the delegates the Ayatollah arranged for him to meet at a Jericho café failed to show. A call from his agent filled the time.

When the agent reported that a role would be filled by the studio's second choice if Kosari could not commit now, he responded, "Look, you couldn't get me a tenth of the publicity this March is generating. They'll wait. Tell them I'll sign in two weeks if — ask for 25% more. Great script — and the female lead is smashing."

Noah and Ruth arrived as he was finishing his call in Farsi. They didn't look like important people, Ruth in a tan sleeveless blouse and slacks, Alessio in a logo-free T-shirt and black jeans. They explained their need for a tourist disguise. Kosari switched to English, perfected by watching Hollywood films that the general Iranian population was blocked from viewing.

"Greetings. Tea? Coffee? I feared you were lost." He smiled with perfectly white teeth that had never needed braces. He looked mostly at Ruth while firmly shaking Alessio's hand.

"The roads were bumpy," said Alessio, responding with an equally firm grip. Kosari pulled back the seat of the pine chair around the gnarly table partly covered with a white muslin runner.

"Coffee," he shouted in Arabic, as the waiter raced to attention, nodded, and scurried to the kitchen.

"An honor to meet you. The Supreme Leader said you wish to discuss the summit. I am a delegate, an honor for a humble actor. What can I tell you?"

Alessio struggled to reconcile Kosari the heartthrob actor with the man suddenly a high-level delegate at an international summit.

"Mr. Kosari..."

"Navid."

"Navid, I report to Pope Sixtus. Your March of the Innocents, what is its purpose?"

Kosari listened intently to Alessio, with a skill honed in countless movies, communicating that this moment is the only one that counts. Ruth and Alessio leaned forward in their chairs, ready to receive a deep revelation from this unique man.

"To tell the truth, I have no idea," Kosari startled his guests. "At the start of every film the director tells me the theme, but this March is ... it's improvisation. The man who engaged me said, 'Advance the cause of women in Islam.' But — no script."

Alessio was unsure what to make of this but took a different tack. "What do you see the March accomplishing?"

"My agent says my ratings have soared. It's been a long road so far but most inspiring. A'ishah's the leader. I am a supporting actor." He projected a facial expression mixing disappointment for having anything other than the lead with piety and obedience to faith.

"And what does she seek?" asked Alessio.

"Should I address you as Father Alessio?"

"Alessio, please."

"I'll be at the summit as well, with the Archbishop of Canterbury," Ruth said, not content to be on the sidelines.

"What a pleasure it will be to join you both next week," Kosari replied with a most charming smile, "as we work together for peace. That is what A'ishah seeks."

Ruth asked before Alessio could resume, "Navid, is the Government of Iran open to recognizing Israel's right to exist?"

"Policy is for the Supreme Leader. I am an artist who only wishes to serve Allah." His broad smile again featured dazzling white teeth.

"You said in the call to the March that you want to unify Islam through this mix of Sunni and Shi'a women." said Alessio. "Is unity the point of the March?"

On that question, Kosari had an opinion.

"You know, Iranians are overwhelmingly Shi'a. I had a dear cousin who was killed in our tragic war with Iraq that accomplished nothing. We sacrificed a million pawns in a senseless power game. If we can stop that from happening again, that would be a victory."

"Peace would be a blessing," affirmed Alessio. "But would Muslim unity then be turned against Israel?"

"A'ishah has never mentioned Israel, only peace."

"Who guides A'ishah? The Army of the Mahdi sponsors the March. Who is that?"

On this question Kosari paused. He glanced down at his coffee, turned to the waiter who was serving only his table, and circled his fingers to indicate another, then looked up at Ruth to answer Alessio's question.

"She talks with a man named Vali."

"Vali Qalil?" asked Ruth, who had researched all she could about AM and noticed a reference to Vali Qalil associated with the mysterious organization.

"Perhaps that is his name," Kosari answered uncertainly.

"Is he the leader of AM?" asked Alessio.

"AM sponsors the March." Kosari nodded. "But who leads AM?" He shrugged.

Ruth picked up, "The name of the group suggests that AM is ready for a final battle, when the Mahdi emerges to lead Islam to victory over forces of ignorance led by the Dajjal. If so, who is the Dajjal?"

"Some say it's Prime Minister Feldman. His one eye makes perfect casting, and you must agree he has not been a friend to Muslims."

"Let's back up. Who/what is the Mahdi?" asked Alessio.

"Ah, the mystery. Allah will reveal the one who has been asleep for hundreds of years."

"In occultation," said Ruth. "A state of hiding, like centuries of being in a coma."

Kosari smiled and nodded as though the camera had moved from Ruth to him. "Let me know when you find him!" said Navid, excitedly. A photograph standing next to the redeemer of Islam would be priceless.

Ruth continued, "Your announcement of the March summed up wrongdoing that precedes the End Time in Shi'a belief — lack of faithfulness, hypocritical leaders, worship of material wealth, oppression of the poor, deceit by the powerful. It was a magnificent speech."

"Thank you," said Kosari, taking a bow for his performance.

"There are those who say the world as we know it is coming to an end. Has there been talk about how the March is part of a final battle to sort those to be saved?" asked Ruth.

That seemed to rattle Kosari, body language expressing the truth that he had no knowledge of such a scheme.

"I hope not before my next movie is released." Kosari laughed and then turned serious. "Many in my country cannot afford a ticket for my films. There are the rich and the poor, far too many poor. I mean it when I say the March summons the women of Islam to reject hypocrites who drove our people into poverty and exalted themselves above the people. But destroy the world? Madness."

Hoping to forge a human connection that would be of use at the summit, Alessio switched topics. "How can the March get to Jerusalem?"

Kosari nodded his head up and down and pursed his lips. "My fear about this March? That it will end in tragedy before reaching its destination."

"How will it cross into Israel?" asked Ruth.

Used to giving interviews to magazine writers, Kosari leaned forward and planted both arms on the table, drawing his unblemished face close to Ruth and Alessio.

"The plan is to find the place where the barrier is weak. I understand that is to the north. A stretch of barren land has no wall, and our marchers can step across this line in the sand that separates the territories of Israel from this part of Palestine, with only a fence to be pierced. Once the March is inside Israel, Israeli forces would not dare drive our women back across the border, as long as they act peacefully, as they will. Then it is only a few days' journey to Jerusalem."

"An area to the north, near Jenin?" asked Alessio, referring to a Palestinian city near the 1947 partition border with Israel.

"Across the border from Tel Megiddo," said Ruth. The translation from Hebrew rumbled through her thoughts. *Tel Megiddo in Greek means Armageddon.*

With that, Kosari abruptly excused himself, saying he was due in Jerusalem to prepare for the summit as the Supreme Leader commanded. He expressed sorrow for missing a week of the March.

The role of a lifetime, thought Alessio.

"I'll be there to welcome A'ishah and the other pilgrims," the film star said as he departed.

Ruth spoke when Kosari was beyond earshot. "Armageddon, where Revelation predicts kings will gather at the end of time."

80

JERUSALEM
Tuesday, May 23

ALESSIO AND RUTH finished their second day in the Holy Land at Askadinya, an East Jerusalem restaurant Kosari recommended. They ordered the special, lamb dressed with mustard, capers, and hearts of palm. Olives, hummus, and a carafe of house red wine arrived first.

"Behold, the mound of olives." Alessio circled his fork above the plate.

Ruth laughed at the reference to the Mount of Olives, where Jesus wept over Jerusalem. She was grateful for the break from a traumatic day. Alessio's friendship was unexpected, a thorough surprise from the cool reception she anticipated from Roman Catholic clergy.

"Aside from surviving, what stood out for you today?"

"It's like when I was a soldier in Lebanon, walking in a foreign land, not knowing if the next step will be on a land mine and everything explodes."

"It found it hard to believe that Navid Kosari seemed in the dark about the Army of the Mahdi. Do you believe him?"

"He is an actor. He is used to someone writing his script," said Alessio.

The lamb was served. "Let me test you," said Alessio with a keen smile. "Behold the lamb — what Bible passage?"

"Easy one," said Ruth. "John, chapter 1, verse 29. My turn — 'Slain from the foundation of the world.'"

Alessio's eyes widened. "Mark?" he ventured.

"It's from Revelation — Chapter 13, verse 8," she said. He looked uncomfortable with his wrong answer. "It's my job to quote religious texts," she reminded him.

"We make a good team," said Alessio, smiling. "I forgot to tell you. Remember I mentioned in our hypothetical story a false manual? It is actually a different word — M-a-n-u e-l, with a capital M."

"Manuel. That could refer to Dom Manuel I, Portugal's King in the great age of discovery, when Portugal had the largest armada in the world."

"When Columbus found America," said Alessio. "But what connection?"

"Manuel expelled Jews and Muslims from Portugal, a few years after Spain. It's said he did this to obtain the agreement of Ferdinand and Isabella to marry their infant heiress. He banished Jewish adults and forced many to leave their children for conversion as New Christians. You can see why the anti-clerical government of Portugal at the time of Fatima viewed him as a villain."

"So what would it mean — a false Manuel?"

"Perhaps that religious cleansing and forced conversions are a false path."

"I know the Holy Father would agree."

"Are you sure? What about his plan to unite Christians in a Vatican cathedral? And the idea that this would attract Jews and Muslims to convert to Christianity?"

Alessio was silent.

Archbishop Okello phoned five minutes before the appointed time. It was Tuesday evening, and Ruth was exhausted. Rather than being her scholarly self, she had without thinking thrown herself in front of Alessio in their brush with death by AK-47. Then she heard an actor forecast Armageddon. They drove through tense occupied territories where gleaming Israeli settlements signaled to ancient Palestinian villages that they should vacate before crumbling into memory's dustbin. They watched Arab children throwing rocks at teenage Israeli soldiers shouldering automatic weapons, beggars squatting by the roadside, shepherds with their flocks as in biblical times.

"Desperate and getting worse that's the bottom line," Ruth told Okello. "A significant number of Muslims, Jews and Christians seem prepared for the end of time itself, each seeing it go their way. One thing is clear — the Pope wants to build a Roman cathedral on the Temple Mount."

"He told me he was forming a plan based on a secret he recently received," said the Archbishop.

"Could it be about the Miracle of Fatima?" Ruth asked, as if it were a lucky guess She didn't feel free to share details Alessio confided.

"I'm amazed at your intuition. He did mention Fatima. Something new from the company that unleashed the Crusades," the Archbishop quipped.

Ruth worried the Pope was fixed on planting the largest flag in the Holy Land. "He wants to unite Christians at the Summit, maybe even Jews and Muslims too."

"If that's the goal, the Summit will be a flop."

"Maybe not. You can play a key part."

"How so?" asked a puzzled Archbishop.

"Anglican churches are a mix of Protestantism and Roman Catholic practices. As an Anglican, you are accepted by both the Vatican and Protestants."

The Archbishop agreed. "We are a small denomination. No one will worry that we are forcing ourselves on others."

"During the Summit you can forge consensus when hope appears lost."

Okello ended the call with a prayer for the summit, a meeting improbable only a week ago.

Ruth collapsed on the sofa, too tired to move to the bedroom. She had just lectured the Archbishop of Canterbury in rather grand terms about his mission at the Summit. With that final thought of the day, she sank into a fitful sleep, with intermittent dreams of an ancient castle intruding, doors creaking and the sense that someone or something was lurking, about to pound on her door.

81

ROME & JERUSALEM
Tuesday, May 23

ALESSIO RECOGNIZED the ringtone as he did his late-night stretches after rereading the day's Gospel passage.

"Holy Father," he greeted the caller.

"All is well, but God's call burns in my soul. I could not wait until tomorrow for your update." Pope Sixtus sounded cheerful despite the late hour. "Is there chipa in Jerusalem?"

"You must bring your own. Jerusalem is nothing like Rome," Alessio replied, thinking of the recent attack rather than the cuisine.

"What needs to be done to make the summit a success?"

Pray for a miracle, he wanted to say but stuck to his report.

"We met with Haim Etzion, leader of the Jewish organization 4K that is raising money to build a Third Temple. Evangelical Christians support that because they think it will call Jesus to return. But he is hiding something, I am sure of it."

"What about the Iranian actor, a delegate? Such an odd choice."

"Kosari said he does not know what individuals are behind the March."

"We will pray for guidance." Sixtus seemed to think the solution was that easy. "Where are you going to mass?"

With a start Alessio realized he had not stepped inside a church since his arrival. "I will go tomorrow," he assured Sixtus. "I need the Church's counsel."

"What troubles you?"

"It has been many years since I spent this much time alone outside the Vatican, and this time...."

"Yes?"

Alessio hesitated, uncertain how much to reveal, even to himself. "With a woman."

Sixtus sighed knowingly. "My son, even Our Lord faced temptations. To be sure they don't become actions, arm yourself with counter-thoughts. When a woman's image comes to you, picture her as the Virgin Mary, mother of God. Your thoughts will turn to pure devotion."

"Thank you, Holy Father."

"I understand temptation more than you might expect. I have regrets, things not reported." There was silence before Sixtus continued. "Father, hear my confession. Bless me, for I too have sinned."

Alessio was stunned at this exchange of authority.

"What was your sin?"

"When I was 17, I fathered a child. I have not seen the child or the mother for more than fifty years. I do not know if they are alive. I am ashamed of turning my back on them."

Alessio grappled for what to say to a man he thought of as infallible. He stumbled into the traditional words, "Let us say together the Act of Contrition. 'O my God, I am heartily sorry for having offended Thee, and I detest all my sins, because I dread the loss of Heaven, and the pains of Hell; but most of all because I love Thee, my God, Who art all good and deserving of all my love.'"

"Amen." The Pope disconnected.

Half a century and no reports, no rumors about his own flesh and blood? We are in a fishbowl now. We must be careful.

82

JERUSALEM & VATICAN CITY
Wednesday-Thursday, May 24-25

AFTER A HARROWING TUESDAY Ruth and Alessio hoped for a quiet Wednesday. In the morning they met with the Israeli Deputy Foreign Minister, an expert at asking what the Pope and Archbishop wanted and avoiding any answers about Prime Minister Feldman's intentions.

"We will protect the delegates as surely as we protect our people," he promised.

"What are the odds of war?" Alessio asked, doubting that Israel's people were well protected by Israel's recent bellicose actions against Iran and its burst of settlement expansion.

The Minister minimized any chance of conflict.

"Zero. Outsiders can be easily misled about what is truly going on here."

After lunch, seeking to understand the range of Jewish opinion, Ruth and Alessio spoke with one of Israel's two Chief Rabbis, the one not invited to the summit because of his statements about the need to "purify Israel." With forced cordiality that failed to mask his disdain for Christian meddling, the Sephardic Chief Rabbi claimed that the Israeli Government has broad support in its drive to encourage Palestinians to leave the Land of Israel.

"Their prospects lie outside Israel. It's in everyone's interest. Once the Jewish State is pure, we can live in peace. They can have their Islamic theocracies and we will have our Jewish democracy."

"Some might call this apartheid," Ruth remarked.

The rabbi scowled. "Not at all. Muslims embrace the Qur'an as their civil code and are fulfilled in an Islamic state. We won't bother them if they don't bother us. A recipe for peace."

Alessio tried to schedule a meeting with the priest in charge of the Church of the Holy Sepulchre, where tradition placed Jesus' entombment after crucifixion. As Ruth predicted, there was no one such person. Control of the heavily visited tomb was divided among competing Christian denominations, with keys to the main entrance held by two Muslim families.

They settled on holding separate meetings with the Church's Greek and Russian Orthodox priests. Both were aghast when Alessio floated the idea that the Roman Catholic Church would seek a presence on the Mount.

"There would be war," said the Greek.

"War with whom?" asked Alessio.

"With everyone. You have spent too much time in Rome if you don't see that it would unite Jews, Muslims and non-Roman-Catholic Christians against you," he warned.

Shaken by the hostile reaction to his Church, he turned to Ruth for support, but she kept a blank expression.

As Ruth and Alessio walked toward the Old City's Damascus Gate where the Jeep was parked, children kicked soccer balls against stone steps. Three women dressed from head to toe in black with eye slits the only opening passed to the left of two men in black suits and white shirts wearing shtreimels, round fur hats of Hasidic men.

Street merchants stocked their stalls with images of summit luminaries and competing flags and refrigerator magnets shouting "Shalom!" "salaam," or "Peace"! Dry heat of late afternoon steered most residents indoors until cool evening air would entice a stroll. But soldiers installing security barriers dispelled any image that life was normal here.

Israeli preparations contrasted with accounts Alessio had read of Italian hill towns during the Middle Ages, when news of plague striking one town meant nothing to its neighbors until death crept into theirs on rat feet and the Black Death became the worry of every soul, each praying to escape the reaper's scythe. Still, he doubted that preparations would be enough to deter the apocalypse in which he was beginning to believe.

He looked at Ruth's profile before turning the Jeep's ignition key as she studied the guidebook map for directions to their final meeting of the day with an Arab-Jewish group seeking reconciliation. A curious scholar, yet also a woman who stepped in front of a gun pointed at him. *She did not look like the mother of Jesus.*

On the flight home on the Vatican jet early Thursday morning Ruth and Alessio scanned notes and worked on reports. "Is the Pope fixed on building a Vatican cathedral on the Mount?" Ruth asked.

"The idea did not receive a warm reception here, did it?"

Ruth coughed. "No, it didn't. If that's the only summit topic, there's little point in going ahead with it."

"You know, he is focused on a New Jerusalem. One idea is to make it an open city, like the Vatican."

"Israel won't give up Jerusalem, Alessio," said Ruth, stating it as fact.

When Alessio returned to his room at the Vatican, he found a note from Sixtus asking for an emailed report that afternoon.

Putting off sharing his discouraging findings, he reprised a rigorous 30-minute exercise routine from Army days, then stepped into a long shower to wash away the dust of the holy lands. Facing his deadline, he concluded the report:

"1. It is very unlikely that any delegate will support a Catholic Cathedral on the Mount.

2. Israel will never surrender control of Jerusalem but wants it open to tourists."

3. Israel feels under siege, like a kettle about to boil over. It will do anything to stop Iran from having a nuclear weapon."

Two hours later in the pontiff's private office, Alessio waited for Sixtus to finish reading his report.

"Disarmed two terrorists," read the Pope as he looked up at Alessio.

"We had no choice. I had to protect Mother Waller. I did not look at those men with Christ's love. My prayer to St. Michael was that I take them down."

Sixtus approved. "Archangel Michael leads God's army in the Book of Revelation. Our Lord put to good use your Army and religious training."

"Redemption," Alessio agreed, feeling guilty for omitting the part where Ruth threw herself in front of him.

The Pope unlocked his desk drawer, used by John XXIII in the days of Vatican II. He removed the Fatima File that Alessio recognized by its label. The Pope drummed his fingers on the folder.

"How can I convince delegates that building a Cathedral over the Rock of Abraham is God's will?"

"Not everyone has your vision." *Or embraces the truth of our Church.*

"The Blessed Virgin Mary told humankind here how to prepare for the Apocalypse." The Pope waved the Fatima File.

"Might there be different ways to read the page?" Alessio began tactfully, yet more assertive than he had been with the prior pope. "Forging three into one — that could mean bridging differences among three faiths rather than uniting three branches of Christianity," recalling one of Ruth's alternatives. He left out Ruth's disparagement of the authority a teenage author of the page should hold.

Unmoved, Sixtus continued, "I read what you wrote about where the March is heading — to Megiddo. Fatima instructs that when Armageddon is near, the sanctuary must be built to welcome Christ's return. This is certain."

83

VATICAN CITY
Thursday, May 25

THE BOOK CLUB began arriving around 6 p.m. at the VIP gate to the Vatican Art Galleries, where they were escorted on a half-hour tour that included the Sistine Chapel, then outside onto the grounds of the Papal Gardens, past the Fountain of the Eagle, into the Ethiopian College where a room was arranged in round tables. Alessio greeted each member as seminarians circulated with juice, wine, and antipasti platters. Saudi Grand Mufti Feisal Al Sheikh asked who would be the evening's guest.

"A surprise," replied Alessio.

Ruth was in a spirited discussion with Rabbi Ehhud Krusch, host of the prior gathering.

"Judaism would not rule out that Jesus might turn out to be the Mashiach?" she probed.

"The Mashiach's identity is unknowable," the Rabbi responded with crinkles deepening at the sides of his eyes.

"Ruth, welcome to your first evening as a member. Rabbi Krusch, Shalom."

At that moment entered a Syrian Sunni imam, colleague of the assassinated Imam of the Umayyad Mosque.

He frowned at Rabbi Krusch, ignored Ruth, then turned to declare, "A crime, the murders in Qom. Why does Israel kill innocents with such savagery? Will the mini-drones be unleashed next on Syrians?"

Rabbi Krusch scowled.

"Israel's leader concluded he had no choice. And Syria kills itself. It needs no help from Israel."

Ruth felt a chill snaking through the room. Usually members aimed for diplomacy and understanding, but spreading tension found its target even within the Book Club.

Rabbi Friedman joined Ruth and Rabbi Krusch.

"How was Jerusalem?" he asked.

Ruth reported highlights without mentioning the highway incident.

"An American Evangelical pastor and twelve followers were arrested for proselytizing. They were distributing leaflets that the Rapture will be a week from Saturday, inviting Jews to be baptized and raised into heaven on Judgment Day."

Rabbi Krusch sniffed.

"The Rapture? Sounds like a romantic movie."

Rabbi Friedman explained.

"It refers to dispensationalists. They believe the faithful will be lifted into the sky on the Final Day when others will be left behind with Satan."

"Like the Millerites of the 19th century," Ruth added, "or today's Seventh Day Adventists, who believe the End is at hand, and they will be chosen to be with Jesus."

Alessio clinked his crystal glass with a spoon. After repeating the script used for the start of each Book Club session, he said, "Several of you asked who our guest and what the topic will be tonight. As a departure from protocol, our guest will announce the question."

A door opened and Pope Sixtus entered.

"My friends, I am honored to be with you."

After the first course was served, Alessio stood to begin the discussion, prematurely for the Club, as the custom was to wait until dessert to commence a group dialogue.

"Let's start as the second course is served. Your Holiness."

"Thank you, Father Alessio. My question is this — from your faith perspective, is the End Time near?"

With recent troubles fresh in mind, no explanation was needed for the question's meaning. Eugenia Portman edged out others to respond first.

"The killings in Qom — the mini-drones are the equivalent of locusts unleashed after the fifth trumpet of Revelation. Armies massed along Israel's borders — they match the line-up before the final battle between Christ and Satan."

The Sunni imam spoke next.

"The great March — a sign to all Muslims. Like Shiites, we believe the heroic Mahdi will appear to join with Isa to defeat the forces of darkness. Our Last Day will bring the resurrection of the dead, the judgment of souls and the fulfillment of Allah's plan dividing the sheep from the goats."

Rabbi Krusch offered, "The destruction in Jerusalem. Tragic as it is, this is a sign that the final Temple is about to rise, an ultimate step before the Day of Judgment, some believe."

85-year-old Russian Orthodox Father Sergei Blogadarov added, "The Cold War has returned but with a fever. This time the Great War will not be fought in trenches but with mushroom clouds that obliterate all life. I refer to my Government and yours," he glanced meaningfully at Rabbi Friedman and Ruth.

Rabbi Krusch stood to respond with a cadence like that of an esteemed professor, slow, incisive, facing the Pope.

"Your question is if the End Time is near. If you mean the end of Judaism, then no, it is eternal as is Israel. If you mean time for the judgment of nations, yes, it is."

The Syrian Sunni imam rose and glared at the rabbi.

"Israel attacks our people, kills Muslim scientists, assassinates our imams. Israel will be harshly judged."

Visibly upset, the Sunni Grand Mufti looked directly at the Pope.

"We are enraged by the Dome of the Rock's destruction by Israel. A final battle is coming. We will be judged by how we submit to Allah's call."

Seeking to lower the heat of words, Alessio asked if the newest member of the Club had observations, adding that they had returned from Jerusalem that day.

"As People of the Book," Ruth reminded, "we are three branches of the same tree. We can be physicians for an ailing patient. We must seek an antidote to the venom of violence."

At Ruth's mention of three Alessio glanced at the Pope, who was deep in thought and oblivious to Ruth's comment.

"After so much bitterness, let us turn to something sweeter," said Alessio, signaling for dessert to be served.

Rabbi Krusch turned quietly to the Pope and asked, "Is your sense of an impending Apocalypse why you called this summit?"

The Pope hesitated, then confided, "I have come to believe that these may be Earth's last days."

84

WEST BANK, PALESTINIAN TERRITORIES & JERUSALEM
Week of May 28

ON MONDAY, a teenage suicide bomber prematurely detonated herself near Nablus after stumbling over a rock before reaching the Jewish settlement that was the assigned target.

On Tuesday, a Shiite attack on a Sunni mosque in western Iraq was the only incident reported. Instead of an anticipated uproar over the Dome of the Rock's destruction, there was an eerie stillness like that before a summer thunderstorm, just before leaves begin to quake, skies darken, and a sudden sweep of air warns the animals of the earth to scurry for shelter.

The Vatican released the astonishing list of summit leaders — twelve from government and religion plus the Pope as chairman and the Grand Ayatollah as dual delegates. The announced agenda was "finding a path to peace."

The March reached the Palestinian city of Jenin, northern point of the Palestinian Territories just south of the Israeli border, with a population of 40,000 sustained by a spring. Jenin was under full Palestinian control, but outside the city Israeli security forces roamed at will. Electrified barbed wire demarcated northern Palestinian enclaves from Israel's pre-1967 boundaries, surveilled by air and sporadic ground patrols.

In the nearby Valley of Jezreel, an area of blackish and sandy soil decomposed from volcanic rock, a single security tower guarded the border in the arid expanse between the mountains of Samaria and the Plain of Esdraelon.

The March refueled on Jenin's outskirts and resumed north towards an opening that AM determined was the best opportunity to pierce Israel's 1967 boundaries. An ancient pathway converted into paved road drew the marchers on a slight elevation upward as it headed in the direction of Haifa, reachable in a day's journey on horseback. A mountain pass lay ahead connecting the Jezreel Valley to the coastal plain of Israel.

The March arrived within eyesight of the border fencing in the late afternoon at a distance from an Israeli guard tower. AM officers disabled fencing and opened a gap large enough for the leading edge of the March headed by A'ishah to cross into Israel.

Within seconds, an Israeli convoy broadcast a bullhorn demanding that the March reverse course immediately. Instead, momentum propelled the marchers forward, and the convoy moved to the side while repeating commands that no further incursion will be tolerated. A'ishah responded by holding her right hand upright and halting her mare. By the time the March paused, it was spread wide within Israeli boundaries. As dusk descended, the great March encamped for the night near a road sign that read "Tel Megiddo — 1 km."

Once the guardian city of a trade route between Egypt and Assyria, Megiddo hosted occupations and battles stretching back 10,000 years. An excavation was a minor tourist attraction atop Tel Megiddo, a UNESCO World Heritage Site. It was here in 609 B.C.E. that Judah's King Josiah fell to Egyptian warriors and where Pope Paul VI met Israel's Prime Minister in 1964. A guidebook described Megiddo as the site of the oldest remains of a Christian church in the Holy Land, with a Greek inscription consecrating it in the third century to "the God Jesus Christ."

An Israeli colonel met A'ishah at her tent and issued a stern demand that she turn the March backward the next morning. A'ishah replied quietly that the March must complete its peaceful pilgrimage to Jerusalem.

The colonel glared. "With or without your agreement, you will leave." With a military 180-degree turnabout, he departed.

On the same day Noah Stoll met Haim Etzion on the shaded portico of the East Jerusalem Palestinian-owned Ambassador Hotel in sight of the Temple Mount. Dressed like a western tourist ready for a guided tour through the Old City, Noah was certain no authorities had any interest in eavesdropping on tourists two days before the Summit would make Jerusalem the planet's greatest concentration of global leadership

Stoll and Etzion reviewed the success of their separate web contests that raised awareness of the Third Temple campaign to majestic heights. Financial pledges poured in to build the winning design. They discussed permit applications and other steps needed to create for the third time a Temple on Mount Moriah.

Acknowledging Etzion's gratitude for NJA support, Noah assured him, "Rebuilding the Temple's an imperative for us both. We may differ over whether the Messiah has already visited, but we both believe he is coming soon."

Etzion nodded without comment on what he considered ecumenical palaver about an apocalypse, unwilling to say anything that could jeopardize the NJA's financial support.

Noah added, "We want anonymity. We ask nothing in exchange except success with the Third Temple."

"As you ask, so it will be." Etzion waited for the catch.

Noah spoke as though reading Etzion's mind. "There is a favor you can grant. We'll distribute leaflets about the Third Temple with a Christian view of what it means."

No problem, thought Etzion. "Be careful. Israeli law forbids proselytizing. But we won't object to your fliers."

They reviewed the design for the Third Temple, with its vaulted ceilings, space for a thousand on the ground floor and balcony, protective glass above the Rock in the design of the Star of David, and other features to make it the greatest Judaic architecture of all time.

Noah raised his cup and clinked it against Etzion's, holding now lukewarm dregs. "I'm having a surprise flown in later today — for the cornerstone."

"What?"

"Let's just say it's a souvenir from two thousand years ago, finally coming home."

85

ROME
Thursday, May 31

THE POPE'S ENTOURAGE of seven left early Thursday morning to the private airport where Vatican dignitaries had use of Alitalia jets. Along with his press secretary, social media advisor, Alessio and two cardinals, the Pope brought along the Vatican architect, the chief of a team that controlled design of Roman Catholic churches throughout the world. The plane lifted off as dawn featured skies a shade of pink turning milky white tinged baby blue and brightening into an azure radiance.

On the ground at the edge of the Roman Forum, a guide waiting for a college class visiting Italy was first to call the police.

"*Vieni presto!*" he shouted into his cell phone, "A death!" The operator asked him to calm down, and the guide exclaimed that he stood before the Arch of Titus, the best-preserved ancient monument in Rome. "They killed it!" he cried.

When police arrived, a television crew was broadcasting close-ups of the damaged part of the Arch. An entire section had been removed, as though a laser torch had cut through the two-millennia-old stone and removed several scenes from the Arch's frieze.

A television reporter interviewed the guide.

"Emperor Titus' victories in Jerusalem in the year of our Lord 70 have been stolen," mourned the guide, as though a dear relative had died suddenly.

"What are the missing scenes?" asked the reporter.

"Roman soldiers taking treasures of the Second Temple in Jerusalem. A golden Menorah is lifted above heads of soldiers as they carry it, silver trumpets, Table of Shew bread. Important relics they brought to Rome," explained the guide.

"Who built the Arch?" asked the reporter.

"Emperor Domitian, brother of Titus. He reigned when the Revelation of John was written. He persecuted Jews and Christians to strengthen paganism's grip."

"Who could have done this?" asked the reporter.

The rabbi hosting the Tel Aviv college group provided two guesses.

"A collector? Many great artworks hang in the mansions of drug lords, who hire thieves to do their acquisitions. Or could it be the revenge of an extreme Jewish sect? In the 1500's, Pope Paul IV declared this Arch is where Jews must annually give an oath of submission to the Christian faith, so it became a symbol of humiliation. For centuries Jews of Rome refused to walk under this Arch."

At the same airport where Pope Sixtus departed for Jerusalem, a chartered cargo plane loaded its single shipment. Crated in a large container, with "Fragile" stamped on all sides in Italian, Hebrew and English, the merchandise demanded special care.

86

JERUSALEM
Thursday, May 31

HALF OF ISRAEL'S 10,000 Roman Catholics greeted Sixtus upon arrival in Jerusalem. The Latin Patriarch, Rome's highest official in Jerusalem, and an Israeli security phalanx whisked the Pope through immigration. Seeing a throng of well-wishers, the Pope insisted on being hoisted to the top of the dark blue van that would take him directly to Notre Dame of Jerusalem Center, where he and his colleagues would prepare for the summit set to commence the next day. He waved to the crowd, thanking them through a loudspeaker for their good tidings, asking their prayers for the Church to be a "bridge to peace."

The Pope and Father Alessio shared the van, along with their driver who they assumed was Mossad or Shin Bet. They had twenty minutes to talk privately without fear of listening devices other than the ears of Israel, so they whispered in Italian.

"We'll announce our gift in the first session," said the Pope. "Lead with generosity of spirit," Sixtus continued. "I sense that you fear rejection."

Alessio gazed at the streetscape, mixed with shopkeepers staring at yet another motorcade passing by without purchase, believers waving flags with yellow and white papal insignia, ecstatic women in tears gulping in air as they saw the Pope, bicyclists and pedestrians annoyed by the commotion and intent on getting to appointments on time. He turned directly toward Sixtus and repeated his report's conclusion.

Perhaps this time the Pope would listen.

"Your donation to repair the Mosque will be applauded. But your call to build a second Vatican will be bitterly resisted."

The challenge hardened papal determination. "Fatima demands it. We must build our Basilica over the Rock of Abraham. There's room. You confirmed that."

"Yes, yes, the Mount could fit 21 football fields." Alessio shifted the subject as the Pope waved to a group hoisting rippling Vatican flags. "Holy Father, do you feel bound to follow what a young girl wrote a hundred years ago?"

The Pope answered quickly, "It is God's wisdom we must follow. Was it not a young woman who bore our Lord Jesus Christ? A hundred years are nothing in divine time. We must unite three into one to prepare for the Last Day."

Alessio sat silently, glancing at the crowds lining the streets with a forest of welcome signs mixed with protest banners like "Free the Prisoners!" and "Palestine for Palestinians!" A jumping man screamed "Go Home!"

The Holy Father was fixed on his improbable vision. He was pursuing the impossible — that somehow this gathering would approve a Catholic Basilica on land sacred to Judaism and Islam. This same Holy Father had a child he ignored in his ambition for a life in the Church. His judgment was beginning to seem anything but fallible.

87

JERUSALEM
Thursday, May 31

FELDMAN FUMED at Beit Aghion in Rehavia, the Prime Minister's official residence. Tensions were as high as Mt. Sinai, armies massed along Israel's borders, Russia promising Iran retaliation if Israel attacked the Fordow uranium enrichment facility. The March had penetrated Israel's borders to Feldman's rage. He gave his Defense Minister a choice and an order. The choice was to resign or fire the idiot who let this happen. The order was to evict the March. The Minister's start of an explanation was snuffed by the sweep of a hand and a glare of disgust, as an aide announced that President Palmer had arrived.

Palmer and Friedman embraced each other like cousins at a family wedding, but the mood was more like a wake. Feldman ushered Palmer into his library filled with mementos of Israel's rebirth and growth into a prosperous nation. Color portraits of every Prime Minister lined one wall. Gifts from Harry Truman, Nelson Mandela and other notables filled the shelves.

"Aaron, I don't envy you. My job's impossible, but I don't know how you manage yours," Palmer began.

"With a good shot of my favorite Kentucky bourbon," replied Feldman, not really joking.

"I brought you a case of Woodford Reserve." Palmer gestured to a box his aide deposited on a side table.

"My friend, your support means everything."

"You can count on it," replied Palmer, simultaneously measuring his limits.

"I don't know if you heard, but the March of the Idiots spilled into our territory last night."

"So I was informed. We can't afford to have that go bloody wrong."

Feldman didn't mention his order that authorized any level of force to push the March back into the West Bank. "You've heard Ayatollah Mousavi picked the movie star as the third Iranian delegate."

"What do you make of that?" asked Palmer.

"A diversion." Shifting to his major objective, Feldman said, "I'll tell the Iranians we can't wait longer. We'll strike Saturday unless Iran backs down, as we agreed."

"It has to be stated as an absolute ultimatum," said Palmer. "The Supreme Leader may need to break with his hawkish President if he wants to stop it."

88

JERUSALEM
Thursday, May 31

WITHIN THE CLOSE of St. George's College, the Pilgrim Guesthouse served as Anglican summit headquarters. It hosted Archbishop Okello, Ruth, the Rev. Canon Willis Dickens, and Bishop Archibald McDermott of British Columbia. Canon Dickens would be the Anglican listening post outside the summit tent while the Archbishop, Ruth and Bishop McDermott attended as delegates.

Deep sleep eluded Ruth Thursday night. Anxious thoughts were like drops from a leaky drainpipe. As one dripped away, the mind conjured another. *What if the world really is about to end?* She imagined a parade of Apocalypse horsemen, Satan's legions, beasts numbered 666, her Zoar Village home bursting into flame, fire scorching the earth and sweeping toward Rome where Gabriel whimpered alone, abandoned.

She turned on the light to banish the dread. She had succeeded in her academic career, specializing in global religious mysticism and in a priesthood that had once been a male domain. But the dread of no more days to come stirred other longings. She wanted to be more than a scholar of curiosities. And she did not want to be alone, with no love to say farewell.

Ruth turned off the travel alarm clock a half hour before the scheduled breakfast meeting, took a bracing shower, dressed in clerical garb. The Archbishop, Bishop, Canon, and Ruth met in the parlor over juice, scones, and clotted tea. After a blessing and a minute of silent contemplation that began and ended with the tap of an African bell as was his custom for meetings, Archbishop Okello began with reports for Canon Dickens and Bishop McDermott.

"Ruth advises that the Pope will make astounding proposals tomorrow. He'll call for building a Vatican basilica where the Dome of the Rock stood. And he'll propose making Jerusalem an open city."

With bushy graying eyebrows raised, Bishop McDermott asked, "A Roman Basilica on the Mount? We may as well leave now."

The Archbishop continued, "He told me he'll sell part of the Vatican's art collection to restore the mosque and might even support a new Jewish Temple between it and the Vatican basilica if that'll gain support for his second Vatican."

"Peace, rainbows and butterflies — we'll live happily ever after," muttered Canon Dickens.

The Archbishop gently smiled. "Thank you, Willis, but we can't be silent observers. We have a role in this drama. Ruth?"

"The Pope's inspired by a secret prophecy. From it he believes that the Day of Judgment is near and that he must unite Christianity in Jerusalem before the Second Coming."

"Since when has Rome concerned itself with the Last Days? That's the play stuff of Evangelicals," Canon Dickens said with a belly-laugh.

"It's not a joke," Ruth replied, glancing at the three men.

"Ruth, you're saying the Pope wouldn't mind Armageddon?" asked Bishop McDermott in disbelief.

Ready to sketch thoughts on a pad, the Archbishop turned to Ruth. "What can we do to avert a final battle?"

"We can prepare our challenge to what the Pope takes as a divine command," she replied. "I have some ideas."

A uniformed attendant entered and announced that Father Alessio Brondini had arrived unexpectedly.

"And he is with Pope Sixtus. May I show them in?"

89

NEAR TEL MEGIDDO
Thursday, May 31

THE ARMY OF THE MAHDI ordered the March to push forward, then turn south toward Jerusalem while staying on the Israeli side of the barrier. Vali Qalil assured A'ishah that despite the bullhorn threat, the Israelis would not dare attack a half million unarmed women.

Tents were disassembled and packed, horses and camels fed and watered, breakfast consumed by the throngs of women, children, and a few men, all dressed in white fading to dust brown. A BBC commentator imbedded within the March remarked that A'ishah and her mare evoked Joan of Arc astride a white horse in her ill-fated 1429 campaign. Live coverage focused on A'ishah, cameras alternating between marchers and Israeli military forces that had massed overnight in an inverted V formation blocking the road to Megiddo. Television viewers watched the March head into a wedge with tank turrets pointing at the March.

At the very moment the BBC commentator recalled how Joan of Arc was burned at the stake without seeing France free of the English, his remarks were punctuated by sounds like exploding firecrackers. Shots rang out, seeming to come from inside and outside the March. Cameras panned Israeli forces in firing mode.

Stampede, wailing, screams, camels, and horses turning and falling, a march turned to riot, women twisting in circles, clutching their children and unable to move forward or back. A scattering of men within the March moved to the front, picking up rocks to hurl and being shot in return.

One photographer captured stills showing two males dressed in white pointing what appeared to be AK-47's at the Israeli troops before crumpling to the rocky ground. Photographers scrambled toward the tanks, hoping to capture front page history but escape the fusillade of fire. They were rewarded with images of red bursts on the marchers' white garments. One cameraman snapped a photo of an Israeli soldier shot in the neck, lying face down in the dust, blood irrigating land that had felt no liquid for months, and so it curdled in small gobs on top of sun hardened dirt, an image Israeli newspapers used in color on half their next front pages.

Searing images immediately appeared on websites, YouTube, and TV news throughout the world. A'ishah halted on her mare, while an Israeli bullhorn repeated a terse demand that the March turn back. But the momentum of the March pushed others against her horse, causing it to lurch forward in awkward steps, despite her effort to stay put.

An Associated Press photographer captured a bullet entering A-ishah's left temple, a stain spreading through her hijab until crimson red, as she fell from onto the stones beneath. Marchers were propelled forward, as her body disappeared to be trampled by the multitude in helpless disarray. Unwilling to move sideways in the direction of the firing Israeli troops and unable to move backwards against the inertia of the force behind, the marchers were trapped.

After a minute of horrific carnage relayed in real time to global viewers, the firing abruptly ceased. Tanks and soldiers maintained their V formation, rifles at stiff ease. Women swirled in agony and confusion until the tanks began to rumble forward. Loudspeakers commanded the marchers to turn back to where they had penetrated the fencing. Tanks pushed the uninvited to reverse in the direction of Palestinian Jenin. A baritone Israeli spokesman instructed that the marchers leave the wounded to medics.

The March shifted into neutral, then reverse and moved toward Palestinian controlled territory. Within two hours the entire mass was south of the fencing.

All that was left was human wreckage and its consequences. A'ishah's horse stood guard while her body was lifted into a Red Crescent van.

90

JERUSALEM
Thursday, May 31

PRIME MINISTER FELDMAN got the good news just after President Palmer departed his residence. "March driven south of barrier" read the post on his secure text device. *Good riddance. One less worry before tomorrow.*

His aide inquired if a problem had arisen, observing worry lines on his boss' forehead.

"No. Place a call to President Goudonov. He's at his hotel by now," barked the Prime Minister.

But television screens on silent mode irresistibly drew the eyes of the leader and aide to a banner in red: "Israel kills 100's of Women's March." "Israel Massacres Innocents" blared another. "A'ishah dead — Kosari in Jerusalem" headlined a third.

Scenes of women falling to the ground with red splotches on white clothes flickered in the background, followed by slow-motion still shots of A'ishah, a woman unknown a month before and now known to the world equally with Queen Elizabeth.

As if in a movie, she sat erect on her horse, beautiful in white garments flowing gently with the wind. Then her head abruptly jerked back and to the right, and she fell to be trampled by terrified marchers.

Feldman swung into damage control.

"Forget Goudonov. Get the Defense Minister," he fumed to his aide, who immediately contacted him as well as Mossad Director Siegel, knowing his boss would need him as well. "And issue a release that we fired in self-defense after terrorists started it. Find footage that proves it."

President Palmer was notified in his limousine returning to the fortified American Colony Hotel. Riding with Secretary of State Shulman and an intelligence officer, Palmer groaned when he received an Israeli report that the Muslim March had been disrupted. Israeli intelligence claimed that infiltrators within the March fired on Israeli soldiers. Two Israeli troops were reported killed. Over 750 deaths from within the March were the initial count, with thousands injured, the rest pushed through the border toward Jenin.

"Get me Sullivan," ordered the President. "A call in five minutes in the secure room," referring to specially insulated quarters within the hotel to which the motorcade was returning. "And link the Joint Chiefs." Turning to Shulman, Palmer muttered angrily, "Aaron botched it."

"We knew Feldman would never let the March enter Israel," said Shulman. "This was no surprise."

"So much for the summit." Palmer shook his head in disgust.

President Goudonov had just finished breakfast of smoked salmon, fried egg, and black bread when Iranian President Al-Rabani called to report that Israeli troops had murdered

A'ishah and thousands of marchers. Goudonov slammed his fist on the table, rattling the coffee cup.

"That damn American-Zionist alliance. We stand with you," he assured Al-Rabani.

He called his Defense Minister. "Are the coordinates set?" Assured they were, he instructed, "Red alert." *The Israelis committed an act of war. Now Russia will stand with our allies against the imperialists.*

Palestinian Authority President Abu Arafat recalled how his relative Yasser's spirit had been formed in the crucible of 1948. He was never seduced by mirages like a "summit" or other pseudo-peace tricks intended only to allow the Jews to seize control of more Palestinian land. Yasser had not fallen for the slick charm of President Clinton in 2000. He always put the interests of the Palestinian people ahead of the false siren of what the West called "peace." But Abu's ancestor had not done what needed to be done, to rally Islam to eradicate Israel or at least topple the occupiers of power in Jerusalem. Palestinians had become the lepers of the Muslim world. The Saudis, Qataris, Egyptians, even the Syrians looked down upon them as though they were distant relations no one would invite to dinner.

This time would be different, Abu told himself. *Helpless, unarmed women and children mowed down by Israeli bullets. A holy pilgrimage met by evil.* Arafat trembled with fury. He concentrated as a political chess board unfolded in his mind, with pawns, bishops, rooks, knights, and queens moving about toward checkmate Israel. The sacrifice of the Innocents was the turning point.

Sunni, Shiite, Sufi — none of that mattered now. All Islam would avenge this sacrilege.

From Army of the Mahdi captains imbedded within the March Vali Qalil received a real-time stream of the Massacre of the Innocents, which AM fed to the Iranian media. Once A'ishah's death was confirmed, Qalil sipped his second cup of Turkish coffee, relishing the moment, momentarily regretting the sacrifice of A'ishah he had arranged, with the Israelis doing just what he expected, assisted by a few plants who initiated fire from within. It was destiny. He would be hailed as the Mahdi once the movie star was eliminated. Then the final battle would be won. Yes, the End Times approach, as Allah ordained. Qalil glowed in ecstatic contemplation.

All for you, Allah. Allah be praised, the Compassionate, the Merciful.

91

JERUSALEM
Thursday, May 31

THE ST. GEORGE WAITER CIRCLED with trays of coffee, tea, and sugared biscuits as the Pope and Archbishop of Canterbury discussed with their aides the proposal for a Cathedral on the Mount. Sixtus is hovering miles from reality, Ruth decided, when for the third time he referred to it as a second Vatican and beatifically declared that this would reunite all the faithful under one roof, his roof. She was heartened when the Archbishop pushed back, arguing that this attempt at Roman primacy would destroy any chance of support from other Christians and would offend Jews and Muslims alike.

"An ecumenical spirit is the way forward," coaxed Archbishop Okello.

Before the Pope could try yet again to convince the Anglicans to support a Roman Catholic basilica, the Anglican Bishop of Jerusalem walked into the conference room looking grim.

"There was an attack on the March of the Innocents. A'ishah was killed."

The news hit like a Molotov cocktail thrown through a stained-glass window.

After the Archbishop and Pope led prayers for the dead and for peace in the Holy Land, Okello turned to Sixtus and asked if the summit should be canceled.

The Pope responded emphatically, "No. We must proceed."

The Archbishop sat quietly.

Ruth broke the silence.

"The March was near Megiddo — Armageddon in Greek or English translation, where the Islamic and the Christian final battle of good triumphing over evil is prophesied to be fought."

Ruth decided that the Pope was not used to speaking to ordained women, probably uncertain whether to call Ruth Mother Waller or Rev. Waller or something else. He turned to her and said, "Go on."

Ruth proceeded.

"Islam, Judaism and Christianity all say the world will end in splendor with the

Almighty's reign on earth. In Shi'a Islam Megiddo is where the Mahdi will defeat the Dajjal, fighting side by side with Jesus."

"I think you said this Dajjal is like an AntiChrist figure, and that some Muslims think that Israel's Prime Minister is the Dajjal?" the Archbishop asked.

"Yes, which is why Muslims could interpret Israel's attack on the March as the start of the final battle." Ruth stopped, as the others stared in horror.

Ruth was grateful when Alessio jumped into the conversation. "In the Book of Revelation and in Islam, the triumph over the Dajjal or AntiChrist comes when people realize they were seduced. We must do something to turn the people away from evil to worship the true God."

The Pope tried using a title. "Reverend Waller, Archbishop, the power of revenge is strong. Tomorrow our load is heavier than we imagined. May Mary, blessed Mother of Jesus, give us pure hearts."

The Archbishop walked the Pope to his vehicle arm in arm. After entering the Vatican van with white and yellow flags on each side, Sixtus was uncharacteristically quiet with Alessio.

"My son, we are on the right path."

"No doubt," Alessio answered by rote, though feeling doubt.

He sat in silence for the brief ride to the Vatican compound overlooking the Old City. The world with all its possibilities might be ending. If he had not become a soldier, if he had not killed a child, if he had not turned to the priesthood, what would have been his path?

For the first time it seemed not a sin to think of Ruth. And it was not as Mary.

92

JERUSALEM
Thursday, May 31

Seated in the Persian carpeted lounge of a boutique hotel that catered to ultra-rich sheiks and business titans of the Arab and Iranian worlds, Ruth felt a moment of awe, as though she had suddenly been admitted to an extraordinary elite. She reported to Noah that delegates would attend the first session despite the March tragedy. "None wanted to be seen as first to flee."

The city was on high alert, curfew fixed for 8:00 p.m., with troops in the streets armed to enforce it. Ruth hesitated to ask if Noah's presence meant that the New Jerusalem Alliance was orchestrating another signal of the Apocalypse or something worse.

Noah hesitated, then whispered, "You may find this hard to believe, but it's time you knew. I'm an advisor to President Palmer. I raised a boatload for his campaign and spent time in Ohio marshaling support among Evangelicals, Catholics, Amish, and other believers who put the ticket over the top. Without Ohio's swing votes, he'd be a retired financier."

"What sort of advice do you give him?"

"He calls me his Secretary of Faith. I'm not ordained. He doesn't want to be tied to any one denomination that could be seen as a slight to others. So I'm the President's faith delegate."

Astonished at this lofty revelation from her high school friend, Ruth said, "You're not kidding, are you?"

"Nope. How are preparations going? Is there hope after what happened to the March?"

"Did you have anything to do with this morning?" Ruth avoided answering.

"Heavens no, Ruth. The NJA's non-violent." He leaned back. "The March had to end at some point, and as soon as it crossed into Israel, force was inevitable."

"Israel's attack could unleash an intifada that'll make the prior ones seem like tepid protests. For Shiites this could be a call for the 12th imam to return as the Mahdi for the final battle."

Noah persisted, "Maybe A'ishah's death will prepare the Muslim world for the message of Jesus, the sacrifice of an innocent wiping clean the slate with God."

Ruth considered Noah's Christianizing hope that the Army of the Mahdi could be viewed like the apostles of Jesus — with victory coming from an unexpected source — sacrifice in death, this time through the sacrifice of women. It seemed an unlikely deviation from Islamic prophecies of armed male combat. She looked up as Noah continued.

"We believe the New Jerusalem's within reach. Our job's to proclaim its coming. The Temple's restoration's a step toward what Revelation prescribes. All that's left is the conversion of 144,000 Jews to accept Christ as Savior."

Ruth stood up angrily.

"There was nothing redemptive about this morning's killings. The world's lurching towards a conflict that could end life on earth. No one will be left behind to build a fountain with living waters flowing around your New Jerusalem. You can't be trying to advance that."

Noah stood to face her. "Slow down, Ruth. The NJA has no weapons. The facts aren't our fault."

"I've got to go — the Archbishop. If we get through this weekend, you can buy me dinner in Rome."

"First meet me tonight at 10 o'clock. I'll come to where you are with one other person. It's imperative."

"Noah, I barely have energy for the Archbishop this evening."

"You won't be sorry." Noah held firm.

"Who else would be with us?" Ruth demanded.

"President Palmer."

Ruth's eyes widened at the thought of being in a room with the President of the United States. *Could this get any stranger?*

She composed herself and said, "What about the curfew?"

Noah replied, "Leave that to me. 10 o'clock sharp. We'll be at the front door of St. George. And if anything goes wrong, call me at the American Colony."

Ruth nodded assent, knowing the American Colony Hotel was across the street from St. George. Leaving the lobby, she watched security men opening trunks and rolling detection devices under the Mercedes that pulled up to the semicircular drive at the hotel's entrance.

93

JERUSALEM
Thursday, May 31

JUST BEFORE DUSK and the curfew, a helicopter with Israeli Air Force markings, camouflage green and a white cobra baring its fangs swept through the skies from the suburban base near the Jerusalem northeast settlements. It touched down at the cargo center, where workers strapped a wooden crate to its underbelly, and the chopper lifted into the twilight as Jerusalem's glow merged with a starry canopy.

The helicopter glided over modern cement sections of the city's sprawl and pierced the center zone. The pilot positioned it directly above Mount Moriah, deserted except for security guards and a few workers preparing for the next day. The chopper descended near ruins aside the Foundation Stone, itself undamaged and open to the elements for the first time in 1500 years. Rubble from the Dome of the Rock remained where it fell, as ordered by the Prime Minister to be visual proof of the daily dangers facing the Jewish people.

Thinking a piece of equipment was being delivered for Friday's opening ceremony, the guards gave a thumbs-up to the pilot, who responded with a search light beam marking where he would place his load. The container was gently lowered to a flat area between Solomon's Throne, miraculously undamaged, and the Dome of the Rock's former location, on the edge of the Mount's floor before it opened to the Well of Souls beneath.

The guards ran a detector over and around the container. "Fragile" said the markings. Otherwise it lacked identifying labels except for a stamped import declaration and in bold capital letters — **"FOR SUMMIT — GIFT RETURN FROM PEOPLE OF ROME."** Unconcerned, security forces left it for others to uncrate the next morning.

94

JERUSALEM / WORLD PRESS
Thursday, May 31 / Friday, June 1

WHEN RUTH OPENED THE DOOR to St. George's College seconds before 10 p.m., she saw Noah and President Palmer hustle across the street inside a cordon of black suited men with earpieces. Noah and the President entered alone, leaving a Secret Service perimeter outside. Ruth led them outside to the Biblical Garden, where fig, pomegranate and olive trees lined a path to seats under a Judas Tree and next to Cypress Cedars of Lebanon. Inhaling the delicate bouquet of lavender, sage, and mint adrift in the light evening breeze, she hoped a tree named for the man who betrayed Jesus was not an unlucky spot.

"Noah tells me you're an expert in the end of the world," Palmer stated brusquely. "What do you make of recent events?"

Uncertain whether the President knew the depth of Noah's involvement, Ruth described signals manufactured by the NJA without referencing it and how each was linked to the Book of Revelation. Palmer seemed entranced by her connection of recent omens to Islamic texts about The Hour. His curiosity turned to alarm when she explained how Prime Minister Feldman fit the one-eyed profile of the Dajjal. But Palmer said nothing about Feldman.

He asked her about 4K.

She could not reveal that she'd met with Haim Etzion or that she knew of Noah's connections to 4K. Instead, she explained that destruction of the Dome of the Rock cleared the way for a Jewish Temple. This matched 4K's public statements about a Third Temple and expelling non-Jews from an Israel with Kingdom of David boundaries. She sensed Palmer might share the same view about conversion, as he listened passively. She pressed on.

"There are Christians who share the same vision of an Israel with ancient Davidic boundaries, but for them Jews will become non-Jews when they accept Jesus as Messiah, uniting the Old and New Testaments."

Palmer listened passively. His final question led to a sleepless night. "Reverend Waller, do you believe we are called to hasten the Second Coming?"

Ruth blanched. *Presidential meddling would be far more dangerous than Noah's group dramatics.*

Seeking to deter him, she chose an academic response. "Mr. President, scholars doubt the passage you mention was written by Peter the Apostle, and the wording in some English versions that we should 'hasten' the Second Coming is a poor translation from the Greek. A more accurate translation is to be prepared for the End Time, in the sense that we should always prepare, should always do the work of God."

"We have prepared. We are watchful," Palmer replied impatiently.

With cataclysmic military might at his command, would Palmer expedite the Apocalypse? Would he unleash fire and destruction so a seventh trumpet could sound?

That night dreams did no favor. Tossed by the sea Ruth treaded water while white gulls seemed to cry "Shore, shore!" But there was no land in sight, only the circulating beam of a faraway lighthouse. Gulping water, she bobbed in the waves, uncertain whether to swim for a remote shore or wait for a rescue that might never come.

She arose before dawn as Muslim calls to prayer misted through the City. Web networks offered gloomy predictions about the odds of the summit accomplishing anything. Prime Minister Feldman's statement was brief, "Israel welcomes the world's leaders to our Capital."

The Megiddo Massacre, as it was quickly labeled in most of the world, or the Megiddo Terrorist Attack as Israeli media dubbed it, dominated the headlines. Saudi Arabia's king broke his usual above-the-fray silence to call for "just retribution — swift in impact, merciful in targets." Angry crowds surrounded western embassies in the Arab world. And yet, Jerusalem itself was eerily calm, as though fears and hopes were shuttered. Those with the power to do something were here. Protected by a curfew, with security patrols forming a cordon around the Mount, the summit tent awaited.

95

JERUSALEM
Friday, June 1

AS THE WORLD'S MOST EXCLUSIVE and secretive gathering, the summit admitted no media. Security drones empowered with micro-video surveillance and energized by laser beams maintained constant operation over the Old City.

The summit tent was a technological marvel of water-resistant fabric enclosing a labyrinth of private spaces and two circular areas — one large enough to accommodate all delegates, the other designed for the faith delegates. Unmarked by any religious symbol, the structure allowed Jews to envision it as a tabernacle from the days of Solomon, Muslims to feel as though the great portable tent palaces of ancient Persia and Arabia or the modern tent cities for Hajj pilgrims had arisen from thin air. Christians could picture a Tent of Abraham for biblical nomads, Evangelicals a revival tent. It embraced faiths without reconciling them. White noise was piped in to shield private conversations. An ongoing sweep minimized any threat of eavesdropping.

Alessio, Ruth and Noah nodded to one another as the summit opened. The Pope welcomed by name the leader of each political and religious delegation, followed by opening prayers of the Ashkenazi Chief Rabbi of Israel, the Grand Ayatollah of Iran and the Egyptian Coptic Pope, each expressing faith that the Lord of All would bless the gathering.

All eyes turned to Pope Sixtus. All expected him to list the topics for discussion.

Instead he began, "Among us are those who hold the power to destroy our planet. Signs are clear — the end of the world may approach. And there are active forces who urge this on." He described the litany of recent events that foretold the coming of the Last Days.

Looking around the space, Alessio watched government leaders shift uncomfortably in their seats. He saw President Palmer tapping a navy pen on his pad, President Goudonov scowling, President Arafat glaring at Prime Minister Feldman.

"Our work," the Pope continued, "is to seek a New Jerusalem. I am called in this holy place to offer gifts, a proposal and a prayer."

"First, the Mosque on this Mount needs urgent repair. I pledge substantial funds to begin the reconstruction. We must all join in this," he said rather than asked.

"And I offer that the one true Church will build a cathedral where we sit today. It will invite all Christians and welcome all others to worship God on this sacred Mount. We must build the Basilica of Jerusalem."

Alessio made a note that the Jewish and Muslim faith delegates seemed to freeze in horror. Prime Minister Feldman's frown inverted to a smile when the Pope added, "There is room as well for a Jewish Temple. Our three great faiths can share this ground — three together — one day to be one.

"My proposal," the Pope paused briefly as the delegates stirred uneasily, "is to the leaders of government. I ask you to declare this holy city to be a universal city, open to all, the territory of none. Jerusalem must be a spiritual jurisdiction." Alessio noticed Prime Minister Feldman's dismay and Palestinian President Arafat's delight.

Alessio was relieved when the Pope made his final point.

"And I have a prayer for peace. I pray we find a path to banish weapons of mass destruction from this region." There was nothing to imply it was time for a climactic battle. Sixtus had listened to him. But no smiles emerged among the government delegates, only icy glares.

Preempting immediate reactions, Sixtus asked the faith leaders to meet with him and for the government leaders to consider his remarks and convene in an hour. The six other religious leaders and their confidantes arose to join the Pope, while political leaders dispersed toward their private rooms within the complex.

Alessio observed glum faces. He completed his notes before moving to the faith delegates' enclave.

Not hopeful.

96

JERUSALEM
Friday, June 1

ALESSIO HURRIED to the space reserved for religious delegates. The leaders formed an inner circle, with two deputies each forming a second ring behind, a configuration the Pope had designed. There would be no supreme primate, a stark deviation from Vatican thinking that put the Pope at the center of everything.

"Unity among equals," Sixtus had explained to Alessio who wondered whether any hope for consensus was shattered by the Pope's provocative proposals.

The delegates clutched a sheet of paper summarizing the Pope's requests, some wearing earpieces for simultaneous translation, others trusting their command of the conference language, English.

The Pope's opening was startlingly brief. "Your thoughts, please."

If unity was the invited guest, a different visitor was present. The Russian Patriarch spoke first, raising his thick eyebrows. "Do you seek a monopoly for the Roman Catholic Church in this New Jerusalem you propose?"

Before the Pope could respond, the Coptic Pope of Alexandria, of All Africa and the Holy See of St. Mark aimed words directly at Sixtus. "My Brother in Christ, while it is a noble thought that a Christian presence be added to this sacred Mount, you suggest that the Vatican is the one true Church to build and operate it."

The Pope responded gently, "We can create a community of Christian worship. If the Orthodox and Coptic branches of our faith wish to have chapels within the Basilica, we will make a place." Alessio watched the Patriarch straighten his back and bristle at the idea of the ancient Orthodox Church demoted to a side altar under a Vatican dome.

Israel's Ashkenazi Chief Rabbi expanded the challenge. "If the idea is to diversify worship in this ancient place, there must be a Third Temple."

The Pope replied, "There is space."

Alessio felt the heat rise as the Imam of Mecca's Grand Mosque leaned forward with narrowed eyelids.

"So the idea is to replace the Dome of the Rock with Christian and Jewish structures?

You called us here for this? Richard may be a fabled hero in England, the Lionhearted is it? But in the 1100's he and his Crusaders slaughtered Jews and Muslims alike in this very place. This Noble Sanctuary has been protected for centuries by people of Islam, and it has been open to all. That must continue."

The Pope tried to reassure, "We can work out these details, my Brother."

"How can this be?" thundered the Imam from Mecca. "A church does not belong here. You propose to take control of the Foundation Stone, where the Prophet, peace and blessings be unto him, ascended to Heaven! I suppose you will decorate this Basilica with human images blasphemous to Islam."

Before the Pope could respond, Iran's Grand Ayatollah shifted the deteriorating discussion. "Let me ask about other ideas you suggest," as he held up the draft. "What leads you to think Israel would give up its capital and surrender its nuclear weapons?"

The Ashkenazi Chief Rabbi emitted a guttural sound, and the deputy to the Sephardic Chief Rabbi glowered at the Ayatollah as though punched in the gut.

The Pope looked upward as if seeking guidance. "It is my prayer that if we agree on what our common God calls us to do, our governments will find a path to peace."

The Ayatollah said, "Is today is the first time you have shared these proposals with government delegates?"

The Pope nodded, "Yes."

After brief silence, the Ashkenazi Chief Rabbi of Israel said, "Any redesign of this area must include a presence welcoming to Jews, Christians and Muslims. My Government supports restoring the Further Mosque. But what to do above the Foundation Stone, where the Dome of the Rock and the First and Second Temples once stood? Definitely not a church. We should study what can be built where."

Alessio sensed the Holy Father's distress that the Summit's outcome might be an interminable task force. Alessio willed the Archbishop to enter the conversation with a moderating influence, as he had urged Ruth to manage. And as if in answer to prayer, Okello's calm voice filled the space.

"Like each of you, I know persecution firsthand. My father's church in Uganda was burned to the ground by a mob bearing the banner of the Prophet. And I saw in retaliation the desecration of a mosque by those claiming to follow Jesus. Violence is never worship.

"I agree with the Ayatollah that our discussions mean little if governments do not embrace the spirit of Pope Sixtus' proposals and shape them in a positive direction. I suggest we allow him and the Ayatollah to convene the political session while the rest of us consider what can be done on this Mount."

With this welcome intervention, Sixtus concluded the initial faith session.

"Let's see where we are in an hour." He arose, and with the Ayatollah he moved to the larger space where grumbling, astonished heads of state were waiting.

97

WEST BANK, PALESTINIAN TERRITORIES
Friday, June 1

AS THE SUMMIT OPENED, Arab and Iranian television coverage centered on an open hearse speeding toward Damascus. It carried the body of A'ishah, shrouded in a kafan, five wrappings of pure white cotton. Women, men and children lined the roadways, beating their chests, wailing, wringing hands, enraged by the loss of a woman unknown a month ago, now mourned as martyred daughter of Islam.

Handwritten placards waved "Death to the Infidels!" — "Israel — Revenge!" — "Dajjal Feldman." "Death to America" and "Avenge!" shouted scattered signs along the route to Damascus.

More numerous were stenciled posters on sticks saying "Mahdi — Return," "The End is near", "Death to the Dajjal" and "Isa — Come." A few read, "Mahdi Kosari — Lead us!"

With a news blackout at the Summit and no leaks occurring, CNN captured the swollen anger of the streets. It ran an interview with an Oxford Seminary Dean, who explained the Mahdi, Dajjal and Isa links to apocalyptic Islamic views. Viewers were shocked to learn that the Mahdi's ally would be none other than Jesus. But the Dean's interview was broadcast only once, in the middle of the night.

Israeli Army units stationed in the northern West Bank were ordered to bolster defenses along Israel's fenced and walled borders, forming an impenetrable barrier to any encroachment on the most populous Israeli lands. This left settler communities virtually undefended. Israeli intelligence tracked troops massed along the Lebanese, Syrian, Jordanian and Egyptian Sinai borders, one report predicting "Attack imminent. Haifa could be overrun in a day."

Aided by a flock of U.S.-supplied drones, Israeli reconnaissance revealed the transfer of three fourths of Iran's air power to its western border, the other quarter stationed at Iraqi air bases on the same airstrips that decades earlier hosted planes attacking Iran during the Iraq/Iran War that took millions of lives. A classified CIA report summarized, "Islamic forces unite as never before since the battle at Karbala in 680 split Islam in two."

A U.S. naval build-up in the eastern Mediterranean ordered by Palmer the week he became President was boosted to maximum strength of carriers, submarines, and other craft. An American request to position forces in Turkey's southeastern Kurdish region was rebuffed by its Islamist president, interpreted by the U.S. Director of National Intelligence to mean that Turkey's leadership too had fallen under the spell of solidarity with Islam because of the martyred March. Battle-ready conventional ground, naval and air forces were at levels unseen since 1944 Europe.

AM leader Vali Qalil directed the March from his hiding place between Iraq and Iran, steering it south toward Jerusalem. AM lieutenants struggled to impose a semblance of order on the chaos that followed Israel's repulse of the marchers from Megiddo. Doctors without Borders rushed to the scene physicians from eighteen countries. An outpouring of support revived the spirits of the remaining pilgrims, estimated at a half million. Imams and other clerics left their mosques to join the March as it aimed at Jerusalem through a different route within Palestinian controlled territory. A Syrian Sunni imam issued a fatwa against Prime Minister Feldman, explicitly branding him the Dajjal.

AM issued a stern web-message, calling on the faithful to prepare for a final battle. AM video clips shown to the marchers featured a tribute to A'ishah by Navid Kosari the night before the Summit opened, sitting on his white mare in Jerusalem, posed with the Noble Sanctuary in the background absent the Dome of the Rock that had been its apex for 13 centuries. Kosari lamented A'ishah's martyrdom:

"Our March and her sacrifice are for a reason. We have revealed the false Dajjal and his unrighteous armies. Our Innocents are a greater power than all the rifles and ammunition he can muster. The Word is our weapon, unshakable and divine. In this final battle you are the elect. Come, join me in Jerusalem. It is a Night Journey to create a New Jerusalem, following the path set by the Prophet, may peace and blessings be his."

As the March targeted Jerusalem, Qalil envisioned the glorious End Time. The people would see him as the Mahdi, he who sacrificed the beloved A'ishah to the glory of Allah.

First, he must eliminate the listless Ayatollah and leave evidence that blames President Al-Rabani.

Next will be the movie star.

Then Vali Qalil will take his rightful place as hero of the new age.

His will be the victory. His will be the glory. For the glory of Allah.

98

WEST JERUSALEM
Friday, June 1

The cell phone blackout on the Mount made delegates fidget in collective withdrawal from a digital drug. The absence of instant reports transformed summit existence into a cloistered life.

President Palmer, Secretary of State Shulman and Noah Stoll left their private huddle room and wandered outside the tent, waiting for the religious delegates to conclude their session. They examined the Foundation Stone, exposed to the skies for the first time in fourteen centuries, a karst limestone slab with markings sacred to Jews and Muslims and an opening to a lower cavern at its southeastern edge.

Palmer shook his head in disbelief. "Jerusalem as a political no-man's land? The UN can't manage itself, much less a city of a million."

Shulman deliberated. "Think of this as a chessboard. You can sacrifice a pawn to the Pope by proposing a 3-religion guard protecting this Mount instead of the Jordanians."

Palmer turned to Noah. "The Pope endorses a Third Temple. What does my Secretary of Faith say?"

Noah's right hand was divided between thumb and fingers slowly stroking from cheek to chin. Before he could respond, Palmer turned back to a disquieted Shulman.

"A friend of Noah's is here, an American woman advising the Archbishop of Canterbury. She's a scholar of the Apocalypse. She thinks some delegates want to bring on war as a purifying fire."

Shulman sneered. "Religion yet again threatens sensible policy."

Noah countered, "God works in mysterious ways."

Palmer put his hands on their shoulders to defuse the tension. "The Lord wants the best for the United States. Noah, see from your friend what the prelates decided."

As Noah left to find Ruth, Palmer said quietly to Shulman, "Don't worry. If there's to be a New Jerusalem, we're best off watching it bloom from Washington. How quickly can we get to Air Force One?"

99

WEST JERUSALEM
Friday, June 1

NOAH PULLED OUT A PAIR of dark wire-rimmed sunglasses against the late morning glare as he searched for Ruth. Gray tombs along the slope of the Kidron Valley ascending to the Mount of Olives seemed ready to release their souls for judgment, he thought. Bullhorn voices from Arab dwellings to the east disrupted his trance. He watched Israeli troops in the distance push back a clutch of Arab youngsters next to the graveyard who were throwing rocks uselessly in the Mount's direction.

Spotting Ruth, Noah rushed to ask for an update on the faith leaders' discussion. "There was an uproar against injecting a Vatican cathedral onto Jerusalem's prime acreage," Ruth summarized.

"Do the faith delegates realize the Apocalypse is knocking on the door?"

"There are some who agree with you. Some Jews believe a Third Temple must be built to summon the Mashiach, the true king to be anointed at the End Time. Is this important to President Palmer?"

Noah replied, "If he thought his actions could bring about a New Jerusalem as the apostle John foresaw it, he would advance it."

Ruth stared at Noah. "We keep coming back to this. It's not for you or the President to play God."

"Second Peter says, 'The day of the Lord will come like a thief, and then the heavens will pass away with a loud noise, and the elements will be dissolved with fire, and the earth and everything that is done on it will be disclosed.' We can't wait like dumb creatures, Ruth. Peter calls us to be '**hastening** the coming of the day of God.'"

"I explained to you yesterday that "hastening" is a mistranslation." Clearly Noah was not moved by scholarship, so she tried a different approach. "Then remember the end of those verses: 'Therefore, beloved, while you are waiting for these things, strive to be found by him at peace, without spot or blemish; and regard the patience of our Lord as salvation.' At peace, Noah, not war."

"As Luke told us in his Gospel, Jesus said, 'I came to bring fire to the earth, and how

I wish it were already kindled.' Think of the NJA as providing the kindling."

"What you're doing is more like arson." Ruth hoped her words struck a target in this battle of cherry-picked Bible verses. Seeing the Archbishop raise his right hand in her direction, she started walking toward him after casting her last rebuke. "President Palmer can serve his God and his country if he finds a way to avoid a cataclysm, not if he brings it on."

Noah walked in the opposite direction toward the hole opened by the Dome's destruction. He tapped the upper right lens of his sunglasses, turning on the nano-microphone imbedded within that linked him with the leader of 4K.

"Haim, the Summit may not last through Sunday. If Israel strikes Iran, a war starts and everyone heads out of here. Palmer can support the Third Temple if other pieces fall in place. No matter what, the NJA will stick with our mission."

"We won't interfere with your leaflets," said Etzion, apparently unconcerned about the imminence of war or the likely collapse of the Summit.

Etzion disconnected and marveled how destiny was unfolding as 4K planned. Having Palmer and Feldman in Jerusalem would help get the Third Temple under way and blunt the swell of global sympathy in the wake of Megiddo.

He made a call, "Etzion here. I have another job, in addition to the restaurant. That's set for tomorrow, right?"

"Yes sir," said the assassin. "The new one?"

"Air Force 1 and its decoy are at the northern military base. Destroy both. And pin the blame on Hezbollah."

100

WEST JERUSALEM
Friday, June 1

AFTER HEARING NOAH'S BRIEF REPORT on the faith leaders' session, Palmer met alone with Feldman before joining the opening session of government leaders. Secretary Shulman and Israel's Defense Minister stood guard at the entrance to the Israeli space, quietly discussing Islamic forces massed along Israel's borders.

"We're ready to strike Fordow," said Feldman.

"Not today I trust. Wait 'til I get back to Washington." Palmer forced himself to add, "And who knows, maybe we can get something positive out of this."

"The enemy wouldn't dare invade while you and the others are here. We can defend a conventional attack. It's a nuclear Iran we can't risk."

"We have your back," Palmer assured.

"We've told the Egyptians and Syrians — one step into Israel and we'll obliterate their capitals. We've said the same to Kosari — we'll hit Tehran if Iran touches our soil."

Palmer returned to his first comment. "You'll hold off today, right?"

"Okay, the Pope bought them a 24-hour reprieve."

"What's your position on the Vatican coming to your town?"

Feldman spit out a laugh. "Suddenly this is the most valuable real estate on the planet. Maybe we'll have an auction. Seriously, we're going to rebuild the Temple. I'll need to figure out whether what the Pope wants could fit between a refurbished mosque and the Third Temple. Not a bad idea really. Good for tourism. Can you believe it, Ike?" Feldman's eyes misted. "The Temple rebuilt on our watch."

"Under your leadership," the President flattered. "Let's see if we can make it part of a deal." He imagined the ease of being elected in his own right after this achievement.

A clang of baritone bells signaled the conference would resume. On the way Palmer met Noah, and they entered the assembly together.

"We're getting close," he said to Noah.

Palmer thought, *Common sense tells me to get out of here. But maybe this will be the End after all. If so, better to be here, here to meet our Savior when He comes in glory.*

101

WEST JERUSALEM
Friday, June 1

The Pope swept into the grand assembly space with his hallmark broad smile amidst an assembly of stern expressions. Heads of state were seated except for Palmer and Feldman, who joined minutes later. Sixtus invited Feldman to open the initial government session.

"Pope Sixtus, honored guests, thank you for visiting our capital, our Jerusalem."

Palestinian Authority President Arafat coughed and crossed his arms, refusing to inhale a mention of Israel's claim to the city.

Facing the Pope, Feldman continued, "Israel wants peace with our neighbors, but some deny our right to exist. Unless that changes, our discussions will be futile. And — Jerusalem is an open city — just look around you."

Glaring at Feldman as though slapped in the face, Palestinian Authority President Arafat snapped, "This from a man who expels my people from our homeland. If the Prime Minister had begun by pledging that Jerusalem welcomes all to live and visit, we might have something to discuss. But to start by declaring Jerusalem belongs to Israel ... is, is ... preposterous."

Russian President Goudonov nodded vigorously. "Israel should heed the Pope's prayer — surrender its nuclear arsenal to free this region of weapons of mass destruction."

Not used to the sidelines, Palmer spoke.

"Let's not recite the same old lines. We can start with Iran pledging here and now that it will stop its drive to acquire a nuclear weapon and open itself to immediate inspections."

President Al-Rabani of Iran jumped from his seat behind his Supreme Leader and shouted, "The only country in this region that has a nuclear bomb is Israel. And now it threatens us after murdering our scientists and innocent marchers! Iran will defend itself."

The Grand Ayatollah sat impassively while Al-Rabani fumed red-faced. The Ayatollah asked, "May we have a recess?"

102

JERUSALEM
Friday, June 1

Goudonov used the break to confer with Russia's allies, the Presidents of Iran, Egypt, and the Palestinian Authority.

"Palmer's trying to look like the forceful leader," Goudonov assured the three.

"American politics depend so much on sound bites," he added contemptuously. Turning to Iran's President, he asked directly, "But — why build a nuclear weapon? A strike on Iran is a strike on Russia. We will defend you."

The Iranian President answered smoothly, "We welcome your pledge. But understand — we are an ancient and proud nation."

Arafat exploded. "Feldman blows up the Dome of the Rock, and suddenly his friend the Pope wants to move his headquarters here? The last time Christians conquered Jerusalem, they put Muslim heads on pikes."

Sitting on either side of his fellow Muslims, Egypt's President motioned to each.

"We stand with you. As does President Goudonov. But let's be smart. The Pope proposes that Israel relinquish control of Jerusalem. Let's push for that. If the price is a new building within the Noble Sanctuary, we can live with that."

Goudonov nodded, "I'll strengthen our hand."

103

JERUSALEM
Friday, June 1

Troubled that Goudonov was walking with an arm around Egyptian President Modri, Palmer cast an eye toward Feldman, who jerked his head to the right to signal a meeting in Israel's huddle room. Palmer dispatched Noah to fetch the woman priest, her name forgotten. Perhaps Palmer and his predecessor erred in suspending the billion dollars of U.S. aid to Egypt, leaving a vacuum Russia promptly filled. But the action was coupled with congressional approval of a formal alliance with Israel, one that gave Palmer a blank check to protect it.

Palmer and Shulman joined the Israeli delegates.

"Israel's not giving up our trump cards," Feldman told Palmer before they sat.

"I don't expect you to," said Palmer. "But what's the harm in dialogue about a world free of nuclear weapons, something far in the future, subject to conditions that will never be met? That was Reagan's ploy during the Cold War."

"That's not on the table," argued Feldman. "Look, it's time to strike Fordow. We know the scientist who survived is working 24/7. I'm giving the green light tonight for act two of Operation Meteor."

"Your call, Aaron. But I wish you'd wait until I'm back home. You can say it was done to further the Pope's goal of stopping the spread of nuclear weapons. On this universal city nonsense — what about a UN presence here? Jerusalem remains Israel's capital but gets protection from a UN peacekeeping force. What better security for Jerusalem than being everyone's city?"

"Including Arafat's capital? Not a chance, Ike. The UN bullies us every time it can."

Palmer did not disagree. "Look, I'll tell Goudonov that a strike on Fordow can buy time to ensure Iran doesn't go nuclear. I'll add that it's not in Russia's interest to retaliate because that would obligate me to hit Russia in response."

"The Rev. Dr. Ruth Waller," Noah announced, entering the space with Ruth. "Deputy to the Archbishop of Canterbury," he explained to Feldman, who was startled to see a woman wearing a clerical color at an event convened by the Vatican.

Palmer asked, "Reverend Waller, would Protestants support a Vatican cathedral on the Mount, a universal Jerusalem and action to stop Iran from getting the bomb?"

Ruth stifled a gasp at the ease of his proposed use of force. "Mr. President, if the idea is to have an ecumenical presence here, and if Jerusalem becomes a center of peace rather than the cradle of war, Protestants should look favorably on both." She ignored the last item.

"Then ask the Archbishop to support the Pope's proposals, including a Jewish temple on the Mount. A nuclear-free zone will take work and shouldn't hold up those steps." Palmer kept his eyes on Ruth as though demanding a "Yes Sir."

Instead he received, "I will convey your message. Anything else?"

"Prayer," said Palmer.

Bowing her head, she prayed, "O God, creator of all, we confess our sin of worshipping violence and pray for guidance on a path to peace."

Feldman retorted, "Peace comes from strength and sacrifice, Reverend Waller. It is built on the bones of heroes."

"Thanks to Judaism, human sacrifice ended for People of the Book when God released Abraham from killing Isaac," she replied, hands shaking slightly from lecturing the leader of Israel.

Noah grasped Ruth's arm and moved toward the exit, saying quietly, "Let me know the Archbishop's position and I'll convey it."

Once in the corridor Ruth whispered to Noah, "God help us if they start a war."

"They can't allow Iran to acquire a nuclear weapon."

"So bombing Iran will make peace, is that it?" Ruth said incredulously. "Russia will bow down and Muslims'll take up the cross?"

"Palmer and Feldman are consummate politicians. They're probably negotiating through back channels. Let's talk of something more pleasant, like dinner with you in Rome when this is over, like old times in Zoar."

Ruth laughed harshly at his attempted diversion. "Sleepy Zoar was nothing like this."

"Here we are together in Jerusalem instead," Noah coaxed.

Ruth looked across the spires of the Old City, sympathizing with their reach for heaven like hands beseeching the skies for deliverance.

She walked to the Archbishop's huddle room without looking back. The biblical Noah dutifully built an ark according to God's instructions when the heavens opened to drench the Earth. The Noah she knew now seemed untroubled that soon the skies would rain fire and there was no flameproof ark.

104

JERUSALEM
Friday, June 1

WHEN RUTH RETURNED to the Anglican delegation's space, she found Alessio and the cardinal from Venice hotly insisting on a second Vatican Basilica with the Archbishop and Bishop McDermott. She heard Bishop McDermott say, "only if it's for all Christians."

The cardinal parried without acknowledging Ruth.

"We are the majority. We want this structure to unite Christians within the one church God calls us to be. It can have chapels for other denominations." He unfurled a drawing by the Vatican Architect showing three chapels scripted as Russian Orthodox, Coptic and Anglican.

The Archbishop frowned, a departure from his usual disposition. "We are here to find unity among all People of the Book. Casting other denominations to the sidelines is not in that spirit. Surely Pope Sixtus is open to a structure expressing all Christendom."

"The Vatican welcomes millions every year to St. Peter's. We will do the same here."

"But," said Bishop McDermott, "women — half of humanity — cannot be priests by your doctrine. You brand ten percent of humanity as inveterate sinners by their sexual preference. You prohibit your members from taking communion from our priests."

Alessio frowned at this attack on his church. He glanced at Ruth, gestured an arc upward with his eyes toward the door. Without a word they went into the hallway.

"It's going nowhere." Alessio was grateful for a chance to debrief with her.

"Not if the Pope sees Christianity as his domain alone."

"We must find a way forward."

"Alessio, we have a deeper problem than putting words on a page. I'm worried Israel's going to strike Iran while we're here, with U.S. support."

"That would be a disaster," Alessio replied, eyes widened. "Surely the USA does not want another war in this part of the world."

"President Palmer believes Israel has a right to strike Iran preemptively. And if war erupts, he's not afraid of the Apocalypse."

"Does he plan to be whisked to heaven as he blows up the planet?"

"I don't know what to predict."

"It's not like you to be uncertain," said Alessio.

"Then you don't know me very well. I study religious matters. I can't forecast how leaders will act."

"The world's fate depends on what people will do in the name of God."

"Look — you need to get Sixtus to give up his Fatima obsession."

Alessio paused. Was it for him to question his superior, to challenge the Holy Father? This had been unthinkable, before he met Ruth. *But now?*

105

JERUSALEM
Friday, June 1

ALESSIO FINISHED notes of the government session with "no hope." The weight of history crushed any breakthrough on the idea of Jerusalem as a universal city or banishing nuclear weapons from the region. Each leader claimed the high ground and blamed others for recent violence. Only EU President Schmidt seemed to express hope that the Summit could succeed.

After adjourning the session and urging that progress be made through individual negotiations, an unusually grim Sixtus learned from Alessio that Israel and the United States might be planning an attack on Iran during the summit. Sixtus immediately sought out President Palmer for a one-on-one talk, but Palmer was with Noah and insisted discussion include him. Sixtus asked Alessio to remain for the conversation.

"Mr. President," the Pope said, "a cathedral here will be a home for all Christians. Can you support my first proposal?"

Noah knew Palmer had neither the desire to debate religion with a pope nor to be open to a charge from Evangelicals that he backed a Vatican monopoly on Jerusalem's Mount. He'd prepared Palmer for this.

The President replied, "Your Holiness, you have ventured where none has dared, and for that I thank you. America will accept a consensus but can't take sides in matters of religion."

Noah nodded silently.

"But Mr. President," the Pope persisted, "Your influence can be decisive."

"We separate church and state."

Noah knew otherwise, at least with this President.

"And the other two proposals. How can we make progress?"

"A world free of weapons of mass destruction — a noble aspiration. Let's recast it that way, as an aspiration. As for Jerusalem, what if we build toward your vision by starting with a United Nations peacekeeping presence here?"

"We are agreed that no aggressive action will occur while we are here, yes?"

"I can't speak for others." Palmer closed his lips tight and straight across.

"Then the Final Day draws close," said Sixtus.

As an Iranian delegate, Navid Kosari had no speaking role and had said nothing privately to anyone since broadcasting his eulogy for A'ishah and the call for the March to head to Jerusalem. He burned inside from Megiddo. Had his incessant thirst for fame made the March a tragic target? Feeling survivor's guilt, he sought wisdom from the Grand Ayatollah.

"What is your wish of us? Shall we end the March now? Before we get too close to Jerusalem to turn back? Declare our mission accomplished?"

"Navid, those who march must not think they are pilgrims without purpose. Their sacrifice won the Battle of Megiddo. They revealed the Dajjal for what it is."

"What?" Kosari said, looking as though he had forgotten a line in a script. "I did not see the Dajjal, or I would have cut him down myself with a sword," as he made a twisting slashing motion with his right arm, mastered by rehearsing for the Saladin film.

"My son, the Dajjal is no person. It is the mirage of military might. This is what struck at Megiddo. The marchers defeated the Dajjal by sacrifice. You emerged as the Mahdi."

"Me, the Mahdi?" gasped Kosari, off script this time with no expression he could summon from prior roles.

"You are what the texts describe. Your white mare, your appearance. I do not anoint you, as only Allah can do that. But our people feel this. You must accept your destiny as The Hour approaches."

Kosari relaxed his shoulders and straightened his back, relieved there was a grand plan in place. He would star in a script of momentous consequence. He began to formulate how the Mahdi behaves, what posture, what gestures. He stretched out his fingers.

The Ayatollah continued, "The March must proceed to this City. Do not relent. But tell me, why Jerusalem? How did you decide this?"

"I thought the order came from you, from AM."

"I do not direct AM. I don't know who does. Do you?"

Kosari was startled, "The communications always came through A'ishah, until yesterday when I received a script for my broadcast."

The Ayatollah patted Kosari's right arm. "Do not fear, Navid Kosari. All has a reason. Jerusalem is the end of the pilgrimage. We must bring about the reign of the righteous." The Ayatollah gazed above Kosari as though speaking to a higher power in the distance. "Go to the March. Guide it here tomorrow. I will meet you at the Qalandia Gate."

The six Israeli delegates met at the request of the Ashkenazi Chief Rabbi, who opened the huddle by asking the Prime Minister for his conclusion about building a Catholic church and a Third Temple on the Mount. For decades the Rabbi embraced the official position of all past Chief Rabbis that the Temple was spiritual not physical. Until now.

Feldman responded, "We can make room for a Christian church here if we get a Third Temple. Let the Christians work out their squabbles."

The other delegates said nothing, and so the Israeli position was unanimous on the Pope's first proposal. The rabbi turned to temporal concerns. "Will you strike Iran?"

"As necessary, Rabbi," said Feldman.

"During this conference?" pressed the rabbi.

Feldman hesitated, virtually signaling the answer, then openly admitted, "More delay risks too much."

"I cannot bless this aggression — and to do it now...."

Feldman gazed into the rabbi's eyes and said in a slow same-pitch cadence, "Do you wait until the adder strikes to defang it?"

106

JERUSALEM
Friday, June 1

ALESSIO PROBED for progress among delegates but found roiling anger. Fearing a plenary session could end in a walk-out, the Pope urged delegates to continue private talks and announced there would be a break at 4 p.m. before returning for a 7 p.m. dinner. "Our discussions remain secret," he stressed.

Military escorts shielded them from the media and crowds cordoned off from a perimeter around the Mount. A press of pilgrims, millennialists, protesters, demonstrators, monks and the curious, as well as pickpockets, encircled the security force.

A cacophony of chanting, shouting, and singing accompanied signs ranging from "The End is Near — Repent" to "Out of Israel Now" to "Out of Palestine Now" to "Holy Feast for Pilgrims — call 0854 1244." Twelve young men dressed in flowing white robes and dragging 12-foot wooden crosses encountered dervishes whirling in delirium near the Western Wall, where Orthodox Jews who claimed it as their domain enjoyed single-file access to the Wall through metal detectors.

Journalists were frustrated. Efforts to squeeze information from media aides for the delegates drew blanks as they were equally stymied in learning what was happening. Tweets and blogs speculating that the Pope had predicted a Second Coming morphed into a frenzy of writings about the End Time. American groups clogging area hotels were interviewed sitting in lounge chairs on rooftops ready for the Rapture. One pre-Rapture gathering uphill from the Mount sang "Nearer My God to Thee" over and over, accompanied by moog synthesizer.

The apocalyptic fervor, layered with international threats and the Holy Father's rigid interpretation of the Fatima secret, plunged Alessio into unfamiliar despair. He exited the summit tent to check the security of the path the Pope would take to descend from the Mount to a Vatican convoy for a brief respite at the Notre Dame of Jerusalem complex.

Retrieving his iPhone at the exit, he connected with news reports and winced reading of an attack that morning on an Israeli village near the Gaza buffer zone, killing a family of seven and injuring dozens in the collapse of an apartment building. He scrolled through the next item about a bomb that fell on a Gaza school next to a mosque, though according to Israeli sources it was a Hamas ammunition depot. There was a photo of a weeping grandfather holding the remnants of his granddaughter's pink backpack, the leveled mosque's minaret tilting in the background. A chronic cycle of violence, one atrocity demanding the next revenge in the name of God who created all.

Alessio shuddered in memory of his own moment as killer soldier, then straightened his shoulders in recognition that this was why he was here now, with a Pope committed to reverse the spiral of hate. He was a protector again. This time there would be no mistake.

As he returned to the Summit guard post that kept delegates' communication devices in a secure holding station, he read a British news report about the March of Innocents moving south.

The Oxford commentator explained, "Islamic visions of the Apocalypse are not that different from Christian expressions. The Book of Revelation predicts that Christ will return to vanquish an unleashed Satan. The Shiite Muslim version is the same, except that it foresees a figure called the Mahdi joining Jesus to defeat the devil, in Arabic the Dajjal. The names change but the core idea's the same."

A leaflet shaped in a synagogue silhouette fluttered to his feet. It proclaimed the Third Temple was ready for construction.

"Permits to be issued soon," it claimed. "With your help, the Land of Israel will again have its Temple." A website listing 4K as sponsor sought donations, followed by a postscript with a biblical reference from the prophet Isaiah, "The cornerstone has been laid."

The Pope and the Cardinal met Alessio at the summit exit to hurry to a waiting van through a corridor of Israeli soldiers shielding them from public view. "Holiness, you should see this," handing him the leaflet.

107

THE OLD CITY, JERUSALEM
Friday, June 1

FOR THE LATE AFTERNOON recess Palmer, Shulman and Noah were escorted by machine-gun toting soldiers in black riot gear to a conference room within the Western Wall Tunnels Museum. The Secret Service cleared the space as a more secure alternative than shuttling between the Mount and the American Colony Hotel. The agents' caution prompted Palmer to revisit with Stoll and Shulman whether to depart immediately for Washington.

"Israel's strike could moot the Summit." His fingers combed through his hair three times, his habit in times of stress. "But I can't be viewed as a coward, turning my back on a pope."

"You're meant to be here for what could be the greatest moment in history," Noah urged.

"Convince Feldman to wait until Monday," Shulman advised.

"He's certain the Iranians are ready to test any day and then it'll be too late," said Palmer. "The strike's tomorrow."

"If all hell breaks loose, we can manage our response from here," said Shulman. "Americans will rally to Israel. If we can get the Iranians to agree to a nuclear-free zone with real inspections, you're a hero. If they refuse, you'll be seen as having tried everything you could and proven right about having no alternative. Either way, you win."

"And if this world ends, what better place to be than here," added Noah.

Again, Shulman stared at Noah as though he was from some other world.

Palmer decided. "We can get to Air Force One in 20 minutes. We'll stay for now."

Just before 7:00 delegates returned to the Mount. Alessio kept count at the entrance for Sixtus, who worried some may flee. The Pope was determined that the Vatican basilica would be built, whatever it took. When Alessio summoned his nerve to ask whether an ecumenical design would be better, the Pope replied flatly "No."

Alessio watched a full moon rise to hover just above the Mount of Olives as a blood orange orb. Accompanying a spectacular moonrise were muezzin-like cantors beckoning in Hebrew from six loudspeakers pointed at the Mount, directing delegates to look toward the southern edge of where the Dome of the Rock once stood as the City's postcard picture.

The tenor chorus was not a Muslim call to *Isha salah*, evening prayer, but a Hebrew summons to the unveiling of an object shrouded in the deepening dusk. Word spread among the delegates that they should gather where laser beams pointed at an object covered with a golden sheet.

The cloth veiled a rectangular form. An invisible thread lifted it to reveal, glistening in the spotlight, a weathered, sculpted slab of white marble — the chunk from the Arch of Titus that had been chiseled and removed from Rome. Now here it lay near the Rock held sacred by Jews, Christians and Muslims alike — the foundation stone where Jews and Christians believed Abraham prepared to slay his son Isaac in obedience to his God, where Muslims knew the son of Abraham to be sacrificed was Ishmael, only to be told by God/Allah that there would be no more human sacrifice, sparing the son and setting Judaism, Christianity and Islam on their collective courses. Even at a distance, delegates could see the bas relief of Roman soldiers carrying off the gold menorah and other sacred objects from the Second Temple when it was destroyed in 70 C.E. Now here it was in Jerusalem, a stolen ancient tribute to the Roman Empire returned to the altar of Judaism, to be a cornerstone for a third temple.

Standing next to Ruth, Noah whispered, "Praise be to God."

Ruth's mouth was open, and then she demanded, "Was your NJA behind this?"

Noah turned to face Ruth, avoiding a direct answer. "Israel is being restored to its roots. The prophecies are being fulfilled."

"This stunt could destroy any last hope for the Summit," said Ruth, shaking her head, anticipating an outraged reaction from Muslim delegates who would view this as the start of a temple on ground held for centuries by the Dome of the Rock.

Four enormous, illuminated balloon figures floated overhead in the shapes of a lion, an ox, the face of a man and an eagle in flight, slowly spiraling before ascending upward and drifting out of sight to the west. Ruth moved to the Archbishop's side near the tent entrance, sensing he was struggling to place the symbolism in biblical context.

Archbishop Okello said, "Revelation, but I can't quite recall which chapter."

"Chapter four," said Ruth, "as a door opens in heaven and a trumpet announces what the New Jerusalem will be, revealing to John seven lamps burning as the seven Spirits of God surrounding the divine throne, and as soon as four beasts appear, the elders bow before the throne, and the book with seven seals is ready to be opened."

The Archbishop stared at the marble block and whispered to Ruth, "Sixtus is taken with the number 7. He told me we must complete our work by Sunday, the seventh day. Did we miss a call on the white phone from Heaven?"

"The Fatima prophecy," said Ruth. She whispered, "He's fixated. He's driven to combine three into one before the final seventh day."

"Prophecies — powerful words, poor guides to action. What can we do?"

"We need to help him find a more constructive meaning of how three into one leads to seven."

As delegates buzzed about the Arch fragment and balloon display, the Pope and his aides circulated with emphatic denials that the Vatican had planned either. The crowd spotted a small plane circling at a distance but close enough for all to read the lettering of a flashing LED banner trailing behind — "LET MY PEOPLE RETURN — AM," referring to the Palestinian claim of homeland. A dinner meant to find unity would begin with unsettling provocations.

A gong sounded. Prime Minister Feldman indicated with a wave of his hands that it was time to move inside. Delegates entered muffling dread over what might come next. Alessio noticed the Prime Minister angrily pointing to the sky and berating his Minister of Defense before turning with a smile, as though nothing of import had occurred.

The meal proceeded without a formal agenda. Delegates grumbled about the Pope's draft. The session adjourned with a benediction by the Imam of the Grand Mosque of Mecca, "Allah, the compassionate, the merciful, we thank you for this time of dialogue. We search for peace on this day of Sabbath, the start of Sabbath for our Jewish friends and for the Sabbath Day of our Christian friends to follow." Feldman glanced at Palmer, who stared back, both knowing it was not peace that would unfold Saturday.

As delegates lingered before departing for adjacent lodging, Ruth reconnected with Noah and Alessio.

"The Pope will appreciate your ideas on what America and Canterbury can embrace," said Alessio. He handed them a sketch of a Vatican Basilica with Orthodox and Protestant side chapels and a Coptic niche.

"The President won't take sides on this," said Noah. "Personally, I think it should include a Temple and a place for all Christians."

Noah wished them a good night as he noticed Palmer gesturing.

Alessio turned to Ruth. "What is your old friend up to?"

"I don't really know him now." Ruth looked down at her shoes.

"Was he your boyfriend?"

"A special friend. He moved away before senior year in high school," said Ruth.

"It is never too late," Alessio teased, perhaps probing.

"No matter if Armageddon takes us all." Ruth shivered.

They walked toward the unveiled marble shimmering in the moonlight. "An ancient marble moved here, Revelation balloons, the March pressing on the gates of Jerusalem. Signs from extremist groups of all three faiths, each aiming to bring on the End Time, each certain its people will inhabit the New Jerusalem."

"Government leaders are the real threat. They hold the weapons," said Alessio.

Ruth leaned forward. "Weapons of war — the Beast. That's what's worshipped."

Alessio turned to join the Pope, who emerged from the tent ready to depart for a waiting van. Ruth caught Alessio's right arm and held it. "If Sixtus insists on a second Vatican here, there won't be an agreement on anything, and the Beast wins."

108

JERUSALEM
Saturday, June 2

A DISMAL HAZE from a sandstorm's aftermath matched Alessio's gloom as he entered the tent Saturday morning. Taking a seat behind Sixtus, he watched delegates file in slowly, dispirited.

Where is hope? he scrawled in his notebook. He thought of Ruth.

After the Pope opened with a short prayer and asked what progress could be shared, Iran's Grand Ayatollah addressed Israel's leader directly.

"Prime Minister, can you renounce in principle weapons of mass destruction? If you will, we have a proposal."

Feldman replied, "Ayatollah Mousavi, your country's President calls for our destruction. I will defend my people."

"As we must protect ours," said the Ayatollah.

"You have no need for nuclear weapons. We do not threaten you."

"Then you have no need for them either," the Ayatollah reasoned.

Feldman deployed the grand gesture. "If Iran renounces any plan to develop a nuclear weapon and pledges it will be immediately and forever open to compliance inspections, I pledge that Israel will never launch a first strike against your country."

The Egyptian President intervened. "We have no nuclear program and can accept this concept if you will also open to inspection and eliminate your stockpile over time."

Feldman dodged. "Once we come to trust one another, my successors could embrace this dream. But first Iran must halt its imminent test of a nuclear weapon and affirm Israel's right to exist as did Egypt years ago."

Standing and slamming his hand on the table, Iran's President Al-Rabani released himself from second-chair status behind the Ayatollah and leaning in front of the Supreme Leader shouted at Feldman, "We won't submit to your outrageous one-sided proposal!"

"Then we have no choice," Feldman shrugged, nonchalantly.

Alessio wrote Nowhere next to his question about hope and added an exclamation point.

109

JERUSALEM
Saturday, June 2

THE POPE called a recess after Al-Rabani's outburst. Noah, Palmer and Shulman retreated with the Israeli delegation to the American enclosure. Before settling around the wooden table, they were surprised to see the Russian President and his interpreter pull back the curtain.

"May I enter?" Goudonov asked in a booming voice, not pausing in his entry. He took a seat next to Palmer, interpreters stooping behind.

"I understand," said Goudonov, his face a foot from Palmer's, "that for your American politics, you must appear to be the strong warrior. But if Israel attacks Iran, that is an attack on Russia also."

Feldman interposed, "We have no quarrel with Russia. You can understand our problem. You would act if Germany were about to acquire a nuclear bomb."

"Germany has the bomb," Goudonov shot back, "on American bases. At this moment I have inspectors at Fordow confirming what we are assured — that Iran is not developing a weapon. We are your best protection. Do not antagonize us."

"We aim to prevent a catastrophe, not provoke one," said Feldman. "You heard me invite Iran's Supreme Leader to pledge open inspections, and he did not overrule his President."

Palmer leaned towards Goudonov in a posture of serious business.

"If Israel takes out Fordow, let's leave that as a matter between Iran and Israel. You and I have more to lose from getting entangled with their affairs than anyone. And consider, it would simply buy time to prevent nuclear weapons from spreading."

"I would rather be Iran's protector than have it join the nuclear club. But I say this for the last time. If Israel strikes Fordow, we will retaliate." Goudonov turned to Feldman, "You are warned. Back off."

Goudonov stood up and turned toward the curtain with his interpreter.

"Wait," said Palmer. "A minute with you. *Pozhalista*," using Russian for 'please.'

110

JERUSALEM

Saturday, June 2

AS SHE WATCHED faith leaders fume about the idea of a Roman church on the Mount, Ruth was not surprised. The summit was fractured into shards of old men contending for supremacy within their corner of the Kingdom. The leaders of the Coptic and Russian Orthodox churches would not be shunted by the Roman Catholic pope to plaques and side altars. The Imam would not share with anyone else custody of Islam's sacred Rock where God spared their ancestor Ishmael. The Pope clung to a vision of all Christianity under his dome. How naïve he had been to expect others to embrace his Vatican-centric vision.

Ruth excused herself to breathe fresh air and found Alessio outside the Anglican space.

"I was hoping to catch you," he said. "The government session makes no progress. Will the faith leaders accept a Vatican cathedral here if there were more space for other denominations?"

"For you, the Vatican is the One True Church. Not for the rest of us. It's one among many. And one we choose not to join."

Ruth's resistance continued to puzzle him. "But he offers every Christian a means of affiliation. Anglicans, Baptists, Russian Orthodox, Coptic Egyptians — all can maintain their rituals and symbols."

"Are we supposed to feel grateful that Rome would open a door that many of us have already walked through?"

He tried a more tactful approach. "Would the Archbishop say a favorable word for the proposal? His Holiness asks."

"In the guidebook, I read about the Jerusalem Syndrome. It grips visitors with delusions of grandeur." Undeterred by Alessio's look of insult, she finished, "I'd be happy to lend it to you."

Alessio was silent.

The women in his dreams never snapped at him.

111

JERUSALEM
Saturday, June 2

WITH VETERAN INTERPRETERS at their sides, the Russian and American Presidents walked outside the Tent for their first one-on-one meeting like heavyweight boxers at a weigh-in. Noah accompanied Palmer.

Palmer took a conciliatory tone. "How can we defuse this? Nothing good will come if Iran gets the bomb. Do you want them supplying your Chechens?"

Goudonov faced straight ahead. "I assured Iran that we are its nuclear shield, but I can't control them." He shrugged. "Our intelligence says Iran is far from having a weapon."

"Mine say the opposite. And Iran won't let UN inspectors into Fordow. Feldman has no choice."

"Then Russia also will have no choice," said Goudonov. Noah thought he sounded regretful rather than angry.

"Some in my country would welcome a final conflagration," said Palmer. "To them this is destiny, to be followed by a timeless age of glory. They call it the Rapture."

Goudonov's eyes narrowed. "Are you among these believers? Or you, Mr. Stoll?"

Noah stood silent. Palmer held a neutral expression. "I believe that one day there will be no earthly struggles. Your Patriarch understands this."

"That sounds like what I was taught in grade school about communism. What a fantasy that was."

Palmer frowned at the comparison of religious belief with a godless system that destroyed generations.

He switched to a stern tone. "If Russia attacks Israel, we must strike Russia."

Goudonov laughed harshly.

"Is this a game of chess? What will your people say when the chessboard is aflame, pawns burned to ash, knights dying from radiation? May we both be forgiven." Goudonov abruptly turned away with the Russian interpreter.

Palmer turned to Noah after waving off his interpreter.

"What now?"

"The glory of God may be revealed," said Noah. But Goudonov's words shook his soul. It was one thing to contemplate a heavenly New Jerusalem, quite another to envision people incinerated or lying in mortal agony. He must find Ruth.

112

JERUSALEM
Saturday, June 2

"THE POPE MUST have forgotten the Reformation," quipped the Archbishop of Canterbury, as he sat with Ruth and Bishop McDermott in the Anglican space. The Pope's call for a second Vatican building on Mount Moriah had provoked bristling opposition. Rabbis and imams called it an architectural Crusade, no less arrogant and insensitive than the barbarous medieval incarnations.

"Your Grace, time to go home," said Bishop McDermott.

Ruth disagreed. "Let's avoid a disaster. We share a common faith in one holy catholic church — with a small 'c.' Your Grace, you could convert the conversation to what a universal cathedral would be."

"But you heard him, Ruth," said the Archbishop. "He's fixed on Rome's supremacy."

"Intentions aren't buildings," she argued. "Let's work together on a design and see what happens."

"Faith's not a matter of committees," scoffed McDermott.

"What do you have in mind?" asked the Archbishop.

Before Ruth could answer, Noah entered the space and asked to speak to Ruth alone. "There's nothing you can't share with us. Noah Stoll, American delegate. Archbishop Okello, Bishop McDermott."

Noah nodded. "Very well. Israel could strike Iran's nuclear factory today, and if that occurs, Russia will retaliate against an Israeli target. No, not Jerusalem," he reassured Bishop McDermott, whose arched eyebrows betrayed personal alarm. "But if that happens, America would be driven to punish Russia, Russia would retaliate, and so on."

Ruth noticed a change in Noah. He delivered his message calmly, like a news anchorman announcing that unemployment rose, not as a zealot praying for a final fire.

The Archbishop responded, "Surely President Palmer isn't about to destroy the world."

"What could happen is beyond any individual's control," said Noah. "It has been prophesied for a long time."

The Archbishop put his hand on Noah's shoulder. "Mr. Stoll, there are those who read the Book of Revelation as a guidebook of what is to come," the Archbishop replied evenly. "But after the Flood, God promised never to destroy the world again. How do you reconcile those biblical passages?"

Noah looked at him blankly.

"Have the great men lost their minds?" asked Ruth. "You're saying this could go nuclear while we're here?"

"Iran did not back down on nuclear monitoring, so Feldman believes Israel has no choice. Palmer agrees."

Ruth shifted to the evangelical language Noah might accept. "Satan is seducing Palmer into thinking he's God's equal, able to decide the fate of the world."

Noah pushed back, "Palmer's a devout Christian."

Ruth lost her struggle to keep from shouting. "Revelation's not a script!"

113

JERUSALEM
Saturday, June 2

AFTER HIS MEETING with Palmer, Goudonov went to the Iranian tent where he found President Al-Rabani alone.

Goudonov was direct. "Look, are you about to test a nuke?"

"We have no need for your protection," said Al-Rabani.

"Answer my question."

"Our scientists work to expand our energy supply, with Russia's assistance for which you are well paid. But are we testing a bomb today? No."

Goudonov gave a slight vertical head shake and pursed his lips. With an engineer's background, Goudonov knew the difference between producing a weapon and supporting a power plant. He appreciated that most politicians relied on others to tell them when a line is crossed. He couldn't tell if Al-Rabani was ignorant or lying.

"Israel will strike Fordow today — that seems certain. When that happens, Russia will honor its pledge to you and hit an Israeli target in response. It can end there, and we'll negotiate terms favorable to Iran."

"Iran is not a child."

"So act like an adult. If Israel and America attack Fordow, we can turn world opinion in our favor. Even the Saudis and Jordanians would join us. Iran is better off playing the victim. Leave it to me."

"We will defer to you for the immediate response if Israel strikes. Our men at Fordow will be blessed as martyrs if that is their fate."

"We keep our word." Goudonov clenched his jaw.

When he returned to the Russian space, he summoned the Defense Minister. "Tell our inspectors to get out of Fordow immediately. Drive west fast. Be ready for the Haifa Maneuver at my order. But first, see how fast our chopper can get us to the air base. I'm going home."

114

MUSLIM QUARTER, JERUSALEM
Saturday, June 2

DELEGATION LUNCHES were arranged at separate restaurants immediately adjacent to the Mount. A tight cordon of machine-gun toting soldiers kept the area safely separated from the rest of the Old City.

Although the threats exchanged among Israel, Russia and America were not broadcast, delegates sensed a breakpoint approaching, a fractured moment that could plunge the world into chaos. From the west sounds of bullhorns and crowd buzz mixed with calls to prayer and shrill ululations. Strains of anguish emanated from the Jewish Quarter. Ruth felt the anarchy of the Tower of Babel recreated horizontally, with Peoples of the Book singing in multiple tongues with no conductor or common score.

The Archbishop had sent a note to the Pope that he had a proposal for what to build on the Mount. As his emissary Ruth would elaborate at the Vatican delegation's lunch.

On their way to the restaurant Ruth and Alessio followed the Via Dolorosa, the path of Jesus' last walk from prison to crucifixion. They passed the grey Crusader-built Romanesque Church of St. Anne near the Lion's Gate, also known as St. Stephen's Gate in commemoration of where the first Christian martyr was stoned to death. They paused in the shadow of the Church of the Flagellation, a 20th century Franciscan construction with a mosaicked dome evoking a crown of thorns. Ruth imagined the world was about to be sentenced to a fatal whipping if a miracle did not intervene.

She and Alessio came to the side door of a Palestinian café, where a table was set for the Vatican delegates plus one. The three-person wait staff glared at her passively. Ruth wondered if that was because she was a woman wearing a clerical collar.

A minute later Sixtus entered with aides, including his off-the-Mount advisors, the Papal Architect, and the Vatican publicity chief. He greeted Ruth with two hands and asked that she sit to his left, Alessio to his right, around a table festooned with Vatican colors. A waiter served hummus and pita bread with tea or juice as the Pope asked about the Archbishop's idea.

How would she address the Pope? As an Episcopalian, she didn't want to call him

Holy Father. Sixtus wasn't her father or her leader, so she began speaking without any honorific. She explained that Archbishop Okello had polled the other faith delegates and confirmed that none supported a Vatican Basilica on the Mount. There was a slim chance for consensus that might allow a church there, but it would need to be for all Christians, not just for Roman Catholics.

The Pope winced at the word Roman.

Ruth continued without a blink. "And a Jewish Temple and a Muslim space are essential to have any hope of having a church approved. All three faiths of People of the Book must share the Mount. Without that, we see no hope for the summit."

The Pope leaned forward and pressed the table with his right fist. "My call for Christian unity must be heard."

Ruth tried to sway him. "You can inspire a unified Christian spirit. A church here could express the simplicity of prayer and reconciliation."

Including women, women as priests, women as worshippers, not just an image of Mary as the Mother of God as a baby.

"And be a martyr in the process. I will be vilified in Rome if I sell Vatican treasures to rebuild a mosque, create a Jewish Temple and install a nondenominational space here." The Pope's expression instantly changed from pensive to cheerful. "But we are open to design ideas. Our architect," he gestured to the bearded gentleman across the table, "could revise our plan. Someone must be in charge or it will be the Church of Holy Chaos."

The wait staff brought to the table dishes to be served family style and placed them at the center. Leaning over the table, a burly mustached waiter prepared to slice the cone of lamb shawarma with a glistening knife. He paused, then flung himself towards the Pope, transforming the blade into a dagger.

Alessio leapt and twisted the knife backwards. It severed the attacker's right ear. Screaming in pain, the assassin scraped Ruth's left arm with the blade before it slid to the floor. Flinging the attacker from the table to the ground, Alessio pinned him in a headlock and elbowed his neck in a sleeper hold until the man lost consciousness, blood spurting from where his ear had been. The other staff fled, leaving the delegates oddly still in their chairs. Israeli security guards rushed in, having heard a clatter. They dragged the senseless attacker to a van flashing blue lights.

Alessio ripped the table runner to stop the flow of Ruth's blood.

Shaken, Ruth tried to remain professional. "Just a graze."

"Thank God," said Alessio fervently, gently but firmly pressing the runner.

"He must not have liked my ideas either," said the Pope.

115

THE OLD CITY, JERUSALEM
Saturday, June 2

A MEDIC from Magen David Adom, Israel's emergency medical service, unwound the table runner from Ruth's left arm. "A surface wound," she announced, allaying unspoken fears.

"Thanks be to God," said the Pope.

Alessio braced Ruth's shoulders as she winced while the medic applied antiseptic astringent to the wound and bandaged it tightly. From an obvious concern that the Summit could be cancelled if word of the attack got out, the Pope asked all present to withhold any public mention of what had happened until the Summit concluded.

As the group returned to the Mount surrounded by heavily armed security in flak jackets, Ruth and Alessio watched large video screens installed along streets beneath the Mount. The screens were erected to broadcast summit results and to mark the security perimeter separating the Mount from the public. News streamed of Israel's bombing of Iran's Fordow facility. Images of devastation, clouds of smoke and strewn debris flowed while commentators reported how the facility had been destroyed by bunker-busting explosives ripping deep into the earth. A furious Iranian officer said that a radioactive cloud was spreading.

They scanned their smartphones. Ruth caught a BBC commentator saying "another Wormwood," capturing a scholar's explanation of Chernobyl's allegorical reference. The reporter cited biblical roots in Revelation's prophecy that after the third trumpet sounded, a star called Wormwood would fall and poison the waters of the world, noting that Chernobyl is a Russian and Ukrainian word for mugwort, a species of artemisia, common wormwood.

An uproar arose from the Muslim Quarter, whose occupants poured into the narrow streets chanting "Death to Zionism" with the Fordow news. Orthodox Jews along the Western Wall raised arms to the skies with prayers of deliverance and jubilation tinged with deep apprehension. As they mounted steps to the Mount, Ruth and Alessio observed Hasidic men fretting in circles near the Western Wall.

Dispensationalist tourists throughout the city huddled on hotel rooftops, affirming that the Rapture was imminent. The final sign had been flashed - irreversible and clear. Now it was surely a matter of hours.

Al Jazeera coverage switched between the Fordow devastation and the March of the Innocents, now a half day's walk from the Qalandia Gate where it intended to enter Jerusalem. Seated on a white horse, Navid Kosari spoke with eyes uplifted to the skies while responding to a television crew.

"A hundred Iranian youngsters on holiday near Fordow were killed and many others," Kosari recited tearfully. "We call upon the righteous to join us as we near Jerusalem."

The Old City's large projection screens shifted to the Umayyad Mosque in Damascus, showing residents pressed around the Isa Minaret, the Jesus Minaret according to western guidebooks as the caption noted. Men with prayer rugs unfurled before the Minaret prayed in a growing chorus, "Return, Isa — Return, Isa."

During the lunch break at an underground situation room unmarked on city maps, Prime Minister Feldman assessed his attack on Fordow with his military advisors. He congratulated the Defense Minister, who reported that the Fordow fortress, thought to ensconce nuclear facilities stretching to a depth of ten stories underground, had been thoroughly destroyed, leaving an enormous crater in the earth.

"There was limited collateral loss, consisting we think of an errant strike on a camp that the drones perceived to be an anti-aircraft installation. We don't know what happened to the Russian inspectors."

Satisfied Phase Two of the operation was a success, Feldman turned to repercussions. "Russia will hit us. Red alert for invasion by Egyptian troops from the Sinai and of Hezbollah, Syrian and Iraqi forces from the north."

The Defense Minister's shoulders slipped a bit in reply. "Our conventional forces are stretched to the limit. They can resist for a short time."

"How long is short?" demanded Feldman.

"A day, maybe two. We may need the Temple Swords," said the Minister somberly.

Feldman nodded. "The air base in the west — that's where the Russians will strike. Leave it appearing active but get our planes in the skies."

The Defense Minister nodded. He understood the calculus of war.

116

HAIFA, AKKO
Saturday, June 2

IN HAIFA, the seaside Israeli city close to the Lebanese border, a noon test of the warning system was a weekly event. But when sirens began blaring at 12:20, Haifa's residents knew this was no test. They rushed to safe rooms and underground bunkers.

Israeli Army and reserve units gathered north of Haifa, around Akko, Acre in Crusader times. Moving in separate columns toward Lebanon, they aimed to blunt a land invasion by allied Islamic forces massed in superior numbers. Israeli fighter jets were aloft to avoid the mistake of the Yom Kippur War when a surprise attack decimated grounded craft. One report to the Israeli commander of the northern force claimed the enemy had crossed the border, but another was firm that the Islamic alliance stood in place inside Lebanon and Syria.

At 12:30 missiles struck without warning the furthest northern Israeli air base. Devastation was total, the air traffic control tower leveled, fuel terminals ablaze, air strips ripped to jagged rubble, uniformed corpses scattered like discarded rag dolls.

Surveillance drones reported to Palmer that Russian bombers inflicted about 500 casualties, which he immediately relayed to Feldman. An Israeli spokeswoman announced that residents of Akko, Haifa and other northern cities should take cover until further notice.

Feldman phoned Goudonov.

"That was an act of war."

Goudonov replied calmly, "We destroyed the base where your bombers that attacked Iran were housed. I gave you fair warning."

Feldman sputtered, "The Americans will retaliate."

Goudonov said, "As will we if that is so."

"Call off the dogs," said Feldman. "Get Muslim troops to pull back two kilometers from our borders, and we can have a truce. Russia and Israel are not enemies. More than a million Russians make Israel home."

"Yes, after abandoning their homeland. History will record that you tossed the first bone to the dogs of war."

Feldman was not used to Russia throwing sand in his face. Thinking furiously, he tossed out, "Palmer and I will meet you on the Temple Mount at –"

"Agreed — at the Noble Sanctuary," said Goudonov, purposely using the Islamic term for the Mount as he disconnected.

Feldman reached Palmer. "Ike, we need to meet."

"I'm going home," Palmer barked into the phone.

Feldman was interrupted by the Defense Minister. "Hold the line, Ike." Seconds later Feldman blurted into the line, "Bad news."

"Wait a minute," said Palmer. Feldman could hear Palmer conferring with someone. "You promised security, Aaron," Palmer spurted. "Air Force One was just blown up, along with the decoy. And it wasn't Russia. Goudonov's jet's destroyed too."

"I just got the same message," said an angry Feldman. "Meet me on the Mount in five minutes."

"Who did this?" demanded Palmer.

"Hezbollah claimed credit a minute ago."

"That can't be, Aaron. Hezbollah's not that stupid."

"We're investigating," said Feldman, dread seeping into him as he contemplated yet another enemy of Israel.

117

TEMPLE MOUNT, JERUSALEM
Saturday, June 2

Events were unfolding that had been the stuff of fiction — the bombing of Fordow, the Russian attack on the Israeli air base, massed armies, the March approaching Jerusalem, destruction of Air Force One and the Russian counterpart.

Feldman and Palmer conferred upon returning from the lunch break, accompanied by their delegates, including Noah.

"We confirmed it was the Russians who hit your base," said Palmer. "Their MIG's returned to Arab air space. And now I'm trapped."

"Ike, you're safer here than leaving. We have to wait it out together on the Mount."

Palmer glared at his old friend. "What's your next move?"

"You stole my question," Feldman deflected.

"I promised Goudonov a response, strategic, unmistakable."

"Meaning what?"

"Better that I don't tell you. This isn't just about Israel anymore."

Goudonov strode into the enclosure, anger marking every stride. "Have you reconsidered?"

Palmer drew his lips tight. "You killed a thousand people."

"And he didn't? You both knew what would happen if Israel struck Fordow." Goudonov stared at Palmer, but his words were aimed at Feldman. "Our response was restrained."

Feldman entered the fray. "Fordow was a nuclear bakery. It wasn't black bread in the oven. Your inspectors surely informed you of that, and we gave you enough warning to get them out of there in time."

Unblinking, Palmer looked at Goudonov. "A response is unavoidable. I will give you one-hour notice to remove civilians."

Goudonov stared back. "We avoided war for 75 years, when many times there could have been a catastrophe."

"You can reverse this," said Palmer slowly, "by renouncing your alliance with Iran and working with us so that it never has a nuclear weapon. Pledge this and I'll postpone our response."

Goudonov considered. "Israel gives up its Temple Swords. I'll tell Iran to back off. Everyone stands down. Agreed?"

Feldman immediately preempted any possibility Palmer would be tempted. "Never. America does not control the Jewish State. We won't abandon our ultimate weapon, surrounded as we are by fanatics."

"Then we each have our part to play," said Goudonov. He took four steps toward the entrance, turned, and added, "I'm leaving now for Moscow."

"I don't think so," said Palmer. "I assumed you heard. Terrorists blew up your plane a few minutes ago. Mine also. And we've been warned terrorists are ready to shoot down a helicopter that tries to get us out of here, and mobs in the streets won't let a motorcade escape. The Prime Minister can't guarantee anyone's safety unless we stay where we are. We're trapped here together."

118

JERUSALEM
Saturday, June 2

"I cut myself. I'll change later," Ruth told Archbishop Okello, Canon Dickens and Bishop McDermott. The Archbishop looked with concern at her bloodstained shirt and asked if she needed medical attention or return to St. George, which she refused.

They debated how the Summit would be affected by the Fordow attack, the Russian response and the destruction of the Russian and American presidential jets, news that jolted the delegates like a lightning strike. The Archbishop remained calm, his patience sharpened as a survival mechanism during the genocidal horrors of Africa decades earlier.

He reported, "I have spoken with the faith leaders. None support a Roman Catholic cathedral on the Mount. The rest is in the hands of the politicians."

Ruth sighed. "Sixtus is fixated on 'three into one,' and to him this means uniting Catholics, Orthodox and Protestants."

"Right," said Canon Dickens. "So when we merge you'll renounce being a priest and take a nun's habit."

Though silently laughing at the image, she proceeded dispassionately. "'Three into one' can have many meanings. It could refer to unity among the three faiths of the Book."

Canon Dickens rolled his eyes and interjected, "The Pope in charge of Christianity, Judaism and Islam. I can picture him in a turban holding a Torah."

Suppressing the ridiculous image, Ruth pressed on. "If we simply say no to building a church here, the summit will collapse. Meanwhile, the Third Temple force may get its victory, and Islam will explode in fury if a Jewish temple replaces the Dome of the Rock."

The Archbishop stroked his chin. "How can we help him re-vision 3 into 1? Ideas?"

"Here's one." Ruth unfolded a paper showing the Bünting Clover Leaf Map. "This is a drawing of the world from 1581, with Jerusalem in the center. You can see Europe, Africa, and Asia as three leaves of a clover, joined by Jerusalem in the middle. What if God calls Sixtus to create a three-in-one complex? Instead of continents, the three leaves can be worship spaces of Judaism, Christianity and Islam, each expressing the unity of one God, celebrated in different forms, connecting here in Jerusalem."

"Maybe this could be a turning point." Okello stared at the map, the world as a cloverleaf with Jerusalem at the centre.

119

JERUSALEM
Saturday, June 2

DELEGATES GATHERED ANXIOUSLY for a briefing by the heads of Mossad, Shin Bet, and the Jerusalem police. Shin Bet's director detailed the missile attack on the Jerusalem military airport where Air Force One, its double and the Russian President's plane were destroyed. Safe departure from the Mount could not be guaranteed.

The police chief scowled while describing enraged crowds. He reported the arrest of a Palestinian Israeli whose car was stopped, the trunk opened to reveal two hand-held missile launchers capable of shooting a helicopter out of the sky. The security officers insisted that delegates remain on the Mount throughout the day and overnight until a safe exit could be arranged early Sunday while most of the City slept.

"Who did this?" President Goudonov shouted.

"Hezbollah claims credit for the airport attack," answered the Mossad chief.

Palestinian President Arafat fumed, "That was not Hezbollah."

The delegates began talking at once.

Feldman stood, saying in a loud voice, "Israel is your host. We failed at the airport. We will not fail you again. To assure your personal safety, we will make arrangements for everyone to remain here overnight."

This quieted the delegates enough for the Pope to declare, "Let's make use of our time to agree on what we can. Let's resume in full session at 3:00."

Delegates had about an hour to meet one-on-one while absorbing the impact, feeling like prisoners caged with others who could be their murderers.

Iran President Al-Rabani fulminated with other Muslim delegates. Despite outward bravado, Arafat did not urge an immediate move of conventional troops into Israel, and the Egyptian President said he was consulting military advisors before sending troops east

— "to ensure victory" was his explanation. Privately the Egyptian and Palestinian leaders agreed the massed Muslim armies should wait, or they themselves could become immediate hostages of arch-enemy Feldman. Lacking unified command, the Arab forces served better as a threat than an invading team.

Feldman met with a deeply troubled EU President Schmidt. In a monotone, each syllable enunciated clearly, she cautioned him against any further offensive action, berated him for a reckless strike on Fordow, and warned that if Israel did anything beyond defending its pre-1967 borders, the EU would throw its full support to the Palestinians. She added, "You must turn this disaster around. One way to do that is to let the March into Jerusalem."

"What?" blurted an astonished Feldman.

"The only way to deflect the furor over the Megiddo Massacre is to invite the survivors into this City to complete their pilgrimage. Muslims will not want to attack their pilgrims. We're safer together than apart."

Palmer had what he took to be an encouraging meeting with the Egyptian President, who promised to hold back the Islamic armies from attacking Israel at least through the summit's conclusion. The Egyptian President committed that if the United States publicly encouraged Israel to give up its nuclear arsenal over time, Egypt would press for a similar pledge by Iran and all other nations of the region. Otherwise, the uproar in the Islamic world would force every Muslim government to join in an attack on Israel's nuclear assets.

"The last thing I want is another war," said the Egyptian President, "but you can understand what my people are demanding."

"You talk with Al-Rabani. I'll talk to Feldman," Palmer responded. Sensing an opening, as this would not require Israel to give up its weapons immediately, Palmer calculated how he could put it.

"Think of it as a prayer, Aaron," he could say to his old friend, *"not an action. We can agree to hope for a world free of nuclear weapons."*

120

JERUSALEM
Saturday, June 2

HAIM ETZION gloried in the destruction of Air Force One, including media reports that Hezbollah claimed credit. He washed an alabaster cup in scalding water to free it of germs for the third time before pouring his fourth espresso of the day. From his Jerusalem apartment in walking distance of the Temple Mount, Etzion called his contact.

"Well done. You'll get your money this afternoon. But the Russian plane?"

Informed it had been too close to the American targets to avoid damage, Etzion relented but scolded, "You failed at the restaurant."

"Regrettable," said the assassin. "But guns were not possible, and the Pope was lucky." They disconnected.

It may all work out for the best, thought Etzion. This way the summit would proceed, all delegates forced to share a hostile night together, when the only possible discourse would be a spiral of recrimination. Shi'a and Sunni delegates would spit hatred at one another, the Pope would be blamed for a disastrous gathering, and they would all go home. It would show how Israel was truly on its own, must purge itself of foreign influence, be free from the contamination of strangers.

Israel will triumph. America and Russia can go to war with each other, and our Government will see that the only way to protect the Jewish people is to rebuild the Temple and push Israel's boundaries to those of King David. Then the Mashiach will appear. Etzion wept with ecstasy at what was unfolding.

As 3:00 approached, Iran's Supreme Leader summoned President Al-Rabani to a private meeting. Confident the Ayatollah would commend his foresight in warning of Israel's villainous act at Fordow, Al-Rabani was shocked by the Ayatollah's rebuke.

"Mr. President, we can achieve here what no one could have imagined possible if we act with the wisdom of the Prophet, peace be upon him. As he taught, defensive jihad is a noble duty, but Islam does not sanction a nuclear weapon. We will use the attack on our soil as a sword of truth. We turn our back forever on a military nuclear program. I will communicate Allah's path of righteousness as our position."

Al-Rabani sat stunned. He, the elected President, was treated as a schoolboy by this cowardly successor of Ayatollah Khomenei. If the cleric insists on being unworldly, he deserves an immediate trip to paradise.

Feldman huddled with Israeli confidantes, who reassured themselves that what had been done was right.

"No looking back," said the Defense Minister. They rehearsed how Israel would repel what was expected, a movement of Muslim forces across the borders. They reviewed every aspect of what would follow invasion.

Feldman came to the final two items. "Are the border trenches ready to be set ablaze?"

"Yes," said the Defense Minister.

"Are the Temple Swords trained on Tehran and Damascus?"

The Minister took a deep breath. "Yes, Prime Minister."

Unspoken was that the Temple Swords were once poised for use under Golda Meir. It had been questioned whether a Prime Minister had the individual authority to deploy a nuclear bomb without the Cabinet's concurrence. No one within the small coterie on the Temple Mount raised the issue this time. Israel's survival hung in the balance.

121

JERUSALEM
Saturday, June 2

WITH DELEGATES TRAPPED at the summit, the ban on outside communications was lifted. Government leaders connected with their capitals to plot next moves. An extraordinary show of security forces held back crowds pressing along a cordon encircling the Mount. Jerusalem was a human pressure cooker, thought Noah. The lid would not hold tight for long.

Midafternoon he met privately with President Palmer, who explained the Egyptian President was working to forestall an invasion of Israel. "Would a truce affect how you read the signs?" asked Palmer.

"The New Jerusalem is near," Noah replied confidently. "We're half the way to God's target of 144,000 conversions to Christ. Truce or not, you can't fail. Either the End will take longer than we think and you bring peace from the uproar, or we'll be ushers for the return of our Savior."

Palmer had relied on Noah since his campaign that began more than three years earlier when Noah's work confirmed the divine path of his political quest. When an opponent led in the Iowa primary polls, Noah inspired Evangelicals, using local pastors to make recorded calls and targeting social network posts featuring images of Jesus himself with a Palmer button to generate the largest turnout in Iowa caucus history. They packed the homes of startled Iowan precinct executives. The bold appeal earned Palmer a victory in the curious Iowan method of choosing a presidential candidate, the caucuses, where showing up in person on a snowy evening was what mattered. When a populist triumphed as the Republican nominee, Palmer was the obvious choice as his running mate. After his predecessor's heart attack, the Oval Office was Palmer's, according to God's plan.

After a long pause Palmer thanked him. "I can feel the End Time approaching, but perhaps it is not for us humble followers to know the hour."

"Yes, Mr. President. But the watchmen are at the towers. If the End is near, we are His servants to help it on its way."

"And what would be the final sign, Noah, the unmistakable signal that the seventh seal is broken, that the final page is turning?"

Noah didn't try to tamp down his excitement. "Saint John foresaw it as a blaze. Six trumpets have sounded. All that remains is the great fire. And then the coming of our Messiah, heralded by the seventh trumpet."

Palmer nodded. Secretary of State Shulman swept into the American space. "Mr. President, Options A and B are ready on your order."

Palmer switched gears from contemplation to command. "What times to impact?"

Shulman replied, "Option A, from off the coasts, 30 minutes."

"And B?"

"Five minutes max."

"Set a meeting with Goudonov - 4:00 sharp. Noah, talk to your friend, the Episcopal priest, and report back on the faith delegates' progress - or lack of it."

Thirty minutes later Noah walked with Palmer and Secretary Shulman to a meeting with Goudonov and his aides. "Mr. President," began Palmer, "Your attack on northern Israel will have our response, as I promised. It's proper to give you fair warning."

Palmer paused, as if searching for a way off the escalator. Goudonov's eyes met Palmer's like an Arctic fox judging its prey. Unable to turn back Palmer continued. "It will be military targets. Let that be the end of our confrontation."

Glowering, Goudonov responded, "If you want war, you will have it. An attack on Russian soil would be a bridge crossed with no return."

Palmer looked at Goudonov as a master poker player eyes an opponent. "Your country's destiny is in your hands. I am playing the hand you dealt when you struck Israel. You can stop the game or play on. You will not prevail." Palmer turned abruptly and departed with Noah and Shulman through the fabric space divider.

122

TO THE EAST OF JERUSALEM
Saturday, June 2

NAVID KOSARI'S MARE was linked by a hemp rope to a riderless pale horse. Led now by Kosari alone, the March was within two hours from the Qalandia Gate. Marchers numbered half million or more, overwhelmingly women, some with children, a scattering of men.

AM's web posts blared "To Jerusalem!" peppered with photos of A'ishah not in the throes of a martyr death but in life exuberantly urging the women of Islam to reclaim its soul, to defeat evil, to bring peace. A bulletin appeared: "The 12th Imam has returned. He and Isa will lead us to glory as a holy dawn breaks over our Land."

At 10:40 Saturday morning, Kosari halted his mare to receive a hand delivered envelope embossed with Iran's flag enclosing a message from the Grand Ayatollah, ending with "I will greet you at Qalandia this afternoon. Come armed only with the Word," wrote the Supreme Leader. Kosari read the letter twice.

As the head of his country had spoken, Kosari issued the instruction to the March commanders, who quickly spread word through the ranks. Marshals patted down everyone, women checking women, men frisking men, to be certain none carried a firearm, explosive device or even a pen knife, honoring the Ayatollah's admonition.

Vali Qalil listened as Iranian President Al-Rabani fumed by phone that he was being upstaged by Kosari and humiliated by the Supreme Leader, who had countermanded Al-Rabani's efforts to launch a united Islamic invasion of Israel.

"The March is at the gates. When Israel turns it back, the fury of our supporters will be overwhelming, unstoppable," Qalil assured him.

"A second great sacrifice is next," said Al-Rabani. "The Ayatollah."

123

JERUSALEM
Saturday, June 2

"TRAPPED LIKE A RAT when I should be a bear roaring in Moscow," Goudonov raged as his aides confirmed immediate escape from the Mount would be suicidal.

The Defense Minister urged a pre-emptive attack on America. "We must take out the Alaskan anti-missile defense."

"That would be like going west to attack Napoleon rather than drawing him into our frozen heartland. No, we know where our strength lies. History must record that the Americans started World War III and that we were righteous in defense. Palmer said it would be military targets. I'd guess one of our nuclear silos, like Solatov."

"So harden the bases?"

"Keep them open for launch. This could be a bluff," said Goudonov. "They're not essential anyway. Putin was smart to mobilize our arsenal. I'll tell Schmidt that any action from Europe will be met with devastating counterattack. Inform the Ukrainians our planes will enter their air space at will. And direct our submarines to speed to the Israeli coast."

"Yes, Mr. President," said the Defense Minister.

"Find the Patriarch," Goudonov barked, and the interpreter rushed to fetch the head of the Russian Orthodox Church. "We'll photograph him praying with me for Mother Russia."

124

JERUSALEM
Saturday, June 2

"THE HOLY FATHER is concerned about you, Ruth. And so am I." They sat in an alcove within the summit tent.

"You're a great bodyguard," Ruth replied, flexing her arm to show how quickly she was healing.

Her compliment flowed through him like rain on dry sand, thirsty after years of drought. Unable to visualize her as Jesus' mother as Sixtus had counseled, he quickly switched to Church business. "The Holy Father remains fixed on uniting three into one, and to him this has a single meaning — bringing Christianity under one roof."

"Mass destruction on the horizon and he's stuck on a cryptic vision? The more pressing concern is 'three into one' as bringing Jews, Christians and Muslims closer together."

"Maybe the Holy Father is right about the Fatima page, and gathering Christians together is what we are called to do, so the seventh trumpet can sound the Second Coming."

"I can't believe it. You're brave enough to stop armed thugs but afraid to challenge your employer, even if he's triggering annihilation of the planet."

"He would not do that."

"Wake up! He'll be doing the devil's work if this escalates." Ruth gave up on not shouting. Noticing the looks she was given by passersby, she lowered her voice. "Not on purpose, but the situation's spiraling out of control."

Alessio looked down at his priest shoes, black Vatican issue. "When I was ordained, I pledged obedience. But I did not promise never to think again." *Or feel again.*

"We're in this together, Alessio."

Yes, we are.

125

JERUSALEM
Saturday, June 2

INTERCEPTED MESSAGES reinforced the Israeli security forces' conclusion that delegate safety required staying on the Mount. Cots and bedding arrived.

The New Jerusalem Alliance circulated leaflets with the blue and white of the Israeli flag urging the people of Jerusalem to go to baptismal fonts appearing throughout the City. The fliers listed mortal dangers facing Israel and promoted salvation through conversion. At each font, a cheerful man and woman dressed in khakis and oxford blue shirts invited visitors to accept Jesus as Savior. "Born a Jew, he is the Messiah," the baptismal couples gently coaxed, invoking Judaism's teaching that a Mashiach would emerge one day, and this could be the day.

Army of the Mahdi supporters circulated through the streets with clipboards emblazoned with the green, black, red and white of the Pan-Arab flag. They sought digital signatures on e-petitions beseeching the Israeli Government to let the March enter the City.

4K volunteers dispersed throughout the Old City stood by alabaster hued vessels and a poster sketch of the winning design, seeking donations to rebuild the Temple. Residents flocked to collection posts. An elderly woman donated a wad of shekels, saying she'd saved for a burial plot, but restoring the Kingdom of David was more important.

The faithful and the fearful packed churches, mosques, and synagogues, some in ecstatic trance, many praying or staring vacantly. Outside each place of worship street vendors hawked candles, crying "Light one for peace!" The entire police force would work the night into Sunday.

The Jerusalem District Police Commander maintained high frequency radio communication with the inter-agency center linking security forces for the summit. Shin Bet's Director told those on the channel that the Prime Minister had offered twelve March leaders safe passage to the Old City on condition the others remain beyond the barrier wall, but the March leaders rejected this gesture as it drew within reach of Qalandia Gate.

"We are protecting not only Israel itself," said the Director. "We have a sacred duty to safeguard the summit leaders — Christian, Jew and Muslim alike."

Palmer and Noah conversed quietly while Secretary Shulman monitored intelligence reports on naval and ground forces in the region. "Stuck here when I should be in Washington," Palmer angrily muttered. "I never should have come."

Noah reassured the President. "You don't run from tough battles. In Psalm 18, King David praises God, 'You armed me with strength for battle; you humbled my adversaries before me.'"

"Would King David lead the charge toward or away from the end of the world?" Palmer asked testily.

126

JERUSALEM
Saturday, June 2

PRIME MINISTER FELDMAN received the Ashkenazi Chief Rabbi for a private meeting. The rabbi's bleary eyes betrayed lack of sleep. As a boy he witnessed the rebirth of Israel as a nation, and now in the December of life he was troubled that its days could be as numbered as his own.

"I am always honored by your presence, Rabbi," Feldman said with a tightly drawn smile.

"Let the March enter Jerusalem." He let the words penetrate.

"Impossible!"

"No less impossible than Israel itself. The March has been a disaster for us. The world holds us responsible for a massacre. Turn it around by letting the women enter Jerusalem to fulfill their pilgrimage."

"Risk the safety of our people? Are you mad?" Feldman asked, incredulous.

"More will go wrong if Muslim women are dishonored. Where in Jewish scripture is there exultation over that sort of battle? What of the fury of Muslim nations that surround us?"

Feldman did not wish to antagonize the rabbi, "I respect your words as they come from your heart. But I must protect our people."

Realizing the conversation was over, the rabbi rose to depart.

"As for the Temple Swords, even if we are attacked, you have no blessing to unleash them." He left, head bowed in despair.

The rabbi was a revered scholar, a living repository of Judaic history. But he was elderly and weak, Feldman saw. Had he forgotten that God gave this Land to the Jews? Did he fear Judaism's great prophecy of the End Time? But a disquieting voice entered Feldman's mind — was the sacred mission of restoring the Land of Israel as it was under King David a seductive mirage in the Judean Desert if the United States and Russia waged war?

127

JERUSALEM
Saturday, June 2

WORD OF EXPLOSIONS in Russia spread through the Old City like a sudden thunderstorm sweeping through an unsuspecting village, drenching residents without shelter. Nuclear combat had faded to an assumed taboo, unimaginable since the Cuban Missile Crisis of 1963. Hiroshima was a novel read by schoolchildren about a device from ancient times, but now the specter of atomic warfare visited again.

"US attacks Russia" was the news flash with fiery eruptions at two Russian ICBM centers — the command post of the Strategic Rocket Forces at Kuntsevo in the Moscow suburbs and the Siberian silo base at Uzhur. Flaming, spark-filled clouds billowed into the heavens. A 30-second amateur's cell phone video posted on YouTube revealed massive explosions in a ring around the command center, ending with a still shot of a sign at the security fencing featuring the SRF's two-headed-Eagle emblem and its motto —*After us it is silence.*"

CNN broadcast, "World War III begins!"

Religious tensions that gripped the crowds melted to talk of Russia and America at war, even as the two presidents were trapped together at the summit.

The Rapture-ready gloried in the news. As they sat in rooftop chairs or lay on blankets ready to be lifted up to heaven, they knew their purchase of one-way tickets to Jerusalem had been the right choice.

President Goudonov summoned his Defense Minister, but just as the aide departed the Russian enclave to find him, the Minister rushed in. "Palmer did not bluff. They attacked our SRF command post and the Uzhur base."

"The count at Uzhur?" demanded Goudonov.

"We had 30 R-36M missiles there," siloed intercontinental ballistic missiles capable of carrying a variety of nuclear warheads, coded by NATO as SS-18 Satans. "I doubt any remain operational."

"And our RS-28 Sarmats?" labeled by NATO as Satan 2's, cruise missiles carrying five warheads that Goudonov's predecessor had announced with fanfare in 2018 as unstoppable, able to evade any missile defense.

"Untouched. Untouchable," said the Defense Minister. "Central command was transferred to the Urals post. Colonel Svobodov confirms operational control, but communication is disrupted."

"Loss of life?"

"Thousands."

Goudonov thought for five seconds and spat. "Topols and SLBM's are all we need," referring to missiles that could be launched from mobile locations scattered across Russia and ballistic missiles aboard submarines. "Get me Commander Korolevsky."

Secretary Shulman reported to Palmer. "Option B succeeded 100%. Minimal casualties. The Siberian Satan base at Uzhur is destroyed. To stop radioactive leaks, they'll have to cover it like a concrete tomb. The command center is out of order, so we have an overwhelming advantage but not for long."

Palmer sat impassively. "Next?" he asked himself out loud, looking as though he was watching a play being performed, uncertain of the next scene.

Shulman answered, "Submarines. That's how the Russians will play now. And their land-based mobile launchers."

Noah listened silently. He understood the President had chosen a less aggressive alternative than a broader nuclear strike, and the tech wizard within him was intrigued. "How did you manage it?" he asked.

"Cyberwar took out the command center. When you control the electrical circuits as we can, you can do almost whatever you want."

"And Uzhur?"

"Laser-guided missiles from our Pacific fleet. They can't accuse us of a nuclear strike."

Archbishop Okello, Bishop McDermott and Ruth joined in prayer.

"Eternal God, in whose perfect kingdom no sword is drawn but the sword of righteousness, no strength known but the strength of love: So mightily spread abroad your Spirit, that all peoples may be gathered under the banner of the Prince of Peace, as children of one Father," Ruth read from her *Book of Common Prayer*. After the silence that followed, the Archbishop asked, "My God, what has Palmer done?"

Bishop McDermott was pale. "Surely he wouldn't start World War III because of Bible passages. People thought the Beast was Emperor Nero, Hitler, but ...."

Ruth could barely speak. "Ephesians: 6:12 says, 'Our struggle is against the rulers, the authorities, against cosmic powers of this present darkness, against the spiritual forces of evil in the heavenly places.'" She paused. "A dreadful force has been released. Apocalyptic symbols have come alive."

Horror silenced Okello and McDermott.

Ruth leaned forward. "We have a few hours to stop this from spiraling into a fireball. Archbishop, you are the last hope." She opened her notebook and began a sketch.

128

JERUSALEM
Saturday, June 2

WITH ALESSIO AT HIS SIDE, the Pope approached Goudonov, extending his arms to embrace the Russian President. "I grieve for your loss and pray for your people."

"Thank you," Goudonov replied coldly.

Sixtus probed, "What can we do to put out these fires of hell?"

"America's strike on Mother Russia demands a response. There is no point in words."

"You can turn the world from violence," said the Pope gently, his eyes searching the hardened face of the Russian President.

"Perhaps you are in the business of miracles. I am not."

129

JERUSALEM
Saturday, June 2

SUMMIT DELEGATES held frantic discussions. With no safe escape from the Mount, they plotted the few moves they could control while nuclear holocaust loomed beyond the power of anyone except Presidents Palmer and Goudonov.

The Muslim leaders agreed to delay sending troops into Israeli territory until the delegates were safely home. They hesitated demanding assurance from Prime Minister Feldman that Israel would not use a nuclear weapon on a Muslim city for fear it might trigger the opposite.

Feldman debated with his Defense Minister what to do with what he called the March of the Terrorists. They settled on an email message to Navid Kosari, repeating an invitation for him to return to the Mount with twelve persons of his selection. Kosari again rebuffed it, demanding that all marchers be allowed into the City, promising with an oath that they would leave Jerusalem Sunday afternoon.

"Have I failed?" Sixtus asked Alessio. What was planned as a gathering for harmony had become a vortex of violence.

Alessio hedged. "You are daring to change the course of history."

"And no one follows. Where are today's apostles?"

"Our Savior must have felt the same here," said Alessio, "when he was crucified on Good Friday."

"He wasn't alone at the Last Supper."

"But he was abandoned and denied in the Garden."

"And he gave his life for us."

"Perhaps you also are asked to give up something," Alessio ventured.

Such as the illusion of yourself as uniting Christians based on nothing more than how you read a young girl's words.

130

JERUSALEM
Saturday, June 2

AS THOUGH SUMMONED by an invisible messenger, Noah, Alessio and Ruth ran into each other in a passageway. Ruth wore a fresh clergy shirt and a jacket that covered her bandaged wound. Pre-dusk shadows lengthened across the Mount as they made their way outside the enclosure.

"We are at the point faith has led us," said Noah. "The New Jerusalem is near."

"The world's exploding into nuclear catastrophe and you seem pleased?" Ruth was aghast.

"I didn't foresee that the 'lake of fire' in Revelation would be nuclear," Noah admitted.

"What does Palmer want?" asked Ruth.

"We want the prophecy to be fulfilled as promised in the Bible."

"And how will this prophecy be fulfilled?" asked Alessio.

"As Revelation says. First, by conversion of 144,000 Jews to the light of Christ. It's happening. Over 50,000 were baptized by this morning, more this afternoon," radiated Noah.

"Baptismal promises by people gripped by fear are not what God wants," Ruth argued.

Noah disagreed. "It's a healthy fear, about how they will spend eternity."

Alessio broke in heatedly. "You want President Palmer to accelerate a catastrophe?"

Ruth resorted to battle with biblical quotations. "The Book of Revelation preaches that a fire will consume only Satan's army that surrounds Jerusalem. It doesn't talk about you throwing on an accelerant. And I thought you wanted to build a Third Temple. That will never happen if all-out war breaks out."

Alessio watched with satisfaction as Noah struggled unsuccessfully for a comeback. He saw Noah struck by Ruth's words, wavering about the sequence of events and what it meant. Alessio seized the moment.

"What if the Supreme Ayatollah could convince Russia not to retaliate? As the Pope's delegate I could make that proposal."

No need to mention the appeal yet to the Holy Father.

Alessio and Ruth hurried to the Iranian space, dragging Noah along. They entered, overhearing the Ayatollah berating President Al-Rabani.

Iran's Supreme Leader turned.

"We beg for a few minutes of your time," said Alessio.

The Ayatollah dismissed Al-Rabani and listened as Alessio presented a papal request that Iran ask Russia to stand down. Noah's presence underlined the obvious point that the Americans would welcome such a move.

The Ayatollah quickly absorbed the point of a ceasefire. "Iran does not ask Russia to use nuclear weapons to defend our people. I will make that clear to President Goudonov."

"I have a request of you," he continued. "I leave to meet the March that is at the wall east of here. Ask the Pope and the Archbishop to join me."

"And the Chief Rabbi?" Alessio asked.

The Grand Ayatollah nodded. "All People of the Book."

131

JERUSALEM
Saturday, June 2

ALESSIO AND RUTH left to convey the Ayatollah's request first to the Archbishop, then to the Pope. Noah escaped the tent and called 4K leader Haim Etzion on his glasses that doubled as a phone. "Haim, you need to do something you won't like. Get through to Feldman and convince him to let the March of the Muslim women into the City."

"What?" blurted Etzion.

"It's essential if you want to build the Third Temple."

"Letting the March in is against all we believe."

Noah held firm. "Letting women walk around a wall doesn't abandon anything. It'll let off steam and show that Israel welcomes visitors. Or do you propose never to allow Muslims to come here? Will you pin Muslim crescents to their clothing? Ban Christians too?"

"We welcome friends but not those who despoil our Land."

"At least discuss it with 4K."

"Don't hold your breath."

Etzion disconnected. He turned back to the 4K meeting that was arguing whether the NJA's financial support of the Third Temple was worth tolerating its abhorrent conversion campaign. They were angry there'd been no notice to 4K about this trick.

When Etzion shared Noah's request with the 4K leadership, there was an uproar. One member shouted, "I told you not to trust them."

"Return their blood money," another yelled.

A third had a different slant. "He's right about one thing. We must welcome visitors. What's the harm in letting them finish their pilgrimage and then leave?"

Etzion slammed his fist on a table. "Let's vote," he said. "Those in favor of asking the Prime Minister to let the March in — raise your right hand." At first only one of the 24, then three, finally six raised hands.

"Opposed?" Twelve shot hands upward. Six did nothing. Etzion declared, "The motion fails."

The rabbi who was 4K's spiritual advisor stepped forward and said, "We must welcome all to Jerusalem. That is a sacred obligation. The marchers should enter, if only for a day."

Etzion answered abruptly, "Thank you, rabbi, but you have it wrong. We must safeguard the Land of Israel."

Outvoted 4K leaders gathered in the back of the room around the rebuffed rabbi.

"We must show hospitality," said one. "Let's go to Qalandia to meet the March."

Etzion glared. "Order — quiet. All who will obey what we just voted, stay. For those who won't, get out — now."

Noah prayed over his encounter with Ruth and Alessio. They were right about one thing. The Third Temple would not be built if the world went up in flames now. The End Time must not be today. Luke reported Jesus saying the moment would be unexpected.

Noah entered the American enclave, where Palmer was conferring with his Secretary of State.

"Mr. President, I have an idea."

"And?" said Palmer.

"Ask the Prime Minister to let the March into Jerusalem."

"You think I should tell our host to welcome a million Muslims? At this time?"

"Yes," he replied, continuing to pray. "We should make time for the Third Temple to be built."

"Perhaps that is God's will," Palmer answered in a burst of tolerance, instantly calculating that letting the March into the City might divert attention from the Mount so he could escape to Washington.

Amen.

132

JERUSALEM
Saturday, June 2

POPE SIXTUS leaned into his clasped hands in prayer. When he heard Alessio and Ruth enter the papal enclave, he opened his eyes and patted the chairs next to him.

"Come, sit. I could use friendly company. How are you feeling?" he asked Ruth.

"The way Isaac must have felt after Abraham untied him and sacrificed a ram to God instead," Ruth replied. "Spared."

The Pope smiled briefly at the biblical reference. "And I feel like Jesus in the wilderness."

"Your intelligence officer reporting," said Alessio. "The March is at the checkpoint on the east side of Jerusalem. The Ayatollah and others plan to greet them there. You're invited to join them."

"The Archbishop is going," said Ruth.

Sixtus sighed wearily. "My Vatican on the Mount — did I misread Fatima?"

Ruth faced the Pope. "Visions are not how-to manuals."

"Father Brondini, what do you say?" asked Sixtus.

Alessio hesitated before suggesting, "Surely if your vision is God's will, others would have heard the same divine message. No one has." He held his breath, awaiting an order to pack his bag and leave not only Jerusalem but the Vatican, maybe even the priesthood.

"I should abandon what I began?" The Pope seemed angered.

"Change course," said Alessio, taking a step back toward reassurance. "3 into 1 can mean bringing the three peoples of the Book out of a wilderness toward peace."

"But Fatima is clear, clear to me," said the Pope, scowling.

Alessio knew this was his moment. To challenge his superior, the Holy Father, the Pope of Christendom. It no longer felt like betrayal of obedience sworn. It was loyalty to a deeper truth. Feeling himself at the edge of a cliff, Alessio leapt. "It's idolatry to worship a piece of paper rather than seeking God in communion with others."

"It's not your place...."

"Holy Father, we have both erred. We have sinned," said Alessio, not needing to remind Sixtus of a secret shared between penitent and confessor.

Long silence ensued. The Pope stared at Alessio as though he'd been slapped in the face. Then he looked downward with a frown, his head supported by a right arm that rested on the chair's arm.

Sixtus looked up. "As Jeremiah prophesied, 'Let the idols be confounded and the images be broken in pieces.'" He arose and walked to his portable altar, picked up a matchbox next to the votive candles, reached into his vestment pocket and pulled out the yellowing Fatima page, held secret for a century. Alessio took the matchbox from him and struck the match. The Pope tilted the page into the flame. He held the burning paper until it was about to scorch his thumb, letting ash flutter to the floor. "We are free from that, as will be the Holy Father who follows me. Let's meet the March."

We are free, Alessio silently agreed.

133

JERUSALEM
Saturday, June 2

IRAN'S SUPREME LEADER entered the Russian space, ushered in without a word by the nervous interpreter standing watch. President Goudonov greeted the Ayatollah, who knew some Russian, having spent part of his youth in Turkmenistan when it was part of the Soviet Union.

"*Chai?*" Goudonov asked.

"*Nyet, spacibo*," replied the Ayatollah. "I grieve for your loss. We pray for the souls of those who died."

Goudonov silently accepted the condolence.

Staring directly into Goudonov's eyes, he said, "I ask you to hold fire."

Goudonov held the gaze, determined not to blink first.

"You Iranians may see everything as Allah's will, sacrifice as victory. For Russians power respects strength. I must act after what America did to my homeland."

The Ayatollah did not back down. "Russia can lead the world in a new direction.

You pledged to defend Iran. I release you from that."

Goudonov refused the offer. "Now it's between Russia and America."

"I will tell the world that Iran asked Russia to refrain. We will show the true nature of Iran, a country of peace, and of Islam, a faith of righteousness."

Goudonov answered, "We act in the immortal interests of Mother Russia."

"Russia is mortal. I see doom."

134

JERUSALEM
Saturday, June 2

THE MARCH PRESSED like raging floodwaters against a dam when it arrived at the Qalandia checkpoint. Navid Kosari stood with a bullhorn before the entrance to the heavily fortified maze of concrete and steel that separates East Jerusalem from Palestinian areas to the north. He beseeched the Israeli border guards to let the women through. An amplified voice from the watchtower responded that without visas the marchers could not enter.

Kosari heard a distant commotion as soldiers on the Jerusalem side turned to face south. Unseen by Kosari, an improbable delegation had arrived.

Seven figures marched as one.

In the middle was the Ashkenazi Chief Rabbi of Israel, an aged figure with foot-long white beard, black suit and flat-brimmed hat, white shirt, and tie striped in gray and black.

To his left was Pope Sixtus VI, resplendent in white robe, atop his head a pretiosa, a white mitre embroidered with a red stripe pointing to the heavens, in his right hand a ferula, a crozier with crucifix of Christ bowing to the earth.

To his right was the Grand Ayatollah of Iran, robed in black with white and gray silk showing at the collar, a black turban atop his head.

To the further right and left were the Coptic Pope from Egypt, the Imam of Mecca's Grand Mosque, the Archbishop of Canterbury, and Russia's Patriarch, each in the regalia of his faith.

Each held scripture with hands outstretched. The Rabbi held the Torah, the Pope a Latin Bible, the Ayatollah the Qur'an, the Archbishop the New Revised Standard Version of the Bible, each pointing his version of the Word in the direction of the border wall and the armed unit that held rapid-fire gunnery. Alessio and Ruth walked directly behind the Pope and Archbishop.

Some Israeli soldiers held their M16 rifles at semi-ease. Others aimed directly at the crowd on the southern side of the checkpoint, fire ready. Jerusalem residents formed a dense semi-circle around the religious leaders.

Silence held sway except for a background buzz from the Old City. An Israeli soldier shouted through a bullhorn, "Halt!" But the seven stepped forward, holding the Word aloft. The bullhorn blared, "Halt! Stop where you are." But the seven slowly moved forward, holding the Word aloft. "A final warning. If you cross the red line, we will stop you." But the seven walked forward, holding the Word aloft. They stepped over the red line, all with their right foot at the same moment, facing straight ahead.

135

JERUSALEM
Saturday, June 2

PRIME MINISTER FELDMAN was arguing by phone with Mossad's Director when President Palmer, Noah at his side, whipped open a curtain and ignoring the conversation said, "Let's talk."

Feldman quickly signed off and greeted his old friend. "Congratulations on the strike."

Without acknowledging his ally's gratitude, Palmer said, "You should let the March into the City, after screening them of course."

Feldman sputtered, "But why would you say this? The March is fizzling out like a balloon losing air. The media have more important events to report than a movie star on a white horse and a gaggle of women."

Palmer bore in on his target. "Aaron, you need to do this, for Israel. You can't be seen as shutting the women out of this city. You can show the difference between violence and compassion, and the world will know which side we're on."

"You sound like a minister," Feldman scoffed. "What got into you, really?"

"This is basic political calculus for our survival," Palmer admitted. "Letting the March in will give me a chance to get back to Washington."

Noah added, "The religious leaders are at Qalandia to meet the March. If there is bloodshed, you're responsible." When Ruth called to invite him to join them, he couldn't believe she was putting herself in such danger. He would do what he could to keep her safe.

"You must be kidding," Feldman said. "Is the Chief Rabbi participating?"

"He's leading it, along with the Pope, the Ayatollah, the Archbishop and the rest," said Noah. "And hundreds of Israelis."

Feldman blinked rapidly, looking down at the portable parquet flooring as though searching for the lost piece of a puzzle. He picked up his secure device and summoned the Interior Minister, who was on the line in a second.

"Moishe, tell the guards to let the Marchers enter - but only after seizing any weapons - everything, even a nail file. They have a one-day visa from me personally. They are welcome to the City, and they must return through the same gate by nightfall tomorrow. Clear?"

Palmer sighed and his shoulders dropped an inch, as though a millstone had been lifted from his neck. "Thank you, Aaron."

"Tell that to my coalition partners — if I have any after this." Feldman shook his head, scowling.

136

QALANDIA GATE, JERUSALEM
Saturday, June 2

IGNORING THE ISRAELI soldier's demand that they stop, the seven prelates took another step toward the barrier wall. None said a word, but a book held aloft by each — the Word holy to each — spoke unmistakably on whose authority they approached. A phalanx of soldiers lined the wall, most frozen in their stance, some shifting uneasily, all poised to fire on command.

When the religious leaders came within fifty feet of the gate, the unit leader stepped forward, M1 carbine in hand. He shouted, "I command you to halt."

The Ashkenazi Chief Rabbi moved forward to greet him with a Torah scroll held in front. "My son, put down your arms. We come in peace to greet our sisters and brothers, so they may worship in our Holy City."

The soldier hesitated. "Rabbi, I understand. But we have orders."

"That has been the defense of many judged by history - following orders. You have a higher calling." The rabbi took another step forward with the other six faith leaders, holding their books aloft.

The guard hesitated, then clenched his jaw and commanded, "Battery, ready."

The faith leaders stepped forward.

I have taken a life, so it's my turn to be shot but not Ruth's. Alessio moved in front of her as a shield.

The units atop and along the wall assumed firing position.

"Aim," the unit leader stated, though his enunciation quivered.

The faith leaders took another step.

A phone jangled. The prelates paused. The leader was still. A soldier hustled to the unit leader's side and whispered. The leader's face melted in relief.

"Rabbi, you may greet Navid Kosari as he enters Jerusalem. The marchers will be admitted. They have 24 hours and will return through this Gate tomorrow afternoon."

The religious leaders lowered their sacred texts and moved forward with the leader to the entrance gate. Navid Kosari and a dozen women in white were greeted first by the Rabbi and the Ayatollah.

"Welcome to Jerusalem," said the rabbi, "a city for all People of the Book."

As ancient Hebraic custom demanded, the rabbi presented them with food and drink offered by his aides. The Russian Patriarch's assistant offered his country's traditional welcome of bread and salt. Others held grapes, water, cheese, and sweets.

As the religious delegates led Kosari and his coterie in the direction of the Mount, a flow of women in dusty white entered in unceasing numbers and divided in western and southern directions. Escorted by Israeli guards and informed they could not enter the walled Old City because of crowds and Summit security, the marchers streamed along the hillsides and streets of East Jerusalem, to encircle the Old City with a band of white. Strangers offered gifts, including candles distributed by men wearing jackets embroidered with 4K and others in blue oxford shirts marked NJA.

The religious leaders headed back to the summit as one. As they turned a corner near the eastern entrance to the Mount, a bearded middle-aged man dressed in a buttoned navy suit, pressed white shirt and pink tie rushed forward. He pulled a silver serrated dagger from his coat. Yelling *"Allahu Akbar!"* he lunged at the Grand Ayatollah. But the Ashkenazi Chief Rabbi swung his Torah in front of the blade that plunged into the wooden frame holding the scroll. Alessio leapt upon the thwarted assassin, slammed him facedown to the ground, and held him in a chokehold until police handcuffed and dragged him to a vehicle with flashing blue lights.

The rabbi supervised as a policeman carefully extricated the weapon from its resting place without further splintering the Torah casing. The Pope comforted the Ayatollah, who seemed more concerned whether anyone else was attacked than what his own fate might have been if the rabbi and Alessio had not intervened. Security forces separated the startled crowd from the dignitaries. Together the faith leaders ascended the Mount where the fate of the world was being decided.

137

JERUSALEM
Saturday, June 2

IT WAS DUSK when the religious leaders returned to the summit on the Mount. Amidst frenzied coverage of America's attack on Russia, news spread virally that the "Magnificent Seven" had faced down the Israeli border guards to usher the March into Jerusalem. Arab and Iranian media featured photographs of the Pope extending his arms in greeting to Navid Kosari and the Ashkenazi Chief Rabbi thwarting the attack on the Ayatollah with his Torah case.

"Prayer Trumps Military Might!" beamed CNN. "Torah Saves Ayatollah!" blared Fox. "Feldman greets Marchers for peace," headlined the Israeli Government's press release, which failed to mention that the Prime Minister was nowhere near where the March entered. Stern Russian television anchors briefly interrupted coverage of the American attacks, military music reminiscent of the Great Patriotic War somberly playing, with a clip of the Russian Patriarch presenting bread and salt to Navid Kosari. This was followed by a blunt reminder of the unshakable alliance between Iran and Russia.

The bespectacled anchorman announced that the Duma unanimously empowered President Goudonov to do "the necessary."

Once gathered in their meeting space, the Pope brought the religious delegates to order with prayer. "May we be as united here as we were at Qalandia."

Alessio leaned forward, ready to record whether the summit would cohere or collapse.

The Coptic Pope spoke. "My brother, we are unified by the Spirit. What is built here must be for everyone."

The Russian Patriarch spoke next. "We will join in creating a Christian presence on this Mount. But no primacy of any one of us."

The perpetually taciturn imam of the Grand Mosque of Mecca looked adrenalized by events. "This ground is holy to Islam. But there is room for a Christian structure within our Noble Sanctuary."

The Ashkenazi Chief Rabbi placed both hands on the table. "The Rock of Abraham is the foundation of all three of our faiths."

"Today is a good beginning," said the Supreme Ayatollah as he looked at Pope Sixtus with a smile, "Can you surrender your dream of a second Vatican?"

Instead of answering, Sixtus turned to Okello. "Archbishop, your thoughts?"

The Archbishop paused for a brief silent prayer, then stood unlike the others who had spoken seated.

"An hour ago, the Word spoke as one and denied violence the victory. Let us celebrate what we hold in common. Let us build here ... the Domes of the Book."

The Archbishop paused, letting the name echo through the delegates' minds. He clicked on a laptop that broadcast a video Ruth had her tech assistant produce at the Anglican Centre based on sketches she created with the Archbishop and Bishop McDermott. The screen showed three domes as clover leaves with a fourth joined at the center.

"Three into one," the Pope murmured.

Archbishop Okello described the drawing of four interconnected enclosures — the three leaves labeled "Islam," "Judaism," and "Christianity" and the center marked "Dome of the Book." He explained how a visitor would choose a doorway into a Jewish, Christian or Muslim worship space and from each one could enter the central rotunda.

The screen shifted to the central space where a visitor could access the Book according to her or his faith.

The Archbishop explained, "The Torah will be available in print or on screens in any language of the visitor's choice. The Qur'an will be in Arabic with translation into other languages. The Christian Bible will be accessible in any language, including Latin and other ancient tongues. There will be braille and audio versions." In the middle of the rotunda encircled by a railing lay the Foundation Stone, the Rock of Abraham.

"We can build the symbol the world needs — that we commune as people of the Book while celebrating our own expressions of its truth. If we can march together, we can create the Domes of the Book. Together we follow the command of our one true God to love one another."

The Archbishop paused, observing the other delegates' physical reactions. The Coptic Pope's head tilted to the side. The Russian Patriarch stroked his beard. The Imam of the Grand Mosque of Mecca moved his head slowly up and down, stretching a neck muscle.

The Russian Patriarch said in a strong voice, "This is a breakthrough. If we participate in the design, I support it."

The Ashkenazi Chief Rabbi smiled broadly.

"As it is said in Deuteronomy, following the celebration of my ancestors when they were released from Egypt and came to this land, 'Then you, together with the Levites and the aliens who reside among you, shall celebrate with all the bounty that the Lord your God has given to you and to your house.' Let everyone be welcome here."

The Imam of Mecca's Grand Mosque pursed his lips and spoke quietly as all leaned forward to hear. "Enough blood has been shed over what the Prophet, may peace be upon him, gave us as guidance to shame us eternally. Enough! I will work for this idea."

The Coptic Pope posed a question, "Who will be the design committee?"

Archbishop Okello replied, "Let's find the best talent. We must avoid the peril of design by committee." All the prelates laughed at this, each having witnessed unfortunate results of groupthink.

"With full participation I support this," said the Coptic Pope.

Eyes turned to the Supreme Leader of Iran, who held a steady, impenetrable gaze from the moment the sketches were unveiled and throughout unanimous acceptance to that point.

"Our world faces destruction as we sit together. And we discuss a building that may never be constructed in a Noble Sanctuary that has been the center of conflict from recorded time." Alessio noted several heads visibly slump. "Our only hope for survival is to show government leaders that a way can be found out of ancient impasse. Iran supports building the Domes of the Book."

This left the Pope, who had stolidly insisted on a Vatican cathedral, a face-saving solution. "Then we are unanimous. We shall create together the Domes of the Book, three separate and united. A blessed outcome. We should ...."

A messenger from Prime Minister Feldman dashed into the gathering space. With pain in his eyes, he announced, "Forgive my intrusion. Russia attacked America. Government leaders are gathering. Please join them — now."

138

JERUSALEM
Saturday, June 2

"DAMN. They got through in North Dakota," the President muttered.

"But our shield worked at Warren," said Secretary Shulman. "So the Russians know they're unlikely to succeed next time. We've shown our overwhelming advantage," Palmer shook his head. "The war now will be from the sea. It can all happen in minutes."

Noah was about to say that this was the final sign, Revelation's beast rising out of the sea, but held his tongue in Shulman's presence. He and Palmer exchanged glances that caused Shulman to ask, "What is it?"

Palmer assessed the damage instead.

"Our Minot command center is destroyed, and the ICBM's there are out of commission. Thank God the Minutemen in Wyoming are untouched," referring to about 150 Minuteman III ICBM's scattered at Warren Air Force Base launch sites, once slated in nuclear reduction talks for conversion to historical relics but still a bulwark of America's land-based nuclear attack force.

"Congress convenes at midnight Jerusalem time," said Shulman. "The leadership's drafted a declaration of war. But it would help to buy time ...."

"Time? It'll be Option A+," said Palmer firmly. "Russia submits to our terms or that's it. I'll speak to Congress from here."

Shulman closed his eyes.

Noah asked, "Option A+?"

"Obliteration. Every base, every mobile launcher, every submarine, every major city."

Shulman pursed his lips. "No step approach?"

"We can't risk it," said Palmer. "But ... let's get back to the summit." Palmer raised his shoulders. "One last chance for Russia to submit."

"Or this world ends in fire and we are made anew," said Noah, ignoring Shulman's glare.

As the American group entered the assembly, they noticed a glum Iranian President Al-Rabani sitting behind the Ayatollah's empty lead chair. Unknown to them, Al-Rabani was furious to learn of the botched assassination attempt on the Ayatollah, but anger turned to dread when Al-Rabani realized that his phone call from AM's leader Vali Qalil had been intercepted, so it was a matter of minutes before the Ayatollah would be informed of Al-Rabani's treachery.

Prime Minister Feldman announced to those present as they waited for the faith leaders to join them, "I admitted the March to welcome all People of the Book to our City. Security forces will escort each of you safely tomorrow to a secure airfield to return home. There was an attack on the Ayatollah as the faith delegates returned from greeting the March, but it was thwarted. Your safety requires that we all remain here tonight."

The leaders were deathly quiet, each knowing of the attacks on Russia and the United States and holding a collective breath.

Silence was shattered when Palmer got to his place. He glared at Goudonov.

"You launched a war Russia will forever regret. Your missiles struck Minot, but our defenses shot you down in Wyoming. You won't get through next time, but we will."

Goudonov was emphatic. "You attacked us. Russia responded. We are even."

"Now you know how we live every day," shouted Palestinian leader Arafat.

Palmer ignored the intrusion.

"State clearly and unequivocally now that you will take no further action, that you will withdraw all forces from this region immediately, and that you renounce all alliances against the United States and against Israel. Pledge this now or the blood of all Russia is on you."

Goudonov stiffened. "You could have left the conflict to this region, but you attacked Russia. That was your death sentence."

Egypt's President shouted, "Gentlemen, Israel started this. The killings at Qom, the strike on Fordow. This is not your fight." He addressed Feldman. "Will you surrender your nuclear weapons if Arabs and Iranians pledge never to have them?"

Feldman shook his head. "To ask that we surrender anything with your troops massed on our borders, to ask that we stand by while Iran acquires nuclear weapons when its President," he pointed at Al-Rabani, "says he will wipe Israel from the map. Really, this is too much."

Al-Rabani looked ready to walk over to Feldman and strangle him with hands already reaching forward and fingers gripping inward. "You Dajjal. Back off or be damned," he shouted at Feldman.

The assembly was about to erupt when the religious leaders entered. They surrounded the government delegates, each standing behind the seated leader most closely aligned by territory or religion.

"Friends, I speak for us all," said Sixtus. "We agreed on what should be built here, a symbol of unity of our faiths. Every nation must cease fire. We surround you with prayer and beseech you — all of you — to order your forces to stand down. Let us have peace."

The faith leaders put their hands on the shoulders of the government leaders, communicating calm through touch and silent prayer. The Ayatollah pressed his hands on seated President Al-Rabani's shoulders.

"Iran," said the Ayatollah, "will do nothing militarily, nothing through this Summit. I ask you, President Goudonov, that Russia do nothing to avenge what Israel did to Iran. We release you from alliance."

"But your President ...," began a puzzled Goudonov.

"I speak for Iran," stated the Ayatollah. "Iran's armed forces follow my orders."

Al-Rabani nodded piously, contemplating destinations that were not Iran.

The Egyptian President sought clarification. "What is our assurance that Israel will not take advantage of a pause?"

Feldman sat silently, then nodded towards Palmer.

Palmer reciprocated with a quick bow of the head, saying, "Let's take a short recess. I pledge that for now America will take no offensive action if Russia commits to the same."

Goudonov nodded agreement without a word.

Palmer pushed his chair back, walked to Feldman and put his right arm around the Prime Minister as they departed together.

139

JERUSALEM
Saturday, June 2

SOLDIERS PATROLLING the Old City's cobblestone and marble alleys and rooftops gripped their automatic weapons. Synagogues overflowed with rabbis and congregants searching Torah for deliverance. Orthodox men in black gathered in circles along the Western Wall passionately discussing defense of their families, their City, the Land of Israel, or sat silently reciting psalms and rocking their heads back and forth, many wearing tefillin, black straps lashed and wound tightly from shoulder to wrist to bind themselves to God. Churches exhausted supplies of votive candles, ancient bronze holders full and glowing, worshippers filling pews and kneeling before side altars with relics, statues and gilt and silver framed icons of martyred saints. Orthodox Christians mixed with Catholic, Protestant, Armenian, Syriac, Coptic and other monks, priests, ministers, and worshippers at the Church of the Holy Sepulchre. Mosques filled with men in socks on prayer rugs and women in balconies. Imams chanted from minaret loudspeakers about akhir al-zaman, The Hour when "The unbelievers among the People of the Book and the pagans shall burn forever in the fire of Hell, but the reward of the righteous shall be the gardens of Eden, gardens watered by running streams, where they shall dwell forever," Qur'an 98:6-9.

The March of the Innocents divided at the Qalandia checkpoint into two streaming lines escorted by Israeli security forces, encircling the Old City from the surrounding heights, each marcher cradling a lighted candle. They faced a sleepless night at the end of a pilgrimage few imagined when joining the March. They almost doubled the resident population.

Roof-top Dispensationalists sat in chairs or stretched out on rugs and blankets, ecstatically looking upward into the moon-lit sky, heartened that Russia and the United States had struck each other's nuclear bases, certain this was the time, the End of Time, about to be swept up to heaven to meet their Savior that very night.

The portable baptismal fonts the New Jerusalem Alliance deployed to convert Jews to Christianity did brisk business. Residents queued to receive water and oil, to recite the Baptismal Covenant in the language of their choice, hedging bets about the afterlife.

The NJA's global convert count rose to 126,500. Noah projected 144,000 by midnight.

Because of 4K's rancorous split earlier in the day, competing fliers in Hebrew circulated throughout Jerusalem. One issued by 4K headlined, "Restore the Land of David. Rebuild the Temple!" The other urged reconciliation, beckoning all to a website petitioning the Israeli government to make peace with the Muslim world

It was Shabbat, the Jewish Sabbath. The Knesset did not meet but members talked privately about the unfolding calamity. An ultra-Orthodox party was furious Feldman let the March pollute the City, and a moderate pro-settlement party feared the attacks on Iran and the Megiddo massacre had united Islam and would lead to slaughter of settlers in Samaria, Judea, Galilee and Golan. A No Confidence motion was in the wind.

Media coverage scrolled flames and destruction at the Uzhur base in Siberia and the Minot ICBM center in North Dakota. From Google Earth imagery the Russian and American locations appeared as smoldering rubble. CNN projected death counts in the thousands in each country and featured a grizzled elderly man in denim angrily mourning the loss of his son, a guard at Minot.

"Crucify them," he demanded, referring to Russians.

The BBC projected a world map and featured a retired Royal Navy Admiral about what was happening underwater. Using a laser, the Admiral pointed to nuclear armed submarines within striking distance of Russian and American urban centers. It was 99% certain the American submarines "can evade interception and destroy 90% of the Russian population in minutes." He could not give a precise estimate of survival odds for the U.S. population — "not more than 20%, I should say," he hazarded.

A retired Russian admiral interviewed by the BBC in his posh London flat asserted, "Do not underestimate the Russian Navy. The fleet can destroy America's coastal cities in minutes. And don't forget Moscow's Topol-M and RS-24 Yars. They move at 15,000 miles per hour and can penetrate America's missile defenses. You saw that in North Dakota. Imagine a strike with ten nuclear warheads next time."

While nuclear game theory dominated the media, Fox featured a panel of nine religious commentators. The Evangelical pastor who had been on the Harry Black show with Ruth, hair slicked back like Billy Graham in his prime, proclaimed, "We are seeing what Revelation prophesied. No need for despair. The glory of God is upon us."

The moderator asked, "How do you know?"

"Just look at the fires of Jerusalem." The screen cut to an aerial shot of Jerusalem appearing aflame with fiery light, a distinct white circle aglow around the Old City from candles. Citing Revelation Chapter 20, the pastor declared, "At the end there will be a

Lake of Fire for those not written into the Book of Life, but the chosen will dwell forever with the living God in the New Jerusalem."

The moderator turned to a Brooklyn rabbi, often accused but never convicted of aiding and abetting violence against Muslims. He had earned a moment of fame two years earlier by leading a march on New York City Council demanding a mosque not be built near a Yavneh Academy, and threatening to smash the cornerstone were it ever laid.

The rabbi answered, "The Land of Israel was given to the **Jewish** People. We must restore its rightful boundaries. With a rebuilt Temple our Mashiach will appear and all nations will face righteous judgment."

A frowning professor of Muslim Studies at Wayne State University responded to a question about the Islamic view of the unfolding cataclysm.

"Shi'a Islam shares a similar view to Judaism and Christianity about the End Time," she asserted. "Details differ, but all three faiths see calamity as a prelude to the Mahdi's or the Messiah's arrival." The screen shifted to Damascus' Great Mosque, where an enormous crowd gathered around the Isa Minaret, beseeching Isa to appear and read out the Book of Judgment.

"Who is this Mahdi?" asked the moderator.

The professor replied, "The Mahdi was born in the seventh century and has lived since in a kind of hiding. He will emerge to lead the final battle against the Dajjal, the devil on earth, if you will."

"The Dajjal, who would that be?" asked the moderator.

"Some say Israel's Prime Minister."

The moderator threw a curve. "So do you see a kind of bringing together of Christianity, Islam and Judaism at the End Time?"

The pastor jumped off his seat at that. "It's the beginning of endless time under Christ Jesus! A glorious moment for all that turn to Him! They will share eternal peace refreshed by the waters of the Living God." He was jubilant as though holding the winning ticket to a mega-lottery.

"The nations will be judged — for their treatment of Israel. God embraces his chosen people," said the rabbi.

The Wayne State academic scowled. "There's no glory to anyone when there's no one left to judge or be judged. You're all nuts."

140

JERUSALEM
Saturday, June 2

FELDMAN PUT HIS RIGHT ARM around Palmer in the privacy of the Israeli space, certain no one was watching except for Noah who accompanied the President.

"I am sorry, my friend," Feldman commiserated, though Noah couldn't tell if it was sincere or a performance. "What's your next move?"

Palmer slid out of the embrace. "Russia accepts the terms I offered or it's midnight in Moscow. I'm buying time for a broadcast to Congress while we target every Russian submarine, bomber base and missile silo that could possibly retaliate. Once that's set, we strike," Palmer stated matter-of-factly.

"Can we help?" asked Feldman.

"You'd better reserve the Temple Swords for yourself. This is America's fight now. Conventional danger is what you face."

"What about a truce?" asked Feldman. "Back to the Cold War?"

"The Russians just made 9/11 look like a mosquito bite. If I do nothing, I'll be impeached and deserve it. We'll teach Russia a lesson that won't need repeating."

"And what if it all turns to hell?"

"We didn't start this," said Palmer.

"Don't blame Israel. What did you think would happen when we took out Fordow?"

Noah stepped in. "If it all turns to hell, if fires rage across the planet, they could be the final step towards a New Jerusalem."

Though what was happening was beginning to look less godly as he watched interviews with the Christian families of the deceased and the hell they were living.

Feldman was speechless.

"Look, Aaron, you need to back me now — all the way," said Palmer.

141

JERUSALEM
Saturday, June 2

WHILE PALMER PRESSURED FELDMAN, Goudonov met with the Egyptian and Palestinian leaders. "Iran backed down," said Goudonov. "If the Supreme Leader means what he said, you're on your own in the Muslim world."

"Jihad," Egyptian President Modri replied. "Our people demand it. We can occupy most of Israel in a day."

The Palestinian leader was ecstatic to hear this. "The Mahdi has returned. How else to explain Navid Kosari and the March? We must join them for the final battle."

Cringing at the religious fairy tale, Goudonov thanked his Soviet education for teaching him the irrationality of religion and how it could be useful for manipulation.

"You'll have naval and air support from us but no ground troops. A decisive intifada, not some 3-day protest. Agreed?"

The two Muslim leaders shook the Russian President's hand, gave him traditional kisses on left and right cheeks, and gripped him by the shoulders with hugs close friends give to seal a solemn promise.

Once alone with his Minister of Defense, Goudonov switched to commander mode. "Where will the Americans strike when I decline their invitation of surrender?"

"GRU predicts the next moves will be against two of our cities, maybe Nizhny Novgorod and Chelyabinsk, where strategic assets combine with large populations. We're blocking cyber-attack on our offensive assets. The Americans won't be able to target our mobile launchers."

Goudonov stretched his increasingly tense neck. "Give the sub commanders freedom to act. If under threat, each may strike first on his own order."

"Yes, Mr. President," replied the Defense Minister. "And Operation Mikhail?"

"Is that a question?" demanded Goudonov.

"On your command," replied the Defense Minister. Unstated was the reality that great cities of Europe and the United States would vanish under mushroom clouds, as would Russia, with no place safe from nuclear explosions that would irradiate the globe.

142

JERUSALEM
Saturday, June 2

"IS THERE A BIBLE PASSAGE that makes this go away?" Alessio asked Ruth, hoping for a miraculous suggestion.

They sat on a bench outside the tent. The air was cool and eerily still. The Old City was bathed in candle glow ringing the town, visible along the ridge of the Mount of Olives across the Kidron Valley. The improbable agreement of the faith delegates to create the Domes of the Book seemed inconsequential.

"Some think Gog and Magog in Revelation refers to Russia, but that would mean that the author John of Patmos envisioned Russia ten centuries before it existed. And it's far-fetched to say the lake of fire means nuclear blasts given the state of science then."

Alessio had come to expect Ruth to respond to crises with scholarship. He settled his gaze on the Mount of Olives and the deathly grey stone cemetery lining its slope, a harbinger of what awaited all humanity.

They watched the City below surge with people in the streets, light, tumult, sound. Large screens in place to broadcast the summit's results flashed reports of a world in timeless suspension, people massed in worship places and city squares, praying, protesting, shouting, stretching hands to the skies, a Russian Orthodox Church ablaze in Brighton Beach, the American Embassy in Moscow attacked by a furious mob, rocks crashing through windows, tires burning, cars overturned. Split images repeated scenes of devastation in Uzhur and North Dakota — utter destruction, cremains.

Ruth began to cry. "I never thought it might end like this."

Not used to weeping women, let alone Ruth, he didn't know what to say.

"So many things I'd hoped for may never happen. Like having a child." Ruth broke down.

Was it like this for women? The men he admired were his colleagues, clergy and soldiers who served under orders and offered their lives for the good of the many, others they would never meet.

Alessio hesitated, then put his arms around her as she wept. *Priests are called to comfort the suffering.*

"Maybe it's too late anyway at my age." Ruth took a breath and apologized for her outburst. Alessio moved away, his arms feeling the loss of her. Was there something he was afraid he would never do?

Television screens below the Mount grabbed their attention.

"Oh, Santo Cielo!" Alessio pointed to the graph of U.S. and Russian submarines in the eastern Mediterranean.

Video technology mapped ten submarines from each fleet grouped around seven vessels of each navy atop the waves, with commentary along the bottom "Nuclear armada face-off," "Nuke-armed subs ready for attack." Russian and American fleets streamed toward each other, the American force from the west and the Russians from the north, where they were fated to collide off the coast of Israel.

"The Beast from the Sea with seven heads and ten horns," said Ruth.

"And Satan mounted as a dragon on the Beasts of the Sea," said Alessio.

"The people seduced by the Beast, worshipping a false god," said Ruth.

Descriptions from Revelation come alive.

"We have to convince your president," said Alessio, "that his adoration of military might is the worship of a false god. It is not Jesus he summons but the Lord of Evil." He began to think of things he desired to do before time ends.

143

JERUSALEM
Saturday, June 2

USING THEIR HIGHEST POWERS of persuasion, the Pope, Ayatollah and Ashkenazi Chief Rabbi cajoled government delegates into session. Trapped together, the leaders seethed with anger but met, knowing they could use the time to assess their enemies and use any sign of weakness to their advantage.

The Pope had not envisioned global destruction as the outcome of his summit. He faced the heads of state.

"Events threaten to incinerate the earth. The Almighty calls upon us all to reverse this course." His eyes moved from Goudonov to Palmer to Feldman.

The Grand Ayatollah underlined the message.

"Iran will possess no nuclear weapon. Despite what we suffered, we will not respond in kind. President Goudonov — you are free of alliance with Iran."

Arafat shouted at Feldman, "Will you give up your Temple Swords and end the occupation of Palestine?"

Feldman replied sternly, "I marvel at your amnesia. Israel, reborn of the Shoah, where Abram became Abraham, home to half the world's Jews, I will protect it. When you call for our destruction, what do you expect?" Feldman glared at Arafat. "We can have peace. Start now by every country in this region recognizing the Jewish State's right to exist."

The Palestinian leader's face was as red as it could be without exploding.

"You speak to me of amnesia? You evict our people and treat us as animals. You marched our grandparents to the east to die in the desert, without mercy, without conscience."

EU President Schmidt slapped her palms on the table.

"Focus. We have one question — whether the world will be destroyed. The European Union asks Russia and the United States to pledge an immediate cease-fire now." She glared at Goudonov, then Palmer.

"The United States," said Palmer, "will suspend offensive action for four hours if Russia swears the same. By then we must have proof that Russia has deactivated its missile system and that its submarine and naval fleet have drawn back from the coast of Israel and away from all U.S. borders." Palmer's face was determined, unflinching.

Goudonov responded, "The American proposal is that we disarm and then the United States might change its ways. Ridiculous. If Israel agrees to a nuclear-free region and the United States reverses its Navy and pledges no strike on Russia, we could agree to a stand-down."

EU President Schmidt seized the moment. "I will work with you both on a truce. Neither of you will act before midnight," she stated.

Goudonov and Palmer grimly nodded affirmation.

144

JERUSALEM
Saturday, June 2

The Ayatollah, Rabbi and Archbishop followed Pope Sixtus into a private space with four maroon velvet padded armchairs arranged in a square, side tables with coffee and tea handy for the night ahead. Interpreters were dismissed.

The Pope got to the point.

"We pray the truce holds. What can we do to find a way forward?" He stroked his chin. "Do we agree on what the Ayatollah said — no nuclear weapons in this region, Israel included?"

"If only Israel has them," the Archbishop reasoned, "its neighbors will find a way to get them. I was the middle of three brothers. We each wanted what the others had. Nations are no different."

"Our Prime Minister can't surrender the Temple Swords. He'd be out of office in a flash," said the Rabbi.

The Ayatollah sat with arms crossed. "Then one day Iran will restart its program, no matter what I say now."

The Archbishop rubbed his bald spot, then broke into a broad smile. "What if we call for a vote of everyone in this region, Israel and Iran included? Hold it the same day in every country on one question: 'Should nuclear weapons be banned in every country on this map?' with the region stretching from Egypt to Iran. If every country votes yes, no leader could ignore that."

The Pope smiled. "It might buy some time, might even work."

"Brilliant. Let's try it," said the Rabbi.

145

JERUSALEM
Saturday, June 2

NOAH LEFT THE TENT to behold Jerusalem ablaze with light. Marchers along the heights and a multitude in the streets below cast a warm glow from flashlights, candles and lanterns that promised darkness would not descend upon this cradle of three great faiths and of its sacred violence. Alessio and Ruth found him in what seemed to be a trance.

Without waiting to catch her breath Ruth grabbed Noah. "How can we stop Palmer from launching a nuclear holocaust?"

"What world are you living in?" he replied. "America was struck as never before, this time in its heartland. This wasn't Pearl Harbor or San Francisco. The dead are people of the frontier, ranchers, wives and mothers, children with corn-blond hair."

"What are you telling him?"

"That this could be the closing page. Time for the seventh trumpet to sound. 138,000 are baptized - only 6,000 more before the Glory is revealed."

In the distance sounded the rumble of thunderheads. To the north fast-moving flat-topped clouds heralded an impossibly early summer storm, lightning striking with skeletal fingers and thunder crashing in applause.

Ruth stared at Noah. She sensed disquiet.

"You know Revelation's chapter 14. 'Those who bear the mark of the Beast will have no rest, day or night, and the smoke of their torment will last forever'."

He replied quietly, "And that is why whatever happens next between Russia and America is nothing compared to what comes next, the river of life flowing in the New Jerusalem, with the Lord God the temple forever after. And for us of the right faith to be here, to be present for the final Revelation!"

"Whatever Bible study you were in left out what happens between Chapters 14 and 22. Consider that."

"What's your Master of Divinity interpretation, O Great Scholar?"

"If you follow Revelation to the letter the way NJA is hell-bent on doing — and I mean hell-bent — it says that Jesus must return to bind Satan, defeat the beasts and reign for a millennium. After a thousand years will there be a final battle. In case you haven't noticed, Jesus and the saints haven't been running the world for a thousand years."

"The Roman Empire fell long ago. That's the defeated Beast."

"In a thousand-year reign of Christ presiding over a peaceful earth the devastation of World Wars I and II would not have taken place."

"How do you know God counts years the same way you do?" Noah's voice sounded less confident.

Ruth prayed he was wavering.

"Right now Russian and American fleets are surging toward each other off the Israeli coast. Each armada has ten submarines with periscopes rising out of the sea — ten horns, and the escorts are seven ships — seven heads. Just like the seven heads and ten horns that Revelation foretells before the final millennium."

We're not just depending on Revelation. We prayed over Bible passages and discerned that these are the final days described in Romans 8:22, 'the whole creation groaning with labor pains,' waiting for redemption."

Alessio looked ready to strike. "In a nuclear World War III, Jesus will have no Israel as a place to return. No Third Temple. All your work up in smoke. Is that your script? One written by the Father of Jesus or the Father of Lies?"

Noah frowned. The Book of Revelation said that only a third of the earth, trees, waters and living creatures in the sea would be destroyed.

"Total annihilation would be a problem."

146

———

JERUSALEM
Saturday, June 2

THE ASHKENAZI CHIEF RABBI spoke to Feldman like a grandfather encouraging his son to care for a grandchild. "Mr. Prime Minister, the faith delegates have agreed to a solution for where the Dome of the Rock once stood."

"The Domes of the Book, is that what you've christened it?" Feldman asked, with stress on the word "christened."

"It is a miracle we agreed," said the Rabbi. "It needs your support. I trust we have it?"

"To join a synagogue to a mosque and a cathedral, as though faith is an amusement park — preposterous! The Muslims can restore their Mosque. We'll build a Jewish Temple here. There are plenty of Christian sites in Jerusalem."

"The Domes of the Book can unite us."

"Not on my watch." Feldman glared to halt further debate on this crazed idea that would become a footnote of failed diplomacy.

Unmoved by his unbending opposition, Rabbi Solomon said, "Can you embrace the idea that Jerusalem should be a universal city?"

"If HaShem would reveal himself and take command, I will yield," said Feldman, "as I would for the Mashiach. Turn authority over to some supranational governor, who would it be? The bumbling Secretary General of the Jew-hating UN? Ridiculous."

Rabbi Solomon parried, "Martin Buber was once asked about the Book of Genesis, to explain how Judaism could justify the notion that this land or any land was forever entrusted by God to any one group of people. Buber answered, 'It seems to me that God does not give any one portion of the earth away. The conquered land is only lent even to the conqueror who has settled on it — and God waits to see what he will make of it.'"

"Rabbi, if HaShem wonders what Israel can make of this place, who am I to disappoint? He gave us this Land of Israel. You've said that many times. We govern it well." Feldman raised his decibel level for the last four words.

The Rabbi turned to a third topic. "And your position on the proposal that this region one day should be free of nuclear weapons? Surely the American and Russian attacks warn of what could happen here."

The Prime Minister's silence was uncharacteristically long. "The Temple Swords are our security guaranty. They deter and so protect us. We cannot allow any other country in this region to possess such a device, especially not Iran."

"Then you recognize that others find abominable what we possess, and they do not."

"We cannot abandon what ensures our survival, at least not until trust is built and peace flows like a river," countered Feldman.

"Then Israel is on a permanent war footing," said the Rabbi. "That is how you lead our people."

"This is our lot, Rabbi. We seek no territory beyond the Land of Israel. We have a sacred duty to defend what is ours by all means."

"And in that lies your weakness, Prime Minister," quietly said the Rabbi. "Military power is a false idol. It is not security. It blocks all paths to peace."

"Excuse me, but I have pressing matters." Feldman turned his back as the Minister of Defense entered.

"What?" Feldman demanded.

The Minister whispered into the Prime Minister's ear, "The Russian subs are near the coast."

147

JERUSALEM
Saturday, June 2

NOAH STRODE with Ruth into the American enclave, where they interrupted Palmer and Shulman mulling reports about Russian missile sites and naval movements.

"Mr. President, may we talk?"

Palmer looked up, annoyed, but after seeing the worried face of his faith advisor and fundraiser Palmer changed to the earnest expression that served him well when confronted by uncertain voters.

"Of course." Palmer waved for Shulman to absent himself.

"There is an aspect of our plan that needs adjustment," Noah began. "This can't be the End Time. There is another stage before the prophecy can be fulfilled."

"What do you mean?" asked the startled President.

"This is the time for binding up Satan before the final millennium."

Palmer understood the reference and disagreed. "Revelation, Chapter 20. Rome fell long ago. Satan's pagan idols were destroyed then."

"Who else but Satan could draw Russia and America into a fight that would ignite the whole world? Revelation speaks of only one third of the earth being burned. The Prince of Darkness has taken on the form of the beast of military might, ready to destroy it all."

"What difference does it make after Russia's attacks?"

Noah continued to appeal to shared beliefs.

"Without nuclear war you can provide time for all people of the Book to know the Messiah, with the Glory revealed on the Temple Mount, linking all three faiths, all led to the destiny God ordains."

Sensing Palmer also lived by selected Bible passages, Ruth searched her arsenal.

"In 1 Chronicles, God denies King David the right to build the Temple because of the blood he shed. If you go to war, you face God's rejection — no Temple, no New Jerusalem."

Palmer snorted in disbelief. "Is the will of God that Russia obliterates America?"

Noah pressed.

"You are like Abraham, willing to sacrifice a son because God commanded it, only to hear God say Stop! Human sacrifice shall be no more."

"Unlike Abraham, I'm not hearing the voice of God or seeing an angel in the room with us," said Palmer.

From the campaign Noah knew the depths of Palmer's devotion to voter perception, currently glued to the image of the American President who bullied Russia into submission. Time for a different image.

"Sir, as your Secretary of Faith, I have to tell you I think God placed you in the world's most holy place with the religious leaders of our day for a reason. This is the opportunity to make a lasting peace. God's will be done." He could see Palmer trying on the garment of God's favorite president.

"Thanks for your advice, Noah. I'll take it to the Lord in prayer."

He walked them to the exit. As the curtain closed, they heard him say to Shulman, "Put a hold on Option A+."

Noah turned to Ruth. "Time for me to join a new Bible study."

148

JERUSALEM
Saturday, June 2

THE AYATOLLAH WELCOMED Navid Kosari as he arrived at the summit tent. Kosari had lingered at the Qalandia checkpoint to welcome the first group of marchers to enter Jerusalem, as media photographers captured the historic moment. Kosari posed as the champion who brought his flock safely to their destination. Some of the women cried and hailed him as the Mahdi. Kosari grinned broadly to hear the CNN commentator report that this title was for the Muslim hero who would gather the faithful for a final battle.

Palestinian leader Arafat embraced him. "You accomplished what none of us could. Now let's smash the Jewish stranglehold on this land."

Egypt's more practical President softened the objective. "We can make Jerusalem, at least the eastern half, capital of a restored Palestine within a universally governed city. We will never again have the world's powers so ready to accept this."

The Wahhabi Imam from Mecca feared the March could strengthen Iran's role and advance Shi'a Islam, detestable to him as a Sunni. But even he was entranced by marchers who ringed the hills holding candles through the night.

"Islam is united. Shi'a, Sunni — we are all brothers," he paused, "and sisters."

Knowing his was the role of a lifetime, Kosari had rehearsed his lines.

"Peacefully we come, our only sword the Word. We are all the Army of the Mahdi. March on to the Day of Judgment!"

The Ayatollah continued.

"We need no physical weapon to achieve justice. We open Jerusalem to all people of the Book. We turn from idolatry, fraud, corruption, falsehood, hypocrisy, shame, and worship of military might. We restore the world revealed to us by the Prophet, blessings be upon him."

The Palestinian and Egyptian presidents looked askance, comfortable with devotional reflection but not giving up weapons.

The Ayatollah sensed their ambivalence. "When we resume our meeting tonight, you will be with us, Navid. You will light the way toward this City as capital of the world."

In Damascus the interim Imam of the Umayyad Mosque watched with mouth agape as a throng of over a hundred thousand gathered around the Isa Minaret, known in the West as the Minaret of Jesus. Television screens displayed an aerial image of candlelight encircling the Jerusalem summit, footage of Navid Kosari and women in dusty white entering Jerusalem, clips of destruction in Russia and America.

The Damascus crowd called in unison waves of sound — "Isa, return. Save us. Mercy."

As midnight approached in Damascus, the crowd hushed when a ghostly glow vaporized atop the Minaret, first appearing as a lighted fog descended from the jet-black sky above, then gradually emerging from the billowing cloud as a vague outline, imperceptible as a figure until it clarified as a human form. A three-dimensional image of a 6-foot tall man in his early to mid-30's, wearing a bleach-white robe, with dark hair and beard, stretched out his hands, a halo aflame overhead.

"Stigmata," the crowd murmured, "the wounds of Isa." Word spread through the assembly, "The Day of Judgment is at hand."

149

JERUSALEM
Saturday, June 2

EU President Schmidt shuttled between Presidents Palmer and Goudonov, urging each to embrace a nuclear truce.

"You're even," she argued.

Neither could rebut that. Schmidt's mediation allowed neither to show weakness to the other. Schmidt was surprised to find Palmer the readier of the two, willing to accept mutual suspension of actions until at least Monday, when each could be home from the Summit. Goudonov agreed after expressing satisfaction that Russia had struck the most recent blow and so could not be accused of being soft.

When Schmidt left Palmer after a fourth session, Palmer asked an aide to summon Noah and Ruth to the American enclave, where Shulman was tracking Russian submarine movements, neither armada having stopped heading toward a collision off Israel's coast.

"I postponed the session with Congress," Palmer told them, "until Monday when I'm back home. We're working on a truce. So let's turn to the rest of the agenda." He faced Ruth, "Where are the faith delegates, Dr. Waller?"

Ruth handed the President text of what the religious delegates had agreed:

- The Domes of the Book will be built where the Dome of the Rock once stood. There will be a Jewish temple, Christian church and Muslim shrine clustered around a central Dome of the Book, rising above the Rock of Abraham, where the Torah, the Bible and the Qur'an will be displayed in common space for worship and prayer.

- The walled Old City of Jerusalem will be governed by a supranational authority as a universal city, open to all, with a United Nations presence.
- There will be a popular vote on a common day in all countries of this region, Israel and Iran included, to decide if the region will be free of nuclear weapons.

All nations will respect the people's decision if it is affirmative in every country.

"What does Israel say?" Palmer turned to Noah.

"That depends on who Israel is," Noah responded. "The Prime Minister probably hates everything on this page. But he knows Israelis want peace. The Chief Rabbi supports this. He thinks only the messianic will oppose it. Including a Third Temple makes it hard to oppose."

Palmer sighed. "Noah, this doesn't sound like our New Jerusalem. And Israel can veto it all. But let's play it out. The American people deserve a president who brings peace to the Middle East." Noah could tell Palmer was trying out his election theme. "Otherwise, we're in a nuclear chess match, leading God knows where."

"God does know where, Mr. President," Noah stated, confident again.

150

JERUSALEM
Saturday, June 2

FELDMAN WAS ON THE PHONE when Palmer entered the Israeli space. He ended the call with "Do what it takes."

Feldman greeted Palmer as he stood to reach out his right hand as though greeting a head of state rather than an old friend. Palmer ignored the formality, sat down and unfolded his hands palms up.

"Aaron, America sealed its loyalty to Israel with the blood of our people. Now burnt offerings must be put behind us, forever."

"Ike," the Prime Minister softened. "Israel is forever in your debt."

"Then let's chart a course out of this together."

"How?"

"The faith leaders, including your Chief Rabbi, drafted this." Palmer handed the three-point sheet to Feldman.

Feldman listened intently as Palmer argued how each item could benefit Israel. "Each is worse than the others," said Feldman, handing the paper back to Palmer.

"You don't need to give up anything today or tomorrow," Palmer pressed. "You'd have years to work out the details if the vote's in favor of no nukes in the region. You'd get a Third Temple and what do you give up? Nothing really. Let the UN pay the bills for Old City police. Not a bad deal."

Feldman countered. "If you can get our enemies to give up nuclear weapons forever, with real verification, you're a miracle man. If it's only a vote you propose, I trust the Israeli people. After all, they elected me, so their good sense is clear. But where would America be now if it had surrendered its nuclear stockpile? Speaking Russian."

151

JERUSALEM
Saturday/Sunday, June 2-3

HOURS OF ARGUMENT led to midnight, leaders bickering over words — could anything be agreed by three faiths, four nations, a union, an authority and the Vatican? The EU President worked frantically to extend the truce beyond Monday, but neither Goudonov nor Palmer would divert his submarines from their collision course off the Israeli coast.

Church bells pealed twelve deep tones. Delegates wandered outside to smoke, to breathe the cool evening air, to give thanks they survived Saturday. A city normally dimly lit was ablaze with March candlelight, throngs in the streets, rooftop Dispensationalists reciting Revelation by flashlight, large screens flashing assaults on the Russian Embassy in Washington and the American Embassy in Moscow, protests and vigils in daylight and darkness depending on time zone. People worldwide massed in urban squares, churches, temples, and mosques, as though counting down the minutes to a new year, except now it could be to the end of time. Prayers aimed at the Mount, where those with power to make history were trapped like scorpions in a box.

The stars were as bright overhead as anyone could recall, with rumbling thunderheads and flashing lightning at a distance to the north. Mecca's Imam asked if one alignment was the Constellation of Orion, and the Coptic Pope replied he forgot what he learned in astronomy class. The Coptic Pope pointed at the Big Dipper.

"That one I know," he said, recalling what life was like as a boy when he could lie on the sands and look upward with no cares, able to journey by fantasy to distant places far from the troubles of Nasser's Egypt. And then he noticed that from the bottom left star of the Big Dipper emerged a light that brightened by the second and streaked from right to left.

"A satellite?" he asked.

The two noticed the Russian Patriarch also looking upward. They pointed to where he was gazing.

"I pray that's not a missile," said the Patriarch. He hurried to where President Goudonov was standing in a cloud of cigarette smoke. The Patriarch pointed upward.

"Is that one of ours?"

Goudonov wrenched his head backward and said, "No. And it's not American either. Missiles don't do that."

The light grew brighter and appeared to drop and slow its right to left trajectory. Delegates looked to the skies, negotiations suspended.

The light from the east floated nearly overhead, its tail two streaks of glowing cinders, forming a Y, with the bottom of the Y moving from east to west and descending as it approached the Mount. As the glow came closer, it cast yellow floodlight over the City and emitted a deafening sound wave causing everyone watching to grimace and hold hands to ears. The earth trembled. Structures seemed to bend to the will of the fiery object as it headed westward.

Alessio was first to reach the Foundation Rock but it was missing. Recently stolen from Rome, the chiseled hunk of the Titus Arch depicting soldiers carrying to Rome the treasures of the Second Temple had toppled into a depression below. He motioned to Ruth, who was standing next to Noah.

"The Well of Souls," Ruth identified the location. "A cave where the dead are said to meet twice a month for prayer, awaiting the Day of Judgment." Forbidden from contamination by human activity, the area had not been excavated since the Babylonian destruction of the First Temple over 2500 years ago.

Noah joined as they peered into the Well. Beaming a flashlight borrowed from a guard, Alessio shone light deep into the cave, where marble from the Titus Arch had crashed onto the rock below, cracking the floor into pieces and revealing an object that had been concealed beneath. A glint of gold caused a collective gasp.

As additional light pierced the darkness, there appeared a golden box with magnificently winged angels facing each other on the lid. It appeared to be one of Judaism's most sacred objects, built to carry the Ten Commandments given to Moses.

Delegates rushed to the edge of the fencing and looked down into the Well of Souls. Word spread that a golden object had been unveiled by the crash of the Titus Arch marble onto the cave floor.

The Ashkenazi Chief Rabbi was ecstatic. He expounded to the crowd, who hushed to hear his every word.

"This must be the Ark of the Covenant. We thought our Babylonian captors melted it for its gold. But our priests must have hidden it in the most secret place of all — its very home — under a rock covering."

Ruth thought for a moment about a Revelation connection. Could whatever had just flown over them refer to Chapter 8's large mountain burning with fire that was hurled into the sea? That was beyond NJA's capability.

The delegates crowded at the ledge, transfixed by the emergence of the golden object. Feldman shouted, "Please return to the tent. We're standing over an unstable area."

Palmer asked, "Was that an asteroid?"

"What else!" said Feldman. "Sorry, Ike. Looks like It could hit the fleets in seconds."

152

JERUSALEM
Sunday, June 3

LIGHTNING FLASHED from the north. Wind whipped the tent. Rain began to spatter. Thunder rolled close. Inside the delegates met in small groups over a revised draft.

Sitting with the Pope, Alessio felt liberated. Not only had he not been fired, but Sixtus had embraced his contrary viewpoint. Alessio's challenge convinced Sixtus to surrender his divisive idea in favor of an ecumenical complex, a cloverleaf with Jewish, Christian and Muslim leaves. While Alessio read the draft, overhead lightning flashed and thunder instantly resounded.

"Even heaven applauds," he said.

"Or condemns it. Let's pray the delegates can accept this," said the Pope, holding the document in a red binder ready for signing. He looked up as though for guidance. "If not, we're out of time."

Sixtus opened the concluding session with a short prayer. Each delegation would be asked to declare its position, yes or no, beginning with the Pope of Alexandria.

"I support it," said the Coptic prelate, "with the Old City map and immediate transfer of authority to the Convocation of the Book," the name given a group that would design the Domes of the Book and propose a supranational board to oversee the Old City.

Sixtus turned to Egyptian President Modri. The former Secretary of an Islamic group that was on the USA's terrorist list decades earlier but who governed as a moderate since replacing a military-backed head of state, Modri stood.

"Egypt supports a nuclear-free zone for our region, and we support a popular vote. This Old City should be a home for all the righteous. We look forward to a worthy replacement for a sacred shrine desecrated by an abominable act of," he paused before saying what came to mind (*Zionist terrorists*) and instead ended with the word "fanatics," his expression revealing the word was not quite what he intended.

Sixtus recognized the Russian Patriarch.

"This is a miraculous gathering," the Patriarch began. "I support this," as he pointed an index finger at the map of the Old City stamped **Universal** at the top. "And the Ark of the Covenant, if that is what has been revealed, must rest within the Domes for all people of the Book," he added, looking at Prime Minister Feldman.

EU President Schmidt followed. "We agree to this text. We Germans know tragedy follows when faith is displaced by worship of military might, when one's own tribe is exalted above others."

Four in favor. Alessio noted Goudonov stone-faced and Palmer frowning.

"Rabbi, your comments, please," said the Pope.

Israel's Ashkenazi Chief Rabbi breathed in deeply and exhaled.

"It is written in Ezekiel that Jerusalem is the center of the Land of Israel and the foundation of the world. To the world it belongs. I will do all I can to support a universal authority for this Old City, one that belongs to all humankind." The Rabbi faced Sixtus, but Alessio knew his target was Feldman.

There was a lull in the rainstorm. For seconds. Then a harder pelt like rocks being thrown onto the canvas overhead. Alessio slipped to an exit and returned in seconds.

"Only hail, heavy hail," he reported to the nervous delegates.

153

JERUSALEM
Sunday, June 3

THE STORM ENDED its assault as ice pellets and torrents of water poured down to the streets of the Old City and Kidron Valley. Crowds that took shelter during the storm began to emerge and look toward the illuminated tent that occupied space once crowned by the Dome of the Rock. Black sky was punctured by a blood orange moon dipping toward the western horizon, casting scant light through a dark city.

Dispensationalists recognized the moon from Revelation 6:12 and Joel 2:31, the sun turning black and the moon to blood before the great day of the Lord's wrath. They left rooftops during the storm but now hurried back, certain this was Rapture day when living streams would prepare to encircle an enthroned God returned to the Holy City. They knew the asteroid was fire from the sky, confirming the coming of the Savior to lift the select group corporeally to the heavens. Many wore their Sunday best. None would be left behind.

Marchers endured the drenched night by shelter extended by Jerusalem residents. Except for those in ultra-Orthodox enclaves, Palestinians and Jews alike extended hospitality. The glowing ring from the March was doused before dawn approached, candles melted to puddled wax.

Haim Etzion fumed that 4K's grand plan to purify Israel was endangered. He'd trusted Feldman — but the Prime Minister had let Muslim marchers into Jerusalem. He had betrayed the cause. Would he allow alien forces at the summit to divert the march of Zion? If so, he would pay the price. Decades ago, Prime Minister Yitzhak Rabin had received his due after signing the Oslo peace accord with the Palestinian Liberation Organization that pledged to destroy Israel. A bullet could find Feldman if he betrayed the faith.

Vali Qalil congratulated himself. AM's success in generating the ghostly 3-D image of Isa at the Minaret the night before convinced millions that the End was near. The March was in Jerusalem. Muslims would embrace Qalil as the Mahdi to lead a united Islam in the final jihad, the call of every Muslim. But the Ayatollah had survived. He worried what would happen if his communications with Al-Rabani were intercepted. And the movie star's ratings had skyrocketed. Was there a backup plan?

NJA elder Sam Turrain sat in the darkness of the Garden of Gethsemane. He stared expectantly at the Golden Gate, blown open after centuries, ready for the Savior to reappear and ascend the Mount, not for crucifixion but to redeem the world, when earthly time would cease and the blessed would see the living God. Sam had overseen the effort that baptized more than 144,000 Jews and marked the name of Jesus in oil on their foreheads. Sam awaited a call from Noah to sound the brass. Russia and the United States were following the script. Only hours remained — and then the timeless glory.

154

JERUSALEM
Sunday, June 3

RUTH SAT BEHIND the Archbishop as one by one leaders were declaring their position on the summit text. Five had said yes. One no could doom the gathering. And the specter of nuclear war loomed over it all.

The Pope called upon President Arafat.

"We seek justice. We can accept other structures in this Noble Sanctuary but not the evil of Israel's Temple Swords. They must be surrendered. If it is military power Israel worships, we will show them the righteous power of Allah."

"Is that a yes?" asked the Pope.

"I will sign if Israel does the same," said Arafat.

Sixtus recognized the Imam of Mecca's Grand Mosque, who Ruth knew was an outspoken antagonist of Shi'a Iran.

"On the Day of Judgment," he began, "the righteous will have eternal reward. Every soul will stand alone, and the *Sijjin*, the Sealed Book, will be read out, separating those whose good deeds and love of justice earned their place with Allah. We support this," he held aloft the text, "with the territory of a universal Jerusalem as Allah created it. In the name of Allah, the Compassionate, the Merciful."

Ruth counted six in favor, with the Palestinian vote ironically contingent on Israel's approval.

"Mr. Prime Minister," Sixtus extended his right hand towards Israel's leader. Ruth felt an early morning chill snake through the assembly.

If Feldman felt isolated, he gave no outward sign. "I can support creation of a center on this Temple Mount open to all People of faith, of the Book as you say. With the recovery of what appears to be the Ark of the Covenant, we need time to consider what will be built here.

"The Old City has no need of a world governing body. Our welcome of the marchers is definitive proof that we govern fairly and protect everyone.

"If our neighbors wish to poll their populations on a question, that is their right. Israel is a representative democracy. We do not hold plebiscites." Feldman said no more.

Ruth saw the Pope thinking whether to ask the Prime Minister if this meant "no," but instead he turned to the Ayatollah in an apparent effort to avoid a breakdown.

The Ayatollah drew in his lips and paused before speaking. "Iran is a peaceful nation. Iran will hold a vote of our people never to possess nuclear weapons. We will contribute to build the Domes of the Book. We support this Old City as a world sanctuary.

"And if Israel will not commit to join in these commitments," he held the text aloft, "we will join others in employing the most powerful weapon of all — the Word of Allah, of God, of HaShem. As it is written, 'Believers, those who follow the Jewish Faith, Christians, and Sabaeans — whoever believes in God and the Last Day and does what is right — shall be rewarded by their Lord; they have nothing to fear or regret.' Iran will sign."

Qur'an 2:62, thought Ruth. Seven in favor. She watched Feldman as he kept his eyes on the Ayatollah, then glanced at Palmer who appeared moved by the Ayatollah, then at Feldman who looked down at his hands.

Russia's President was next. Goudonov stretched his shoulders upward as though aroused from a stupor and assumed the commanding posture of a man in charge of his country and himself.

"Russia and the United States killed each other's citizens for the sake of this region, and Israel equivocates over trivial details. Shame. The Jewish people suffered a catastrophe from Hitler, but we lost seven times their number to defeat that devil. We know what it is to be attacked, to endure efforts to humiliate and contain our people.

"So, what is the way forward?

"First, we have agreed with the United States to withhold further action until Monday noon." Glaring at Palmer he added, "We shall see.

"On these proposals this is Russia's position.

"The Domes of the Book can be built. Russia will contribute generously.

"The Old City will be governed by a body appointed by the faith leaders present, who will design rules for permanent universal control. While this is worked out, Russia will send peacekeepers here through the United Nations. We invite all countries to participate. Israel will agree or face the anger of a united world.

"There should be no nuclear weapons in this region. If Israel will not let its people vote on this, we will place nuclear assets in the care of our neighboring allies, positioned at an equivalent distance from Israel's border as those pointed in their direction from Israel."

Goudonov ended with a chin protruding as though daring a boxer to hit it.

Ruth despaired at the Russian tone, though couched in agreement to the protocol.

Again, the Pope did not ask whether the statement was a yes or a no. Instead, he gestured to the Archbishop of Canterbury, his expression pleading that his ally reverse a downward spiral of rhetoric.

The Archbishop stood.

"For some signs of the Apocalypse have flashed. Fire from the sky, trumpets and images at the Vatican, twelve marble gates with Israel's tribes inscribed, mass killings, an asteroid that crashed upon the sea disabling monstrous submarines, thunder and hail, a darkened sky and blood red moon.

"And we sense worship of the Beast in Christian terms, Armies of the Dajjal and the Mahdi in Islamic terms, regathering of the Jewish people according to the Torah. In all three of our faiths the End Time may be near. But it is not for us to know when that time will be, and certainly it is not for us to cause it. To give Apocalypse its true meaning — Revelation — revealing the holy plan — let us commit to God's reign of peace and justice on this earth."

He looked in Palmer's direction.

"We can worship the Beast of Military Might, or we can embrace a New Jerusalem." He looked to Feldman. "We can have Shoah, this time for the whole world, or we can summon justice like the prophets." He turned toward Arafat, "We can treat another as the Dajjal and wage a battle, or we can act so on the Day of Judgment we are judged as righteous to the end.

"Our task is to do what is right and entrust the rest to the Almighty." The Archbishop walked to the Pope, took the red binder, drew his gold pen and signed the paper.

Ruth looked about. Had the Archbishop's remarks found their target? After a ten second silence, the Pope said, "President Palmer, your position please."

Palmer looked to the right and left and said, "May we have a short break?"

"Let's resume at 5:45." Dawn was about to break over Jerusalem.

"Noah, come with me," whispered Palmer.

155

JERUSALEM
Sunday, June 3

SECRETARY SHULMAN was on a secure line with Director of National Intelligence Sullivan and the Vice Admiral of the 6th Fleet.

"Assessment," demanded Palmer when he and Noah entered the American enclave.

"We can't assure a knock-out of Russia's strategic assets. They'd detect a launch in seconds and hit our major cities. Unlikely our shields could prevent a catastrophe. So Option A's a crap shoot. The asteroid disrupted both fleets. We're in no shape to eliminate their subs, and they have the same problem."

"Alternatives."

"Step by step escalation? That would be like jumping across the Grand Canyon in several leaps. A better choice is an immediate mutual stand-down. The risk is the Russians don't honor it and strike us first. But we'd know the second a missile launches, and we could destroy their whole country. The Vice President called. She said the War Declaration has 99% support. It's held for a vote as soon as you're back."

"Got it." Palmer turned and left the tent with Noah.

As the moon dipped below the horizon all was still and dark except for a dim glow of window light from dwellings of an Old City about to awaken.

Usually a machine of yes or no after puzzling through a decision tree, Palmer seemed uncertain. He faced Noah.

"What do you think, my friend?"

"I think we misinterpreted Revelation, that nuclear destruction was Satan creeping into God's script."

"Let's build the Third Temple," Palmer decided, "and go ahead with the Domes of the Book. The other two points will take years to work out, so why not be on board. The American public will love it and give us seven more years to steer it in the right direction."

They noticed Iranian President Al-Rabani stealthily descending the stairs to the base of the western wall, wrapping a scarf to hide his face.

"Don't only women cover themselves?" asked Palmer.

156

JERUSALEM
Sunday, June 3

INSTEAD OF HEARING the Russian fleet had advanced to the Israeli coast, able to checkmate any move by America at his command, the Russian submarines had retreated in the wake of the asteroid strike.

"Cowards," Goudonov roared. "That was nothing compared to the Siberian winters when I was in the Red Army along the Chinese border."

The Defense Minister patiently explained that the fleet's computers were incapacitated, and Admiral Morozov's dashboard could not locate the American vessels or assure accurate strikes. The assessment was no better for Russia's aging 500-plus land missile launchers. Despite public bragging about its superiority, Goudonov knew Russia had let its strategic force atrophy. Work progressed on RS-27X ballistic missiles configured to evade American and European defense systems, but they were not fully deployed. The RS-24 missiles armed with non-nuclear warheads had destroyed targets in North Dakota, but most were intercepted.

Even if the Americans thought Russia could obliterate a few U.S. cities in a nuclear conflict, Goudonov was not assured of that. He was certain Russia would be annihilated in an all-out exchange. Russia was outmatched.

"If the U.S. and Russia destroy each other, China will pick up the pieces," Goudonov muttered. "What's the sense of that?"

Russian Patriarch Florovsky entered the enclave. Wearing a white domed hat embroidered with a golden Orthodox cross, a white stole dangling above a black robe, the Patriarch placed his hands on the President's shoulders and prayed silently.

"How will I be seen if we abandon our Muslim allies?" asked Goudonov.

Old enough to have spent more than half his years in the Soviet Union when the Church was not the revered institution it became after 1991, the Patriarch answered carefully.

"To your allies you can quote the Qur'an, 41:34: 'Good deeds and evil are not equal. Requite evil with good, and he who is your enemy will become your dearest friend.' We cannot burn our homeland to ash."

Goudonov barely dipped his head, wanting to be seen in prayer or able to deny it, whichever was most useful with a future audience. He was a man who rose through the ranks of the Soviet Army and then the KGB, ascended under Yeltsin and Putin, and now bore the mantle of Russia's destiny as a world power second to none, or so it would strive to be. He knew how to survive.

157

JERUSALEM
Sunday, June 3

DELEGATES GATHERED ANXIOUSLY for the last session. Disagreement could unleash the beasts of war in a final blaze engulfing each nation and faith.

Palmer and Noah met Feldman outside the tent.

"We play the cards we're dealt," Palmer stated. "If I put my chips on nuclear war, we end up with a smoldering planet. We're not going to strike Russia again.

"Now let's look at your hand. You're surrounded by leaders who survive by keeping their populations enraged at you. And what friends will come to your defense?

"Just as Christians must relinquish the idea that Christ will reign over the earth any time soon, so Israel must give up its mystical dream of restoring the realm of King David. Israel doesn't need to control the Old City. It's a tourist park. What difference will it make if the UN is stuck with the bills? The tough choice is your Temple Swords, but you won't use them, and you can drag that out for years. All you risk is allowing a vote. You lose if you don't go along."

Feldman blanched.

"Reread 1 Chronicles, chapter 28." Palmer turned about and strode to the assembly.

Feldman stood alone. He remembered the passage. King David planned to build a home for the Ark of the Covenant, but God denied him because David was a warrior who had shed blood. Instead, God reserved the building of the Temple to David's son Solomon, free of the stain of war.

Almost miraculously, the Ark had returned, architectural plans were drawn, funds were raised, and space was available for a Third Temple. Would not signing the declaration jeopardize HaShem's choice of Aaron Feldman to build it, alone?

When Feldman returned to the assembly, only Iranian President Al-Rabani was missing. The Pope glanced at the Ayatollah, who gave a slight shrug of his shoulders and motion of his right hand indicating no need to wait.

Before the Pope could call on Palmer to resume, Russian President Goudonov stood up and stared at the American President.

"Russia decisively answered the American attack. We are satisfied. Therefore, I have ordered our nuclear assets to stand down and our fleet to change course. Russia will sign the protocol if you will do the same."

The Russian Patriarch across the way bowed his head in joyous prayer.

Palmer rose from his chair.

"President Goudonov, America stands down. We have each suffered enough. It is done."

Delegates turned their heads, wondering if that was all the American President was going to say.

But Palmer added, "No matter our faith, we are all sinners who must seek repentance." Christian voters would appreciate his next move, repentance sourced from spiritual wisdom and strength. Calculating Goudonov would reciprocate and envisioning the sound bite he added, "And we ask forgiveness for Russian lives lost."

Goudonov sighed. So many lives lost over such a small spit of land. With a sorrow he didn't know he could feel, Goudonov replied, "We regret the loss of life in America. May we each be forgiven."

Palmer was surprised to feel himself moved by Goudonov's response and the remorse it stirred in him. He walked toward Goudonov, who arose and met Palmer half-way, just behind the Pope's chair. The men extended their right hands and clasped them vigorously for several seconds staring into each other's eyes as icons to the soul.

A grace descended. Alessio made the sign of the cross.

Palmer asked Archbishop Okello for the red binder and placed it on the table for Goudonov and himself to sign, as they did to a thunderous standing ovation of the delegates — except for Prime Minister Feldman who remained seated in what appeared to be a deep trance.

As the leaders of Russia and America returned to their chairs, the other delegates came forward and signed the protocol. One signature was lacking.

Pope Sixtus asked, "Prime Minister, does Israel concur?"

The first morning rays from the east pierced the translucent tent and brought Feldman to attention. Images of Yitzhak Rabin, soldier turned politician, Feldman's boyhood hero came to his mind. He pictured Rabin in his early days as a Freedom Fighter imprisoned by the British, as Israel's Fifth Prime Minister, as Nobel Peace Prize recipient. Feldman recalled being near the viewing stand during Rabin's 1995 assassination, shot by an ultra-Orthodox zealot. If he said yes, Feldman could be next. But if he said no, he might not preside over building a Third Temple, even if part of a cloverleaf. And Palmer had made clear America would not protect Israel from utter isolation.

Feldman turned to President Arafat.

"If we journey together as People of the Book, there is no limit to our future."

He faced the Pope and began, "I have no singular authority. This will need the Knesset's review." He arose and approached the binder, black pen in hand. He signed. "Let's convene talks about all issues, so life can become normal."

Pope Sixtus reached behind to grip Alessio's arm.

"A miracle," Alessio agreed and crossed himself again.

The Old City's bells began to announce the hour. After six peals, a single trumpet sounded across the Kidron Valley. A second joined from the west, then a chorus of brass encircled the Mount for a fanfare in a major key, a triumphal melody more resplendent than Olympic codas. Melody blended with counterpoint, motifs hearkening back to the psalms of King David, intertwined with early Christian chant, followed by a cadence of Muhammad's time, then to a blend of all three, each successive stanza one tone higher than the prior. The chorus resounded as the Sun completed its rise over the Mount of Olives.

Beautiful, Ruth sighed. She would thank Noah. The NJA got it right this time.

Delegates sat motionless throughout the hymn of brass. After a glorious finale, the Imam of Mecca's Grand Mosque spoke. "The trumpets. The meaning from the Christian Bible?"

Sixtus called on Ruth, introducing her as an expert on Revelation according to John of Patmos.

"In Revelation, the seventh angel blows his trumpet to herald the return of Christ to reign peacefully on earth. Those who destroyed the destroyers of the earth are rewarded. The chapter concludes, 'Then God's temple in heaven was opened, and the ark of his covenant was seen within his temple; and there were flashes of lightning, loud noises, peals of thunder, an earthquake, and heavy hail.' Those present see a new heaven and a new earth, and a new Jerusalem." Ruth smiled, "We have nothing to fear."

The Pope lifted his arms upward.

"Praise be to the God of Abraham, of Moses, of Jesus, of Muhammad, to the compassionate and merciful Creator of all."

158

JERUSALEM
Sunday, June 3

THE MOST WATCHED NEWS conference in history began at 9 a.m. Jerusalem time. Reporters and camera crews took hastily marked placements. Israeli soldiers and Waqf guards flanked a riser and podium.

Chief delegates walked in a line from the tent that dazzled white from the brilliant rays of a cloudless morning. Pope Sixtus stood at the podium. To his left sat Prime Minister Feldman, then Palestinian President Arafat. On Sixtus' right sat Iran's Grand Ayatollah, who was next to the Ashkenazi Chief Rabbi of Israel. President Palmer sat on the far right as the cameras viewed the group, at the extreme left President Goudonov.

The Pope announced, "The Presidents of the Russian Federation and the United States of America."

Goudonov and Palmer strode to the microphones and shook hands. President Palmer announced a permanent cessation of hostilities.

President Goudonov declared, "Never again will an alliance become the trigger of mass destruction," describing the agreed stand-down as "victory for all." They embraced.

Pope Sixtus resumed the podium after standing applause. Aides distributed the summit's unanimous release, and the Pope read the startling accords. A nuclear-free-zone plebiscite would be held on the last day of September in all countries of the region. The Domes of the Book would be built to provide each faith a separate worship space, connecting to a central domed sanctuary where sacred texts would share a commons, with the Foundation Stone, Abraham's Rock, at its center. Delegates pledged funds to build it and restore the Al Aqsa Mosque. The Old City would become a universal city. EU President Schmidt announced that she would host the foreign ministers of Israel and the Palestinian Authority in Berlin next month to discuss how greater Jerusalem could become a shared capital. Prime Minister Feldman revealed that the Ark of the Covenant had been discovered, concealed for centuries within the Wells of Souls.

The Pope invited the faith leaders to stand with him. They gave a benediction in different tongues but a common cadence.

"May the peace of God, Allah, HaShem, through a grace beyond all understanding, dwell within us. We commit our hearts and souls to the work of peace and bless all who embrace it. Amen."

Rooftop crowds that had been ready for the Rapture thinned, Dispensationalists disappointed that their one-way tickets to Jerusalem had been a miscalculation. Throngs in the streets talked excitedly, many with tears streaming, others bent in prayer, circles of Orthodox men in black debating the meaning of the Ark of the Covenant's return. Marchers began their homeward trek.

Before he boarded a plane for Tehran, a reporter asked the Grand Ayatollah why Iranian President Al-Rabani was absent from the conclusion. "There will be new elections" was the response.

Haim Etzion and what remained of the 4K leadership met to watch the news. The announcement that Domes of the Book would be built wrecked the dream of a Third Temple and a pure Israel. Feldman would pay for this. There would be a Day of Judgment.

As world leaders departed, shielded by a legion of security, residents lined the streets waving palm branches, banana leaves, and other sprigs of green. Noah, Alessio and Ruth found themselves the only delegates left on an emptied Mount, as crews untangled cords and removed equipment.

"Professionally, I don't know what to think," Ruth confessed, recalling the asteroid, the heavy hail, and the submarines, beasts of the sea. "Some of the signs were NJA theatrics, but others came straight from Revelation. On the other hand, no one would confuse UN rule with the reign of Jesus, and the earth and sea weren't destroyed as the Book predicted." The threat had shaken her personal life as well, bringing up longings she had long packed away.

Ruth turned to Noah. "Are you disappointed that all your Bible verses didn't come true?" She hoped he'd learned — no more cherry-picking the Bible for direction.

No such luck. His certainty resumed.

"The NJA got some of the details wrong but we were basically right about the signs of a turning point in God's history. There will be a New Jerusalem. And President Palmer asked me to be its U.S. ambassador."

"I can't believe it. The Archbishop asked me to be Chief Missioner for the Anglican Communion's representation to the New Jerusalem Authority."

This changes things, thought Alessio. He had turned down the Holy Father's request that he become the Vatican deputy to the New Jerusalem. The Pope had asked him to reconsider. *The answer would now be yes.*

Before he boarded a plane for Tehran, a reporter asked the Grand Ayatollah why Iranian President Al-Rabani was absent from the conclusion. "There will be new elections" was the response.

Haim Etzion and what remained of the 4K leadership met to watch the news. The announcement that Domes of the Book would be built wrecked the dream of a Third Temple and a pure Israel. Feldman would pay for this. There would be a Day of Judgment.

CPSIA information can be obtained
at www.ICGtesting.com
Printed in the USA
BVHW040500020622
638544BV00004B/6/J